Save Our Country

Matt Drozd

Matt Drozd Books.com

Copyright registered @2024 Matt Drozd

All rights reserved. No part of this book may be used or reproduced by any means, graphic, mechanical, or electronic, including photocopying, recording, taping or by any information storage retrieval system without written permission of the author except in the case of brief quotations in critical articles and reviews.

Matt Drozd Books may be ordered on major book sites which can be found on www.mattdrozdbooks.com

Images from Library of Congress, White House website, Wikimedia Commons, Unsplash

TABLE OF CONTENTS

CHAPTER 1, Roots 5
CHAPTER 2, The Encounter 11
CHAPTER 3, First Love 20
CHAPTER 4, Boxing Lessons 25
CHAPTER 5, Discovered 36
CHAPTER 6, War of Independence 42
CHAPTER 7, War Hero returns 54
CHAPTER 8, True Love 64
CHAPTER 9, A Sad Loss 70
CHAPTER 10, Winds of War 78
CHAPTER 11, Time marches on 86
CHAPTER 12, Enter Politics 92
CHAPTER 13, Nominations 102
CHAPTER 14, Marching orders 121
CHAPTER 15, Super Tuesday 124
CHAPTER 16, The Candidates meet 128
CHAPTER 17, Swing states 132
CHAPTER 18, Border Crisis 134
CHAPTER 19, Debate Eligible 141

CHAPTER 20, Top ten Presidents	144
CHAPTER 21, President's resume	156
CHAPTER 22, Party Platforms	165
CHAPTER 23, First Presidential Debate	182
CHAPTER 24, Assassination Attempt	202
CHAPTER 25, Biden Abdicates	206
CHAPTER 26, Campaign Promises	210
CHAPTER 27, The Silent Majority	216
CHAPTER 28, Unorthodox Partners	222
CHAPTER 29, Trump and Harris Debate	231
CHAPTER 30, On the road again	241
CHAPTER 31, The Votes are Counted	261

CHAPTER 1

Roots

It was a rainy-thunderous day at Monticello. Lightning flashed  across the sky followed by a torrential downpour and thunder. Thomas Jefferson was in his library when he was summoned to one of the slave cabins. Upon his arrival, there were several women slaves attending to the birth of a young female slave in her early twenties. In those days, it was not uncommon for an owner to be especially concerned about the birth of new children among their slave population. The birth of new children was as valuable and profitable to the owner as his crops. (Photo1)

Jefferson became especially interested in this young woman because he became extremely fond of her when she served him in the mansion. Like Sally Hemings, she was a beautiful young woman of mixed blood. She had stunning olive-like eyes with velvety curly hair and a figure that was petite and athletic. Her soft demeaner and personality of light humor charmed anyone she encountered. Whenever she walked into a room to serve guests, all the men's eyes locked on her. Because of her and Jefferson's closeness and friendly attitude towards one another, some on the plantation wondered if it was Jefferson who fathered her child, but Jefferson knew it was one of his plantation managers who he fired because of misconduct. Prior to the birth of her child, she begged Mr. Jefferson to look after her baby should anything happen to her when giving birth. "Like countless enslaved women, Sally Hemings bore children fathered by her owner, Thomas Jefferson.

Female slaves had no legal right to refuse unwanted sexual advances. Sally Hemings was also the child of an enslaved woman who was impregnated by her owner. At least two of her sisters bore children fathered by white men. "Mixed-race children were present at Monticello, in the surrounding county, across Virginia, and throughout the United States. Regardless of their white paternity, children born to enslaved women inherited their mothers' status as slaves." (1)

"Of the Jeffersons' six children—five daughters and one son—two died in infancy and only two daughters, Martha, and Mary (called Patsy and Polly by the family), survived to adulthood. Their last child, Lucy Elizabeth, died of whooping cough in October 1784. " (2) The sad loss of his children may have prompted Jefferson to be that more tentative to the young slave woman.

"Jefferson directly profited from the labor of enslaved people on his four farms. Jefferson bought and sold human beings. He purchased slaves occasionally because he needed labor to work on his plantation. Despite his expressed scruple" against selling, he sold more than 110 in his lifetime, for financial reasons. Jefferson was once quoted as saying "I consider a woman who brings a child every two years as more profitable than the best man of the farm," Jefferson remarked in 1820. "What she produces is an addition to the capital, while his labors disappear in mere consumption." (3) Adding another slave through the birth of this child could have also been a reason for his interest.

Jefferson was focused on the birth of the child and impatiently awaited its arrival. He stood at the cabin entrance listening to the cries of the young mother giving birth. Some of the slaves who served the main house lived under its South Terrace. The cabin that housed the young mother was one room with lofts, measuring about 12 by 14 feet. The roof was made of pine slabs and had a wood chimney with dirt floor. A root cellar was dug into the floor to store vegetables. "(4)

Leaning against the cabin wall dripping wet, you could sense his sincere concern. Several slave women served as midwifes but knew little about how to deal with complications that arose from childbirth. The screams of the young woman grew louder, and one could sense the need for urgency. When the child evolved from the womb, the mid wives exclaimed that it is boy and at the same time cried out that the mother had died. Hearing this, Jefferson slid down the wall to his knees holding his face in his hands with tears in his eyes. The death of the young woman reminded him of his wife's death. Staring at the mother and child, Jefferson ordered that the child be placed in his arms and that the mother be given a proper burial with religious services. Jefferson desperately wanted to save this child because of losing the only son he fathered with his wife Martha. One may conclude that he harbored guilt that he could not do more to save the child.

Wrapping the child in his cloak, he gently carried him to the cabin of Sally Hemmings. The rain still pouring down on him, Jefferson used his cloak to shield the child from the rain. Walking into the cabin, Sally Hemmings gave Jefferson a puzzled look. Still not addressing him informally, Sally questioned Jefferson. "Mr. Jefferson, why do you bring this child to me? Is the mother not going to take care of him?" Jefferson looked helplessly at Sally and answered. "His mother died at childbirth, and I am reluctant to entrust this child's care to anyone other than you Sally. You have always been so kind and loving to our children and asked little of me over the years. I trust you implicitly with this child's life." Seeing the sweet face of the child, Sally took the newborn in her arms.

Jefferson was determined to leave the child with no one else but with his trusted Sally Hemmings. He admired the way she treated the children she bore with him. "Though enslaved, Sally Hemings helped shape her life and the lives of her children. Unlike countless enslaved women, Sally Hemings was able to negotiate with Jefferson. Jefferson may have been far more tolerate of Sally because "she was the child of Martha Jefferson's father, John Wayles, and Elizabeth Hemings, an enslaved woman, thus making Jefferson's wife Martha and Sally Hemings half-sisters." (5) In Paris, where she was free, the 16-year-old agreed to return to enslavement at Monticello in exchange for "extraordinary privileges" for herself and freedom for her unborn children. Over the next 32 years Hemings raised four children—Beverly, Harriet, Madison, and Eston—and prepared them for their eventual emancipation. She did not negotiate for, or ever receive, legal freedom in Virginia." (6)

The forlorn look on Jefferson's face and shaking from the chilly rain prompted Hemings to be more compassionate towards him. "I will raise him under the condition that you keep your word and free our children Mr. Jefferson." Jefferson agreed by slowly nodding his head yes. "In addition to freeing our children, I will make certain that you, our children, and this newborn will have light duties on the plantation. When doing so, however, I want you to never reveal that I have taken a personal interest in this child. I want everyone to believe that I simply placed him under your care because he has no parents." Sally shook her head yes.

One might surmise the reason that Jefferson did not free Sally Hemings, and their children is because he may have genuinely loved Sally. Sally had her chance to be free while living in France. Should she have not returned to America, the French laws that outlawed slavery would have made her a free woman. On the other hand, one would wonder if it was because she feared the practice of slavery in France may have been reinstated. In fact, Napoleon Bonaparte did reinstate slavery in 1804. Being a young teenager with no formal education or training, she would have had a tough time supporting herself. Whatever the case, Jefferson gave his promise to free the children of Sally Hemings if she would return with him. During her stay in France, she tended to Jefferson's young daughter, nine-year-old Mary. Sally performed the duties of an enslaved household servant and lady's maid. Jefferson still referred to her as his daughter's maid." (7)

"Besides Sally Hemings and her children, hundreds of people were enslaved at Jefferson's Monticello but the details as to how they lived were lost over time. George Washington's Mt. Vernon provides more detailed information on how enslaved people were treated. Enslaved families were often separated great distances from one another when working in the fields. Their daily food rations included corn meal and salted fish. Those performing more visible work, such as servants, were provided with more quality clothes than those working in the fields.

"The enslaved were housed in rough one room log houses measuring 225 square feet, about the size of a large storage shed. Two families would sometimes be housed in a two-room log house, heated during cold winters by a wooden fireplace. As many as eight people could be housed in one room sleeping on pallets or on a dirt floor. A visitor to Mt. Vernon, Julian Niemcewicz, observed that "the husband-and-wife sleep on a mean pallet, the children on the ground, a very bad fireplace, some utensils for cooking, but in the middle of this poverty some cups and a teapot." With clean water scarce, hired and enslaved laborers received rations of rum." (8)

"Enslaved people had no legal rights, no autonomy, and could be separated from their family by being sold at a moment's notice. They were considered property and not people. To keep enslaved people from rebelling, white lawmakers passed a series of slave codes governing their status, rights, and treatment. Any violators were severely punished including whipping, branding, and maiming. Those who were enslaved could be bought, sold, rented, and inherited just like assets or livestock. Owners faced no reprisals for abusing their slaves even if they killed one while inflicting punishment. A child of a slave was born into slavery for life and could not legally marry." (8)

Besides being field workers, enslaved people worked as valets, chamber maids, and nannies. They helped their masters and mistresses dress and bathe, arranged their hair, cleaned, and mended clothes, and were messengers. "Unlike some of his contemporaries, such as Robert Carter III, who freed nearly 500 people held slaves in his lifetime, or Washington, who in his Will freed all the enslaved people he legally owned, Jefferson formally freed only two people during his life, in 1793 and 1794." (9)

Before Jefferson left the cabin of Sally Hemings, she grabbed him by the arm with a puzzled look on her face. "What do you want to name this child Mr. Jefferson?" Jefferson stood with his hand on his cheek and the other behind his back. "Good question Sally. Everything has happened so fast; her mother did not live long enough to name him." After walking around the cabin straining to produce a name, Jefferson's eyes lit up. "Upon my father passing away I needed and sought out someone who could mentor and tutor me. "It is at William and Mary where I became good friends with a learned professor by the name of William. I spent a good deal of time with him both in and out of class. I want this child to have similar beliefs as he taught me and to have a strong desire to better himself. I will name him William in honor of my tutor."

After leaving the child with Sally Hemings, Jefferson stood outside the cabin in the rain for an hour or two before returning to his mansion. As the rain dripped from his hat and cloak, he thought about how much he regretted and was saddened by the death of his wife Martha which was possibly attributed to giving birth. It made him more resolved to honor the young mother by ensuring her child's successful development. Especially as the newborn was in effect an orphan. Jefferson became very troubled at the thought of it. As promised, Sally Hemings took loving care of William while Jefferson was entangled in pressing obligations.

As was the custom of the day, neither Adams nor Jefferson personally campaigned for the presidency. Rather, the campaign battles were waged between the political party newspapers, a propaganda device rooted in the anti-British pamphlets of the American Revolution. One factor that elevated Jefferson's chances of becoming President was the country's general mood. Consequently, Jefferson enjoyed a lot of popular support for his opposition to Adams's policies." (10)

CHAPTER 2

The Encounter

Upon William reaching the age of six, Jefferson had him assigned as one of his house boys at the mansion. Their first encounter was traumatic for both. This is the first time Jefferson would lay eyes on the boy since he was born. Jefferson had left the office of the Presidency to be taken over by James Madison. Seeing Jefferson working at his desk, William tip toed into the library. Being awestruck with the fact that this was his first encounter with his owner, William did not look directly at Jefferson. Jefferson, however, was following William's every move by peering behind one of his books. Jefferson saw a lot of his mother in him. William was tall for most boys his age and extremely handsome. His hair was black and curly, and he had excellent posture like his mother. Jefferson was pleased to see that William had grown into an extremely handsome young man with an athletic frame. Having a Caucasian father and mixed mother, the boy was more Caucasian in skin color but had distinguished features that mirrored that of his African American ancestry. His clothing was typical of most slaves except they were very loose on him. He had to roll up his pants leg and shirt sleeves. His demeanor appeared inquisitive and thoughtful.

Before starting his dusting chores, William spanned the entire library in awe. He slowly walked along the endless shelves of books showing great interest. He pulled one from the shelf and started to scan through its pages. After observing William going about his work for quite some time and the interest he appeared to have in his collection of books, Jefferson thought it was time to recognize him. Jefferson cleared his throat loud enough to capture his attention. Sitting back on his chair, Jefferson acknowledged the young William. "Good evening young man. Are you the one they sent to maintain my books?" Startled when Jefferson spoke to him, William dropped a heavy book in his hand. Jefferson stood up from his desk and walked over to help William. William was already bent over to pick up the book. As he rose, Jefferson was standing next to him. William's eyes stared downward towards Jefferson's feet and then scanned the rest of Jefferson's body until his eyes were at the level of Jefferson's chest.

"Jefferson was a slender man; had the air of stiffness in his manner; his clothes seem too small; he sits in a lounging manner, on one hip, and with one of his shoulders elevated much above the other; his face has a sunny aspect; his figure has a loose, slack appearance. Jefferson was six feet two and a half inches high, well proportioned, and straight as a gun barrel." (1)

Looking down on William, Jefferson starts the conversation by asking the boy his name even though he already knew it. "My name is William, Mr. Jefferson." "Who gave you such a stately name William? Why, that is a good question, I really do not know Mr. Jefferson." "I really do not want to stop you from conducting your daily chores William so I will not keep you back from them. "Thank you, Mr. Jefferson." William went about dusting the books. He was so infatuated with the books that he stopped to read the outside cover as he dusted them. Jefferson pretended to be scanning some papers on his desk while he watched William go about his chores.

While carefully dusting the books Jefferson so cherished, Jefferson noticed how William treated them with the utmost respect. He observed him open some of the books and seemed to read a few lines. Jefferson cherished his collection of rare books and William's behavior was interesting to him.

"Jefferson collected three libraries in his lifetime. He started the first in his youth, but it was destroyed when his mother's home, Shadwell, burned in 1770. The second, and largest, of his collections was comprised of some 6,500 books, and in 1814 he sold it to the United States government. This set of books formed the nucleus of the Library of Congress, replacing the collection that was burned by the British during the War of 1812." (2-3) "After the sale, Jefferson began amassing a third library for the amusement of his retirement years. By the time of his death, the book room held some 1,600 of his favorite books." (3) Many books bear Jefferson's ownership markings as well as the original Library of Congress bookplates. Congress purchased Jefferson's library for $23,950 in 1815. In the year 2020, it would equate to $328, 279. (5)

"In Thomas Jefferson's day, most libraries were arranged alphabetically. But Jefferson preferred to arrange his by subject. In practice, however, Jefferson shelved his books by size. A second fire on Christmas Eve of 1851 destroyed two thirds of the 6,487 volumes Congress had purchased from Jefferson. Through a generous grant from private donors, the Library of Congress is attempting to reassemble Jefferson's library as it was once sold to Congress. Some sharp debates occurred in Congress about the wisdom of purchasing the books." (6) "Although the broad scope of Jefferson's library was a cause for criticism of the purchase, Jefferson extolled the virtue of its broad sweep and established the principle of acquisition for the Library of Congress. Jefferson began a second collection of several thousand books, which was sold at auction to help satisfy his creditors." (7)

"Jefferson wrote only one full-length book, Notes on the State of Virginia, first published in 1787, which was a collection of his observations about the natural, animal, and human characteristics of his native land" (8) Perhaps we could speculate that his tutoring in God and nature by his good friend and professor William Small that prompted Jefferson to write such a book. "One can imagine how priceless a book owned by Thomas Jefferson would be today when just one document signed by Thomas Jefferson is selling for at least $82,000." (9)

Sitting at his desk, Jefferson continued to watch in awe as William delicately pulled books from the shelf to dust them. He opened each one, glancing with fascination at the illustrations while struggling to read some of the passages. It was when William pulled down a science book and seemed to spend more time perusing its contents that Jefferson walked over again to talk with William. William was so engrossed in the book that he did not notice Jefferson towering over him again. This would be the second time Jefferson would have words with what he considered his charge without acknowledging his relationship with the boy. "Good afternoon again young man." As always, William's eyes slowly moved from the book to Jefferson mid-section. William being only four feet in height was intimated by a man who was much taller than himself at six foot two. William anxiously acknowledged Jefferson's presence by apologizing for opening the book. "I am sorry Mr. Jefferson; I meant no harm to the book." Jefferson smiled at the boy while patting him on the shoulder at the same time. "Do the books interest you William?"

At this point in time, William had no knowledge of the key role Jefferson played in forging the nation. Awestruck by the fact that Jefferson was talking with him yet alone acknowledging his existence, William at first blurted out his words. "Yes Mr. Jefferson, I am very interested in your books." Jefferson turned towards William and kneeled on his one knee so as not to intimidate the boy. "Where did you learn to read? You seemed to read from each book, what did you find of interest in my books?"

Although there was no rule of law against teaching a slave to read, the boy pondered whether he should reveal who was teaching him for fear that the person may get into trouble. William was not aware that Jefferson was incredibly supportive of people given the opportunity to educate themselves. "Even though there is no record that Jefferson provided instruction for his slaves or encouraged them to learn their letters, several enslaved men at Monticello could read and write. There are surviving letters and documents in the hands of woodworker John Hemmings, blacksmith Joseph Fossett, and James Hemings." (10)

As William was taught never to tell a lie, he knew that he had to be truthful. After Ms. Hemmings and the blacksmith taught me some basics, Mr. Jefferson, I stayed here in the library after you retired for the night and improved my reading by reading some of your books. I asked them to teach me because I was curious about what is written in your books. For instance, I really enjoyed reading this one book by Laurence Sterne's "A sentimental journey through France and Italy," Jefferson's eyes lit up, as that was one of his favorite books. " (8) "Why did you pick that particular book William?" "It was about far off lands Mr. Jefferson. Someday I want to a visit those lands." Jefferson smiled at William and nodded his head in agreement. "I hope you are not going to punish them for teaching me. They taught me to read at the end of the day when all our chores were done." Placing his hands on the shoulders of William, of course, not William, I think it is admirable that they are taking the time to teach you to read."

"Jefferson understood the importance of education. In Virginia, only the children of wealthy men, such as Jefferson, could attend school. Teachers were paid by parents, and their job was to prepare young men for college." (12) "More generally, education was especially important to Jefferson and, as part of the general law revisal at the time of the Revolution, he recommended adoption of a broad educational system with a primary school for boys and girls, academies (secondary schools), and a university. In Jefferson's scheme, primary schools were to be free to students (both boys and girls), and the best male students were to attend the academies and university at public expense. He told his allies in the formation of the University of Virginia (UVA) that if it was a choice between public primary schools and the University, he would choose the former "because it is safer to have a whole people respectably enlightened, than a few in a high state of science and the many in ignorance." (13)

As congress was on hiatus for several months, Jefferson was able to spend considerable time enjoying a prolonged stay working in his beloved Monticello library. Late in the afternoon of each day, young William would tap on the library door waiting for Jefferson's approval to begin his chores. A broad smile would come across the face of Jefferson. He never denied his entrance. When young William entered, he went straight to dusting the vast volumes of books in Jefferson's collection.

When it came to arranging his books, Jefferson followed a modified organizational system created by British philosopher Francis Bacon (1561–1626), and that was to divide them into categories of Memory, Reason, and Imagination—which

Jefferson translated to "History," "Philosophy," and "Fine Arts"—and further divided into forty-four "chapters," the collection placed within Jefferson's fingertips the span of his multifaceted interests. The books from Jefferson's library were then the largest private book collection in North America. Now they are part of the Rare Book and Special Collections Division of the Library of Congress." (8)

Jefferson marveled at the fact that a young boy his age would take the initiative to not only learn how to read but have a desire to absorb so much knowledge. Jefferson spent an hour or two giving William a personal tour of his library and some of the books he was dusting. As the day ended, William was so infatuated with what Jefferson had shown him, he forgot it was dinner time. Jefferson ended their time together by reminding him. "Do you realize what time it is William? It is time for you to have your evening meal. Before you go, I will show you some of the things I invented." "Jefferson is credited with inventing a macaroni machine, a revolving chair with a leg rest and writing arm, and new types of iron plows created especially for hillside plowing. He also designed beds for his home that were built into alcoves on webs of rope hung from hooks, as well as automatic doors for his parlor. He created other devices for use in his home as well, including a revolving book stand with adjustable book rests and mechanical dumb waiters that allowed him to pull wine up to the dining room from the cellar." (14-15) William thanked Jefferson for his time and scurried away to his dinner.

"Morning meals were prepared and consumed at daybreak in the slaves' cabins. The day's other meals were usually prepared in a central cookhouse by an elderly man or woman no longer capable of strenuous labor in the field. The peas, the beans, the turnips, the potatoes, all seasoned with meats and sometimes a ham bone, was cooked in a big iron kettle and when mealtime came, they all gathered around the pot to share the meal." This took place at noon, or whenever the field slaves were given a break from work. At the day's end, some semblance of family dinner would be prepared by a wife or mother in individual cabins. The diets, high in fat and starch, were not nutritionally sound and could lead to ailments, including scurvy and rickets. Enslaved people in all regions and time periods often did not have enough to eat; some resorted to stealing food from the master. House slaves could slip food from leftovers in the kitchen but had to be careful not to get caught, for harsh punishments awaited such an offense." (16)

As William turned to walk out the door, he turned to Jefferson and said that the plantation overseer told him to never bother Mr. Jefferson when he was in his library. "Please do not tell the overseer that I came into the library while you were at work Mr. Jefferson." Jefferson smiled at the boy as he leaned back in his chair. "You are welcome to come back anytime William even if I am here. The only time that would be inconvenient, however, is when I have visitors." "Do not worry Mr. Jefferson, I will never bother you when you are busy with other people."

William joined Jefferson quite often over the next several months, both enjoyed their time together. Jefferson looked forward to the boy's visits, each time pulling another book off the library racks for them to read together. He would read part of a chapter and then tell William to read one, helping him to pronounce and understand the more difficult words. It was especially fulfilling for Jefferson as his mornings were filled with receiving mundane emissaries and government officials. Jefferson would ask William challenging questions. Jefferson would point to his books and ask William to pick one they could read together. He would then ask William to take the book over to his desk where he set up another chair close to his.

"William, who was the first president of the United States and what was his role in the revolution? William quickly responded, "why everyone knows that it was George Washington who led the Continental army to victory Mr. Jefferson, and you were the third president who wrote the document that gave everyone the inspiration to join in the revolution. Increasingly, Jefferson began to appreciate William's thirst for knowledge. He came to the realization that because his schedule was so hectic, he did not have the free time to spend on educating William. This prompted him to search for a suitable learning environment. He previously arranged private tutoring for his daughters and the same for the children he fathered with Sally Hemings. Jefferson did not want to send William to the same Tutors for fear that people may think that he fathered William with another slave.

William also asked many questions of Jefferson, some of which were far beyond those which a child of his age would ask or comprehend. Their visits became more like that of a father and son than that of an owner and his slave. As time went on, Jefferson realized William was far more advanced than children of his age. He kept pondering how to nurture William's talents without anyone noticing his interest in the boy. Recalling that he started his elementary education at a one-room schoolhouse when he lived at the Tuckahoe plantation, Jefferson felt the same educational environment would be a good place for William. "Jefferson began his formal education at the Tuckahoe plantation in a one room schoolhouse because his father was heir to this grand estate. When he left Tuckahoe, the eight-year-old Jefferson began his classical education. Jefferson, who spent seven years of his childhood at Tuckahoe, came to formulate his moral viewpoint of slavery." (17) "In the small one-room schoolhouses of the 18th century, students worked with teachers individually or in small groups, skipped school for long periods of time to tend crops and take care of other family duties, often learning little. Others took private lessons with tutors instead." (18) As a member of the gentry class, Thomas Jefferson received a good formal education. In his autobiography, Jefferson wrote that his father, Peter Jefferson, "placed me in the English school at 5. years of age and in the Latin one at 9. where I continued until his death." (19)

Jefferson decided to contact the current Tutor who taught in the one room schoolhouse at the Tuckahoe plantation to see if he would organize a school in Charlottesville. Charlottesville's population was only about 3,000, but it had surpassed Scottsville as the largest town in Albemarle County and home of several factories, banks, and hotels, as well as six newspapers. The Tutor agreed to do so if Jefferson could guarantee him at least ten students. After Jefferson agreed, the Tutor arrived one month later and began to look for a suitable building for his schoolhouse. The building the Tutor finally found was not the typical schoolhouse.

It was a former residence in the downtown area of Charlottsville. Several grades would be in one room with one teacher. Individual desks or a row of desks for the students would have been used. There was a chalkboard on the wall, and some type of stove to keep youngsters warm. In Jefferson's day, the one-room schoolhouse was usually in rural areas or small towns. America's one-room schools still exist, although they have dwindled from 190,000 in 1919 to fewer than four hundred today." (20, *Library of Congress photo 3*) "The schools in those days typically taught reading, writing, and arithmetic, history, geography, and math. The school buildings were also used for church service, town meetings or community affairs." (21)

CHAPTER 3

First Love

Jefferson had William enrolled by his Plantation overseer with the understanding that it was not to be revealed that William had any connection to Jefferson or that he was a slave. As Charlottesville was in serious need of a school, the Tutor was flooded with parents who wanted to enroll their children. Before he unpacked his bags, he had twenty students enrolled. It was an easy commute for William to reach the schoolhouse, approximately four miles. The teacher was jovial and extremely patient with their students, the first day was a matter of introductions. The student body consisted of eight boys and twelve girls, all around the same age as William and all Caucasians except for William. With little color to his skin, he easily passed for Caucasian. His slight tan from being in the sun gave him a radiant handsome look. With more girls than boys, William was pleased with the odds in his favor. He quickly became infatuated with one little girl, and she likewise took a liking to him. Her given name was Kathy, and her long blond hair and blue eyes put her above all the other young ladies in William's eyes. Her family was upper middle class, and her grandparents were known as they helped settle Charlottesville. They owned no slaves and were not supportive of the slave trade or using them as free labor.

William was told by the overseer that Mr. Jefferson was giving him this opportunity on the condition that he would not tell anyone that he was a slave on the Jefferson Plantation. William was shy and Kathy a bit forward. She took the initiative to introduce herself to him. "Hi, my name is Kathy and what is your name?" William was extremely nervous and shy but finally blurted out his name. "Aah, my name is William." "Where do you and your family live William." Wanting to be as truthful as possible, William thought before he spoke. "My family was hired to work on one of the plantations. We just moved here last year, and it is terrific that my parents found a school for me." William was saved by the bell with the teacher calling the class to order.

Kathy was an incredibly beautiful little girl, the boys in the classroom were all vying for her attention. One of the boys, John, who was somewhat of a bully, kept pushing the other boys away when they tried to talk to Kathy. John's family was among the wealthiest in the town and were good friends with Kathy's family, who were also well to do. In sharp contrast to Kathy's family, John's family were slave owners and supported such bondage. Unlike John, Kathy never flaunted her wealth. She was a very down-to-earth young lady and never looked down her nose at other students. Despite the interference by John, William and Kathy formed a close friendship.

One day at recess, John decided he was going to embarrass William in front of Kathy by having a fight with him. In those days, children liked to play leapfrog, tag, hide and seek, sack and relay teams. John decided the best way to instigate a fight was to organize a relay race and then trip William. John stood on the sidelines while William and his team ran from one end of the playground to the other. As William ran past John, John stuck his foot out to trip him. William picked himself up off the ground and gave John a shove. John grabbed William by his shirt and pushed him to the ground. "Don't blame me because you are clumsy William." William quickly jumped up and came after John. John simply stepped aside and punched William in the eye, giving him a black eye. Just then the bell rang for the children to come in from recess. Standing over William, John gave him a kick in the side and a warning. "I will continue this at the end of another school day. William went to his desk while the teacher came over to examine his bruised eye. "What happened to your eye William?" William looked over at Kathy to keep from staring at John. He knew that if he told the teacher the truth, he would be branded as a squealer among the other children. Looking up at the teacher, William quietly gave his explanation. "One of the swings came back and hit me in the eye." What John hoped to accomplish backfired on him. The other children now held William in high esteem for his courage to not expose John as the culprit. Kathy gave William an approving smile and a thumbs up.

At the end of the school day, John confronted William and knocked him to the ground, as the other kids watched in horror. When William tried to be independent, two of John's friends pushed him back down while John continued to throw punches. Kathy called out to John to stop but he was intent on bringing William down in the eyes of Kathy and his fellow students. Kathy finally spoke up. "Stay down William! Leave him alone John, he has had enough! John ignored Kathy's pleas and after inflicting one last blow, John again warned William about his fate. "This is only a start William. From here on, you are my punching bag. Whenever I want to take out my frustrations, you will be my punching bag." This time John let William get up. He was hurting so much that he had to roll over on all fours, resting on his hands and knees with his face pointed towards the ground in embarrassment. Kathy helped him get up and wiped some of the blood from him.

William returned to Monticello to take up his duties in the library. After what happened to him at school, he was hoping that Jefferson would not join him in the library. After William spent an hour dusting some of the books, the library doors swung open and in walked Jefferson. "Good evening, William." "Good evening Mr. Jefferson." William turned away to hide his black eye. William was concerned that he may be punished by not allowing him to school. To his dismay, however, Jefferson suggested that it was time for William to learn the game of chess. "Chess was one of Jefferson's favorite games, and one that he taught his granddaughter to play" (10) "Great Mr. Jefferson, I always wanted to learn the game. Many times, I would watch you play with a friend." Jefferson cleared his desk and placed the chess board on it. As he set each chess piece in place, he explained how they moved to William. William became so engrossed in watching and learning how each moved that he quickly forgot about concealing his black eye.

Jefferson paused from the chess instructions. Looking up, he noticed William's black eye. Grabbing hold of William's chin, Jefferson exclaimed in horror. "Good god, William, where did you get that shiner." Never wanting to lie to Jefferson, William fessed up. "I got it in a fight at school Mr. Jefferson, but please realize that I did not start it." William then proceeded to tell Jefferson how John tripped him on purpose. To the surprise of William, Jefferson did not admonish him for fighting. Instead, he asked William "what was the other boy's size, did he also suffer any bruises? What prompted him to trip you and who threw the first punch?" William filled Jefferson in on all the details of the altercation including that the other boy wanted to embarrass him over a girl. He did not tell Jefferson that John intended to do the same to him following the end of each school day. Thinking about how he once got in a fight over a little girl, Jefferson's had to refrain from smiling as he thought about his encounters as a youth. At the same time, however, he was angered about William being bullied. "You better go back to your cabin and put something cold on that eye. I will have some ice brought over. William excused himself and headed back to Sally Hemings quarters. He knew that she would also question him about his black eye. Upon entering her quarters, the expression on Sally's face was horrific.

"Sally Hemings may have lived in the stone workmen's house when she—like her sister Critta—might have moved to one of the new 12' × 14' log dwellings further down Mulberry Row. After the completion of the South Wing, Hemings lived in one of the "servant's rooms." (2) "Evidence that Sally Hemings lived in one of the spaces in the South Wing comes from Jefferson's grandson Thomas J. Randolph through Henry S. Randall, who wrote one of the first major biographies of his grandfather. Randolph did not specifically point out the exact room, but the description related through Randall suggests that Sally Hemings and her children occupied one of two rooms in the South Wing." (3) "Sally was a lady's maid (also described as chambermaid and seamstress) and her sons Madison, and Eston, were carpenters while Harriet was a spinner. (4) There is not a lot of detail as to the appearance of Sally, but an enslaved Monticello blacksmith gave some description. "Sally was near white in color, very handsome, with long straight hair down her back. "Owning quite a few slaves, one might ask if Thomas Jefferson was a racist? "Although he made some legislative attempts against slavery and at times bemoaned its existence, he also profited directly from the institution of slavery and wrote that he suspected Black people to be inferior to white people" (5). "Throughout his life, however, Thomas Jefferson was publicly an opponent of slavery. Calling it a "moral depravity" and a "hideous blot," he believed that slavery presented the greatest threat to the survival of the new American nation. (6)

Sally and her children were very fond of William and likewise, he felt the same about them. As soon Sally Hemmings and her children saw the bruises and William's black eye, they circled around to comfort him. After hearing the plight of William, Sally had to restrain her older sons from going off to find the bullies. Instead, Sally prepared a tasty meal from the food that Jefferson provided. Jefferson may not have elevated the living standards of Sally and their children to that of a privileged class, but he always made sure they had light duties and were given ample supplies.

Everyday John and his two friends would meet William to give him another thrashing and every day without saying a word to William, Jefferson agonized over his bruises when they visited one another in his library. William was quickly mastering the game of chess but due to his aches and pains, as well as Jefferson's skills, it was difficult for him to concentrate. Not able to bear seeing the hurt in William's eyes any longer, Jefferson finally spoke up. "Enough is enough William. Saturday I am going to teach you how to deal with this bully." At first, William thought Jefferson was going to teach him how to defend himself, but little did he know, Jefferson had someone else in mind.

CHAPTER 4

Boxing Lessons

Jefferson and other plantation owners purchased coal from a man who was also the bare knuckles champion of England, Tom Cribb. Cribb was all England Champion from 1808-1822.

Bare knuckle boxing originated in England. It is a full-contact combat sport based on punching without padding on the hands. (*Library of Congress photo 4*) "The difference between street fighting and a bare-knuckle boxing match is that the latter has an accepted set of rules, such as not striking a downed opponent. The rules that provided the foundation for bare-knuckle boxing for much of the 18th and 19th centuries were the London Prize Ring Rules. (1)

Cribb supplemented his income by brokering coal and frequently traveled to America to sell it to plantation owners. Over the years, he became a close friend of Jeffersons. It just so happened that he was meeting with plantation owners in Virginia this week. Learning that he was close by, Jefferson invited Cribb to spend the weekend at Monticello and join him for dinner on Saturday. Jefferson's message further explained the reason for his invitation so that Cribb would not think it presumptuous of what he was going to ask of him. Cribb accepted because it was considered an honor to receive an invitation from someone of such high esteem as the likes of Thomas Jefferson.

Jefferson told William about Tom Cribb's background on the night of his arrival. "Normally I do not condone fighting William, but it sounds like this bully is not going to let up. I think that Tom Cribb can be the answer to your problem. He has held the heavy weight bare knuckles championship." William could not believe that Jefferson was condoning his fighting. Not wanting William to think that it was acceptable to fight, Jefferson set the record straight. "Normally I do not condone fist fighting William, but I abhor bullies." He needs to be taught a lesson.

Just then, one of Jefferson's servants came in to announce the arrival of Tom Cribb. Hearing this, William eagerly awaited his entrance. Trying to envision what he looked like, William thought he must be a giant of a man with big fists. At that moment Tom Cribb entered the library. To the surprise of William, Cribb was only partially what he envisioned. At five foot nine, however, he weighed approximately two hundred pounds of solid muscle. His muscles bulged from his clothes and his neck had to be at least sixteen inches.

Upon his reaching out to shake William's hand, his hands were so large that they engulfed William's. His grip was so strong that it almost made one's eyes pop out of their sockets. Cribb did not realize that his handshake was that deliberating. Having experienced the strength of his handshake, Jefferson simply waved him a greeting.

After Jefferson and Tom exchanged some small talk and discussed the coal business, Jefferson turned the conversation to boxing and his reason for inviting him to dinner. "I realize you may be tired of your ride from the coast Tom, but I was wondering if you would be kind enough to spend some time this weekend giving young William some boxing lessons?" Surprisingly, Cribb looked William up and down wondering why he wanted to learn to box. Kiddingly he poked some fun at William. "Are you thinking of going into the fight game young William? "Perhaps you want to take my title someday." Thinking Cribb was serious, William cowered behind Jefferson and quickly exclaimed. "No way Mr. Cribb, I would never think of stepping into a ring with you!

Cribb laughed and seemed to take an immediate liking to William. On this special occasion, William was invited to join Cribb and Jefferson at the dinner table. As this was the first time William was even allowed in the dining room let alone sitting at the dinner table with Jefferson, he sat quietly with a fixated look.

He listened while the two men exchanged small talk and discussed business. Finally, they turned to the plight of William.

Jefferson described how three thugs bullied William. "The boys are bigger and older than William. They wait for him every day after school to shove him around and provoke a fight." Cribb turned to William asking, "did you provoke these bullies in any way William and if not, why are they harassing you?" William looked away in silence at first. He was embarrassed to give an explanation but then spoke up. "It was over a pretty girl by the name of Kathy. The ringleader does not want me to talk to her. Kathy and I have become close friends.

Cribb sat in silence for a while and then spoke. "William, your predicament reminds me how I was bullied when I was about your age. I took the bullying for a long time before I decided to do something about it. I was much smaller than the other boys in my neighborhood and was meek. After getting knocked around by two boys who always ganged up on me, I decided to do something about it. I started to help my father lift hundred bags of grain onto a delivery wagon and ate enough to gain another ten pounds. In about two months, I was solid as a rock and much broader but still the same height. I then started to go to bare knuckle fights that were held in a local barn. I studied how the fighters threw punches and how they blocked them."

"The next time the two thugs came after me, I stood my ground instead of running from them. My not running away shattered some of their self-confidence before the first punch was thrown. I then went after the biggest of the three, hitting him in the vulnerable parts of his body. The other one was so stunned by my aggressiveness; he froze. After the big guy went down, I started after the other one kicking him in his knee while using my elbow to hit him on the side of his head. He picked himself up and ran away as fast as he could. As the bigger guy started to get up, I gave him my hand and then proceeded to drop him back to the ground with one last punch. Those two never bothered me again. I guess I should thank them. Their bullying gave me the initiative to become a bare knuckles fighter. I made a lot of money from people betting against me when I fought."

"One thing that is against you William, is time. You do not have the time necessary to beef yourself up, but you do have enough time for me to show you how to defend yourself and stop the bully in his tracks."

At that, Jefferson glanced at his great clock. "One of Monticello's most memorable features is Jefferson's Great Clock, which was designed by him, built by Peter Spruck in 1792, and fully functional today. The clock, with both an interior and exterior face, dictated the schedule of the entire plantation, inside the building and out. On the outside wall, the clock has only an hour hand, which Jefferson believed was accurate enough for outdoor laborers." *(2 Library of Congress 33)*

Jefferson glanced over at William after seeing the time. "It is way past your bedtime William, and you are going to need your rest to start your boxing lessons early in the morning. Tomorrow and Sunday, you are excused from your chores so you can work with Mr. Cribb. You will start your lesson at 6:00 in the morning in the stables. William went to shake the hand of Cribb to bade him good night but remembering his grip, William waved him good night.

The morning came fast for William. His bed in Sally Hemmings cabin was on the floor to the right of the door. Sally's room was barely large enough to accommodate Sally's children, let alone William. William woke earlier than usual, excited to meet up with Tom Cribb. The sun crept in through the cabin door. In ordinary times, slaves had two regular meals in a day. After laboring from early daylight, breakfast was at twelve o'clock. When the work for the remainder of the day was over, they had their dinner. In harvest season the daily meals were increased to three.

This morning, however, Jefferson sent for William to join him and Tom Cribb at the breakfast table. He wanted to start a regimented diet to give William more strength. To assure that William was eating the right food, Jefferson had a place set at his breakfast table for William.

Upon finishing their breakfast, Jefferson looked outside to decide whether to work with William outside or in the stables. It is July and the hottest month. "I will try to determine the weather for today, Tom. The month of July is usually extremely hot at Monticello and the stables usually hold a lot of heat. It may be better to work in the clump of trees surrounding the house." "For more than fifty years, Thomas Jefferson was a systematic weather observer, Monticello was the focus of his efforts to understand the American climate. Before 1776, the date of his earliest surviving meteorological diary, he was carefully assembling information on the weather.

As one of the first systematic observers of the American climate, Jefferson tried to enlist others in his activities and even envisioned a national network of weather watchers. He realized that, for the formation of a reliable theory of climate, many others would have to provide what he had: years of "steady attention to the thermometer, its prevalent winds, quantities of rain and snow, temperature of mountains, and other indexes of climate." (3)

After some calculations, Jefferson confirmed that it would be best to teach young William in the shade of some nearby trees. An obscure location would also avoid questions from other workers as to why William was not working, especially as their winter workday was nine hours long, while in high summer it lasted fourteen hours. On the other hand, enslaved workers at Monticello could pursue their own activities in the evenings, on Sundays, and holidays." (4)

Upon meeting William for his first lesson, Cribb pushed him unexpectantly to the ground. "Normally, I would punch my opponent when they are not looking William, but I just wanted to demonstrate what is called the sucker punch. "The first blow is known as the sucker punch and that is when you punch your opponent without warning before he punches you. Such an aggressive action gets your opponent off guard and with any luck, dazes him enough for you to strike a follow-up blow. Cribb reaches out his hand appearing to help him up. William grabs ahold only to feel Cribbs other hand pushing hm in his face, forcing him back to the ground. Cribb then positions his body over William, pinning him to the ground, waving his fist in William's face. "That is your follow-up lesson to the sucker punch William.

Take advantage of your opponent while they are on the ground by plummeting them with punches. "

"Next, I am going to tell you what does and does not work when you are in a fight William. First, Fighting should always be a last resort. always try to talk your way out of a fight. There is a time to negotiate, and a time to walk away. If you are already under attack, that is the time to fight. You cannot stand still. You need to move your body to gain a superior position over your opponent, taking his eyes off the position of your fists. Do not take the fight to the ground. This gives one of your opponent's friends the opportunity to kick you in the body or worse, in your head. Never close your eyes or turn your face or head away from your opponent."

You cannot win a fight by defending alone. "You need to aggressively go after your opponent with a flurry of punches. Remember to use your entire body, it is a weapon and use it as such. You need to rotate your body and use footwork." (5)

The next day being Sunday, Cribb accompanied Jefferson to one of several churches he frequented. "Jefferson was baptized and raised Anglican (married and buried by Anglican ministers), but he rejected many of the tenets of that church. He regularly attended church of various denominations, but he declared that "I am of a sect by myself." In simple terms, Jefferson was a theist." (6) A theist is someone who believes in a God who intervenes with the universe.

After returning from church services, Cribb worked with Thomas for a few more hours. Jefferson watched the two of them train and felt comfortable that Cribb was on the right track. After William's last lesson, Cribb assured him that he was ready to take on the Bullies.

Having to meet with another plantation owner a day's ride from Monticello, Cribb had to leave early Monday morning. William woke early to say goodbye to Cribb. Cribb was traveling by horse and buggy and was just ready to leave when William appeared.

By the time he reached the stables, Cribb was mounted on his horse ready to ride down the road. "Sorry to see you go Mr. Cribb.

Hope you have a safe and pleasant journey." Having grown fond of William, Cribb climbed out of his carriage to give William a hug. Thinking this was a man who was the bare knuckles champion of the world, William was taken aback as to how warm Cribb was towards him. Unbeknownst to William, Cribb lost a son about the same age as William. This could have been why he took a special liking to William.

Cribb stepped back and again placed both his hands on the shoulders of William. "You are going to be okay William. You just needed some confidence and fighting technique. Hopefully, I was able to accomplish that in the two days we sparred!" William positively nodded his head, exclaiming that he did make a dramatic difference. "When will you be coming back this way Mr. Cribb?" "Not until the end of the year William."

As Cribb rode out of sight, William waved goodbye with a tear in his eye. William went about his chores that day with an anxious feeling that he was going to have to meet up with John and his two friends the next day. Jefferson sat in his library struggling to focus on his work but kept thinking about what William had to face tomorrow. A haunting vision was going through his mind of three bullies ganging up on William. A solution to even the odds suddenly dawned on him. He called for Sally Hemings to join him in the library. Upon entering, Sally sensed that Jefferson was stressed about something, so she waited for him to speak first. "Sally, these ruffians are going to gang up on young William tomorrow and I think we can even the odds."

Sally looking confused asked, "are you going to show up after school to protect William Mr. Jefferson." "No Sally, you know that I cannot do that, but I know who can." We can send Eston and Madison for some supplies, and they can stop by the school at the end of the day. Their presence can make certain none of the other kids pile on."

Caring about the wellbeing of William and knowing the strength of her two sons, Sally quickly gave her approval. "Give me your shopping list and I will have Eston and Madison ready to go tomorrow afternoon." Jefferson smiled and asked Sally to sit and talk." (8)

Not to say that Jefferson forced himself on Sally but "coerced sex was a widespread, feared, and traumatic aspect of enslavement. This is hardly surprising, for it would be difficult to construct a context more conducive to sexual exploitation than American slavery. Masters could condemn the living children or future progeny of slaves to bondage or hold out the emancipating them in return for satisfying service." (9)

The next morning came fast for William. He lingered in his makeshift bed for a few minutes before getting ready for school. All he could think about was confronting the three bullies. He was confident that he could handle John but knew it would mean trouble for him if the other two piled on. Upon entering the classroom, John and his two friends stared at William with hate in their eyes. William stayed inside during recess to avoid a confrontation with John and his friends. The teacher excused his students after completing the last lesson plan.

As usual, William started his journey home from the rear of the schoolhouse. John and his two friends were waiting. All the other students, including Kathy, were nearby expecting the worst. As John's two friends took hold of William while John prepared to hit him, Kathy tried to intervene. John simply brushed her off. Pointing his finger at William, John reiterated that he was going to beat him every day after school. "Are you ready for your daily thrashing William?" The expression on William's face was sullen and lost. At that moment, he lost heart in defending himself. Just as John landed the first blow upon William, Eston and Madison showed up.

They quickly grabbed John's two friends by the scruff of their necks and Madison exclaimed "this fight seems a bit unfair. Let us see how you do without your hoodlum friends." Eston and Madison being much bigger and stronger than John's two friends, the only thing for them to do was to stand aside. John threatened Eston and Madison with reprisals for their getting involved. "You are nothing but slaves and need to stay out of this. If not, I will find and report you to your owner." Madison and Eston just smiled at John and held their ground.

"You go right ahead and when you find out who owns us, we think you may not be so quick to contact him. Especially as he does not like bullies." Now it was only John and William facing one another. Just as they were about to fight, another hand reached in and grabbed William. It was John's father who stopped by to take John to their plantation to complete the chores that he did not finish. With John's father restraining William, John gave William a staunch punch in the stomach. As William buckled over, another hand took ahold of John's father. Turning to see it was Tom Cribb who had ahold of him and knowing of his being a champion bare-knuckle fighter, fear gripped John's father. Cribb was very assertive. "Sir, I think it best to allow these two young men to settle their disagreement on their own. Your son needs to be taught a lesson."

William could not believe that Cribb had shown up on his behalf. This boosted his confidence and determination more than anything else. John, used to getting his own way, tried to sucker punch William but this time William was ready and saw it coming. William deflected the blow and delivered a punch that sent John to his knees with an uppercut to the chin for good measure. Williams' defensive move was exactly as it was taught to him by Cribb. John cascaded to the ground painfully holding his stomach. William pounced on top of John preparing to plummet him with punches. Holding John down, he raised his right in preparation for his follow-up attack.

William thought it not honorable to continue his attack but wanted to at least bring a point home. "Have you had enough John?" Seeing the determination in William's eyes and not wanting any more pain, John thought it best to ask for mercy. "I do not want any more. I give up William. The students encircling the two burst out in cheers. They liked William more than John because some of them had been bullied by John and his two cohorts. After John gave in, William in gentlemanly fashion extended his hand and helped John to his feet.

John got up but did not acknowledge William's kindness. He was still resentful of Kathy taking a liking to William rather than to him. William went over to thank Eston and Madison for backing him up. They gave William a pat on the back and praised him for his self-defense skills. William then turned to Cribb. "Thank you so very much for coming to support me Mr. Cribb. I could never have done this without you, and I am incredibly grateful for what you did today. I thought you would have been well on your way to your next meeting." Placing his hands on Williams' shoulders Cribb said. "I thought you might need someone to act as your second."

Being late for his next meeting, Cribb had to excuse himself. He also wanted to catch up to John and his father. When John and his father saw Cribb approaching them, they were concerned that he might beat on them. Cribb put up his finger to signal for them to stop. John and his father turned around with great concern on their faces. "Sir, I would hope that the bullying by your son and his two friends has ended here and now. If not, please rest assured that I will return to discuss this matter with you in person." John's father backed up in fear. Taking his son by the ear. "You can rest assured that his bullying stops here and now, right John." Tongue in cheek, John spoke up. "You can rest assured Mr. Cribb that we will no longer be bullying anyone."

By the time William returned to Monticello, Eston and Madison had already reported the results to their mother and Mr. Jefferson of how William defended himself. As usual, William reported to the library to take up his chores. Jefferson was sitting at his desk making believe that he was hard at work. Showing any indication that he knew the outcome of the fight, William would know it was he that sent Eston and Madison. He wanted William to think that he stood up on his own. Deep down, however, William thought it was Jefferson who deployed them.

William was so excited and relieved about the outcome that he forgot the protocol of a slave addressing his owner. He quickly pulled up a chair alongside the desk of Jefferson with unrestrained excitement. "I wish you were there Mr. Jefferson. Eston, Madison, and even Mr. Cribb showed up. I did exactly what Mr. Cribb taught me, and the outcome was in my favor. I will never have to worry about being bullied again. I cannot begin to tell you how relieved I am and how much I appreciate what you did for me."

Clearing his throat without showing any emotion, Jefferson needed a diversion to hide his joy for William. He pointed to the chess set. "All this is good, but it is time for another game or two of chess William. You seem to have quickly mastered the skills of chess. From here on, we are going to keep score." They played three games. Jefferson was amazed that William beat him to one out of the three. Jefferson looked at William with awe and with a puzzled look on his face "How did you manage to defeat me, William? Have you been practicing?" "By watching your moves Mr. Jefferson, I learned a lot."

Time marched on. William would meet Jefferson at least once a week to play chess. It was not long for the two of them to be evenly matched. Jefferson grew fonder of William and looked forward to their visits. He started to place visits with William as a priority over visits with others. After chess became too much of the norm, Jefferson decided to teach William foreign languages. Thomas Jefferson could speak in four different languages. William quickly picked up speaking and reading some of the languages.

CHAPTER 5

Discovered

As time went on, William and Kathy were now young adults. They became closer, frequently visiting one another at the plantation of Kathy's parents. Kathy always wondered, however, why William never invited her to visit his home and introduce her to his family. Despite the many encounters between William and Kathy, John harbored hopes that Kathy may someday opt for him over William. Kathy had two brothers and one younger sister by the name of Jane, an adventurous child.

Every time William would visit, Jane would fondly taunt him. She would sit with William teasing him relentlessly. Despite her being mischievous, William kept thinking that Jane was a very jolly, amusing, and attractive fourteen-year-old. She was great fun, talkative, and full of life. A rebel who was inquisitive and not afraid to challenge others including her parents and siblings. Jane was highly intelligent and beautiful to behold, with long blond hair down to her waist.

Kathy had reached the age that women started to court. Being a slave and of mixed blood, William knew he could not formally court Kathy let alone ever marrying her. "In 18th-century America, the typical age of marriage for middle-to-upper class white women was 22 and 26 for men. Women began courting as early as 15 or 16, but most delayed marriage until their early twenties. Women had the right to refuse any suitors and were not occupied with running a household. This was why women began courting at such an early age but did not usually marry until several years later." (1)

In the case of Kathy, she had already turned down several suitors, including John who was persistent in his advancements towards her. John even asked her parents for permission to court her, but they were reluctant to intercede. "We are leaving it up to Kathy as to who she wishes to see John." Kathy was becoming anxious as to why William was waiting to ask her parents if he could formerly court her.

Regardless of him being a slave, William did not fit the bill in any way whatsoever according to acceptable couple matches in those days. Some key considerations helped high society couples "get it right" when finding their life partner. First up, finances: a family's fortunes would be furthered if a daughter married well. Another guideline was finding compatibility rather than fleeting romance. Divorce was not acceptable. "People were still marrying very closely within their own social circles. It was not uncommon for first cousins to marry. They would have the same family background, upbringing, and parity of status. All features of a good match, keeping property within a family." (2)

"In those days, a single woman could never be alone with a gentleman. It was imperative for a chaperone to always be present, supervising meetings and time spent together. A single woman could never begin a conversation with a man without having a formal introduction first. No physical contact of any kind was allowed during courtship. During the engagement period, couples were allowed to hold hands and take unchaperoned walks and carriage rides. Victorian woman focused on fulfilling her duties as a wife and mother." (3) In the case of Kathy and William, they already violated this protocol knowingly by her parents. Again, Kathy's parents thought nothing of the visits of William. He was looked upon as a trusted friend and not a suitor. Conversations at Kathy's family dinner table did on occasion, come up about William. Many questions about him went unanswered.

Her younger sister Jane was of immense help by talking about what she saw as William's great attributes. "William is of good character and compassionate. He is highly intelligent, well read, and versed in more than one language. He can talk on most subjects and is a great conversationalist." Kathy and her parents looked on in amazement as Jane checked off the qualities of

William. One would almost think it was she that desired William more than Kathy.

Meanwhile, William was struggling with how to gain his freedom. When next reporting to perform his chores in the library, William noticed Jefferson scanning an original copy of his Declaration of Independence. He thought this was an opportune time to ask Jefferson about his freedom. It was Jefferson who not only wrote the declaration, but he helped to arrange its printing and distribution among the powers to be. "Today, there is only one copy of the engrossed and signed Declaration of Independence, in the National Archives in Washington DC. Sealed in a gold-plated titanium frame, with bulletproof glass and innovative safeguards against light and moisture, it remains under constant surveillance by armed guards and security cameras. This copy was produced and signed several weeks after the Declaration of Independence was first published.

"It is estimated that John Dunlap, the printer, produced two hundred broadside copies of the Declaration of Independence, the first printing of the text. Of that original number, there are twenty-six known copies of the Dunlap broadside in the world today. The Dunlap broadside did not include any names besides John Hancock and Secretary Charles Thomson. The first broadside to include the names of the signatories was the Goddard broadside, printed in January 1777. (4) A broadside copy is a large sheet of paper printed on one side. (*Library of Congress photo 5*) By asking Dunlap to print the Declaration of Independence which was against the rule of the King of England, Thomas Jefferson was asking him to join him and the signers to commit treason."

William walked over to stand next to Jefferson without saying anything at first. The two simply stood admiring the document. After five minutes went by, William started the conversation. "One thing that puzzles me Mr. Jefferson is how you said all men are created equal, but you and many plantation owners enslave people of my kind." Jefferson's eyes widened with surprise that William would ask such a question but restrained himself from reprimanding him.

Jefferson was conflicted, deep within himself for there was the realization that William had a valid point. On the other hand, Jefferson did not want to have a rebellion among his slaves by letting one of them question him. With his hand on his chin, Jefferson decided to give justification for what many perceived as his being a hypocrite. "I cannot give you a straight answer William and at the same time, I cannot justify why some of my actions conflict with what I authored."

To my recollection, "A statesman from Virginia, put forth a motion calling for the Congress to declare independence. John Adams, Benjamin Franklin, Robert R. Livingston, Roger Sherman, and me were then instructed to draft a resolution." *(5)* "As for slavery, I have been publicly a consistent opponent of slavery. I called it a moral depravity and a hideous blot and believe that slavery presents the greatest threat to the survival of the new American nation." *(6)*

Hearing this philosophy from Jefferson himself, William felt confident enough to indirectly ask him for his freedom. "If you believe all this Mr. Jefferson, why don't you free people like me? I would work extremely hard to guarantee the survival of the nation and Monticello." Jefferson was once again taken back that such a young person as William offered common-sense argument.

"Please realize William that despite my advocating for abolition, the reality is that slavery is becoming more entrenched. I am also in deep debt and cannot afford to hire workers. My only hope of sustaining Monticello is to keep my expenses low and that means to not free my slaves. All the slaves on this plantation know of my promise to free the children of Sally Hemings but if I would also grant your freedom, it would create much disdain among the other slaves."

From what Jefferson just said, William knew that his hope of gaining his freedom was hopeless. He also knew that he needed to stop badgering Jefferson for fear of angering him. "I understand Mr. Jefferson and will not bring up the subject anymore. I thank you for allowing me to ask the question." Jefferson just nodded with a smile.

For the next several weeks, William continued his same routine of visiting with Kathy at her family's plantation. Kathy's sister Jane was always waiting to taunt him. The exchanges between William and Jane blossomed into a close friendship. Always lurking in the background was John, looking for an opportunity to gain Kathy's favor by discrediting William. Then one day he concocted a scheme to have a friend follow William.

Following William across some pastures and through a clump of trees, the friend was surprised to learn that William's journey ended at Thomas Jefferson's Monticello. Perplexed as to whether William was visiting or lived on the plantation, John's friend *(Photo2)* climbed over a back fence into the fields where Jefferson's slaves were working. Approaching two of them, he gave them a description of William. He was surprised as to what he heard. "Yes sir, we know that boy. He was born into slavery. Why do you ask mister?" Not wanting to give away the reason for asking, he gave an excuse that he wanted to give back a book he borrowed.

John's friend could not wait to tell John what he learned; He went straight to the plantation of John's family. John was working for his father cleaning up one of the barns. "John, you will not believe what I learned about William. He is a slave on the plantation owned by Mr. Jefferson." Dropping his shovel, John was speechless. He knew that this meant that Kathy's family would never allow William to marry their daughter. "I can't wait to tell Kathy's parents." He then hesitated. "No, first I am going to talk to William tomorrow when he visits Kathy."

The path that William takes to Kathy winds along a creek and then over a hill through pastureland. John was waiting for him leaning up against a tree. "Good afternoon, William. Do you have a minute to talk?" Remembering the beating he took from William the last time they fought, he did not want to provoke him into another fight. William stopped in his tracks and gave John a puzzling look. "It is rather strange that you want to talk to me now when you once turned your back to me." John gave William a weird smile. "Did you get all your chores done for Mr. Jefferson?" William face turned red; he was speechless. "How did you find out me John?" (*Library of Congress photo 6*)

Pacing back and forth, John pointed his finger at William. "Work for Jefferson? You are owned by him. You are a slave, William! When are you going to tell Kathy and her parents? Don't you think they deserve to know that you are a slave?" William had no comeback. Being a descent and honest young man, he knew that John was right. Looking intently at John, William poses a proposition to him. "If I stop seeing her, will you promise to keep it to yourself?" Even though William felt John was not a good fit for Kathy, there was no other choice. William waited for John's response. "Alright William, I will keep your secret if you keep your promise."

William returned to Monticello, lying awake that night with tears filling his eyes to the point of being bloodshot. The next morning, William showed up at Jefferson's library where he noticed a newspaper lying on the desk with the word war in the headlines.

CHAPTER 6

War of Independence

"In the early1800's, there were two hundred newspapers being published in the United States. At the beginning of the century, journalism in cities was dominated by the political and mercantile press, which tended to cater to groups of elite readers. But the 1820s and 30s saw the establishment of many new papers intended specifically for working men, free blacks, women, immigrants, and Native Americans, as well as for religious denominations, professions, or political causes" (1) Because Jefferson was of that gentry class, he received every publication of interest to him. "Anyone with a printing press and a flair for the written word could publish a newspaper. One newspaper especially defined by its era was *The War*, a New York-based publication that ran from 1812 to 1815. The newspaper's very existence was precipitated by the War of 1812, and the description in the masthead proclaimed it as "being a faithful record of the transactions of the war." The editor declared that not only would the paper "support a love of country, but it would also educate its readers in "the art of war." *(2)* "Families of soldiers and sailors found the most current news in publications like *The War*, which offered a broad overview of the conflict, including laws and negotiations, military movements, and descriptions of armaments as well as the types of sea-going vessels. The headline of the newspaper talked about "The War of 1812". *(2)*

William asked Jefferson to elaborate on the war and how it started. Sometimes referred to as the "Second War of Independence," "the War of 1812 was the first large scale test of the American republic on the world stage. The war that finally broke out in 1812 was the result of nearly fifteen years of tension between the young United States and various powers in Europe.

Americans in favor of open conflict, known as "War Hawks," were especially strong in the South and West. *(3)* "With the British Navy impressing American sailors (taking of men into a military or naval force by compulsion, with or without notice), and the British government aiding Native American tribes in their attacks on American citizens, Congress, for the first time in our nation's history, declared war on a foreign nation: Great Britain. Battles prevailed on the high seas and British soldiers invaded America, captured Washington D.C., and burned the White House." *(3)*

A factor that was weighing on William's mind was that he may be able to gain his freedom by volunteering for the war. He knew the British offered freedom for slaves who fought for them but because of William's loyalty to America and Jefferson, it was out of the question for him to join the ranks of the British. "To encourage participation in the War of Independence, however, some white slaveholders had promised emancipation for military service." *(4)* William also saw that the war may be his opportunity to get away and fulfill his end of the bargain he struck with John. He wanted to avoid at all costs Kathy and her family learning of his being a slave. He was also willing to sacrifice himself so Kathy could marry someone else.

William followed a strict code of honor whereas John did not. When John gave William his word to not revealing his identity, he knew that he was going to break it to make certain that William was entirely out of the picture. He could not wait any longer to tell Kathy's parents. It was early morning when John arrived at the plantation of Kathy's parents. As he finished explaining all that he knew about William, the parents sat in shock. They then called Kathy into the parlor so that John could tell her. Kathy slumped in a chair with her hands in her face. Just then, Kathy's younger sister Jane came into the room. After learning what was said about William, she spoke up in his defense. "What does it matter? Did our religious upbringing not teach us to be benevolent towards others? Has William always been kind and considerate towards our family and Kathy? Just because he may be of mixed blood, his soul is still pure!

William returned to the library the next day stressed out as to how he was going to broach the subject of enlisting in the army with Jefferson. Then it dawned on him that Jefferson played a role in trying to avert the war. His questioning Jefferson about it would provide an opening to request his permission to sign up. "Any new developments on the war Mr. Jefferson?" Jefferson threw a newspaper on his desk. "The British have entered Washington!"

Jefferson lamented that "When James Madison was elected to the presidency in 1808, he instructed Congress to prepare for war with Britain. On June 18, 1812, buoyed by the arrival of "war hawk" representatives, the United States formally declared war on Britain. Citizens in the Northeast were opposed to the idea, but many others were enthusiastic about what is being referred to as the nation's "Second War of Independence" from British oppression. This war will be the first large scale test of the American republic on the world stage." *(3)* "When he was President, Thomas Jefferson attempted to protect and defend American sovereignty and commerce against Europe's two major powers, Britain, and France. *(4)*

"Sometimes I feel it was my fault for not averting the war, William." William tried to justify Mr. Jefferson's part in the war. "You should not blame yourself for something that did not start under your watch Mr. Jefferson. Many of our youth are being called upon to fight for our nation. I think that I should follow their example and join to protect what you and others have started." Jefferson sat in amazement at what William just said and was torn to let William enlist.

Because he blamed himself for the war that befell his nation in the early days of its infancy and he respected the wishes of William, he felt obligated to allow him to go even if it meant his life. Besides, he reminded himself that "he served for nine years as a colonel in the Virginia Militia at the start of the Revolutionary War. He reported directly to the governor in preparing the county militia for mobilization and provided militia soldiers" (5)

Jefferson slowly rose from his desk and for the first time, placed his hands on the shoulders of William while William bowed his head in reference. "If this is your choice, then so be it,

William. I will give you leave to serve but you must give me your word that you will return to your duties here at Monticello once the war has ended." "I give you my word Mr. Jefferson. I will return whether alive or not." Jefferson cringed at what William just said about the possibility of not returning alive. "I prefer you returning to me alive William." "Roughly 15,000 Americans died in the War of 1812. Roughly 8,600 British and Canadian soldiers died from battle or disease." (6)

Receiving the approval of Jefferson, William left to gather what little belongings he possessed. Before he took his leave, he asked Jefferson's permission to say goodbye to some of his friends. Jefferson gave his permission freely. He ran over to Kathy's plantation. At the entrance that he usually took when visiting Kathy, he found Kathy waiting for him. "Tell me it is not true what John told my parents William? "John told you about me Kathy. Our agreement was that he would not reveal anything to you or your parents. I should have expected nothing less from him."

Mr. Jefferson gave me permission to fight in the war but did not grant me my freedom." Kathy looked at William in desperation. "Is there anything that we can do William." "Our only way around it would be for us to flee to one of the free states." "I cannot go against the wishes of my parents William." And I cannot go back on my word to Mr. Jefferson Kathy." Kathy and William gave one another a final hug and kiss goodbye. As William walked away from Kathy, they both kept looking back at one another until both were out of sight.

William packed his bags the night before he left. For his last night, Jefferson directed him to sleep in a guest room of Monticello. He had a selfish reason for having William use one of the guestrooms. He did this so William could not slip away without saying goodbye. William slept little that night thinking about Kathy and the war. The morning sun shone through the window. He woke an hour before the start of the day as he did not want to wake anyone and encounter emotional goodbyes. He tiptoed out and walked across the front lawn towards the road.

"In those days' waterways and a growing network of railroads linked the frontier with the eastern cities. Produce moved on small boats along canals and rivers from the farms to the ports. Large steamships carried goods and people from port to port. Later Railroads expanded to connect towns, providing faster transport for everyone." (7)

William was to report to the town hall in Charlottesville where he would start his journey to meet up with his regiment. As he walked down the road, he heard someone calling out to him. As he turned, he saw Jefferson on horseback in the distance waving for him to wait. Alongside Jefferson was one of his slaves with a horse drawn wagon. Jefferson and the wagon road up to William. "Did you think you were going to sneak off without saying goodbye William?" "No sir, I just did not want to bother anyone. You know you are always on my mind Mr. Jefferson."

Jefferson looked at William with a blank look. Reaching down into his pocket, Jefferson pulled out some money. As he leaned down from his horse, he handed it to William. "Take this William, it will make your journey much easier." "Oh no Mr. Jefferson, I can't accept your money." "You have no choice, William. Take it! James is going to give you a ride to Charlottesville." William slowly reached out to take the money that he desperately needed. "Thank you so very much Mr. Jefferson. I am going to really miss our chess games and our language lessons." Jefferson reached into his saddlebags and pulled out two books. These books are written in French. You can brush up on your French while away." William climbed onto the wagon to start his journey into Charlottesville. As he climbed into the wagon, Jefferson reached out to pat him on his shoulder goodbye. It was a sad scene for both. Both men had a tear in their eye. As the wagon rode down the road, William could see Jefferson still sitting on his horse. (Photo library of Congress 6)

Initially William reported to Fort Niagara on Lake Erie. "After Britain's war with France ended in early 1814, the British turned their attention to the United States, sending fresh troops to invade the U.S. and secure Canada." (8) "During the colonial wars in North America, a fort at the mouth of the Niagara River was vital. The fort was captured by the British during the War of 1812 until being ceded again to the United States in 1815 as a peaceful border post. Old Fort Niagara served as a training station and active barracks from the Civil War until the last army units were withdrawn in 1963."

"Most, but not all, of the men recruited for a particular infantry regiment were from the state of recruitment. Those who enlisted in the army at the beginning of the war had a five-year commitment, though later recruits were given the option of enlisting for the duration of the war. At first the bounty was $31 and 160 acres of land, but because enlistments lagged, Congress gradually increased the incentives to $124 and 320 acres of land. "(10)

Upon his arrival at Fort Niagara, he was told that he was being reassigned to General Andrew Jackson's armies in the south. Little did William know that Jefferson had contacted General Jackson to have him reassigned under his command so he could keep a watch on him.

"During the War of 1812, General Andrew Jackson led his troops through enemy territory to victory in several tide-turning battles. In doing so, he aided our nation's victory in the war. This led to the procurement of millions of acres in the present-day southern United States, including Florida." (11) News traveled slowly across the country. Deployment of Jackson's militia to defend New Orleans had not reached Jefferson. Defending New Orleans could become one of the bloodiest battles of the war. If Jefferson knew, he would have diverted William to an assignment in an area far from harm's way. Jefferson should also have known about Jackson's reputation for being an aggressive combatant but for some reason, it slipped his mind. "The British, however, were planning a major offensive against U.S. southern ports, including the wealthy port of New Orleans. Hearing of the move, Jackson raced to strengthen the defenses at Mobile and then invaded neutral Spanish Florida to drive off a small British force. He next marched his army to New Orleans to defend the city, arriving on December 2, 1814. Jackson made several controversial decisions. He declared martial law in the city, welcomed the aid of Jean

Lafitte and his pirates, and even formed a regiment of armed free blacks as equals. The British force came within sight in about ten days." (12)

Jackson ordered his executive officer to find and send William to his headquarters. In the meantime, Jackson was staging his army to defend New Orleans and if necessary, launch a counterattack against the British. Upon Williams' arrival at his headquarters. Jefferson was leaning over a table reviewing battle plans with his commanders.

William was mesmerized when he first set eyes on Jackson. Jackson was tall and gaunt--6 ft. 1 in. but weighing only 140 lb.--and carried himself in a ramrod-straight military manner. His face was long and thin, and his eyes were clear, dark blue. He had bushy, iron-gray hair, brushed high above his forehead. Noted for his terrible temper, his favorite expletive was "*By the Eternal*!" The cartoonists of the day immediately seized upon this curse and nicknamed him Old Hickory." (13, *White House Web Site Print*)

William could not believe why a high ranking general like Jackson would personally be interested in a soldier holding the lowest rank in the military. Jackson wanted to respect the wishes of Jefferson and would not reveal his connection to the past president. "What is your name son and where do you hail from? Nervous and reverent, William had great difficulty finding words. Finally, he got over his fears and spoke up. "My name is William Sir, and I am from Virginia.

Can I ask you a question General Jackson?" Jackson looked puzzled that William wanted to ask him a question. Most young recruits cannot muster enough courage to do so. Jackson slowly nodded yes. "Feel to ask me any question you wish." Having difficulty looking into the eyes of a great general like Jackson, William looked down in humility to put forth his question. "Why does a great general like you wish to meet a lowly private like me?"

"I do when new and especially young recruits are assigned to me William. If there are large numbers, I have my chief of staff make a random selection of one or two from the bunch. This is how my chief of staff selected you, William. By meeting new recruits and learning about their backgrounds, I have a better understanding as to the makeup of my militia and how best to position them. Now I have a question for you. Jackson continued his questioning of William. "What did you do before you enlisted in the army, William?" "I managed a library that housed rare books Sir. Many of them were from a rare collection by a high revered statesman." Jackson did not want to ask him who was the statesman for fear of tipping his hand that he was a close confident of Jefferson. Instead, he directed one of his officers where to assign William.

"So, you organized a library, William?" "Great, I am going to assign you to personally maintain these battle maps and plans. It is an extremely critical assignment! Do you think you can handle it?" "Yes sir, I will not let you down." Even though it was a noncombatant assignment, it was a crucial role to protect the documents and organize them when called upon.

In the meantime, the military supply units were busy arming the soldiers. "Most of the firearms used by soldiers in the War of 1812 were small arms weapons.

The next few days General Jackson hurriedly moved his militia in place to rebuff the British. "In 1812, things predicatively did not go well for the Army, as it invaded Canada, which was then known as British North America. The U.S. Army was poorly trained and led. It had significant logistical weaknesses." (15) "The force Jackson led to oppose them was made up mostly of militia with some Choctaw allies and a few professional soldiers – more of an armed war band than an army. His men did have combat experience, they mostly had irregular warfare on the frontier. In sharp contrast, The British troops sent to New Orleans were hardened veterans of the Napoleonic Wars. Well trained, professional, and deadly, they had fought in some of the fiercest conflicts the world had seen over the past twelve years." (16)

"Jackson received word that the "British fleet arrived near Ship Island, some sixty miles east of New Orleans, on December 8. After disposing of an American flotilla on Lake Borgne,

Cochrane and the temporary army commander decided to ferry the British infantry through the nearby bayous and approach the city from the south.

"Jackson boldly marches out to meet the enemy. In a daring nighttime assault, the Americans strike the British camp. A sharp but inconclusive fight ensues and after several hours, Jackson disengages and withdraws two miles north to the Rodriguez Canal. A marine battery is established on the right bank of the river." (17)

In the meantime, unbeknownst to Jackson, William is mistakenly assigned to a unit on the front lines, a unit that will receive the first assault by the British and sustain major casualties. Not wanting to desert his post, William says nothing about his being wrongly assigned. While waiting in place, William makes friends with two other recruits. Michael and Mark enlisted in their home states of Tennessee and Kentucky. As William learned upon his arrival in New Orleans, "Each Regular Army infantry regiment was recruited from a particular state (or states). The system for paying the troops broke down from the beginning. At the start of the war privates were paid $5 a month, non-commissioned officers $7 to $9, and officers $20 to $200" (18)

Michael and Mark were recruited involuntarily at the objections of their respective families. While the three huddled together waiting for the call to charge forward, they made a pact to notify their families if any one of them did not survive. William did not mention to Mark and Michael that he was an orphaned slave and the only ones that may care about learning of his demise would be Thomas Jefferson and Sally Hemings. He did not give the name of Jefferson for fear that he would be reassigned to a noncombatant unit. In any event, they exchanged information as to their next of kin. The first assault by the British finally comes but fails. Once again, William and his unit find themselves waiting. Christmas is only days away.

"On Christmas Day, British General Sir Edward Pakenham arrives and assumes command of the British expeditionary force. Annoyed by his subordinates' inability to defeat Jackson and capture New Orleans, Pakenham moves his army to the Chalmette Plantation, about five miles southeast of

New Orleans. Over the course of the next five days, Pakenham makes two attempts to breach Jackson's troops. Both are repulsed by the Americans. Left with few options and buoyed by the arrival of reinforcements, Pakenham decides to launch a major assault.

"The British attack gets underway before sunrise. Devastated in front of Line Jackson, the remnants of the British force withdraw to beyond range of the American guns. Despite the limited success of Col. Thornton's attack against the marine battery on the right bank, Pakenham's successor, Maj. Gen. John Lambert, is unable to salvage the British effort and recalls Thornton's force." (17)

During the "fog of war," William and his two friends are caught in the middle of the onslaught. They fight hard against the British while desperately trying to stay alive. The British train their cannons towards the defensive lines of the Americans and fire several volleys. One lands near William and his two friends, wounding all three with William being inflicted with the least wounds. At first, William could not move, and everything was spinning around him. He had difficulty hearing because his ears were ringing from the cannon balls exploding around him. The repercussion of the cannon balls froze him and muffled all surrounding sounds including the voices of Michael and Mark. He turned his head towards his two friends only to see them bleeding from the impact which hit closer to them than himself.

Finally, William was able to crawl over to them. His first came to Michael. William tried to look for any signs of life but there were none. Michael was unresponsive and his eyes were wide open. He then moved on to Mark who was still alive but in severe pain. "Mark, can you hear me?" Mark moved his head to the side and barely had the strength to nod his head yes. While the two of them laid on the ground, the British volleys kept raining down upon them. William knew that if they stayed there, they would eventually be plummeted with more cannon shots and surely perish. The only chance they had was to move behind the front lines.

William suffered shrapnel in his one arm and upper left leg. He had the mobility to walk but knew if he stood, he would become a walking target for the British marksman. To avert being hit again, he rolled on his back and wrapped his gun belt around the upper body of Mark. Inch by inch, he pushed with the hills of his boots dragging Mark to the rear. Once he was out of the reach of enemy fire, he stood and straddled Thomas on his back. William reached what little medical treatment was available.

"An American soldier during the War of 1812 was far more likely to die from disease than in battle. In fact, fully three-quarters of the war deaths resulted from disease, most commonly typhoid fever, pneumonia, malaria, measles, typhus, smallpox, and diarrhea. Medical practices were rudimentary and often harmful. Military surgeons often resorted to so-called "heroic" treatments. Those treatments often seemed crude and sometime barbaric to modern eyes. Bleeding, the deliberate opening of vein to remove blood from a patient. Such practices were seldom helpful and often made the patient's condition worse. Among the items found in a surgeon's medicine chest were opium and alcohol, useful for pain management, and quinine.

Army medicine also suffered from some basic organizational shortcomings. The War Department was ill prepared when the conflict broke out in 1812. Officials had no standardized system of accounting for or replenishing its medical supplies, or for evaluating the competency and training of its medical staff." (19)

Both William and Mark were fortunate in that there was a young field medic that was trained in some innovative techniques to stop their bleeding. As William and Mark laid on a stretcher side by side, the battle waged on. William reminded Mark about the pact they made to inform their families if they did not survive. "I will see that Michael's family is notified William. I will make sure they know he died bravely and in combat." William nods in agreement. At that instance, another volley of cannon hits nearby, shaking the ground with a thundering sound.

As cannon fire from British ships rained over Fort McHenry, "Francis Scott Key pens a poem which is later set to music and in 1931 becomes America's national anthem, "The Star-Spangled Banner." The poem, originally titled "The Defense of Fort McHenry," was written after Key witnessed the Maryland fort being bombarded by the British during War of 1812. Key was inspired by the sight of a lone U.S. flag still flying over Fort McHenry at daybreak, as reflected in the famous words of the "Star-Spangled Banner": "And the rocket's red glare, the bombs bursting in air, gave proof through the night that our flag was still there."

"Eventually, the British did not venture another run at Jackson and his troops. Despite the British's catastrophic defeat, they continue to bombard Fort St. Philip near the mouth of the Mississippi River for another week. They finally withdrew from New Orleans on January 18. The American victory swiftly resounds with news of the ratification of the Treaty of Ghent, which brings the War of 1812 to an end. Americans hail Jackson as a hero. The victorious battle propels Jackson towards the presidency" (17)

"Soldiers wounded in America's first wars, the Revolutionary War, and the War of 1812, were given pensions to compensate for their loss and inability to labor. Soldiers with limb loss and other serious disabilities were provided up to half-pay for the rest of their lives. Some veterans were given land grants, which could be sold in cash if one so desired, as compensation for their injuries and wounds. Besides these financial benefits, veterans received little else which forced them to rely on family and friends as the primary sources of care and support (21)."

CHAPTER 7

War Hero Returns

It took about six months for William to recover from his wounds and receive his discharge papers. Although the field medic did a Yeomans job of stopping his bleeding, William needed the attention of a surgeon to fully heal his wounds. Even though he was eligible for compensation because of his wounds, William was debating whether to accept any monetary compensation because he felt it was his duty to defend America. He would accept the land grant but being a slave, he did not know if he was allowed to own land. Mark on the other hand, took monetary compensation and land in Louisiana because of the severity of his wounds.

William and Mark were preparing themselves for their journey home. The day of their departure, Mark looked at William and asked the inevitable question of him. "Why don't you take the compensation and land grant William?" "I do not know if it is proper to take compensation for defending America Mark. Besides, I am not a free man."

Mark looked stunned at what William said about not being a free man. "What do you mean, you are not a free man William?" "I am a slave who belongs to an owner of a plantation in Virginia Mark. Besides, I do not even think that slaves can own land." Mark stood there with a puzzled look on his face. "But the color of your skin is just like mine, a bit darker but you look like any other man to me. In fact, I do not care if you are a slave. To me, you are a true American and friend who deserves the same rights as any American." After William gives Mark more details about his life and enslavement, Mark asks William for his contact information. Upon receiving the call for them to report to their wagons for their trip back to their homes, the two men hug one another and exchanged addresses. Looking at William's address, Mark exclaims. "Monticello? I have heard of Monticello before." Mark repeats his address without explanation.

The wounded were given transportation back to their respective states. The severely wounded were transported by wagons and the other injured were given money to purchase a boat and stage passage. William was anxious to return to see what had happened with Kathy and wanted to resume his sessions with Jefferson. He secured passage as far as the Steamboats could take him and then switched to horse drawn carriages. Learning that the war was over, Jefferson anxiously waited to receive word about William. Days had passed and as the sun was setting, one of the house servants came into the library to alert Jefferson that there was a wagon coming up the road. Hoping it was William, Jefferson sprung from his desk and went out to see who was coming. As the wagon drew closer, Jefferson recognized that it was indeed William.

The driver dropped William's bag as he disembarked from the wagon. His first reaction was to look around the plantation while giving a big sigh of relief. Not wanting to show any emotion, Jefferson called for William to join him on the porch. William immediately obeyed and jogged up to the porch where Jefferson greeted him with a steady handshake and then could not resist hugging him. "Welcome back William. Come and join me in the library for a bite to eat. I want to hear all about your escapades." Jefferson could see that William bore some wounds because he was bleeding through some bandages in need of changing. Jefferson called for one of the house servants that knew how to bandage wounds.

After the house servant removed the old bandages, Jefferson was taken back at the sight of William's wounds. For now, he was glad that William made it back alive. Jefferson had some meals prepared and listened to William talking about his war experiences for hours and the time he met General Jackson. When William was finished talking, Jefferson rose from his chair and walked over to his bookshelves with his hands folded behind his back. He then turned to William. "I want to commend you for keeping your word to me William. Some slaves that voluntarily joined the army were granted their freedom, but you kept your word to return. You could have traveled straight toa free state like Pennsylvania where slavery has been abolished.

"In the end, the War of 1812 did not provide greater opportunities or equality for free blacks as they anticipated, nor did it initiate a wave of emancipation for enslaved Americans seeking freedom. Their patriotic efforts had not reshaped white minds about what role they should play in society, and public memories of the war ignored their contributions. New prejudicial racial distinctions replaced class differences among blacks. For African Americans, the "forgotten war" delayed their quest for equality and freedom. "(1)

Five northern states agreed to gradually abolish slavery, with Pennsylvania being the first state to approve, followed by New Hampshire, Massachusetts, Connecticut, and Rhode Island. By the early 1800s, the northern states had all abolished slavery completely, or they were in the process of gradually eradicating it. (2)

Jefferson continues his dialogue with William. "First, I will arrange for you to see my surgeon. We need to heal your wounds as soon as possible. Secondly, I want to reward your loyalty. Over the years, I have watched how quickly you grasp complicated tasks. You have a great mind William, and it is time to broaden your horizons. I will pay your tuition to attend my Alma Mater, the university of William and Mary. Although it concentrates on the studies of Divinity, Philosophy, Languages, and other good Arts and Sciences; it was there that I acquired a taste for architecture. You will not be able to start until next year, but the timing is good because the University of Virginia will begin offering classes shortly thereafter. You can transfer to my university after spending your first two years at William and Mary." Laughing aloud, Jefferson proclaims his disdain for the founders of William and Mary. "Of course, we will have to overlook the fact that William and Mary were founded long ago by British monarchs." "King William III and Queen Mary II of England signed the charter for a "perpetual College of Divinity, (3)

Despite the pain from his wounds, William beamed up with joy. "Thank you, Mr. Jefferson. You do not know how much this means to me." At the same time, William thought that Jefferson may soon grant him his freedom. It was not, however, granted by Jefferson at this time. The main reason Jefferson did not want to free William was because William may have wanted to leave Monticello. Jefferson gave him time off to do whatever he wished and to allow enough time for a surgeon to properly heal his wounds. As Jefferson talked on, all William could now think about was Kathy.

Jefferson sent William to Charlottesville for some supplies. While in one of the stores, he felt a tap on his back. "Hello William. It has been a long time. Where have you been keeping yourself?" William turned and looked right into the eyes of Kathy. He stood in complete surprise until he finally could get out a word or two. Kathy stood with a longing look on her face, as she was still in love with him. "Hi Kathy. I was away on military duty." William's arm was scarred from the wounds he sustained. Kathy ran her hand down his arm over the scars with some alarm. "You sustained some serious wounds, William. Hopefully, you are all right now." "Much better. How are things going for you Kathy." "I am still thinking about us William." That is the one thing William did not want to hear. He had put a lot behind him but still had feelings for her. Kathy was not about to let it go, however. "I wish things were different William. If my parents had not found out about your background, we may have been able to get beyond everything." "Are you kidding Kathy? They would have stopped us and had me jailed."

"The only alternative would have been for us to escape to a free state in the North." Kathy was taken back by what William had just said. "There is no way I would go against the wishes of my parents William!" Reality just hit Kathy. She backed away, putting some space between them, and shaking her head No.

"Without money and no place to live, how would we have existed if we ran off William? With you being a slave, they would hunt you down and prosecute me if they found out that I went of my own free will."

"Enslavers in those days would put up flyers, place advertisements in newspapers, offer rewards, and send out the law to find them. An important part of that system was the Fugitive Slave Act passed by Congress in February 1793. The Act made it a federal crime to assist those who had escaped slavery or to interfere with their capture. It allowed the pursuit of "persons escaping from…their masters" everywhere in the United States, North and South." (4)

William just looked at Kathy with a forsaken look on his face. As he stood there not saying anything, Kathy's mother came over to get her. She looked at William with a distained look. Not acknowledging him, Kathy's mother tugged at her arm. "Come on Kathy, it's time to go." William watched them until they were out of sight. When the summer ended, William prepared to leave for college. Jefferson made sure he had enough money to get him through the school year.

The next two years went fast for William. Jefferson was busy establishing the University of Virginia. After returning to Monticello, Jefferson suggested that William take off a year before starting his next year at the University of Viginia. William was assigned to perform the same duties that he had before going to war and the college of William and Mary. At a distance, he still longed for Kathy but knew deep down that it was time to move on and put her in his past. He prepares to leave for the newly founded University of Virginia.

His first week is orienting himself to the University and selecting his courses. He would become one of the first students to attend the University of Virginia. "The history of the University of Virginia opens with its conception by Thomas Jefferson at the beginning of the early 19th century.

The university was chartered in 1819, and classes commenced in 1825. Initially, some of the students arriving at the University matched the then-common picture of college students;

wealthy, spoiled aristocrats with a sense of privilege which often led to brawling, or worse. This was a source of frustration for Jefferson, who assembled the students during the school's first year, in October 1825, to criticize such behavior." (5)

William thought he could better support Monticello upon his return by taking some courses related to agriculture. As William did not fit the mold of coming from a wealthy aristocratic family and still being a slave, he did not hide his detest for slavery. He quickly became a target of those in favor of it. Debates on slavery raged throughout the campus.

While walking across campus to attend one of his classes one day, William came across a shouting match between a young female and a large congregation of students. At the forefront of the students leading the argument was a large male student. Outside the university, people participated in the sports of the day. Shooting and fishing contests were part of the colonial experience, as were running, boxing, and horse racing.

William recognizes the man shouting down the young woman as being one of the top boxers in the area. Taking a closer look, he thought he may have also recognized the young girl. She was petite and stunningly beautiful, with big blue eyes, long blond hair cascading to the middle of her back and possessed an athletic build. Suddenly, the man shoved the young lady so hard, she fell backward to the ground.

Being a gentleman as he was, William would not have any of this. He immediately jumped in between them to protect the young lady from further abuse, warning the man to back off. Helping the young lady to her feet, William admonished the man for his unacceptable behavior. "You should never lay hands on a lady good sir. It is not very gentlemanly of you and besides, your twice her size." The man looked at William while shoving him and the young girl again. "Who are you to tell me to back off mister. Your more my size. You mean I should not push her like this." Once again, the young girl fell to the ground. Watching her fall irritated William that he lost control of his senses.

William immediately went into attack mode and took the bare-knuckle stance taught to him by Cribb. The young girl's abuser looked at William and laughed. "Do you have any idea who I am? I am one of the most skilled boxers in the area. You need to apologize to me for interfering in our conversation. If not, be prepared to suffer the consequences." William just continued to stand in his fighter stance without saying a word. He just thought about how he had to deal with a bully when he was much younger. In this case, this bully did not know what he was up against.

While continuing to laugh at William, the bully taunts him more by using his hands to continue pushing the young lady. He then turns to William and started shoving him and then tries to sucker punch William. William ducks under the Bully's swing and lands a straight punch to his stomach and an upper cut to his chin using his knee. The bully grunts and falls to the ground in pain. Two of the bully's friends are amazed at how William uses his entire body to fight and are too fearful to come to the Bully's aid. William pounces on the Bully and while holding his knee on his chest, he raises his fist threatening to land another punch to his face, demanding satisfaction.

"I think you need to apology to this young lady for being such an ignorant person lacking gentlemanly manners." Fearing that William is going to hit him again, the bully holds his hands up to protect his face while at the same time begging for mercy. "I had enough. I apologize, I apologize!" William then helps the bully to his feet, brushing off his coat. William commended him for apologizing. "Now that is the gentlemanly thing to do when addressing a lady. I hope that you will remember this next time you argue with a lady."

William turns to the young lady to make certain that she is okay. Looking into her enticing blue eyes, William ponders where he has met this lovely lady before. "I hope you are okay Miss. For some reason, I think we have met before." William is taken back when the young girl takes ahold of his hand. "Do you not recognize me, William? William scratched his head not only trying to recognize this young lady but why she was there in the first place, as women were not admitted to the University. "Otterbein was the first college that opened with women as both faculty and students and was another Ohio school involved in the liberation of runaway slaves." (6)

The only exception to the no lady policy was a summer agriculture class at the university which provided instruction in animal stock judging. "Throughout much of its history, the University of Virginia was a "Gentleman's University," an idea rooted in the institution's traditions, history, and principles as established by its founder, Thomas Jefferson. Jefferson intended for his university to educate "Southern Gentlemen" – no provisions were made for either Black people or females. This exclusivity persisted well into the twentieth century." (7)

William kept staring into the enticing eyes of the young lady but could not place her. She gave William a big hug and laughed as she exclaimed. "It's me, it's me William, Jane." William's eyes widened and was completely caught off guard. He now realized why he could not recognize her. She was so incredibly young when he knew her. Now she has blossomed into a ravishing woman.

Jane reached up and gave him a kiss on the cheek. William blushed. "Jane, I cannot believe what a beautiful young woman you have become. Excuse me for what I just said. I mean, you were always a pretty young thing. What are you doing here?" "I came to do some research in their university's library William. My father sent me to see if I could find any information on agriculture. As you know, our plantation is close to the campus." "I am so glad to see you, Jane. How is your family?" "Their doing fine William." Jane gave William a rundown on each of her family and eventually came to what William feared the most. "Kathy and John are engaged to be married."

Jane then lamented about how sad it was that she could not attend the University. "Why the university does not admit females is beyond me William. I should carry a sign saying the university discriminates against woman, marching up and down in front of the Rotunda building." Jane was a rebel and was always ready to go against the established ways. Scratching his head while he thought for a few minutes, William suggested a solution to address her concerns. "I know what we can do Jane. You can study with me at the end of the class day."

Jane's eyes lit up. "That is a great idea, William. My chores are finished by three in the afternoon, and I can be here before four." Sounds okay to me Jane. Classes start on Monday, and I will look for you at the end of the day. We can meet at the front door of the Rotunda and find a quiet place to study. I will also take good notes." Jane waved goodbye as William watched her petite figure as she walked down a path towards her Plantation.

Monday came quickly for William. "The University of Virginia officially opens its doors on March 7. Only five professors, all foreigners, and a few dozen students are present this first day, but two more professors (Americans) arrive a month later, with more than one hundred students in attendance by the end of the initial year.' (8) "At the time of the University's opening in the 19th century, instruction included ancient languages, modern languages, mathematics, moral philosophy, natural philosophy, chemistry, law, and medicine. Jefferson opposed the granting of degrees on the grounds that they were "artificial embellishments." William's first day included moral philosophy. In addition to not admitting women, "Jefferson intended to establish an institution that would be, in his words, based on the illimitable freedom of the human mind." (9)

Being a slave himself, it was difficult for William to see the slaves being used as free labor at the University. When his philosophy teacher discussed Jefferson's intention that he wanted the objective of the university to be "based on the illimitable freedom of the human mind," William felt compelled to challenge his professor. When doing so, he did not want to criticize Jefferson, so he inferred that it was the university's philosophy. "If the university wants its students to have freedom of the mind, isn't that philosophy hypocritical when it uses slave labor?"

There was a rumbling of both support and opposition to what was just said by William. Interesting enough, however, the professor chimed in support of allowing William to express his opinion. "You have a very valid point, William. Someday it will change. For now, all I can do as a teacher is instruct and allow debate on the pros and cons of slavery."

William thought it was an opportune time to inject some of his insight. "I would ask you and the class to keep an open mind to what I am about to say Professor."

William started to describe the life of a slave to the class. Close your eyes and walk in the shoes of a slave. Slaves were torn away from their families and friends, never to see them again." "Slave traders violently captured Africans and loaded them onto slave ships, where for months these individuals endured the "Middle Passage"—the crossing of the Atlantic from Africa to the North American colonies or West Indies. Many Africans did not survive the journey." (10) "Life on the fields meant working from sunup to sundown six days a week and having food sometimes not suitable for an animal to eat. Plantation slaves live in small shacks with a dirt floor and little or no furniture. Life on large plantations with a cruel overseer was oftentimes the worst. Work for a small farm owner who was not doing well could mean not being fed. Any slave found guilty of arson, rape of a white woman, or conspiracy to rebel was put to death. However, since the slave woman was chattel, a white man who raped her was guilty only of a trespass on the master's property. Slaves could not assemble without a white person present. Marriages between slaves were not considered legally binding and owners were free to split up families through sale."

William continued his description while some students squirmed in their seats. Except for a few students whose families were owners of slaves, most students in the class were not aware of a slave's plight. Many students wondered how he knew so much about the life of a slave. Upon completing his dialogue, there was complete silence in the classroom. Immediately after the teacher dismissed the class, William met Jane outside the classroom.

CHAPTER 8

True Love

As planned, they went off to find a quiet place to study. It was a beautiful warm summer night. The sun was just setting behind the silhouette of Jane. William was captured by her beauty. The sun lit upon her blond hair making it glow that much more. A short distance from the Rotunda, they found a shaded spot under a large oak tree. Jane had brought along a large quilt that she knitted for them to sit on. Each lay facing one another. William spread out his books and notes that included the lesson plans for the day. Their facing one another gave them a feeling of warmth

Both became infatuated with what they read and became so enthralled in the material they went beyond what the Professor assigned for the next day. Time flew by fast. After they finished the first day, they took time to share some of their hopes and dreams. Both sat leaning their backs against one another looking up at the blue sky. The sun was just setting on the distant horizon and Jane reached back with both her hands caressing the hands of William. "What do you want out of life William?" One would never have known that they came from diverse cultures and heritages. They made a handsome couple and appeared free as the wind. William pondered what Jane had just asked.

"First and foremost, I want to be a free man. I want to know what it feels like to not be owned and have my own free will. I no longer want to see other human beings whipped or to see families torn apart by selling them separately to other slave owners. I want people like me and woman like you Jane, to have access to education. I fought for this country and would like to be granted citizenship like many others who did not." "God does not discriminate. Everyone is judged the same when you meet God.

People who go to church every week while going against the basic beliefs of fairness and equality are hypocritical. You would think they would be scared to get into line to meet God. Lastly, I would like to experience true and passionate love, finding that special lady that will share my life and raise a loving family with me. Someone who will stand up for me and likewise I will do the same for her." Jane sat up. "I agree that you and others in bondage should have all that William."

"Thank you, Jane, and what about you? What do you want out of life." Jane did not need any time to think about how to answer that question. "What I want is not much different than what you want. I am fortunate to having my freedom but want more rights that are afforded to men. Like you, I hurt inside when I see how slaves are treated. It is time for our country to grant slaves their freedom by abolishing slavery. I too want to find that special person that shares my dreams and is passionately in love with me."

William started to feel more than friendship towards Jane and wondered if she felt the same towards him. For some reason, it seemed different from his feelings for Kathy. The sun was starting to set, and it was time for Jane to return home. "My family will be wondering where I am William. I need to go now." "Not by yourself Jane. I will at least walk you to your plantation's entrance. As they walked through the pass, the sun accentuated the beauty of Jane. Their interaction also gave him a glimpse into her soul, and he very much liked what he was seeing.

William stopped when he and Jane exited the wooded path, just before the entrance to her plantation. Jane turned to William. "You have come this far William. You are welcome to walk me to the house. I do not care what my family thinks. You are a good friend and a good man who should be welcome anywhere." "I was rejected once before by your parents and do not want to feel that same pain again. Nor do I want to cause you any hurt." Thanking him for studying with her, she simply reached up and kissed William on the cheek. "See you tomorrow, William."

William and Jane met every day at the end of classes to go over the lesson plans given by his teachers. Jane was impressed by how fast he comprehended the lesson plans, and he felt the same about her. Every day, William would walk Jane home and Jane would give William a hug and a kiss on his cheek. As the days drew on, William and Jane became more infatuated with one another. Neither had the courage to say how they were starting to feel for fear of being rejected.

At the end of the first year, the university decided to host a reception to commemorate their one-year anniversary. Many were invited, including people from the surrounding areas. The honored guest was to be their founder, Thomas Jefferson. Jane came with her family, including Kathy and her now fiancé John. Accompanying the family was a young man not known to William. All who attended were awestruck that Thomas Jefferson would be on campus. In addition to Jefferson, several other dignitaries attended including Andrew Jackson.

The ceremony was opened with the playing of the Star-Spangled Banner, bringing up many memories for William when he served in the war of 1812. All proudly stood at attention while it played. It had been a year since Jefferson and William set eyes on one another.

William was taken aback when Jane came over and greeted him with a hug. Out of the corner of his eye, William could see Jane's father approaching them with the other young man they brought. "We meet again William. Hope all is well with you. I do not know if you have met Charles who we have committed to marry Jane." William was awestruck. This was the second time William's heart was broken. He never even had the chance to express to Jane how he had fallen in love with her. William congratulated Charles and Jane and retreated to the place they met at the end of each school day. The moon was full, and the night was warm. William sat under the oak tree, reflecting on his misfortune. The orchestra played some romantic waltzes.

Suddenly, he saw a shadow cast by the moonlight over him. Turning, he saw Jane standing before him. As he stood to acknowledge her presence, the orchestra played a romantic waltz. Violin tremolos rang through the night air. Taking William's hand, Jane asked him to dance with her. "I never danced or even know how to dance Jane." "Just follow my lead, William."

Dancing with Jane was like dancing with an angel. As the moonlight shined on her hair, Jane suddenly laid her head on his chest while swaying to the music in place. "It has always been you William, ever since we first met when I was a little girl. I never met Charles until tonight."

Looking into his eyes, Jane could see his frustration. "Over this past year, I have grown to love you deeply Jane. I now know the meaning of what it is like to be passionately in love. My love for you, however, does not wipe away what still lurks over my head. I am not a free man and to boot, I have nothing to offer. Your parents will never accept me." Jane gave him a hug and exclaimed that it did not matter what her parents thought. "The situation is much different now than it was with my sister."

"Unlike my sister, I am willing to run away with you, wherever you want me to go. We can start a new life together." "No Jane, I am not going to let you endanger yourself for me. Even if Mr. Jefferson did not send bounty hunters after us, your parents may report us to the authorities. If they caught us, I would be returned in leg irons, and you would be branded a criminal. I could not live with myself if that happened to you." We must end our feelings for one another here and now Jane. William took Jane by the hand and led her back to the reception, insisting that she go in first to avoid suspicion. As she walked away, a tear came to her eye.

William waited until Jane walked to the center of the ballroom before entering. Just before she reached her parents, she suddenly turned around and walked back to grab the hand of William. Jane's parents, John, Kathy, and her young suitor stood there in shock. After gaining their composure, Jane's parents went over to pull Jane away from William. Refusing to move from William's side, Jane stood her ground.

The guests could hear her parents berating Jane and William for their public show of affection for one another, especially a slave. John also started in on both Jane and William. People were staring at the commotion being made by John and Jane's parents. Kathy just stood at a distance, not coming in their defense. Being the gentleman that he was, William simply stood there without defending himself. Suddenly, William felt a hand on the back of his shoulder. It was Jefferson. He came over to rescue William from any further embarrassment. Looking around the room, Jefferson proclaimed that William was like a son to him. "This young man has gone far beyond the call of duty to defend his country."

General Jackson came over and placed his hand on William's other shoulder. "I can attest to the sacrifices that this young man has made for our country. He could have stayed safely at my headquarters during the battle in New Orleans. Instead, he chose to join my troops on the front line where he became seriously wounded. His actions are testimony to the creed of service before self. Looking at John and Jane's father, Jackson admonished them both. I did not see you two gentlemen beside him on the battle fields. We need to applaud William for his service."

Suddenly, the room broke out in applause cheering on William. John and Jane's father had no choice but to join in applauding William for his service to the country. Jane beamed with pride as she stood by William. From a distance, you could sense Kathy's regret that she did not stand by William way back when, especially as she knew John was half the man as William.

People realized more than ever that the former president of the United States was extremely close to William and that a highly decorated general and future president of the United States also revered him. Jefferson took William aside. "You have done well William. In fact, you have done more than most men have done. I am proud of you."

"Thank you, Mr. Jefferson. As the two talked, Jane walked over to stand by William. "By the way, this is a good friend of mine Mr. Jefferson, her name is Jane." Jefferson greeted Jane with the protocol of a gentlemen and Jane returned the gesture by making a curtsy. Jefferson made a slight bow while William stood there with pride. All looked on with amazement at the interaction between William and Jefferson. Looking closely at Jefferson, William thought he looked pale, but he thought it was not his place to mention it.

A diagnosis by Jefferson's doctor confirmed Jefferson was not in good health. "Dr. Gordon Jones believes the mercury poisoning helped to exacerbate Jefferson's chronic bowel problems." (1)

After spending time with William, Jefferson went back to the festivities while William danced with Jane. At the end of the evening, William maintained that for Jane's sake, she needed to find someone else to marry. "I will not put you in a position where you may be breaking the law and alienate your parents, Jane." Jane slowly walked away in tears.

After everyone left the reception, William returned to sitting under the oak tree saddened over losing Jane and the possibilities for his future. The next few months were unbearable for him. Every day he would go to the spot where he and Jane studied, reminiscing about the time they spent together. After the way he pushed her away, he had no hope of ever seeing her again.

His only ray of sunshine was when he received a note from his friend Mark, urging him to join him in Louisiana. Mark wrote that he received a large tract of land and checked on the possibility of William receiving the same. The granting agencies assured him that William was eligible and there was another tract of land adjoining Marks'. "The eligibility for the grant was restricted to enlisted men and noncommissioned officers. The size of the grant was fixed at 160 acres. The government set aside six million acres in Michigan, Illinois, and Louisiana for the war of 1812 recruits." (2)

Mark wrote that his family had agreed to loan them enough money to purchase both tracts. William replied that he could not make a commitment because of his promising Jefferson he would not leave Monticello. Mark sent a second message that he would hold both tracts of land for them if he changed his mind.

CHAPTER 9

A Sad Loss

It was July 1st, 1826, when an urgent message was sent to William for him to return to Monticello as soon as possible. William started immediately without taking anything with him. The trip from the University to Monticello was close. Concerned about the urgency, William did not bother looking for transportation. He ran, taking some short cuts that he used when younger. Upon reaching the road leading up to the mansion, he paused when he saw numerous carriages.

Entering Monticello, William was told that Jefferson did not have long to live and asked for him. Waiting outside Jefferson's bedroom for his turn to go in, William learned that the people with Jefferson: "the attending physician, and the husband of Jefferson's granddaughter. Jefferson was lying in his bedchamber which was the most private space of an intensely private man, maximizing light and space with its alcove bed, triple sash window, and skylight."

When he was told that Jefferson was calling for him, William went in and stood at the side of the bed. William knew that this was the end for his benefactor and mentor. Normally when visiting Jefferson in his bedroom, he slept sitting up rather than lying down. "Jefferson was partial to "alcove beds" wedged into walls; he slept sitting up to aid digestion and respiration." (2) This time, William found a weak Jefferson, lying on his back. Jefferson's eyes lit up when he saw William. "I want a word with William. Please clear the room."

William stood there in silence as everyone left the room. When Jefferson started to speak, his voice was waning. William kneeled placing his ear close to Jefferson. William's heart was so heavy it felt unbearable. Jefferson reached out for William's hand and spoke. "You have been like a son to me William. I know you have wished to be a free man, and I should have told you this before. You have been a free man for quite some time." William's face flushed with surprise. "I could not have asked for a better father Mr. Jefferson. You have always been so kind and a great mentor to me. What do you mean I have always been a free man?"

Struggling, Jefferson rolled to his side and motioned for William to come closer to him so he could better hear what he had to say. "After you became so depressed at the loss of your first love due to your not being a free man, I decided that you were never going to feel that pain again and wrote a document that gives you your freedom. I intended it as a gift once you had earned a degree and had skills that would support your life once leaving Monticello. I have been on the verge of insolvency for quite some time and cannot help you financially. I did not want you to struggle and fail. You are now equipped to be self-sufficient William."

"Where is the document Mr. Jefferson." "It has been under your nose all the time William. You will find it under my chess board on my desk (Photo 3) in the library where you sit many a day. In the drawer next to the chess board is a small amount of money you can use to carry you over for a while. One more thing. To gain full citizenship, you will need a last name. In that document, I wrote that you have the permission to use my name."

"I thank you Mr. Jefferson for all that you did for me. I am so grateful that you have eliminated any doubts I have as to why you did not grant me my freedom sooner. Now knowing why, I will always have fond memories of our times together." William then reached over and placed his hand on Jefferson's hand. "I am going to miss you Mr. Jefferson." Looking at William, Jefferson had a bit of fun left in him. "Perhaps we can continue our chess games when you meet up with me in the afterlife William."

Just then the doctor came in to tell William it was time to give Jefferson more medication and allow him to rest. Preparing to leave, William asked Jefferson if he could lean over to give him a hug. Jefferson gave his approval by nodding his head yes. William leaned over and gave Jefferson a gentle hug. A tear came to the eye of both men. Standing up to leave, Jefferson grabbed William by his hand. "Take care of yourself William." Walking towards the door, William turned towards Jefferson. Both men gave each other one more look as William quietly said, "I love you Mr. Jefferson." "Likewise, William."

William walked over to Sally Hemings cabin to wait for the end. The next day on July 4th, at 4 in the morning, Jefferson spoke again. "Randolph writes that Jefferson called in his enslaved domestic workers and addressed them with his last spoken words." What he said to them, Randolph unfortunately does not reveal. Jefferson lingered until 12:50 in the afternoon." Thomas Jefferson's funeral was a simple affair. He was buried in the Monticello graveyard at 5:00 p.m. on July 5, 1826, a rainy day. At his own request, the ceremony was simple and quiet. No invitations were sent, but friends and visitors were welcome at the grave." (3)

"Thomas Jefferson died with debts of $107,000, which is roughly $2 million today. How did he get into this financial disaster? Jefferson's debt was not entirely due to business failures, poor investments, or a shopaholic wife. Jefferson inherited a significant amount of debt from his father-in-law in 1774. He may have been rich in land and slaves, but farming was not a debt solution. Of course, some of it was due to his overzealous spending. He lived beyond his means, blowing large sums on construction projects, furnishings, and decorations for Monticello.

Jefferson also had a taste for fine French wine, which did not come cheap. During his eight years as president, his personal wine bill was over $10,000, or $150,000 in today's currency. That would mean a lot of credit card debt for someone today! Jefferson also co-signed a loan for a friend in 1818 for $20,000 which is roughly $300,000 plus in today's currency. Unfortunately, his friend passed away shortly thereafter, and Jefferson was forced to take on the unpaid debt." (4)

William joined in laying Jefferson to rest in the family graveyard. "Before his death, Thomas Jefferson left explicit instructions regarding the monument to be erected over his grave. In this undated document, Jefferson supplied a sketch of the shape of the marker, and the epitaph with which he wanted it to be inscribed:

"... on the faces of the Obelisk the following inscription, & not a word more: "because by these," he explained, "as testimonials that I have lived, I wish most to be remembered." (5)

Here was buried Thomas Jefferson
Author of the Declaration of American Independence
of the Statute of Virginia for religious freedom
& Father of the University of Virginia

(*Library of Congress Photo 4*)

Following the services, his thoughts turned to Jane and the offer by his friend Mark to join him in Louisiana. Now that he was a free man and had something to offer her, he was ready to ask for her hand in marriage. He quickly went to Janes plantation only to find that the family was not home. Upon asking one of the house servants as to their whereabouts, he learned that the family was at the local church preparing for Jane's arranged marriage. All William could think about his last words to Jane, telling her to find someone else.

William stopped a man on horseback holding the reins of another horse. William recognized him as a former schoolmate friend of his. Telling his friend of his plight, the friend handed him the reins of the other horse and told him to return it later. William rode as fast as he could to the church where he found many carriages lined up along the roadway leading up to it. He quickly went inside to find many people waiting for the bride to walk down the aisle. Jane's family, including Kathy and her new husband John, were seated in the front row. Janes father and the bridegroom were standing at the altar. Just then, the music started, and Jane, dressed in her wedding dress, entered the rectory at the rear of the church.

Surprised but happy to see William, she became focused on him rather than on the ceremony. She walked right to him and took his hand in hers. "Is this what I think it is William." William nodded his head yes and took her in his arms. Immediately the Groom rushed to pull William away from Jane. "What do you think you are doing Sir?" The families of the bride and bridegroom surrounded the two of them. You could sense the anger of Jane's father and that of the groom's family. Jane's mother did not know what to think. Kathy's husband John tried to intervene but recalling the beating he took from William when they were young, he backed off.

Pointing a finger at William, Jane's father told him that he needed to leave now! This is the man Jane is going to marry. You are nothing but a slave." William handed him the document signed by Jefferson, granting him his freedom. Jane stepped between her father and William. "I should have stood up to you back then father. It does not matter if William is a free man not. I have loved William since I was a little girl and want to be with him." She then turned to the Groom. "You are a wonderful man and will make some lucky girl a great husband someday, but I do not think you would want to marry a lady who loves someone else."

The Groom stood there in shock until his grandmother murmured some words to him. Looking at her, William asked her what she said? "I said you need to deck him! Before William could turn to look at the Groom, he felt a blow to his jaw. The Groom used the same sucker punch tactic taught to William by his good friend Cribb. William fell to the floor. He could have easily walloped the Groom but out of courtesy to him, refrained from defending himself.

The groom, his family, and friends filed out of the church while Jane's family and friends remained in place not knowing what to do. Jane's father motioned for William and his family to come into the rectory. As soon as the door closed behind them, Jane's father was reading William the riot act. "I do not care if you are a free man. There is no way you are going to take my daughter from us without having anywhere to go or any means to support her." William stood quietly while Jane's father ranted on. After her father ran out of words, Jane spoke up in defense of William.

"William has always been honorable, a kind person, highly intelligent, and an extremely hard worker. That gives him a huge head start over many other suitor's father."

Still harboring a torch for William, Jane's sister Kathy came to her defense. "I agree with Jane, William has proven himself. Do you realize that he is among the few people in this country that went on to attend an institution of higher learning? You did not even do that father." Finally, Janes mother chimed in. Looking at how loving William and Jane were towards one another; she could not resist saying her peace. "Look at them together." "Few of us have experienced the passionate love that bonds them together. Looking at William, Jane explains her whereabouts those many days she studied with him. "William gave me the opportunity that is not afforded to us ladies Mother. We would study together every day after class to go over his lesson plans. During that time, there was not one time William asked me for anything but my friendship. Our friendship grew into love."

Again, Jane's father reiterates his concern for William not being able to support his daughter. Clearing his throat while waiting for his turn to defend himself, William describes the land offer made by his friend, Mark. Jane's father continues his concerns. "That's all well and good but land alone does not put seed in the ground and food on the table." William humbly retorts the argument of Janes' father. "One other benefit I did not mention sir. Because I was seriously wounded, I also receive a monetary pension for the rest of my life." "Soldiers having suffered wounds were provided up to half-pay for the rest of their lives." (1) That income from my pension will support us while we build one of the largest and best farms in the east.

For a few moments, Jane's father looked William up and down trying to figure him out. He stood looking from William to Jane and then to the rest of the family. It was unheard of for a white woman to marry a free Black person or biracial man. As his thought process was wearing out, he could see that Jane had become very anxious. He then opened the rectory door leading into the church and saw his family and friends were still patiently waiting for an explanation. Turning to his wife, she could see that he was looking to her for a suggestion. Janes mother looked at William and Jane standing there with expressions of frustration and asked them to confirm their feelings towards one another. "Do you love our daughter with your whole being William and do you feel the same about William Jane?"

Both Jane and William simultaneously said yes. Jane's mother looked at the family anxiously waiting for an explanation. "Then there is only one thing to do and that is to go on with the marriage ceremony but this time it will be William. William and Janes eyes lit up.

"The actual wedding day for white 18th-century Americans looked quite like the weddings of today, although it should be noted that most weddings did not take place in a church as it could be difficult to travel to one, especially those living in rural areas. The custom of the father giving away his daughter, the exchanging of rings, and having a reception were all practiced in eighteen century America. Typically, the reception was held at the bride's house where games and dancing entertained the guests. So, some of the wedding rituals and traditions we partake in today were in existence prior to 1800." (2)

As Jane walked down the aisle with her father, William beamed with joy. The guests were shocked to see that there was a new groom waiting at the Alter. Still carrying a torch for William, Jane's sister Kathy kept thinking that she should have stood her ground when her parents forbade her to see him anymore. Instead, she wound up with John, who she did not love.

Following the church service, the wedding party and the guests went to Jane's home for a reception. After the reception, William and Jane retired to their room to prepare to leave for Louisiana in the morning. As the sun shone through the window, William and Jane were already dressed. When they descended the stairs, Jane's family hugged them goodbye.

At the time William and Jane traveled, people traveled primarily by horseback or on the rivers. Later, crude roads were built and then canals. What takes hours today took them weeks. Upon their arrival in Louisiana, they were greeted by Mark. He took them to a home he built on his land grant. Early next morning,

Mark took William and Jane to the land that was granted to William. William and Jane worked extremely hard over the ensuing years to build their future.

Along with Mark, they grew their estates by acquiring adjoining lands. Remembering what it was like to be a slave, William made sure that his hired hands were well cared for and paid a livable wage. As a result of his kindness, the workers became loyal and hard workers. Jane gave birth to three children, two girls and a boy named Nathaniel. The girls were born in their first five years of marriage and the boy was a late-in-life child. Over the following years, Mark and William became one of the state's largest landowners.

CHAPTER 10

Winds Of War

It was 1859 and war was inevitable. "For more than 80 years, people in the Northern and Southern states had been debating the issues that led to war: economic policies and practices, cultural values, the extent and reach of the Federal government, and, most importantly, the role of slavery within American Society. Against the backdrop of these larger issues, individual soldiers had their own reasons for fighting. Their motivations included a complex mix of personal, social, economic, and political values that did not necessarily match those of their respective governments." (1)

"It was the economics of slavery and political control that the Civil War was fought. The Southern states wanted to assert their authority over the federal government so they could abolish federal laws they did not support, especially laws interfering with the South's right to keep slaves. Another factor was territorial expansion. The South wished to take slavery into the western territories, while the North was committed to keeping them open to white labor alone. Meanwhile, the newly formed Republican party, whose members strongly opposed to the westward expansion of slavery into new states, was gaining prominence. The election of Abraham Lincoln, Republican, was a clear signal to the Southern states that they had lost influence." (2)

One night sitting by the fire with Jane and Mark, William spoke of his concerns. "I am overly concerned that our country may be drawn into a civil war between the north and the south and if Louisiana chooses to fight on the side of the south, our family may be placed in peril. In fact, I am certain that Louisiana will choose to fight with the southern slave states. Slavery has become highly profitable, and the value of slaves is continuing to rise."

"Slavery was now legal in Missouri, and the new state added pro-slave members to Congress. By 1860, there were more than 100,000 slaves in Missouri, and slaves were valued at over $44 million (about $112 billion today). Louisiana remained a slave state after it was purchased, and New Orleans a critical trading hub. "(3)

As William continued expressing his concerns, he glanced at his three children who were sitting off to the side. "Our son Nathaniel is fast approaching eighteen and one of my biggest concerns is that he will be drawn on the side of the south and be forced to fight for preserving slavery. We cannot let this happen. The more I think about it, the more it makes sense for us to move to a free state like Pennsylvania, where slavery is abolished."

Mark, who had no sons and only daughters, spoke up. I can understand how you feel, William. If I had a son, I would not want him forced to fight in any war. Let me suggest a plan to protect Nathaniel. I will watch over your plantation and send you a stipend every month. That will allow you to move to the free state of Pennsylvania. We will draw up a formal document maintaining your ownership and designating me as the overseer so I can conduct business on your behalf. After the conflict is over, you can then move back here if you wish. Whether you return or not, you can rest assured that your interests will always be here for you and your descendants. You saved my life William, and I will protect yours." Having great trust in Mark, William nodded in agreement.

For the next month, William and Jane prepared to move their family to Pennsylvania. They purchased a three-hundred-acre farm just outside the small town of Gettysburg, Pennsylvania for less than one-thousand dollars. The money for the purchase came from the income producing land in Louisiana managed by Mark. The soil was rich, and the land came along with mineral rights, farmhouse, and with a barn. The land was fertile, the harvests yielded enough income to support their family. It did not take long, however, for William and his family's worst fears became a reality.

"Once Abraham Lincoln was elected president, many in the south saw his election as a threat by the northern states. "Influenced by South Carolina's decision to secede from the Union, Louisiana voters elected delegates to the State's secession convention. The secessionists outnumbered unionists two to one, and the militant attitudes of the public and the press further influenced the convention's vote. Members signed the ordinance of secession, making Louisiana the sixth state to secede from the Union." (4)

"Shortly thereafter, Jefferson Davis, a former U.S. Senator and Secretary of War, was elected President of the Confederate States of America by the members of the Confederate constitutional convention. At the beginning of the Civil War, twenty-two million people lived in the North and nine million people (nearly four million of whom were slaves) lived in the South. The North also had more money, more factories, more horses, more railroads, and more farmland. On paper, these advantages made the United States much more powerful than the Confederate States. However, the Confederates were fighting defensively on territory that they knew well. They also had the advantage of the sheer size of the Southern Confederacy. Which meant that the northern armies would have to capture and hold vast quantities of land. Still, the Confederacy maintained some of the best ports in North America—including New Orleans, Charleston, Mobile, Norfolk, and Wilmington. Thus, the Confederacy was able to mount a stubborn resistance." (5)

"By the time Lincoln took office on March 4, 1861, rumors were circulating of a threatened Confederate attack at Fort Sumter. Northern Republicans, backed by an abolitionist press, demanded military action. "Reinforce Fort Sumter at all hazards!" became the northerners' cry. Lincoln agreed to re-supply the fort, but with food rather than weapons. Fort Sumter fell. Now the lines were drawn, in the Senate and across the nation. "Every man must be for the United States or against it," proclaimed Senator Stephen Douglas. "There can be no neutrals." (6)

By not properly reinforcing Fort Sumter with sufficient troops to allow it to be taken over by Confederate troops, the Confederates were bolstered in their efforts to secede from the Union. What might have quelched the rebellion by the confederates before it became a full-blown war, now ignited a civil war.

Troubling to William was that Nathaniel was of the age to be thrust into the middle of it. From his experiences in the war of 1812, William knew all too well that his son could become a casualty of war. With Congress having difficulty recruiting volunteers, they had to implement inducements.

"The U.S. government answered this lapse with financial inducements and the threat of conscription. Since the early months of the war, volunteers had been rewarded with a bounty of $100, much of which was deferred until the soldier was honorably discharged, but the bounty seems to have been a significant lure for men from poorer families. The Militia Act of 1862 required individual states to draft men if their enlistment quotas fell short. In 1863 the federal bounty was also increased to $300, to boost volunteering and reduce the number of men that may be drafted. Men who responded to these bounties hailed principally from the lower economic strata of society." (7)

To the dismay of William, his son received a draft notice to report for duty. William wanted to shelter his son from the ravages of war. He nor his son, however, did not want to do the same as wealthy families, which was to pay a substitute to go in his place.

During the Civil War, the U.S. Congress passes a conscription act that produces the first wartime draft of U.S. citizens in American history. The act called for registration of all males between the ages of 20 and 45, including aliens with the intention of becoming citizens. Exemptions from the draft could be bought for $300 or by finding a substitute draftee. This clause led to bloody draft riots in New York City, where protesters were outraged, that exemptions were effectively granted only to the wealthiest U.S. citizens. (8) According to the law, Nathaniel could not be drafted before he turned twenty.

Nathaniels draft notice directed him to report to General Hooker's army of the Potomac, which was recently defeated by Confederate General Lee at the Battle of Chancellorsville.

"After his celebrated victory over Maj. Gen. Joseph Hooker at the Battle of Chancellorsville, Gen. Robert E. Lee leads his troops north in his second invasion of enemy territory. The 75,000-man Army of Northern Virginia is in high spirits. In addition to seeking fresh supplies, the depleted soldiers look forward to availing themselves of food from the bountiful fields in Pennsylvania farm country, sustenance the war-ravaged landscape of Virginia can no longer provide. Hooker also heads north, but he is reluctant to engage with Lee directly after the Union's humiliating defeat at Chancellorsville. This evasiveness is of increasing concern to President Abraham Lincoln. That was why Hooker was relieved of command in late June. His successor, Maj. Gen. George Gordon Meade, continues to move the 90,000-man Army of the Potomac northward, following orders to keep his army between Lee and Washington, D.C. Meade prepares to defend the routes to the nation's capital, if necessary, but he also pursues Lee." (9)

When Nathaniel arrived to join Meade's army, he was amazed to find a huge encampment of tents. Nathaniel was not given any training because unbeknownst to Nathaniel, Meade was busy preparing to defend Gettysburg against the advancement of Lee's army. Nathaniel was thrust immediately into harm's way by being assigned to Pickett's army. It was ironic that Nathaniel was going to defend a town near his family's farm. Little did he know that his family could see the flashing of artillery from their farm. While waiting for orders to advance or defend, Nathaniel had the opportunity to become friends with two other young soldiers his age. Like him, they were not seasoned fighters and had no idea what they were doing or what was the objective. All they were told was to keep vigil for an attack by the confederates over the ridge they were defending. While silently talking amongst themselves, "a barrage of confederate soldiers started an assault. Along with the two young men, Nathaniel kept firing into the onslaught of confederates.

When the rifle and artillery smoke cleared, Nathaniel was appalled by the dead and wounded bodies strewn about him. All he could think about was how fast everything happened to him. Just a few days before, he was on his way to this peaceful town not knowing what carnage awaited him. Looking to his right and left, he saw one of his newfound friends lying dead.

Suddenly, he felt dizzy. Looking down at his chest, he saw a slow oozing of blood coming through his shirt. Ripping open his shirt, he saw a piece of shrapnel sticking in his side. Pulling it out, he screamed in pain. One of the medical wagons heard him scream and rushed to tend to his wounds. "Though the mortality rate was higher for soldiers wounded on the battlefield, field dressing stations and field hospitals administered care in increasingly advanced ways. Once a soldier was wounded, medical personnel bandaged the soldier as fast they could, giving them whiskey and morphine to ease shock and pain.

"If his wounds demanded more attention, he was evacuated via Letterman's ambulance and stretcher system to a nearby field hospital. A modification of triage that was implemented during the civil war is still used today. Field hospitals separated wounded soldiers into three categories: mortally wounded, slightly wounded and surgical cases. Most of the amputations performed at field hospitals were indeed horrible scenes, but the surgery itself was not as crude as popular memory makes it out to have been. Anesthetics were readily available to surgeons, who administered chloroform or ether to patients before the procedure. Though gruesome, amputation was a life-saving procedure that swiftly halted the devastating effects of wounds." (11)

In the case of Nathaniel, the field medical personnel classified his wounds as slight and bandaged them accordingly. Thinking all was clear, Nathaniel laid back against one of the tombstones. To his dismay, however, there was a follow-up assault by 12,000 Confederate soldiers trying to breach the center of the Union line along Cemetery Ridge. The word went down the Union line to hold their position and fire at will. At the same time, a barrage of artillery shells shattered the Confederate's attack. Nathaniel started firing despite the rapid onslaught of the confederate troops.

As he looked around, some of the union troops had to resort to hand-to-hand combat. Finally, the fighting subsided, and calm came over the cemetery ridge.

Nathaniel fell to one knee with blood coming from the other leg and his side. Medical people combed the battlefields for the wounded. (Photo 5)  Coming across Nathaniel, they realized that someone made a mistake. "You should never have been left on the battlefield. Your wounds are significant, and they should have taken you to the field hospital. Gently, they lifted Nathaniel into their wagon and took him straight to a surgical tent. Immediately, the surgeons pulled more shrapnel from his side and a bullet from his leg. He was then taken to another tent to rest and heal.

Suffering great losses, Lee had no other alternative but to lead his army on an agonizing retreat to his home state of Virginia. After surveying the battlefield, it was determined that "more American soldiers became casualties at the Battle of Gettysburg, 51,000, than in the Revolutionary War and War of 1812 combined." (12) It took Nathaniel a month to heal before he could get up from the hospital bed. Word was spread around the union encampment that President Lincoln was coming to dedicate a national cemetery at Gettysburg. The battle at Gettysburg was said to be the turning point of the civil war but there were still battles. As a result of his wounds, Nathaniel was honorably discharged and given a pension.

"For Union soldiers, the amount of the pension depended on their rank and their injury. Dependents (widows and children) of soldiers who were killed on duty were also eligible. No one got rich from these early pensions. A "totally disabled" private received just $8/month at first. But amounts increased as it became necessary to recruit soldiers to a war that was no longer popular, and pensions served as recruiting tools."

Nathaniel wanted to stay in the encampment but as he was no longer a member of the Union army, he had to leave. When he reached the discharge point of the encampment, he found his mother Jane waiting for him. "Because of his connections, your father was able to find where you were assigned Nathaniel. It was amazing to us that you fought a battle that was close to our farm. When he found out where you were, your father wanted to fight alongside you but was told he was too old and frail from his prior war wounds."

"Knowing your father's resolve and commitment to country, you can imagine how it infuriated him when he was turned down." Janes eyes welled with tears, "your father is extremely ill and may not have long to live. We must come home at once; your father wants to see you before he dies." Hugging his mother Nathaniel was grieved his father meant everything to him.

Nathaniel and his mother returned home to find that William had deteriorated further. Nathaniel and his mother went to his bedside to give him comfort. Looking forlorn, William struggled to tell them what they needed to do upon his demise. "It will be up to you Nathaniel to take over for me. Jane knows where to find everything. In the basement, you will find my personal belongings that I stored from childhood. I would ask that one of our ancestors down the road be named Thomas, after my mentor and benefactor Thomas Jefferson.

William and Jane had gone through all the family history found in the basement, including William being a slave owned by Thomas Jefferson. They talked about how much they loved one another before William drew his last breath. Jane and Nathaniel cried while each holding one of William's hands.

CHAPTER 11

Time Marches On

"After General Lee's army surrendered at Appomattox Court House on April 9, 1865, the defeated Confederates returned to their homes to face an uncertain future. The postwar prospects of Robert E. Lee were no clearer than those of his men. When he left Appomattox, he began a journey that would take him away from a soldier's life in the field and eventually to Lexington, where his talent for leadership would serve him well as president of a small college." (1) "He took little pay for serving as its president because he wanted to make amends for what transpired in the civil war. Perhaps his greatest contribution to the United States was his effort to reunite the country following the American Civil War. The Arlington National Cemetery website notes that his property came into the hands of the government when a property tax dispute, amounting to just over $92.07 cost the Lee family their home and in January 1864, the U.S. government purchased the property for $26,800 at public auction." (2 *Library of Congress print 15*)

On January 1, 1863 (following a preliminary proclamation) Lincoln signed the Emancipation Proclamation, declaring it to be "a fit and necessary war measure." It states that "all persons held as slaves within any State or designated part of a State, the people whereof shall then be in rebellion against the United States, shall be then, thenceforward, and forever free." (3)

"The Emancipation Proclamation and Thirteenth Amendment freed all slaves in the United States. African Americans in the South faced new difficulties: finding a way to forge an economically independent life in the face of hostile whites, little or no education, and few other resources, such as money. Houston Hartsfield Holloway, "...we colored people did not know how to be free and the white people did not know how to have a free colored person about them." (4)

"For its part, the federal government established the Freedmen's Bureau, a temporary agency, to provide food, clothing, and medical care to refugees in the South, especially freed slaves. Special boards were established to set up schools for African Americans in the South, and Black and white teachers from the North and South worked to help young and old become literate. Some African Americans in the South were encouraged to move to North where jobs would be available. Extending the vote to Black Americans was hotly debated." (4)

Along with his sisters and their spouses, Nathaniel stayed on the farm, growing it into one of the highest producing farms in the area. He married a local girl and together with her raised a son and a daughter. His one sister never married, and the other did not have any children. Nathaniel and his wife lived a long and prosperous life until his wife died from unknown causes in 1920. Nathaniel lived for another five years until he met his maker in 1925. Their daughter never married but their son met and married his true love in 1920. The lineage went on and eventually a great grandson of William named David married Sarah at the age of twenty-two.

When Sarah became pregnant, they searched for names. David's wife quickly produced some girl names, but they were stuck on the name for a boy. After nine months of pregnancy, David rushed his wife to the local hospital expecting her to give birth soon. When they arrived, they were the only ones in the maternity ward. Within the next two hours, there were many arrivals of pregnant mothers. After an eight-hour wait, David's wife Sarah finally gave birth to a healthy baby boy. The nurses prepared to discharge her while David sat in the waiting room. When the nurse came with the discharge papers, she asked David and Sarah what they would like to name their son. David gave the nurse a perplexed look. "We had a name if our child was a girl but not if it was a boy. We will get back to you soon with a name."

The nurse gave a determined look to David. "What do you mean, you will get back to us. You cannot leave the hospital without giving us a name. We need to put a name on the birth certificate." David kept walking towards the exit with his wife and child. "I promise we will get back to you in a day or two." The nurse just stood at the door with paper in hand and her mouth wide open in disbelief.

Arriving home, David thought he might find some answers in his family's history. Somewhere he knew that his father told him before he died that he had some family bibles and diaries that were kept religiously by his great Grandmother Jane. What his father did not tell him is where they were stored. Thinking they may be in the attic of their farmhouse; he went up to the second floor and pulled down the steps that led to the attic. As far as he knew, there had not been anyone in the attic since he was a small boy. At the top of the stairs, there was a pull cord to turn on a light. When he tugged on the cord, it was shocking to see all the artifacts and clothing his ancestors had stored.

The clothing dated before the civil war days with one complete union uniform that stood out immediately. David surmised that this belonged to his great ancestor Nathaniel. There were numerous antique trunks, some marked and some not. Luckily for David, none had locks except the one marked personal. David decided to open some of the ones without locks first. He was pleased to see that he only had to go through three to find the one that contained family bibles and diaries. He scanned some of the bibles to see what notations were made in it. Finding no answers, he then went through the diary dated around the time his fathers' Great grandfather died. After reading many pages, he came across one of Jane's handwritten notes where William asked a descendant name one of their sons Thomas in honor of Thomas Jefferson.

David's eyes widened and his curiosity peaked when reading what his great grandfather had asked. Seeing this, he pulled from the trunks Diaries and Bibles. He sat in the attic for hours reading about William's father-son-like relationship with Thomas Jefferson and where William felt obligated to have a family member name a child after Jefferson. The reason for no other family member ever discovering the close relationship William had with Thomas Jefferson was because everyone was too busy working on the farm to take the time to find and read the bibles and diaries.

Sitting in the attic for hours reading some of the bibles and diaries only touched the tip of the iceberg. There was far too much to read even if he dedicated weeks to doing so. Whatever the case, he found the answer to the name for his newborn son. Hopefully, his wife will agree to the name. David turned out the light on all the memories and descended the stairs to talk it over with his wife. He proceeds to tell his wife what he found in one of the trunks and one of the last wishes of his ancestor William to have a descendant named Thomas. "What do you think honey?" Sarah ponders naming a boy Thomas with the last name of Jefferson. "I like the name, but do you think that people will make fun of him?" "Maybe, but he will certainly stand head and shoulders above the rest." "Sarah agreed; the decision was made.

The early years of their newborn son were uneventful. Although young, he was highly intelligent and astute, far more than most children his age. The country became infatuated with a young candidate running for president, John F. Kennedy. Along with his father, Thomas took a great deal of interest in the nomination and campaign of Kennedy.

He became hooked on watching the campaign unfold. Earnestly, he watched each of the four debates between Kennedy and Nixon. Some believe that those who listened to the first debate on radio thought that Nixon won verses those that watched it on television thought Kennedy won. "The first Kennedy-Nixon debate captured over sixty-five million viewers resulting in a major impact in the election's outcome and outreach. One of the most discussed issues with the 1960 debates was the notion that people who listened to the radio were more likely to vote for Nixon while people who watched the debates on television were more likely to vote for Kennedy. One of the explanations to this phenomenon was a presidential candidate's physical appearances during the debates with Kennedy appearing better on television than Nixon." (5)

Thomas became so engrossed in the presidency and what it could do to help the people that he dreamed of someday becoming the president. When President Kennedy was shot, Thomas was only in elementary school. Along with millions of Americans, he watched the televised funeral service. Jaqueline Kennedy was quoted as saying, "There will be great presidents again.... but there will never be another Camelot again (6) At night, before we would go to sleep, Jack liked to play some records; and the song he loved most came at the very end of this record. The lines he loved to hear were: *Do not let it be forgot that once there was a spot, for one brief shining moment that was known as Camelot."* (7)

Despite the tragic end to the Kennedy presidency, Thomas continued to dream of one day entering the political arena. After high school, Thomas entered college. While there, he fell in love with a beautiful girl who would later break off their relationship and break his heart.

His family tried everything in their power to consol him but to no avail. One day, his father handed him a diary from his great grandfather. "I thought you might find what he wrote interesting Thomas." Reading the diary, Thomas learned more about the plight of his ancestry, especially about his great-great grandfather William. To heal his broken heart and forget a lost love, he voluntarily signed up to fight in the war of 1812. There was no war going on at the present, but Thomas thought enlisting in the army would provide a diversion from his broken heart.

Thomas military orders directed him to report to Fort Knox for basic training. – Fort Knox stores precious metal bullion reserves for the United States. Highest historic gold holdings were 649.6 million ounces" (8) After being discharged from active duty, Thomas returned home, completed his college degree, and accepted a job with General Motors.

After working a year at General Motors, Thomas was fortunate enough to land a job as their youngest Program Controller with ABC world News in New York For the next three months, Thomas dedicated himself to learning about television operations. During his first month on the job, he encountered an opportunity to see a president of the United States in person. President Nixon was going to a function at a New York City hotel.

The event rekindled Thomas's interest in politics and the mystique of the Presidency.

The agent's story was of particular interest to Thomas when President Richard Nixon addressed the nation in a live televised broadcast to make an unexpected announcement: he had accepted an invitation from Beijing to become the first U.S. president to visit the People's Republic of China. "The surprise announcement was the result of months of top-secret diplomacy between the Nixon White House and Beijing. Nixon, always a fan of the "big play," was optimistic that his trip to China would be the kind of seismic geopolitical event that changed the course of history.

President Nixon's trip to China in 1972 ended twenty-five years of isolation between the United States and the People's Republic of China (PRC) and resulted in establishment of diplomatic relations between the two countries in 1979." (11)

Thomas was assigned to coordinate the broadcast operations and engineering of ABC News in New York. ABC worked with CBS and NBC to arrange for satellite feeds as well as travel and hotel accommodations to reduce their operating costs. The satellites gave them the capability to feed news stories back to the United States for airing on their evening news casts. President Nixon planned to be in China for approximately seven days. The president's trip to China again reignited Thomas' burning desire to hold an elected office.

After living in New York for a year, Thomas took a date to a Broadway performance of "Prisoner of Second Avenue". "The story revolves around the escalating problems of a middle-aged couple living in New York City. The main character has just lost his job after 22 years in his job, and now must cope with being unemployed in middle age during an economic recession. (12)

Walking out of the theater, Thomas visualized that he could end up in the same position as the character in the play. He immediately started making plans to leave New York.

CHAPTER 12

Enter Politics

Upon arriving home, he moved in with his parents and started to decide what he was going to do with his life. A local woman who was chair of the Republican party told him that they needed a candidate to run for a state legislative seat. The dominate voter registration was Democrat. Not feeling comfortable with either party, Thomas decided to register and run as an Independent.

Not knowing anything about running a campaign, kittle did he know that it was impossible to get elected as an Independent,

Thomas and the opposing candidate made headlines on key issues. The area encompassed the largest steel mills in the world. Thomas pointed out that the mills would not always be there, and Pennsylvania should legalize gambling. People criticized him but his prophecy proved right. The mills shut down and gambling was legalized years later. Without money and party support, he lost.

His next venture into politics was running as an independent again for a state senate seat in a district which covered the city. By running as an independent, Thomas thought it better to adhere to his values of serving the people rather than having to do favors for the political party and a select few. Moreso than winning, he wanted to emphasize the adversities faced by the people.

As before, voters cast their vote predicated on name recognition and party affiliation. Most voters are also one issue voters and do not do their research on candidates. There once was a former mayor of Pittsburgh and governor of Pennsylvania, who made a statement about the importance of having a known name when running for elected office. (1)

When once being interviewed about a controversial subject by the news media, he would say, "I do not care what you say about me, just spell the name right." He was inferring to the fact that people vote on name recognition more so than on issues.

Waging political campaigns are a strategic science and can be deceptive depending on the candidate and their backers. Reportedly John Kennedy may never have been a congressman let alone president if it was not for having two opponents with the same name. Kennedy won because the vote for the other candidates were divided between them, giving Kennedy the most votes.

After his initial fling into the political arena, Thomas decided that he was going to take a run at another office. Even though his views were more moderate leaning right, he changed his party affiliation from Independent to Democrat so he could run against the majority whip of the Pennsylvania State Senate.

Many democratic strongholds went for Thomas. Although the incumbent had the democratic machine and money behind him, he did not have the energy to keep up the pace set by Thomas and his young committee. Thomas started his campaign in the winter before the primary election in May. He campaigned during the evenings and in one of the coldest and snowiest times on record, knocking on the doors of over twenty thousand houses.

Lack of campaign funds, lack of campaign experience, and having a third candidate in the race to cut up the vote were the primary causes for Thomas's loss. With a bit more of the first two and elimination of the third, Thomas would have easily won.

Years later, Thomas entered a marriage that ended in an amicable divorce. Their marriage resulted in their having two wonderful sons. Once his sons enrolled in school, Thomas read an article by Rand Education noting that teachers can affect our youth for generations to come. "As to how teachers can influence their students, "research suggests teachers can affect hundreds of students over the course of their careers, and their students in turn can pass these effects on to other people." (2)

It was then that Thomas decided to run for the school board. By running for the board, he felt he could take a firsthand look at the makeup of the Boards. He found that Board members are more than policymakers; they are advocates for students and their parents. During his tenure, he saved the school district $50 million dollars in capital outlay plus a million a year in operating costs by consolidating seven elementary schools.

After completing his term on the school board, the Republican committee asked him to run for a county council position in a county having a population of over one million people. Aside from his career and politics, Thomas always dreamed of being commissioned an officer in the military but thought because he was over the age for commissioning. Suddenly, America came under attack on 9-11. Having the desire to support the cause, he accepted a commission as a first lieutenant and later assigned to the Joint Chiefs of Staff at the Pentagon.

Thomas was discharged from active duty one week prior to the general election. It only gave him one week to campaign. Four hours after the polls closed, Thomas was losing to his opponent. Thinking he had lost, he received a phone call from his friend, Martin Michaels. "Congratulations on your win Thomas." Thomas thought he was kidding. "Come on Martin, I lost by one hundred votes." "No Thomas, you won by a hairline, forty-five votes."

Two days after the election, Thomas's opponent challenged the election. Many people on adding machines sprang into action in the back room of the election department. Each side was allowed to have observers. The whole scene resembled the counting of chads in Florida when Bush and Gore were remarkably close. The recount took a couple of days. At the end, Thomas still won the race by slightly less than fifty votes.

Thomas's tenure on council proved disheartening. The opposing Democratic party had the plurality and always won their side of the argument. When there were meetings having a hot subject, they resulted in public hearings and lengthy debates.

To make his tenure on council more interesting, Thomas kept putting up motions to educate people on issues and shake up the council. A motion could not be enacted into law but would be sent to whatever political power had oversight. An example of two such motions was that Western Pennsylvania should secede from eastern Pennsylvania and become its own state. When people laughed at him, he explained that he meant to divide the state diagonally. That would put all the marcella shell in the West and its residents would not have to pay any taxes because they would benefit from the revenues. Another motion he put up was to send hard core prisoners to be incarcerated in other countries. By doing so, he argued it would deter senseless killings and save the taxpayers money.

After serving on and off for six years in the defense of our country during 9-11 at the Pentagon, Thomas returned home to find his girlfriend left him for someone else, Thomas thought he would try dating sites. His two sons sat down on each side of him purveying the dating web sites of eligible ladies. He would quickly scan over the ones he thought were not for him. He came to one where the photo was not too complimentary of the young woman. It was a very formal photo of her in a lab coat. Turning the page to continue looking, his sons forced him to go back to her. "What are you doing? It is only a cup of coffee." Reluctantly, Thomas read her background and looked at other photos of her. One cute photo of her at the bottom of the page caught his eye. Thomas phoned her. Her name was Abbey.

She suggested meeting over a cup of coffee. Thomas thought she might not have a date tonight even though it was Saturday night, normally a date night. "How about a movie tonight?" "Okay Thomas, I will meet you at the movie theater." Having a long wait at the theater, Thomas thought he might have been stood up. Finally, a cute little lady in a white ski jacket appeared.

Even though the movie was a comedy, Thomas saw a tear come to the eye of Abbey. Leaning over to give her a hug of comfort, he asked her if she was okay. "I am fine Thomas. I really needed a lighthearted movie like this, but I am thinking of my friend who has been inflicted with a serious illness.

Next, Thomas asked her to join him at a party at a posh club in celebrating the election of President Obama. As both were more conservative in their political views, the event did not seem to fit their philosophies. What caught Thomas's attention was while he went to the restroom, Abbey warmed herself in front of the fireplace. Thomas could not take his eyes off her athletic silhouette dancing against the fire. Along with her sincere caring for others and her beauty, Thomas thinks that this may be the lady for him. Upon driving Abbey to her car, she reached up and gave Thomas a kiss on his cheek, which further solidified his feelings towards her.

On one of the subsequent dates, Thomas invited Abbey to his house for dinner. Thomas had a radiant log burning fireplace in the living room. After dinner, Abbey climbed onto the couch and snuggled with Thomas watching a movie. For Thomas, it was like being in heaven having the warmth of her lying next to him. Holding one another in front of the fireplace gave them an opportunity to talk. It was there that they learned much more about one another and how their families were alike. Eventually, both drifted off to sleep. When they awoke, the snow outside deepened. Thomas invited her to spend the night at his home. So as not to put Abbey in a compromising position, Thomas offered her his bedroom while he slept on the couch. After he took his turn in the bathroom, he headed for the couch to find Abbey waiting for him. Without saying a word, he took her by the hand and they both slept in the bedroom snuggling.

Many a time, Thomas would refer to himself as Dom quixote and his friend Jim as his Sancho Panza. Thomas and Jim were still not convinced that Donald Trump was the right person to carry the presidential banner for the Republican party.

After Thomas decided to not run for another term on County Council, Jim suggested that they go to the presidential primary in New Hampshire to learn more about the candidates. Thomas concurred and started doing some research two months before the primary. He discovered that to get your name on the New Hampshire ballot for president, you simply had to pay a $1000 fee and one signature, your own signature. Thomas decided to place his name on the presidential ballot.

There were many diverse types of people that wanted their name on a ballot for President, some more serious than others. One unusual person was Vermin Supreme. "Supreme's 2024 campaign is his ninth run, pursuing the Republican, Democratic and Libertarian nominations. Famous for wearing a rubber boot on his head, Supreme has made numerous headlines for his advocacy for time travel research and human-pony chimeras." (3)

When Thomas and Jim arrived in the capital of Manchester, Concord, the town was abuzz with news media and candidates.

Candidates were traveling throughout the state on their customized campaign buses (Photo 6) with their names printed all over them. As most New Hampshire primaries, a snow blizzard was raining down on the town and the temperatures were below freezing. Daily elevated temperatures are around 35°F, rarely falling below 21°F or exceeding 49°F. Because of the extreme cold, few people were walking on the streets, making it difficult to meet people or hand out campaign literature.

Thomas made up a couple thousand campaign cards but unlike other states, discovered it was almost impossible to hand them out at the polls. New Hampshire has stringent restrictions where you can stand while handing out campaign literature at polling places.

Looking for a restroom, Thomas gained access to the capital building. While inside, he met workers and discussed his candidacy with them. It turned out that many of them voted for him. Campaign buses were descending on the town. Trump rented the local convention hall to hold his campaign rally while Cruz went to a VFW. "Politico described the 2016 Republican primary in New Hampshire as a "topsy-turvy" campaign that saw "an all-out assault" on "establishment" politics."

Just prior to the Republican convention in Cleveland, Thomas received a phone call from his close friend Martin, who asked him if he wanted to go to the Republican convention in Cleveland. One of the delegates to the convention loaned him their passes for an hour or two. Thomas jumped at the chance. Upon their arrival, they found a lot of activity going on around the convention hall.

They did not get a glimpse of any major candidates but it wetted Thomas's appetite to stay engaged in politics. "The convention formally nominated Donald Trump for president and Indiana Governor Mike Pence for vice president." (4)

When Trump ran in 2016 and 2020, Thomas was not especially fond of him because he thought he had too much of an ego. He supported and worked hard to get him elected anyway because he did not like his opponent's left-wing stances. Thomas and his friend Jim would stand on the sides of roads holding large Trump signs.

Jim was a member of the Constitution party and was one of their hardest working volunteers. He was borderline fanatic when it came to supporting a candidate. Thomas and Jim stood ready to support viable candidates that reflected their political beliefs.

During the 2016 presidential campaign, Thomas went into Republican headquarters to pick up some signs and literature for Trump and Senator Toomey. While there, he met a campaign volunteer named Matt. He and Matt entered a conversation about independent voters not having a say in choice of candidates for local or national political offices or their being ignored by elected officials due to their not being organized. Realizing they shared much the same political philosophy, they decided to discuss it in more detail over dinner.

Returning to Allegheny County Republican headquarters (RCAC), they both noticed that a huge amount of Trump and Senator Toomey over 500 signs were laying in the Republican headquarters. Realizing that election day was fast approaching, Thomas and Matt volunteered to give them out when Trump spoke at the old county airport the next day. Thomas said he had a friend, Jim, who had a pickup truck and would call him to bring his truck to the RCAC headquarters the next evening.

Thomas and Matt showed up on time. As requested by Thomas, Jim showed up with his pickup truck. The three of them loaded all thousand signs and took off for the old airport. When they arrived, the cars were backed up for miles to see Trump. Likewise, the line to get into the hangar was so long, you could hardly see the end. Jim pulled his pickup on the side of the road and both Thomas and Matt stood on each side of the road. The cars were crawling so slowly that they were able to give them the signs.

After handing out the last signs, Jim asked Thomas and Matt if they wanted to get in line to see Trump. Looking at one another and then Jim, Matt gave a sarcastic answer. "There are only two people that I get in line for Jim are not here, that's God and Mother Theresa. Let us go somewhere and exchange more ideas over a cup of coffee, Thomas and Jim. After visiting for two hours, Matt and Thomas agreed that they would meet sometime in the future."

A few months passed when Jim asked Thomas to help him drive to the national constitution convention again. Despite how far the drive was, Jim refused to fly because his political convictions for some reason prevented his supporting homeland security. It took them over eight hours to reach the convention in St Louis.

It was not Thomas's intention to attend the convention, but he thought it may be interesting to do so. Once being a democrat, republican, and an independent; Thomas identified himself as a moderate that leaned right. "Similarly, an annual poll on values and beliefs conducted in May by Gallup found that 38% of Americans identify as "conservative" or "very conservative" on social issues, compared to 29% of respondents who identified as "liberal." (5)

Driving all this way with Jim, Thomas thought it was an opportune time to put in his two cents. Even though he was not a voting member of the constitution party, they gave him the opportunity to speak when he raised his hand. "These are troubling times for our country. Your party and other parties like the Libertarian party are always putting up candidates that cannot win. By putting these candidates up, you defeat candidates that share most of your values and beliefs. Why don't you get behind a candidate that can win?" None agreed or disagreed.

Several months later, the democratic County chief executive was getting ready to run for his third and final term. Because the republicans had no candidate, Thomas volunteered.

Thomas was invited to numerous meet the candidate nights. One such event was in the middle of an African American neighborhood. One of the candidates even pointed to Thomas and remarked. "He is the only white man here tonight!" When it came

Thomas's turn to speak, he thought he would use what Clint Eastwood once used at Republican Convention. Thomas started his speech challenging the audience. "Do you know why there are not elected officials here tonight? It is because they know that they have your vote in the palm of their hands." Pulling up three empty chairs and pointing to it while saying, "Isn't that right Mayor, isn't that right Mr. County Executive, isn't that right Mr. Councilman."

As he said it, he could see people in the audience nodding their head in agreement. After completing his presentation, he listened to other candidates. All were running for city council while the incumbent did not even show up, or any elected official for that matter. One candidate who had an outstanding job with the mass transit system, was the last to be present. He questioned Thomas.

"Do you support reparations for African American people?" Thomas thought for a few minutes before answering. "What about people who legally migrated from Europe to the steel valley and received no support whatsoever. My grandparents with six children went to board the boat to America. My Aunt was turned away because they thought she had an air infection. My grandmother never saw her alive again. When they arrived in the steel valley, they were discriminated against and received no financial support or jobs. They worked hard to make it. What about them?"

"Also please note that back in the days of slavery, there were only a handful of states that practiced it. Why should people of free states have to pay or people alive today that had nothing to do with slavery? Lastly, many young men are now victims of reverse discrimination. They must sit by while many are promoted before them. So, you see, trying to implement reparations in a fair manner is not doable. The candidate who questioned Thomas about his stance looked at Thomas and in a discriminating way himself simply said, "But you are a white man!"

After the meeting, Thomas stopped by his parents on his way home. Sitting with his father in their living room, Thomas described his being chastised as the only white man in the room. His father laughed and stood up to fetch a document he found in one of the trunks stored in the attic. Handing it to Thomas, he asked him to read it. His father sat patiently waiting for his son's reaction. Thomas sat with an astonished look on his face. "Is this true father?" "I should have shown it to you sooner Thomas, but I wanted you to succeed in your own efforts, not because you claim minority privilege and your ancestry can be traced to a slave. You also should be proud of your European heritage."

Thomas sat there in bewilderment wanting more information. It was late at night, and he was too tired to look through the trunks. "I have not even gone through all the trunks handed down from our ancestors Thomas. Someday, the two of us will root through them."

The next morning, Jim picked Thomas up to do some campaigning. All Thomas and Jim could do was to stand on major highways waving campaign signs. The sign messages included "Cut Taxes, Term Limits, and Veteran. Without Thomas having any campaign money to deliver his message, the incumbent won.

The next race Thomas entered was to fill a vacant US Senate seat. Others who decided to run was the talk show host, Dr. Oz. Thomas threw his hat into the ring for the vacant Senate seat, but because of the number of candidates in the field and lack of money, he had no intention of staying in the race. He wanted to voice some critical issues. At one meeting, Thomas put forth a point, "Do you realize that all these people who want to be our next U.S. Senator are spending millions in Ads against one another. If they really cared about our country, they would sit down at a table and pool their money to defeat the liberal candidate." Many in attendance urged him to run.

After Thomas got his points across, he pulled himself out of the race. The result was that Dr. Oz won the primary but because his opponent tagged him as a carpet bagger, he lost.

CHAPTER 13

Nominations

Jim once again pleaded with Thomas to drive to the 2024 national constitutional convention out West. "You want me to drive over two thousand miles Jim!" Jim gave him that "why not" look of his. "I will do most anything for you Jim, but I am not fond of driving two thousand miles." Because he did not want Jim to go alone, however, Thomas agreed to go with him by train.

At the end of the first day of the convention, Thomas discussed with Jim his point about the minor parties like the Constitution party getting behind a candidate that can win. Jim was not in total disagreement with Thomas, but he said that the constitutional party has its own agenda and wants its own candidates. "Why don't you change your registration and become the standard bearer for the Constitutional party Thomas?" "Do you realize that you would need an enormous amount of money to travel the entire country, Jim. Jim responded "so what. Just think if you win."

Even though Thomas was not a registered voter of the constitutional party, Thomas was permitted to sit in on the convention and address it at times. When it came to discussing a presidential nominee for their party, Thomas thought it was a good time to again voice his concerns about third parties taking votes from credible candidates of like mind.

"Why not throw your support behind a candidate that can win?" The national president spoke up. "I recall your putting forth that suggestion one other time. "I for one was not in favor of it then but put forth your proposal." Thomas did not back down. "I will bring some information to tomorrow's meeting."

Returning to their room, Thomas and Jim looked online for third party candidates. One such party got his attention and that was Teddy Roosevelt. "The title for highest share of votes ever earned by a third-party candidate in American history is still held by Theodore Roosevelt during the election of 1912. After serving nearly two full terms in the White House, Theodore Roosevelt opted not to run for a third term in 1908. When Roosevelt's close friend and hand-picked successor, William Howard Taft, failed to advance his reform-minded agenda, Roosevelt challenged him for the nomination.

"Although Roosevelt overwhelmingly won the most votes during the primaries, the Republican National Convention nominated the more conservative Taft to stand for election. A bitter Roosevelt broke with the GOP ranks to form the Progressive Party, nicknamed the "Bull Moose Party" because Roosevelt often declared himself "fit as a bull moose.

Roosevelt and Taft ended up splitting the Republican vote, which led to an easy victory by Democrat Woodrow Wilson." (1)

"Wealthy businessman Ross Perot shook up the 1992 presidential election, much as Donald Trump did in 2016. Indeed, the parallels between Perot and Trump are striking. Ralph Nader ran as the Green Party candidate and received 97,488 votes in Florida." (2)

The next day, Thomas presented what he found at the convention. Appealing to their sense of patriotism, "Thomas started with a quote from Abraham Lincoln," "We must stand together and set it back on the course envisioned by our forefathers."

"Never before in our history have we faced issues that threaten the very existence of our great country. We are faced with illegal immigration due to porous borders and non-enforcement of immigration laws, runaway inflation, teaching our children against our beliefs, discrimination and reverse discrimination, mass killings, elected officials violating our constitution, people being chastised for their religion beliefs and right to speak freely, elected officials not voting the will of their people and padding their pockets, our streets laden with crime due to non-enforcement of our laws, a useless and do nothing congress refusing to enact term limits, a miss-directed foreign policy that pits us against our allies, draining of our resources to fund senseless wars not of our choosing, outsourcing of jobs, violation of laws set in stone by the constitution, and a flawed energy policy making us dependent on foreign oil. All this is only the beginning. "

"Moreover, we sadly have two front runners where one is controlled by an extreme faction of progressive left-wing liberals while the other is extremely far right." We need a president that can reach across all factions and unite America. Thomas ended with another quote from Abraham Lincoln. "A house divided against itself cannot stand."

Not knowing until now what Thomas was going to present, Jim sat in amazement. Suddenly, one of the delegates stood up. "I nominate Thomas Jefferson as our candidate for President." Jim jumps up and seconds it. Apparently impressed with what Thomas just said, all the attendees voice an affirmative to Thomas's nomination. Thomas stands up waving his hands. "Whoa, it was never my intention or desire to run as your candidate for president. I cannot accept your nomination. You hardly know anything about me!" Jim stands up. Little did you know Thomas, I have been touting your credentials since the last two conventions."

Jim started handing out the campaign election cards used in New Hampshire when Thomas was on the same ballot for president as Trump in 2016. "What are you doing Jim? I am not accepting their nomination." As the attendees were looking over the cards, Thomas sat down and leaned over quietly talking to Jim. "You did what Jim! Remember our discussion about the feasibility!"

The attendees would not let Thomas off the hook. They kept prompting Thomas to accept their nomination. Thomas just sat there in deep thought before answering. "Let me take a serious look at the possibilities tonight. Anyone who runs as a third-party candidate cannot win without substantial money and backers."

At the end of day two of the convention, Thomas and Jim went out to a local restaurant for a bite and mulled over what had just happened. Sitting in deep thought and talking with Jim about the day's events, Thomas finally spoke up about whether he should accept the nomination of the Constitutional party. "Did the Constitutional Party get their presidential candidate on every state ballot Jim?" Jim grimaced a bit and then answered. "No, they did not get all the states." Thomas pointed at Jim. "How can you win an election with that Jim?" Jim rolls his eyes.

"We must change the thinking of third parties if they ever hope to win a major election Jim. Let us go back to the room and do some research." Sitting in the room, they first looked at a Gallup poll to ascertain how many voters in America consider themselves independents and want a third party. They found that sixty-three percent of U.S. adults currently agree with the statement that the Republican and Democratic parties do "such a poor job" of representing the American people that "a third major party is needed, this is a seven-percentage increase from last year." (3)

Looking at Jim, "People have been hopelessly complaining across America about what has happened to our country. There is not a coffee shop that I go to where a conversation about how dissatisfied people is with our elected official. There is a silent majority out there that wants their voices heard Jim. Do you know who coined the word "Silent Majority"? Jim looked at Thomas with a puzzled look on his face. "No, I do not Thomas." "It was "Richard Nixon, calling on the "great silent majority" for their support." (4) We should be the voice for the silent majority.

The convention started at its usual time in the morning. After a full breakfast, Thomas and Jim walked into the convention meeting area with all eyes on them. This time Thomas had put together a power point presentation. After the morning business was accomplished, the convention chair turned to Thomas. "What is your answer regarding our nomination Thomas?" Thomas stood up and asked them to drop the visual screen behind the podium. "Before I answer, I would like to put forth a presentation and then pose some questions." The chair gave him the go ahead.

Thomas discussed what the Gallup poll revealed about a good percentage of voters categorized themselves as independents and moderates. He then goes on to discuss size of the third parties in the United States. Your party is ranked fifth largest with only 137,000 registered voters. "As of August 2022, there are 310 Libertarians holding elected office: 193 of them partisan offices and 117 of them non-partisan offices. There are 693,634 voters registered as Libertarian in the thirty-one states that report Libertarian registration statistics." (5) "Gallup found that voters who identify as libertarians ranged from 17 to 23% of the American electorate. As I have said at many a meeting, Gallup polling last month found that a record 49% of Americans see themselves as politically independent — the same as the two major parties put together." (6)

Thomas points to a map of the United States he found online showing the states each party had accessed to place their Presidential candidates on the ballot. "As far as getting third party access to the ballot for their presidential candidate, the Libertarian party was able to get their candidate on the ballot in all the states while your party was able to get your candidate only on 29 states ballots Even with the Libertarian party being the third largest, their presidential candidate only garnered 1.2% of the national vote in 2020 which was a considerable drop compared to the 3.3% their candidate received in 2016." (7) "Your candidate barely made a showing, and he may not have received all the votes of your party."

Thomas now gets more emphatic about his point. "What this all means is that without a consortium of third parties, you will not even get to first base. You need to align yourselves with another third party like the Libertarians. If the Libertarian Party is to make a respectable showing, they will need to do the same. Bottom line is this, I will only accept your nomination if you are willing to align yourself with the Libertarian party and back me as an independent rather than being affiliated with any one political party!"

People start raising their hands with questions. "We have always fielded a candidate under the banner of the Constitution party. How do you propose to talk the Libertarians into joining together with us?"   Thomas had a good comeback argument. "You can continue to field a losing candidate, and, in the end, you will never have a say in national politics or join another party and at least have your concerns aired on the national stage. Do not lose sight of what is near and dear to you the most and that is preserving the basic premises of the constitution! By backing an independent who shares your values, you will play a key role in changing the destructive course that radicals have set for our country. As far as getting the Libertarians on board "Jim and I will work that out by presenting our case at their national convention in Washington DC. First, however, we need a resolution from your party that states your party will form the coalition.

Thomas pulled up his laptop to place on the overhead screen a personal letter from a former Chairman of the Joint Chiefs of Staff thanking him for his service to our country. What really caught their eye was the sentence that said, "As a result of your efforts, the chiefs and I were better able to carry out our responsibilities of providing military advice to the President and the Secretary of Defense" You could hear positive comments coming from the attendees. The party chair puts forth a motion "If Thomas can build that coalition, I say we agree to the stipulations put forth by him." Jim second it and the committees from each state ratified the motion. As to nominating a Vice President candidate, the party pledged to let Thomas pick whoever he wished.

At the end of the convention, Thomas and Jim started their return home. Both were quiet for quite some time. Neither of them could believe what had just happened. Especially Thomas who kept thinking about the daunting work ahead of them and virtually not a dime to start the campaign. Looking over at Jim, he asked him what he thought. "I am thinking what you are thinking Thomas. How are we going to convince the Libertarian Party to unite with the Constitution party to back a candidate? Also, where are we going to get the money to kick start a national campaign? Heck, we do not even have any expense money for campaign literature and travel." Thomas thought he would lighten up the conversation by kiddingly saying. "This is another fine mess you got me into Jim."

Upon returning home, Abbey greeted Thomas with a hug and kiss. Thomas told her what had happened at the Constitutional party convention. Like most Americans, Abbey, and Thomas both were concerned about what was happening to their country. Biden's approval ratings were plummeting, and Trump was tied up defending himself in court. Both were making statements that either angered or bewildered voters, including the two of them.

Thomas and Jim started to look at campaign strategies. They wanted to see how the Constitution and Libertarian party philosophies might mesh with one another. The Libertarian party has a membership of approximately seven hundred thousand members. Like the Constitution party, the Libertarian party had conservative values. It is comprised of people who want limited intervention of the government into their lives.

The Libertarian party had many members who leaned more conservative and may have been registered Republican before changing their registration to Libertarian.

Thomas and Jim planned to attend the Libertarian's annual meeting which was coming up soon in Washington DC. "According to their web site Jim, anyone is welcome to attend. It may be best, however, for us to have someone introduce us at the meeting. There was a Libertarian, Dave, who once contacted me about running under their banner in the general. I will contact him to see if he will introduce me at the Washington DC meeting." Thomas briefed Dave on what had transpired at the Constitutional meeting. Recalling how hard Thomas fought for his constituents, Dave agreed to use his influence with the Libertarian party.

Thomas arrived in Washington with David and Jim the day before the Libertarian party's convention. Upon entering the convention hall, the next day, David asked the chair to place Thomas on the agenda in the afternoon. Thomas and Jim had prepared another power point slide show. They sat in on the morning session until it came time for Thomas to present. Thomas slowly rose and walked to the podium looking back on Jim who was egging him on. Standing in front of the hall, Thomas started his presentation with the same salient points he presented at the

Constitution Party's national convention, including nominating someone to run under the banner of being an independent.

After presenting the pitfalls America is up against, he gave a summary of how he supports a good deal but not all of what the Libertarians set forth in their 2022 Libertarian party platform. "Hold that all individuals have the right to exercise sole dominion over their own lives and have the right to live in whatever manner they choose, so long as they do not forcibly interfere with the equal right of others to live in whatever manner they choose. Parents, or other guardians, have the right to raise their children according to their own standards and beliefs. Government force must be limited to the protection of the rights of individuals to life, liberty, and property, and governments must never be permitted to violate these rights. Affirm the individual right recognized by the Second Amendment to keep and bear arms." (8)

Thomas then looked away from the screen and abruptly stopped talking to present his plan. He told the delegates his reason for coming to the convention was to seek their nomination for president under the condition that they would join with the Constitution party. His request shocked the attendees to the lull of silence in the Hall.

The questions and comments then came with a flurry. More than one of the delegates remarked that Thomas was not even a registered Libertarian. Another questioned his stance on the basic principles of their party and if he was aligned to their party platform. Dave then spoke up. "I would like to point out that if Thomas did not share many of our beliefs, our local committee in Pennsylvania would never have endorsed him." Thomas thanked Dave for his comment and then followed up with a thought. "I would venture to say that not one of us in this hall agrees with every issue of the Libertarian party or with each other. Like many voters out there, I would hope that none of us are one issue voters. In today's world, the big picture for America is now turning into a horror film." Thomas then paused again. "My credentials speak for themselves. Google my name and we can then resume our conversation tomorrow if you allow me."

As Jim and Thomas reviewed their notes and what transpired that day, Jim looked up at Thomas. "You are not going to give up, are you Thomas? Without you, my party will again field a losing candidate. Without people like you standing up for what's right, America will continue down a path contrary to the basic principles of our constitution!" Looking at Jim in earnest, Thomas shook his head no. "You know me better than that Jim."

Thomas, with Jim by his side, entered the convention hall the next day with the look of a confident and determined man. After the morning business was put aside, the chair called on Thomas again to say to present his case before the delegates took a vote on whether to nominate him or not. Thomas went up to the podium and stood for a few minutes thinking what he should say. He decided to start with a quote. "Abraham Lincoln was once quoted as saying." "I am not bound to win, but I am bound to be true. I am not bound to succeed, but I am bound to live by the light I have. I must stand with anybody that stands right, and stand with him while his is right, and part with him when he goes wrong." (9) "I would paraphrase his quote by saying that Jim and I have never been bound to any one political party just so we can win. Rather, we are bound to live by the light of that which is the right thing to do for our country. The bottom line is that we may not be bound to win but as Americans, we are bound to try. We are living in trying times and if we must reinvent our party to right the wrongs being done to our country, then it is our sworn duty to do so. To quote John Kennedy, *"Those who dare to fail miserably can achieve greatly."*

"To quote the preamble of your party, "As Libertarians, we seek a world of liberty; a world in which all individuals are sovereign over their own lives, and no one is forced to sacrifice his or her values for the benefit of others." "By joining us, you can put into action that which is written in your preamble."

The delegates gave Thomas a resounding applause. After the exuberance subsided, one of the delegates stood to put forth a motion to nominate Thomas as their candidate. Dave started to second his nomination when he was interrupted by another delegate. "Before nominating Thomas as our presidential candidate, I would like to know where he is going to get the necessary contributions to launch a respectable campaign." The gavel signaled the day's end.

Back at the hotel that evening, Thomas receives a phone call from his father asking how things went regarding his nomination. Thomas said that the Libertarian party was hung up on whether he could raise enough money to launch a respectable campaign. Upon hanging up, Thomas's father gave more thought to the money issue. He recalled something he read in one of their great ancestor's diaries about land he owned with a close friend in Louisiana. He went back into the basement to look through more of his great grandmother's trunks. After going through three of them, he found in one of the bibles an agreement written between William Jefferson and his friend whereby they owned considerable land in Louisiana. Searching online, Thomas's father found an oil company under the same name as William's partner. Calling the number revealed that the oil company was owned by a family bearing the same name as William's friend who fought alongside William in the war of 1812. It turned out that the net worth of the oil company was worth over one hundred million dollars.

Having discovered this, Thomas's father called an attorney located in the same town as the oil company, asking him to investigate the matter. By the end of the next business day, the attorney excitedly called back to inform Thomas's father that he found a document filed in the courthouse dating back to the 1800's. The document clearly validates that Thomas's family had a claim to one-half of the oil company's assets. Their share was estimated at fifty-million dollars. The attorney had notified the oil company of the claim, and they said they will honor it. Thomas's father dropped the phone in shock. After thanking the attorney, Thomas's father called Thomas to inform him of the good news and to make a pledge to loan the campaign ten million dollars. Thomas looked at Jim in disbelief of what his father just said.

While writing what to present the next day at the convention, the news reported that a Chinese weather balloon entered the air space of the United States and was unchallenged by the military while it floated across the North American continent. "President Joe Biden ordered the action to shoot it down but after it drifted over heavily populated areas.

Thomas was deeply concerned that the Department of Defense allowed the balloon (Photo 7) to transverse a good portion of the United States before shooting it down Because the thought bothered him so much, he decided to write an OPED letter.

"By delaying the destruction of an unidentified manned or unmanned aircraft as soon as possible, the Department of Defense and the president places our people in harm's way and fails to protect our sovereignty. It also opens the door to follow-up intrusions. I believe it was imperative for the Pentagon to take out the Chinese surveillance balloon sooner. If such an unidentified flying object were carrying an explosive or biological weapon, whoever launched it could have caused mass casualties by detonating it upon it reaching a heavily populated area. According to international law, a country has every right to deny access to its air space. During the 9-11 crisis, the military protocol was to shoot down any aircraft that did not properly identify itself and did not communicate its intent. I would ask the President why he and the Pentagon did not act sooner. More importantly, we need to take notice that an unmanned aircraft easily breached our air space without immediate detection. Such a breach in our air space bodes an examination of where our surveillance systems may be flawed."

Day three of the convention found Thomas and Jim back in their seats at the Libertarian convention. When the chair turned the floor over to Thomas, Thomas stood up. "Mr. Chairman, my father is willing to loan our campaign ten million dollars if the Libertarian party nominates me as their candidate and agrees to form a coalition with the Constitution party. This time, there was a clammer from the delegates to be the first to nominate Thomas.

A frenzy of excitement broke out among the Libertarian delegates. The chair of each state rose to ratify Thomas's endorsement.

"To get on the ballot, a candidate for president of the United States must meet a variety of complex, state-specific filing requirements and deadlines. These regulations, known as ballot access laws, determine whether a candidate or party will appear on an election ballot. These laws are set at the state level." (10)

After the Chair closed the convention, Thomas and Jim started on their way back home to find a manager for their campaign and start the wheels in motion to organize a hard-hitting campaign committee and strategy.

That night, Thomas came across two interesting books, the first was "The Selling of the President" by Joe McGinnis. The book gives insight into the taping of television ads for the 1968 Presidential Campaign. The book's cover depicts a photo of Nixon on a pack of cigarettes. It describes the marketing of Richard Nixon during the 1968 presidential campaign and as the cover suggests, Nixon was marketed like you would market a pack of cigarettes. It became one of the most-influential books on presidential campaigns. (11)

"Richard Nixon narrowly lost to John Kennedy in his bid for the presidency in 1960 and then lost while running for the governorship of California two years later. "The 1968 Presidential campaign occurred during one of the most tumultuous times in American history. In an environment teeming with anger, violence, and hostility. The Vietnam War and the resulting protests, along with the political assassinations of Martin Luther King, Jr., and Robert F. Kennedy, contributed to these historic difficult times." (12)

The other book was "The Making of the President 1960". "The book traces the 1960 presidential campaign. Much of the narrative describes politicians' looks, voices and personalities; but it also contains thought-provoking discussions of trends in American life and politics." (13)

Speed reading the two books, Thomas tries to produce some common campaign strategies that worked for Nixon and Kennedy. American people formed an unfavorable opinion of Richard

Nixon, viewing him as an ugly, boring, cold man. As it was apparent that his old image could not win, the common take away on selling of Nixon was "an exposé of how Nixon's advertising team remade his public image to resemble that of a good and decent man. The book explains how Nixon's advisers created a series of commercials in which Nixon did not have to appear or speak much. The commercials consisted of crowd-pleasing still photographs with Nixon's voice in the background, designed to divert the audience's attention away from the words of Nixon and toward the emotional appeal presented by the photographs. The last part of the book details campaign memos and texts for the actual television ads. Revealing the influence that image making can have on political campaigning, it serves as a prime example of how politicians must carefully devise an image to garner votes." (14)

What caught Thomas's interest in the book, "The making of the President," was the one chapter detailing the reasons behind Americans' ways of voting and ways of life. Nixon's campaign exhausted its resources by campaigning in every single state in the country, including in places where the Republicans either had little chance of winning, or had too few electoral votes to produce a lead in the polls. Some historians and political analysts have since determined that Kennedy's successful use of television as a communications platform secured his victory in the election. Further interpretations claim that Nixon's shortcomings highlighted the increasing obsolescence of non-visual campaigning in American politics, especially radio."

After analyzing the two books, Thomas decided to look at how Ross Perot was able to garner 19% of the election when he ran as an independent when he ran against George Bush and Bill Clinton. It was summed up in an article he found on History.com. "Perot followed the populist model set down by William Jennings Bryan in his (unsuccessful) campaigns for the presidency. Like Bryan, Perot reached out to working-class and middle-class Americans who felt ignored by the political establishments within both parties. Bryan argued for the interests of the "common man."

Nearly a century after Bryan had run, Perot changed the dynamics of the race by focusing on similarly populist issues voters felt had been overlooked or discounted by both President George H.W. Bush and Arkansas Governor William J. Clinton." (15)

The next morning, Thomas turned his attention to finding a campaign manager. Online he finds additional information detailing the profile of a good campaign manager. "Campaign managers are usually hired by word of mouth from a network of people with experience working on campaigns with whom the candidate is familiar, often a close confidant of the candidate." (16)

To start, Thomas felt it important to find a credible campaign manager. With his campaign more a fluke, he thought it might be wise to select a manager that was more aggressive, hands-on, and used unorthodox campaign tactics. The only one that he knew could fit the role and is a "close confidant" was his friend Martin Michaels.

Thomas knew that it was going to be difficult to convince Martin to take on the role of campaign manager. When telling others about his friend Martin, he described him as the real life "uncle buck." Uncle buck was the character in a movie played by the actor John Candy. In the movie, Uncle Buck was portrayed as a bull in a China shop. He wore a heavy full-length coat and a hat that looked like one worn by the comic strip character Snoopy in Peanuts. Uncle Buck drove a large vintage car that backfired when he drove it. Like Uncle Buck in the movie, Martin was like a big teddy bear with a heart of gold. He would do anything for people. He could be very abrasive at times, always saying what he thought even though it was like hitting someone over the head with a sledgehammer. Although Martin was a registered democrat, his thinking was of the old-style democrats and was moderate in his political philosophy.

Thomas set up a breakfast meeting with Martin. When they met, the good news was that Martin was in a jovial mood. After chit chatting about family and political issues, Thomas got down in business. "I need you to sign on as my campaign manager

Martin." Martin's eyes widened and quickly replied. "Campaign for what and how much do I get paid?" Thomas explained how he and Jim built a coalition of the Constitution and Libertarian parties to place his name on the ballot as a presidential candidate in all fifty states. Martin looked at Thomas and exclaimed. "Are you crazy? Do you realize what it will take to run a national campaign, and you want me to be as crazy as you by becoming your campaign manager!" After a lengthy debate, Thomas could not predict the outcome.

As Martin started for the door without an agreement, Thomas thought his choice for a campaign manager was doomed. Just when Martin reached for the door, he turned around and returned to the table. Pointing to a calendar in his briefcase and holding up his phone, the next words out of Martin's mouth gave Thomas much hope. "We need to get started right away. There is so much to do and little time to do it. Even though it is quite far off, we also need to look ahead to get you eligible for the debates." Martin went over the three main requirements to be eligible to debate prior to the general election. "The requirements are established by the Commission on Presidential Debates (CPD). It is the organization that organizes, and establishes guidelines for general elections, presidential and vice-presidential debates."

"To receive an invitation to debate, a candidate must: (if) be Constitutionally eligible to hold the office of President of the United States; (ii) appear on a sufficient number of state ballots to have a mathematical chance of winning a majority vote in the Electoral College; (iii) have a level of support of at least fifteen percent of the national electorate, as determined by five national polling organizations, using the average of those organizations." (17)

Thomas interjects some campaign strategy. "I have email distribution lists that reach thousands of reporters throughout the nation. Like what I did when I was on county council, I could write some attention-grabbing news releases and OPED letters (opposite of the editorial page of a newspaper). "Your writing is excellent Thomas but in addition to the press releases and letters, we need to get you out on the road pressing flesh." Thomas beamed in. "What about buying a used touring bus and campaigning the same way as a few other presidential candidates? Again, Martin nodded his head in agreement and left to start putting the wheels into motion.

The next key person to recruit was the Treasurer. Thomas thought about another friend Ed, that he could trust as a close confidant. Ed was an attorney; someone he could count on to pay attention to detail when it came to reporting. Upon agreeing to be his Treasurer, Thomas thanked Ed and assured him that he will be paid for his services." "You do not have to pay me anything."

Next Thomas needed someone to recruit and coordinate volunteers. There were only two people perfect for the job and that was Suzy and Mary. Both were the king of the volunteers. As Thomas and the two ladies worked on several campaigns together, they signed on and were ready to hit the ground running.

While working on their campaign strategy, Thomas and his team got word that the Hamas had attacked Israel.

"JERUSALEM (AP) —A stunned Israel launched airstrikes in Gaza, with its prime minister saying the country is now at war with Hamas and vowing to inflict an "unprecedented price." (18)

Martin and Thomas wondered if this would have any effect on their campaign strategy. Because Thomas always believed that citizens of a particular country should owe primary allegiance to the country where they live and work, he felt compelled to write another OPED letter on dual citizenship.

"Of the 22 million-plus immigrants legally admitted into this country between 1961 and 1997, almost 75 percent, are from multiple-citizenship-allowing countries according to the center for immigration studies. If this is the case, why should America be responsible for dual citizens who are taken hostage or incarcerated in another country? All countries should be sympathetic to releasing hostages taken by terrorists and should assist wherever possible but when a dual citizen is taken hostage in the country bearing one or other of their citizenships, then it should be that country that takes the lead in freeing them."

One week went by before Martin was on the doorstep of Thomas's to give him the green light to announce.

"It is time to announce your candidacy for the presidency of the United States Thomas and with your name being Thomas Jefferson, I can think of no better place than in front of the Abraham Lincoln memorial in Washington DC. Send out one of those press releases you are so good at setting the date for next week. Thomas wrote the news release to include some eye-catching points. "A coalition of third parties will introduce their presidential candidate in front of the Lincoln memorial. Their choice of candidates will reveal a first in the history of their parties.

Thomas, along with Abbey and Jim, met Martin with a large entourage of supporters at the Lincoln Memorial. The national chairs of the Libertarian and Constitution parties stepped up to the podium in front of the major news bureau reporters. Libertarian chair spoke first. "Sixty-three percent of U.S. adults agree that the Republican and Democratic parties do "such a poor job" of representing Americans that "a third major party is needed." (19)

Next to speak was the chair of the Constitution party. "We are going to give the American people what they want, a third independent party. The Libertarian and Constitution parties are pleased to announce our nomination for President of the United States, a descendant of an American slave. We have nominated Thomas Jefferson as our candidate for President."

Next to speak was Thomas, who gave his qualifications to hold the office and what he and the two parties wished to accomplish if elected to the highest office in the land. When asked if his philosophy paralleled that of any of the other candidates running for the presidency, he emphatically said no. He explained that one was too far left, and the other was too far right. His reason for running was to return America to the basic values it was founded upon and to preserve what was written in the constitution. The news media found their story extremely news worth. News of their candidacy spread across America and were now known as a contender, but not being taken seriously yet.

Upon hearing of the news about the independent candidates, Presidents Biden and Trump contacted their campaign headquarters to learn about their new opponents. "Democratic officials, saw the outsider as a dangerous wildcard that harkens back to 2016, when Green Party nominee Jill Stein may have enabled Trump's razor-thin victory by winning a small portion of the vote." (20) A third-party independent may cause you the election by detracting votes. We just will not know until polls can tell us more.

Trump's people thought back when George H.W. Bush ran for president and the independent candidacy of Ross Perot, a wealthy and well-known businessman, may have caused him reelection against Clinton. "American presidential election held on Nov. 3, 1992, in which Democrat Bill Clinton defeated incumbent Republican Pres. George Bush. Independent candidate Ross Perot secured nearly 19 percent of the vote—the highest percentage of any third-party candidate in 80 years. "(21)

Not taking the independent candidates seriously, Presidents Biden and Trump did not step up their campaign. Thomas, however, were on the move. After going over the strategy developed by his campaign team and Martin, the plan was to concentrate their initial campaigning in those states and cities that were the most conservative and swing states. After extensive research, they produced ten states that have the most conservative electorate. They included Wyoming, "West Virginia is the second-most conservative state in the U.S. 45% of voters identify themselves as conservative. Oklahoma had only four blue counties in the whole state during the 2018 midterm election, and it voted Republican in fifteen of the last sixteen elections. North Dakota is a Republican stronghold, and Idaho has not elected a Democratic presidential candidate since 2000. Kentucky has not voted for a Democratic presidential candidate since 1996 and is becoming more conservative. Alabama has voted Republican in the last eleven presidential elections. South Dakota has not voted for a Democratic president since 1964, and Tennessee has only voted for a Democratic presidential candidate four times." (22)

Thomas was upset when the news media reported that Presidents Trump and Biden failed to protect classified documents by storing them in unsecure places. Thomas knew firsthand the importance of protecting highly classified information. While serving at the Pentagon, je signed papers stating that if he failed to do so, he could be tried and incarcerated. As the story on the two presidents played out, Thomas saw an opportunity to write another OPED letter.

"Like many Americans, I sadly watch while current and past leaders may receive no punishment for violating laws they helped to create. Sitting and past presidents must stand the same test as any American and not be given special dispensation. Those of us who served in the military were made to sign documents that stated we would be incarcerated if we or stored classified information in unsafe places. As Presidents command our armed forces, they need to set an example. What should concern us even more is the reluctance of elected leaders to admonish a President of their same political affiliation. By their not doing so, they are also culpable. I liken such practices to a fairy tale where the king's constituents were fearful of reprisals if they told the king he had no clothes. As the result of the actions of Presidents Biden and Trump not protecting classified documents, they stand stark naked in the eyes of us and other nations of the world. It is the sincere hope of "we the people" that there are bipartisan Americans and news media that have the courage to severely admonish these two men."

Talk shows and newspapers started to cover Thomas and read his resume on air saying that he is qualified to be President.

Thomas and his entourage continued traveling throughout the country greeting prospective voters. The road to the White House is long, expensive, and exhausting. Today, a candidate's every word, every action, and even their perceived thoughts are paraded before the public. However, many of the methods for persuading voters remain the same.

Next stop was Charleston, West Virginia. Thomas told his team how former West Virginia senator Byrd campaigned. "Not having much money, he fiddled his way across West Virginia to win his Senate seat. "(23) Time was fast approaching for the debates. To prepare for the debates, Thomas thought it prudent to research how the candidates stacked up against one another.

CHAPTER 14

Marching Orders

Trump had easily won the Iowa Caucuses. "While primaries are run much like general elections – lots of polling places, a secret ballot, many hours to vote – Iowa's caucuses are more like neighborhood meetings. Democratic voters debate issues and candidates, eventually cluster in "preference groups" to elect delegates." (1)

During an open primary or caucus, voters do not have to be registered with a political party to take part in its primary or caucus. During a closed primary or caucus, only voters registered with that party can take part and vote. "Semi-open" and "semi-closed" primaries and caucuses are variations of the two main types." (2)

With the Iowa caucuses behind them, Thomas held press conferences and appeared on talk shows. He and Kennedy became favorite topics of the news media and talk shows. The media likened them to David trying to take down Goliath, not knowing what the ending results. In this battle, however, Goliath may overcome David.

Before moving on to other states, Thomas and Abbey returned to campaign headquarters to work on strategy with Martin and key members of their campaign committee. While they were gone, Martin and the committee were busy working on a strategy that would pave the way to the debates.

Martin pulled up a strategy printed in FairVote.org. The Obama campaign highlighted four main strategies for winning a second term. There are the West Path which focuses on Colorado, New Mexico, Nevada, and Iowa, and the Midwest Path, which prioritizes Iowa and Ohio; the South Path, which concentrates on Virginia and North Carolina, and the Expansion Path which hypothesizes Obama winning Arizona and Virginia, while presumably Romney would take New Hampshire and Pennsylvania. All four plans consider the states that Democrat John Kerry won in his 2004 presidential bid. Many states in the South and Midwest have voted almost exclusively for Republican Presidents. (3)

After reviewing the Fair Vote, they looked at what key factors caused Romney's loss. Martin projected an article from the Boston Globe titled "The story behind Mitt Romney's loss in the presidential campaign to President Obama." One of the gravest errors, many say, was the Romney team's failure, until too late in the campaign, to sell voters on the candidate's personal qualities and leadership gifts. Obama had more than 3,000 paid workers nationwide, compared with five hundred for Romney, and hundreds of thousands of volunteers. They were literally creating a one-to-one contact with voters, something that Romney did not have the staff to match. Democrats said they followed the trail blazed in 2004 by the Bush campaign which used an array of databases to "micro target" voters and a sophisticated field organization to turn them out. Obama won in part by updating the GOP's innovation. Romney's team worried that unless he opened up, he would too easily be reduced to caricature, as a calculating man of astounding wealth, a man unable to relate to average folks, a man whose Mormon faith put him outside the mainstream." (4)

Looking intently at the committee as well as Thomas and Abbey, Martin gave his reason why he is going over the campaign strategies used in prior presidential elections. "Lessons learned! We can learn a lot from what presidential candidates did in the past." Referring to Thomas, "You need to personally campaign in those states that Obama gave up for loss and those targeted battleground states identified by Romney. We will form a stronger bond between the Libertarian and Constitution parties in the other states to reach voters for enhancing the support we need to gain access to the debates. Afterwards, you can then turn your attention to campaigning in the other states. First, we need to focus on those states where we can quickly gain voter support."

"Unlike what Romney failed to do, we need to build an army of volunteers across the United States. We also need to keep you out front Thomas and accessible to not only the news media but to the people. Accessibility to the people will help us build that army of volunteers."

The campaign staff of the two main parties were keeping close tabs on the progress of the independent consortium. Presidents Biden and Trump started asking their campaign managers how the independents stood in the polls.

As for Thomas, he did not waste any time. It was not too far off in the future when the CPD was going to take its poll to see who qualified to enter the debates prior to the general election. Thomas and his team stepped up their pace of campaigning in all the conservative and swing states, stopping in every town and city. They did not take one day off. Two prior presidents logged enough miles to travel to the moon, over 238,000 miles. Thomas and his campaign team had already easily beat them.

CHAPTER 15

Super Tuesday

Their next line of attack for the presidential candidates, including Thomas and Kennedy, was to do a whirlwind tour through the southern states following the granddaddy of them all when it came to presidential primaries, Super Tuesday. "Millions of Americans in other areas headed to their polling places in March. They vote on a day known as Super Tuesday, which received its nickname because it marks the date when the greatest number of states hold their primaries and caucuses. The states that conducted elections on 2024's Super Tuesday include Alabama, Arkansas, Alaska, California, Colorado, Iowa, Maine, Massachusetts, Minnesota, North Carolina, Oklahoma, Tennessee, Texas, Utah, Vermont, and Virginia." (1) The states casting votes on Super Tuesday comprise 40% of the U.S. population.

While Thomas and Abbey were on their way to campaign in the south, the News media released a story on Trump's mishandling of highly classified documents. Later, it was discovered that Biden did the same. Thomas became infuriated with such careless acts. When he was on active duty, he had to sign papers vowing that he would not mishandle classified documents. If not, it stated that he would be incarcerated. He started writing another OPED letter.

"Like many Americans, I sadly watch while current and past leaders may receive no punishment for violating laws they helped to create. Sitting and past presidents must stand the same test as any American and not be given special dispensation. Those of us who served in the military were made to sign documents that stated we would be incarcerated if we or stored classified information in unsafe places. As Presidents command our armed forces, they need to set an example. What should concern us even more is the reluctance of elected leaders to admonish a President of their same political affiliation. By their not doing so, they are also culpable. I liken such practices to a fairy tale where the king's constituents were fearful of reprisals if they told the king he had no clothes. As the result of the actions of Presidents Biden and Trump not protecting classified documents, they stand stark naked in the eyes of us and other nations of the world. It is the sincere hope of "we the people" that there are bipartisan Americans and news media that have the courage to severely admonish these two men. "

His OPED was published across the U.S. and talk shows also called him for an interview. Thomas laid out how classified information was to be guarded, stored, and declassified. The first rule is that the only people that should have access to top secret classified information are those that need to know what is in the information. Secondly, it must be stored in rooms where people can access by using codes, eye, or hand identification. Depending on the classification level of the documents, people having access to them must possess the same level of security clearance and have a "need to know" what's in the document.

"Executive Order mandates that classified information may not be removed from official premises without proper authorization." (2) Thomas's OPED letter hit home for the two top contenders to their party's nomination.

President Trump's campaign manager knew they had to press on with their campaign strategy regardless of how well they did in New Hampshire, Iowa, and the Super Tuesday states. Trump was embroiled in defending against inditements filed against him. His campaign was struggling for positive new coverage even though he was ahead in the polls. As other presidential candidates were stomping for votes, Trump was spending his time in court.

President Biden's campaign manager came in with the same newspaper that touted the surprising results of the independent write-in votes. "It is not just that voters continue to say Biden is too old or not up to the job, though that keeps coming up in Democrats' focus groups. It's a malaise about the president that operatives keep noting that goes beyond a slew of national polls – including one from CNN last week – that show a negative view of the president's performance." (3) With thirty some senate seats up for reelection and the hold on most of the congress hanging by a thread, the republicans are fearful that Trump could not only lose the presidency, but he could lose the senate and the house. His record of endorsing losing candidates in the last election leads one to doubt if he is the one to lead the Republican ticket.

Robert Kennedy Jr. has put forth his platform, much of which can be found on his web site. "He is concerned that the American credit card debt is three hundred billion more than when the last president took office. On key issues, he states that it is time Americans got a President who cares about *their* economy, and not the war economy or bank economy. A secure border is a crucial element of a compassionate immigration policy. He wants to protect our environmental infrastructure including the water we drink and the air we breathe. He is quoted as saying My uncle once said that the United States will never start a war, does not want a war, we do not now expect a war, this generation has had more than enough of war, hate, and oppression." (5)

A big concern of followers of Kennedy is that him being a Kennedy, his name and image may attract assassins that could deliver the same death knell that befell his uncle and father. Kennedy's campaign has reached out several times formally asking for Secret Service protection, only to be repeatedly denied. According to protocol, The Secret Service has the authority to provide major presidential and vice-presidential contenders and their spouses within 120 days of a general presidential election. It is ironic that Kennedy has been denied security when President Biden keeps a bust of Kennedy's father in the oval office.

"The Secret Service does not determine who qualifies for protection, nor is the Secret Service empowered to independently initiate candidate protection. Protection is authorized by the Department of Homeland Security Secretary after consultation with the Congressional Advisory Committee. There are many factors that determines whether a candidate qualifies as a major candidate such as the candidate making a public announcement, campaigning on a national basis, the secret service conducting a threat analysis, polling at 15% for 30 consecutive days (20% for a third-party candidate), is a formal party nominee, and is a vice-presidential running mate. Title 18 states that Secret Service also is authorized to protect spouses (6)

Every time a major candidate had secret service protection; the town was in lock down mode. Security blanketed the town, and the candidate was surrounded by police and security people. It reminded Thomas of a long time ago when he was in New York. He was walking down the Avenue of the Americas when a horde of what looked like one hundred New York police officers walking lock step across the street in the opposite direction as him. It looked like a nest of bees protecting their queen in the middle of the swarm. A closer look revealed it was Jimmy Carter walking in the middle with his world-renowned grin on his face with his teeth visibly seen. It looked like the keystone cops. When the swarm came to a street crossing, the entire pack of police would lean forward in a sudden stop. Jimmy Carter would also lean and spring straight up.

Every time Thomas or Kennedy walked among throngs of people, they were concerned for their safety and their loved ones. They were haunted by the assassination of John Kennedy and Robert Kennedy.

Thomas's bus cris-crossed the Super Tuesday states. He and his supporters outdistanced the grass roots efforts of the major candidates. At every stop, Thomas was greeted by an entourage of supporters.

CHAPTER 16

The Candidates Meet

After covering much of the South, Thomas and his team moved on to some of the New England states.

The first city they campaigned in was Boston. The timing was perfect. The week they arrived was the week for one of the biggest festivals in Boston, the Boston Harbor fest. It is one of the biggest festivals in the country, spanning five long days and a draw of 300,000 people. Much of it is staged on the Esplanade along the Charles River. Thomas and Abbey walked among the people with Jim and two other staffers close behind passing out campaign literature. Before leaving Boston the next day, the team wanted to visit the Kennedy library.

What they found at the Kennedy library was exhilarating. One can Immerse yourself in the dynamic history of the Kennedy Administration and gaze at President Kennedy's Oval Office and his personal desk. "Beginning in 1939 and ending with the Nixon administration in 1974, taping systems have played an intriguing role in U.S. presidential history. John F. Kennedy was the first president to record his meetings and telephone conversations." (1)

As they completed their tour of the library, they noticed a few people surrounded by other visitors. There were television cameras and news people also in the group. Looking closer, they could not believe that it was Robert Kennedy Jr. addressing the news media. He was giving a news conference and chose to give it in his Uncles Library. Thomas and his team went over to listen to what he had to say. As they stood there, Kennedy kept looking over at Thomas while giving his news conference. After he completed it, he motioned for Thomas to come over to him.

Surrounded by Admirers, Kennedy pointed a finger at Thomas. "You're that guy that is running as an independent for the presidency, Thomas Jefferson." Looking at Kennedy in wonderment, he nodded his head yes and then began to speak. "I can see a lot of your father in you, Mr. Kennedy. Like his father, Kennedy leaned back on one heel and held his hand up to his chin. "Why do you want to run for President Thomas?" "I would hope to think I am running for the same reasons as you Robert and that is to bring back the fundamentals that America was founded upon. Your uncle and father inspired me early on when I was a young kid."

"You are right Thomas; I am running for the same reason. I do not feel the current president is on the right track and the Democratic Party is not the same. "I can make the argument that President Biden is the much worse threat to democracy, and the reason for that is President Biden is the first candidate in history – the first president in history that has used the federal agencies to censor political speech, so to censor his opponent," Kennedy pointed to his removal from social media platforms, which he attributes to pressure from the Biden administration, as evidence of the president's efforts to censor political speech. He added that if he had to label one a greater threat to democracy than the other, he would choose Biden because he feels the president has been "weaponizing the federal agencies" against his opponents. The chance for me to change the nature of governance in this country, to restore democracy, to restore our nation's moral authority abroad, give us a foreign policy that is not based on war or projecting military power abroad, but on projecting economic power and moral strength." (2)

"Please note that I am not running on the coat tails of my father or my uncle. Although I believe in all what they stood for, this is a different time and different party when they were alive. I have been following your campaign. Have you followed what I stand for Thomas?" Thomas quickly replied, "I have been following your campaign and the two of us seem to have similar beliefs and political philosophies." "Then why don't you step aside Thomas and give me a clear path?"

"I would ask you to do the same Robert. My name may not be as recognizable as yours, but my credentials and qualifications are as strong!" Kenndy retorted. "That may be determined if we both make it to the debates Thomas. Let us exchange contact information and stay in touch. Where are you staying while in Massachusetts?" Thomas points to his bus in the parking lot. "That has been our home since we started and will continue to be until the end of the campaign. Occasionally we check into a hotel."

Looking around at the many photos of the Kennedy clan surrounding the two of them, Thomas points to a photo of the famous Kennedy compound in Hyannis Port. "With your grandmother gone and all her immediate children, do you still make your home in your family's compound?" "The Kennedy Compound consists of three houses on six acres of waterfront property on Cape Cod along Nantucket Sound in Hyannis Port, Massachusetts, in the United States. With eleven bedrooms, a sauna, a pool, a tennis court, and a basement movie theater, it eventually became known as the Big House. The Kennedy Compound became a U.S. National Landmark in 1972, but none of the homes are open for public visitation. Ethel Kennedy still owns and resides in the home she lived in with her late husband, while the Big House was donated to the Edward M. Kennedy Institute." (3)

My mother still lives at the compound. Perhaps you would like to stop by to see it while campaigning in Massachusetts?" Thank you for the invitation, Robert, but I do not want to impose on you or your mother. Besides, we need to save all the time we can for campaigning. Let us plan to get together if we both make the debates." Kennedy nodded in agreement, shook hands, and both men started to walk towards their vehicles. Thomas stopped and turned around calling out to Kennedy. "I once walked your grandmother in New York city for fifteen blocks from St. Patrick's Cathedral to your aunt's apartment. She promised to send me the book she wrote but she forgot. Instead, I received a photo of your uncle John with her signature on the back addressed to me." Kennedy smiled and yelled back. "I will bring a copy of her book for you the next time we cross paths. Kiddingly, Thomas jokingly quipped back. "Your grandmother was going to give it to me for free." Robert replies with the same answer as his grandmother did, "Will do if you make a contribution to the cause." "I will do so Robert!" As an advocate of supporting education and research on mental retardation, Mrs. Kennedy authored a book to support the cause. Thomas boarded the bus and finished his canvas of Boston and left for the South.

CHAPTER 17

Swing States

After completing his campaign tour through Vermont and Massachusetts, Thomas's entourage turned their sites back to the southern states. First stop was Virginia. Virginia used to be a red state but with a registration of only 44% republicans, it has now turned blue. Despite it now having a shade of blue, Glenn Youngkin won the Virginia governor's race, becoming the first Republican to win statewide office in a dozen years. From Virginia, Thomas and his team went on to Georgia. Georgia had supported Republican presidential candidates for decades before 2020 - Georgia last voted blue in 1992. This suggests that Georgia is gradually becoming bluer. As reported by CBS during the last presidential election, "Mr. Biden added the state's sixteen electoral votes to his tally, bringing it to 306. He is the first Democrat to win Georgia since Bill Clinton." (1)

The next states Thomas visited that were all grouped together. They were Arkansas, Alabama, Tennessee, and North Carolina. Trump won North Carolina by a 1.34% margin over Biden, making him only the second Republican incumbent ever to carry North Carolina and lose re-election.

Thomas and his team then started the long trek across county, turning their sites on California, Colorado, and Utah. The trip across county would have been long and arduous if it were not for their being able to campaign along the way. "California is considered a safe blue state in presidential elections, due to significant concentrations of Democratic voters in large urban regions such as the San Francisco Bay Area, Sacramento, Los Angeles, and San Diego. As predicted, Biden easily carried California in the past 2020 presidential election, earning 63.5% of the vote and a margin of 29.2% over Trump." (2) Like many states, one would have to assume that outside the cities, the vast part of California land mass is more republican.

Utah has often given the GOP nominee one of their largest victories in the nation, having awarded George W. Bush and Mitt Romney over 70% of the vote in 2004 and 2012, respectively. However, Trump only won Utah with 58.1% of the vote and a margin of 20.5%, which although an improvement on his 18.1% margin over Hillary Clinton in 2016, is still relatively narrow compared to past Republican nominees. Trump performed strongly in rural areas, as well as in some larger counties." (2)

"Once considered a swing state that used to be Republican-leaning, Colorado has been trending Democratic since the early part of the 21st century due to changing demographics" (2)

Even though it was given that California is a solid blue democratic state, and Colorado is trending toward being democratic, Martin explained to Thomas that he needs to spend time in those states to assure that he will have the 15% voter support for accessing the debates. Martin went on to reiterate that "the cities tend to vote more liberal where the rural areas are more conservative. In view of this, you need to concentrate your efforts in the smaller cities and rural towns." Thomas and his team thought it best to line the states up to optimize their time. After Colorado, they traversed Utah and then spent some time in Nevada before going on to California. After California, they drove the southern route, working their way to Texas. Before reaching Texas, they covered the rural areas of Arizona and New Mexico. It was a whistle stop tour but one that would hopefully pay big dividends when it came to qualifying for the debates and attracting more contributions.

Besides Biden, only two Democratic presidential nominees in the past 72 years have won Arizona in the general election – Bill Clinton in 1996 and Harry Truman in 1948." (3)

CHAPTER 18

Border Crisis

When in Arizona, Thomas stopped by the local library to see if he could find anything on the Arizona border crisis. He finds a news clip by PBS dated as recent as September of 2023. "The Border Patrol's Tucson Sector, which oversees the area, in July became the busiest sector along the U.S-Mexico border for the first time since 2008. It is seen migrants from faraway countries like Pakistan, China, and Mauritania, where social media is drawing young people to the new route to the border that begins in Nicaragua. There are large numbers from Ecuador, Bangladesh, and Egypt, as well as more traditional border crossers from Mexico and Central America." (1-2*Library of Congress Photo 17*)

" Right now, we are encountering people from all over the world," said Border Patrol Deputy Chief Justin De La Torre, of the Tucson Sector. "It has been a real emergency here, a really trying situation. During a recent visit, Associated Press journalists saw close to one hundred migrants arrive in just four hours at the border wall near Lukeville, AZ, inside Organ Pipe, as temperatures hit 110 degrees Fahrenheit (43.3 degrees Celsius). The next morning, several hundred more migrants lined up along the wall to turn themselves in. Tucson Sector registered 39,215 arrests in July, up 60 percent from June. Officials attribute the sudden influx to false advertising by smugglers who tell migrants it is easier to cross here and get released into the United States." (1-2)

While campaigning in New Mexico, Thomas finds a newspaper dated Sept of 2023 highlighting the illegal immigration crisis in New Mexico. The headlines read "New Mexico border city says it's suffering consequences of illegal immigration." "Sunland Park, in the far southeast corner of the state nestled up against El Paso, Texas, to the east and Ciudad Juárez to the south, is one of the safest and fastest-growing cities in New Mexico. But the leader of the community of 17,000 that shares a border wall with Mexico, shown last week, says the failure of the federal government to address illegal immigration is causing the burden to fall on the city's limited infrastructure and resources." (3)

After spending a couple of days in New Mexico, Thomas, and his team head towards Texas. "Republicans have carried Texas in each of the last ten presidential elections. Texas has voted Republican in every presidential election since 1980, and the Republican candidate always does better in the share of the popular vote in Texas when compared to the nation." (4)

Texas has a population of over twenty-nine million people and covers a land mass of over 268,000 square miles. With such a large population, Thomas and his team started on the western border and moved south. He especially wanted to see where the illegal immigrants were crossing. "Texas lawmakers have already gotten to work on the fourth special session of the year where Republicans will once again attempt to pass an immigration law that would make it easier for state and local law enforcement to arrest and prosecute people who cross the border.

Sen. Charles Perry, R-Lubbock, and Rep. David Spiller, R-Jacksboro, filed identical immigration bills — Senate Bill 4 and House Bill 4 — that would empower Texas peace officers to arrest undocumented immigrants and require that a state judge order the person to leave the U.S. to Mexico in lieu of prosecution." (5)

Thomas and his team pulled into San Antonio which is reportedly where a large influx of the illegal immigrants is coming across the border. As his bus traversed through the city, Thomas could see how the influx of illegal immigrants has taxed the resources of the city. Inside the immigration center, "it's a sort of organized chaos, where restless kids run and play while their parents — last week, they were mainly migrants from Africa, Haiti and Central America — stand in line for food, talk to volunteers about travel options and nervously thumb through the pages of immigration paperwork many of them can't read because they don't speak English." (6)

"Most of the Central Americans and Haitians know where they are going and have relatives waiting for them. Many of the Africans, though, either have no idea where to go or know only the names of cities, like Chicago and Portland, Maine, whose names roll uneasily off their tongues." With the Africans, they are like, "we made it across the border, now we don't know what to do," What money they did have, they spent it on the journey." (6)

Thomas also found a recent press release from the office of Governor Abbott, dated May of 2023. "Since the launch of Operation Lone Star, the multi-agency effort has led to over 373,000 illegal immigrant apprehensions and more than 28,000 criminal arrests, with more than 25,000 felony charges reported. In the fight against fentanyl, Texas law enforcement has seized over 402 million lethal doses of fentanyl during this border mission.

Operation Lone Star continues to fill the dangerous gaps left by the Biden Administration's refusal to secure the border. Every individual who is apprehended or arrested and every ounce of drugs seized would have otherwise made their way into communities across Texas and the nation due to President Joe Biden's open border policies. With President Biden ending Title 42, the Governor is enhancing Texas' unprecedented border security efforts with the tactical deployment of hundreds of Texas National Guard soldiers to join the thousands already deployed as part of Operation Lone Star and serve on the new border force for targeted responses as the nation braces for a spike in illegal immigration.

With the ending of Title 42 on Thursday, President Biden is laying down the welcome mat to people across the entire world, but Texas is deploying our new Texas Tactical Border Force," said Governor Abbott. "The Texas National Guard is loading Blackhawk helicopters and C-130s and deploying specially trained soldiers for the Texas Tactical Border Force, who will be deployed to hotspots all along the border to help intercept and repel large groups of migrants trying to enter Texas illegally." (7)

Another article of interest to Thomas was on the Migration Policy Institute web site. "The 2.5 million encounters of migrants occurring at the U.S.-Mexico border in fiscal year (FY) 2023 represent a new historic high, topping the prior year's record. Less attention has been given, however, to the significant change in migration patterns evident in the data, with migrants from beyond Mexico and northern Central America representing 51 percent of irregular arrivals at ports of entry, the first time ever." (8)

A concerning thought crossed Thomas's mind after he read a Reuter news article dated Jan of 2023 which read "President Joe Biden visited the U.S.-Mexico border on Sunday for the first time since taking office (Biden took office Jan 2021), tackling one of the most politically charged issues in the country as he prepares for a re-election bid." (9) In sharp contrast, "Since he took office in January 2017, President Donald Trump has visited the border in California, Arizona, and Texas five times." (10)

When President Biden visited the Border, "The president's flight was met by Texas Gov. Greg Abbott, a persistent critic of Biden and his administration for the federal response to migration on the US southern border. "In a sign of the deep tensions over immigration, Texas Gov. Greg Abbott, a Republican, handed Biden a letter upon his arrival in the state that said the "chaos" at the border was a "direct result" of the president's failure to enforce federal laws. Biden later took the letter out of his jacket pocket during his tour, telling reporters, "I haven't read it yet." (11) The president who caused the chaos at the border needed to be here. It just so happens he is two years and about $20 billion too late," Abbott told reporters at the airport. "He needs to step up and take swift action, including reimbursing the state of Texas toward the money we spent but providing more resources for the federal government to do its job. Also, this is nothing but for show unless he begins to enforce the immigration laws that already exist." (12)

On their bus ride back to the northeast, Thomas did research on his laptop. He wanted to look at immigration comparisons. According to articles he found on illegal immigration, "the United States hosted, by far, the highest number of immigrants in the world in 2020, over fifty million people born outside of the States residing in the country. Germany and Saudi Arabia followed far behind at around 16 and 13 million, respectively. There are varying reasons for people emigrating from their country of origin, from poverty and unemployment to war and persecution." (13)

"Every country regulates immigration in its own imperfect way. Some countries have populations that are 80 percent foreign-born but offer no pathway to permanency. Other countries put up huge barriers to citizenship except for people whose parents were born there. "In many ways the U.S. immigration system is a relic of the past," said Justin Gest, a professor at George Mason University who studies comparative immigration policy, referring to how public opinion has changed since 1965, when the family-based system was established. "It is far more generous than the spirit of the United States is today. South Korea and Japan are so stringent with immigration that they make the United States look lenient. This is partly because of a desire to preserve their cultures, a goal echoed by conservative groups in the United States." (14)

The population of unauthorized immigrants in the United States has been estimated to be around 11.39 million people, a number which has seemingly stabilized after a period of rapid growth. However, studies show that the amount of alien encounters by the United States Border Patrol has significantly increased in the last few years, with 2,214,652 registered alien apprehensions and expulsions recorded in 2022. In addition, there were 568 immigrant deaths recorded near the southwest border in the U.S., the greatest number reported by the United States Border Patrol since 1998, suggesting that illegal immigration may be on the rise again. Currently, Mexico is the leading country of origin for most unauthorized immigrants in the U.S., with California being home to the highest number of illegal immigrants in the country. The most illegal immigrants returned in the U.S. are from the Philippines, followed by Mexico, India, China, and Canada. (15)

"Republicans and Democrats differ over the most pressing priorities for the nation's immigration system. Republicans place particular importance on border security and deportations of immigrants who are in the country illegally, while Democrats place greater importance on paths to legal status for those who entered the country illegally – especially those who entered as children, according to a new Pew Research Center survey. As the number of people apprehended for illegally crossing the southern border has reached record levels, 73% of Americans say increasing security along the U.S.-Mexico border to reduce illegal crossings should be a very important goal of U.S. immigration policy. "(16)

Thomas read the research to his team. Much of it was convoluted to the point that it was difficult to ascertain what were the best approaches to dealing with illegal immigration. Whatever may be the case, however, most Americans were not in favor of immigrants entering the United States Illegally.

He next wanted to find out what were the constitutional duties of our government when it came to protecting our country. He found that a Texas Congressman Arrington put forth a resolution in the House affirming Article I Section 10 of the Constitution, which recognizes states' sovereign power to defend themselves against invasion. "The Constitution is clear: Section IV Article 4 says the federal government "shall protect each of [the states] against Invasion," said Rep. Arrington. "When the federal government fails to fulfill this constitutional duty, Article 1 guarantees states the sovereign power to repel an invasion and defend their citizenry from overwhelming imminent danger." This resolution affirms that states do not have to be passive victims of this Administration's border security failures; rather, they should exercise their sovereign, constitutional right to defend themselves." (17)

As to whether the President has the authority to close a Border and if any President ever closed a border, he found a Congressional Research Service report. "Federal statutes grant the Department of Homeland Security (DHS) general authority over operations to secure the border and specific authority to close temporarily "any port of entry" when necessary to protect national interests. Other statutes give the President broad authority to suspend the entry of non-U.S. citizens." (18)

Media articles discuss at least four occasions when past presidents have restricted operations at ports of entry. "The measures taken on at least one of the occasions covered in the articles—the aftermath of President Kennedy's assassination in 1963—may have constituted a full closure of ports of entry on the southern border for the afternoon and evening of November 22, 1963. President Reagan ordered the closure of nine ports of entry "for a matter of days" after the abduction of a Drug Enforcement Administration (DEA) agent in Mexico in 1985. Two other times—President Nixon's "Operation Intercept" and President George W. Bush's post-9/11 measures, the restrictions consisted of extensive inspections that brought border traffic to a standstill." (19)

President Trump's Border wall, it is "a series of piecemeal barriers that vary in size, shape, and age. Sections of "wall"  include low fences, high barriers, dividers with steel slats and areas with checkpoints and pedestrian passages. Other parts of the border have no structures at all, demarcated instead by rivers or mountains."
(*Photo 8)* Thomas, wrote another OPED letter.

"Unarmed invasion of our Borders."

"In times of crisis, four presidents ordered the closure of our borders. The 9-11 terrorists entered our country illegally by using forged passports. One can only wonder how many terrorists or criminals could be embedded among the illegal immigrants. Resources of our border towns have been taxed beyond catastrophic proportions. Article 1of the constitution guarantees the states the sovereign power to repel an invasion and defend against imminent danger. The illegal immigrants might be likened to "unarmed invaders." With millions of apprehended illegals, the president should exemplify his predecessors and empower border states with the authority and resources to defend themselves."

CHAPTER 19

Debate Eligible

Following weeks on the road campaigning in states from the East to the West coast, Thomas's bus rolled into his hometown. Thomas was not going to let any moss grow under his feet. So as not to overtax his volunteers and hired staff, Thomas and Jim took off by themselves to spend some time campaigning in Ohio and parts of Illinois. It was a remarkable sightseeing Thomas and Jim pulling up in this huge bus with only two people aboard. While in Ohio and Illinois, Thomas wanted to visit the mausoleums of Presidents McKinley and Lincoln. The ironic thing about them is like John Kennedy, that they were both killed by an assassin's bullet.

After holding a news conference at the Mausoleum of William McKinley in Canton Ohio, Thomas went on to Lincoln's tomb to hold another. "Counterfeiters tried to kidnap his body shortly after his death so they could exchange it for one of their incarcerated colleagues. "Early in 1876, an engraver of counterfeit plates, had been sentenced to 10 years in the state penitentiary. To pressure the governor to release him, a small-town crime boss recruited two members of his gang to kidnap Lincoln's body." (1) At that time, it was not illegal to abduct a body. The plan was thwarted, and Lincoln's body continued to be preserved intact.

Ironically, it was at President Lincoln's tomb when word came in that Thomas and Kennedy had not only garnered the polling percentages they needed to qualify for the debates, but they surpassed it. Cameras and television crews surrounded Thomas for his comment on the good News. Thomas simply said, "I intend to continue campaigning and wait to receive official word from the Commission on Presidential Debates (CPD!"

"I want to also congratulate Robert Kennedy. He and I are not that far apart when it comes to what we envision for our country." As he spoke, a call came in from the Kennedy headquarters. Excusing himself, Thomas stepped off to the side while the cameras were still filming, and the microphones were picking up his words. Kennedy started the conversation by congratulating him on a great showing in the polls. Thomas started to return congratulations when Kennedy interrupted him. "Your showing was much more impressive than mine. I have name recognition where you are a newcomer to the national scene. It is incredible what you did! I am really looking forward to joining you in the debates." Thomas said likewise and returned the compliment. "During my tour of the country, I have heard good things about you from people of all parties including independents. We can meet up for dinner at the debates or not long thereafter." The phone connection was getting weaker and the clatter from the news media and supporters was starting to drown out their conversation. Thomas ended with, "Hope to see you soon Robert."

Noticing the phone conversation, the news media started to give a flurry of questions to Thomas. "What was that all about. Why is Robert Kennedy calling to congratulate you, Thomas?" Thomas just looked at the reporters, shrugging his shoulders, he replied. "Why not? I met him on the campaign trail, and we share a good deal of the same philosophy. He is a gentleman and cares about our country as much as me!" The reporters returned to their questioning of Thomas.

Thomas goes on with his revelation. "Amazingly the American people do not give much credence to who would be second or third in line to occupy the white house should something catastrophic happen to the president. The scary thought is that the vice president of the United States is just one heartbeat away from becoming President should the sitting President die in office. There were fifteen vice presidents who ascended to the office of president, eight of which dawned the presidential mantle upon the death of their president, and four of the fifteen were later elected president. One can only hope that whoever is selected to be vice president is as capable and competent as the one who is elected as President."

"Sadly, we have said about many a president, is this the best we can find throughout a large country such as ours? Our choice is often relegated to the lesser of two evils. If we were to hire a president rather than elect one, what should we be looking for in that person? How should their job description and resume look and how should a job description be authored and by whom? When doing so, we should not forget that we are not just electing a President. We are electing a team, which includes a vice president, a first lady and cabinet. As far as the first lady of the land, we would imagine them having much influence. Whoever the President surrounds themselves with can have positive or negative influence as to the outcome of major decisions."

Thomas brought the news conference to an abrupt end by pointing to Lincolns tomb as an example of what he just said. "One of Lincoln's famous quotes says it all "I must stand with anybody that stands right, and stand with him while he is right, and part with him when he goes wrong." "With that being said, I must now depart from your interviews and return to my headquarters."

His arrival at headquarters was met with applause and jubilation. Wanting to prepare himself for the debates, Thomas thought it prudent for him to research on what were the top ranked presidents and what attributes made them so great. Looking at Martin, Jim, and Abbey; he asks the question. "What do you think makes up the character of an ideal president?" All three shrugged their shoulders. Looking puzzled at Thomas, Martin quirks. "That would take a lot of research Thomas." "Then I better get started to see if I fit the mold." To start, Thomas feels that the best place to look is how renowned scholars ranked them. Perhaps their findings will reveal whatever qualities one needs to be a great president. He found a credible survey by the Siena College Research Institute.

CHAPTER 20

Top Ten Presidents

"For the seventh time since its inception in 1982, the Siena College Research Institute's (SCRI) Survey of U.S. Presidents finds that experts rank Franklin D. Roosevelt, Abraham Lincoln, George Washington, Theodore Roosevelt, and Thomas Jefferson as the United States' top five chief executives. The 141 participating presidential scholars agree with their peers over the last 40 years naming the same five leaders as America's finest. "(1)

The criteria in the Siena College Research Institute were based on such characteristics ranging from integrity to executive ability. In most surveys, William Henry Harrison and James Garfield were not rated because of their dying within months after taking office. In the USPC poll, the rankings of the president were predicated upon five criteria as follows: vision/agenda-setting: "did he have the clarity of vision to establish his overarching goals and shape the terms of policy discourse?"

Domestic leadership: "did he display the political skill needed to achieve his domestic objectives and respond effectively to unforeseen developments?"

Foreign policy leadership: "was he an effective leader in promoting US foreign policy interests and national security?"

Moral authority: "did he uphold the moral authority of his office through his character, values, and conduct?"

Positive historical significance of legacy: "did his legacy have positive benefits for America's development over time?"

"Some of the other criteria in determining the most effective president were ability to communicate effectively, solid relations with congress, court appointments, handling of the economy, ability to compromise, willingness to take risks, executive appointments, imagination, domestic accomplishments, integrity, executive ability, foreign policy accomplishments, leadership ability, intelligence, avoiding crucial mistakes, and the last would-be luck."

Sienna college also reported on some other salient findings of the scholars. (2)
- 44-35% believe office of President has become too powerful.
- 1% say our system of checks and balances is not working.
- 5 63% argue in favor of electing the President by popular vote.
- 69% believe that by 2032 a woman will be elected president.

Another survey of presidents as to how they were ranked was performed by C-SPAN in 2021. They surveyed a cross country of approximately 142 historians, professors, and other professional observers of the presidency. When C-SPAN conducted their first Historians Survey of Presidential Leadership in 2000, they worked with a team of nationally recognized historians to establish the survey's framework. Their ratings were based upon ten qualities of presidential leadership: public persuasion, crisis leadership, economic management, moral authority, international relations, administrative skills, relations with Congress, vision setting on agendas, and the pursuit of equal justice for all and performance within the context of the times. (2)

The following is a brief overview of the top fourteen presidents ranked by the results of a sweeping survey of historians, political scientists and presidential scholars maintained by Siena College Research Institute. (3) Since 1982, SCRI has ranked presidents across twenty categories, from integrity to executive ability:

1. Franklin D. Roosevelt (1933-1945)

Historians laud Franklin D. Roosevelt for his extraordinary popularity and his devotion to economic justice. (*Library of Congress photo* 19) Assuming the Presidency at the depth of the Great Depression, Franklin D. Roosevelt helped the American people regain faith in themselves. He brought hope as he asserted in his Inaugural Address, "the only thing we have to fear is fear itself." (3).

Roosevelt believed that a balanced budget was important to instill confidence in consumers, business, and the markets, which would thus encourage investment and economic expansion. As the economy recovered, tax revenues would increase making budget balancing even easier. This traditional view that deficits were bad was also supported by opinion polls. (4)

"FDR was a quick study. He possessed an insatiable curiosity, a boundless appetite for knowledge that combined with his capacity to absorb a striking range of facts through conversation. FDR possessed the charisma and self-confidence to connect with large numbers of the American people. He possessed noblesse oblige, a sense of patrician duty or responsibility toward others, and a strong character. He had a sharp vision of America and her role on the world-historical stage, possessing the political skills to get his vision communicated and his programs enacted." (5) According to the Miller Center at the University of Virginia, "historians laud Franklin D. Roosevelt for his extraordinary popularity and his devotion to economic justice

2. Abraham Lincoln (1861-1865)

Among all the U.S. presidents, Lincoln is almost always in the top five for crisis leadership ability, his dedication to keeping the United States together and for pursuing equal justice for all. The outstanding attributes of Abraham Lincoln's character are best described by the Lincoln Heritage Museum. "Abraham Lincoln is an exemplar and a model of virtue perhaps more than any person in world history other than religious figures. Even when Lincoln attained the high political position of president, he treated others whom he encountered with honest, humility, courage, justice, and grace. He learned from his mistakes and learned how to compensate for his own personal shortcomings. His life examples provide powerful lessons: being honest in all dealings; possessing a never-ending quest to learn; facing fears and overcoming defeat; treating others with compassion, kindness, and respect as you would like to be treated; standing up for, and standing firm in, what is right; and rising to the highest heights if willing to work hard." (6 *Library of Congress Photo 20*)

What made him great in our eyes is what he professed, stood by, and the examples he set that all presidents should follow today. He never seemed to falter or stray from the words of truth he himself spoke in many of his speeches.

3. George Washington (1789-1797)

The nation's first president ranked highly for his moral authority and overall performance within the context of his time.

"George Washington's leadership during the Revolution and Constitutional Convention, unimpeachable character, and his demonstrated willingness not to abuse power made him the ideal presidential candidate. (7, *White House Web Site*)

"Of all the founding fathers, George Washington alone demonstrated fully the threefold characteristics of a visionary leader and the intellectual and moral capacity, over a lengthy period and during manifold difficulties to maintain coherency between long range ideas and goals and short-term actions. Another major strength of Washington is that he had excellent judge of character. This strength proved invaluable to winning the Revolutionary war. He was exceptionally good at assembling a 'military family' around himself and when he became president, he formed a small cabinet where its secretariats were people having the expertise to exercise their offices. Each was responsible for areas most important to growing our nation. While the current presidential cabinet includes sixteen members, Washington's cabinet included just four original Secretary members: Thomas Jefferson (State), Alexander Hamilton (Treasury), Henry Knox (War), and Edmund Randolph (Attorney General)." (8)

"What made Washington a great leader was his understanding of what had to be done. His style of non-partisan leadership perfectly fit the needs of the new republic. He warned against "the spirit of party" in his Farewell Address, but it went unheeded. Soon party politics would dominate American democracy." (9)

4. Theodore "Teddy" Roosevelt (1901-1909)

Theodore Roosevelt ranked highly for public persuasion and other presidential attributes. "With the assassination of President McKinley, Theodore Roosevelt, not quite forty-three, became the youngest President in the Nation's history. He brought new excitement and power to the Presidency, as he vigorously led Congress and the American public toward progressive reforms and a strong foreign policy. He took the view that the President as a "steward of the people" should take whatever action necessary for the public good unless expressly forbidden by law or the Constitution. He won the Nobel Peace Prize for mediating the Russo-Japanese War, reached an Agreement on immigration with Japan. He crusaded endlessly on matters big and small, exciting audiences with his high-pitched voice, jutting jaw, and pounding fist. (10 *White (House Web Site Photo)*

"Teddy Roosevelt made the President, rather than the political parties or Congress, the center of American politics. He had a unique relationship with and responsibility to the people, and therefore wanted to challenge prevailing notions of limited government and individualism; government, he maintained, should serve as an agent of reform for the people. Roosevelt also revolutionized foreign affairs, believing that the United States had a global responsibility and that a strong foreign policy served the country's national interest. In terms of presidential style, Roosevelt introduced "charisma" into the political equation. He had a strong rapport with the public and he understood how to use the media to shape public opinion." (11)

During Theodore Roosevelt's political career, the United States evolved from a weak, domestically oriented nation to a country with imperialistic aspirations, from a conservative nation to a more progressive one, from a nation bent on destroying its natural resources to one that had begun to preserve them.

5. Thomas Jefferson (1801–1809)

Jefferson was ranked highly due to his involvement in the founding of our nation and his unique vision as president.

"Jefferson was an eloquent correspondent but not a fluid public speaker. When serving in the Virginia House of Burgesses and the Continental Congress, his primary contribution was his pen rather than his being an orator. Yet at the youthful age of thirty-three, he drafted a document that would change the course of America history and cause Britain to lose its most valuable, the Declaration of Independence. When Jefferson assumed the Presidency, he slashed Army and Navy expenditures, cut the budget, and eliminated the tax on whiskey. All that he did was to reduce the national debt by a third. (12, *Photo from white house web site*)

A note about Jefferson and leadership. "First, he was reluctant. When he said he had no more desire to govern than to ride his horse through a storm. Jefferson meant it. Second, he seems to have learned early on to check his ego at the door. There was a kind of selflessness about Jefferson's leadership: quiet voice, understated arguments, no drama, and almost excessive willingness to hear from everyone else and seek consensus. Third, Jefferson was an actual Utopian visionary who genuinely believed in the severely limited government. He believed in no formal government at all, that each of us would be a fully self-actualized being who governed him or herself, and then beyond that, all we would really need was a post office. Fourth. Jefferson was a patient leader. He reckoned the time was on America's side, that most things can probably be left alone, and that precipitous action is almost always the worst possible response to a problem or a crisis. Finally, Jefferson believed in peace, not peace at any cost, but peace if in any honorable way possible. He regarded war as ancient, medieval barbarism and savagery. Jefferson said, "peace is my passion." (13)

6. Dwight D. Eisenhower (1953-1961)

Eisenhower, a celebrated commander in WWII, saw his energies as president largely devoted to the onset of the Cold War. He obtained a truce after years of war in Korea, continued the desegregation of the U.S. armed forces, and sent federal troops to enforce a court order desegregating public schools in Little Rock, Arkansas. (*Photo from White House web site*) "Eisenhower demonstrated the following good character traits: Being honest and truthful without being spiteful. A person who does not lie, cheat, or steal. Respect: Treating both people and property with courtesy and honor and acting in a manner so that others respect you. Responsibility: Being reliable, dependable, and accountable in your actions. Not blaming others if things go wrong. Perseverance: Not giving up, even when something is hard, and you feel discouraged. Using self-discipline to follow through even when you feel like quitting. Courage: Facing one's fears in difficult and challenging situations. The ability to accept disappointment and move forward despite it.

Cooperation: Working effectively and peacefully with others to accomplish common goals. (14)

Addison Leadership notes five bold leadership qualities of Dwight Eisenhower: (15)

- Teamwork, love, care for one another through tough times
- Practicing optimism and leading by example
- Managing your ego and the ego of others for the cause
- Knowing your purpose and selling others on the mission
- Accepting responsibility and blame when things go wrong.

7. Harry Truman (1945-1953)

Historians praise Truman for his foreign policy leadership. Though unpopular when he left office, he has grown more highly regarded by historians over the years. "The character traits of President Harry Truman can be described as open, frank, honest, independent, forceful, modest, confident, and decisive. It has been speculated that the Myers-Briggs personality type for Harry Truman is an ISTJ (Introversion, Sensing, Thinking, Judgment). A reserved, well-regulated, and serious character and a strong traditionalist. Harry Truman Personality type: logical, organized, sensible, thorough, and dependable." (15) "Assuming the presidency in the final months of World War II, he inherited a worldwide catastrophe. Truman shouldered the burden of leadership in a rudderless world. With courage, integrity, and humility, he vindicated the American conviction that an open society can produce leaders equal to any challenge. Truman was quick to make decisions about problems that confronted him. He was quick to take responsibility for his actions as reflected by the sign on his desk "The buck stops here." (*16, Photo Wikimedia*)

8. Lyndon Johnson (1963-1969)

Among some presidential historians, Johnson tops the charts for his pursuit of equal justice for all Americans. "One of the most notable techniques of Johnson's career was his ability to share a respect for both the Democratic and Republican Party. The understanding of government that Johnson possessed delineated his knowledge to be able to lead a nation. Being able to transfer from vice president to the president of the United States shows that he easily adapts to new environments and can make positive change in areas he was not accustomed to." (18)

"No one can lead who does not first acquire power, and no leader can be great who does not know how to use power. The trouble is that the combination of the two skills is rare. Successful leaders somehow manage to do both—accumulate power and use it to some great end. And few leaders have done both so well as the 36th president of the United States, Lyndon Baines Johnson. For most of his career, Johnson was an archetypical politician, trading favors and flattery in generous measure. He was manipulative and devious, searching out and exploiting the weaknesses of colleagues and rivals alike. Yet once Johnson achieved the power he so ruthlessly sought, he turned into a visionary of breathtaking scope." *(19, Photo, White House Web Site)*

8. John F. Kennedy (1961-1963)

Historians Credit Kennedy most for his public speaking skills and his vision He also rates well for crisis management and his handling *(Photo Wikimedia Commons)*international relations. John Kennedy's brief time in office stands out in people's memories for his leadership, personality, and accomplishments. Many respect his coolness when faced with difficult decisions--like what to do about Soviet missiles in Cuba in 1962. Others admire his ability to inspire people with his eloquent speeches. Still others think his compassion and his willingness to fight for new government programs to help the poor, the elderly and the ill were most important. Like all leaders, John Kennedy made mistakes, but he was always optimistic about the future. He believed that people could solve their common problems if they put their country's interests first and worked together. (20, photo from Library of Congress 22)

According to an article that appeared on LinkedIn by Gary Burnison, CEO of Korn Ferry, John Kennedy possessed all of what he "deemed the Twelve Absolutes of Leadership. (21)

- LEADING: aligning, motivating, and empowering others.
- PURPOSE: enables a nation to make decisions in unison.
- STRATEGY: the ability to adapt to changing conditions.
- LEARNING AGILITY- learn from experience and apply that learning to new, first-time situations.
- PEOPLE –Assembles a mosaic of talents to work together, complement one another, carry the organization forward.
- MEASURE -the President set forth a challenge ultimately measured by that achievement.
- EMPOWER-The bridge from planning to action is empowerment of others, not yourself.
- REWARD-is not about money, it is about milestones.
- ANTICIPATE – As a leader you need to create a vision but must anticipate the future that others cannot yet envision.
- NAVIGATE – Is to perpetually set a strategy in an ever-changing environment.
- COMMUNICATE –a leader's information highway, it flows freely in each direction – in good times and especially in challenging ones.
- LISTEN – Listening as a leadership skill involves observing with one's eyes and ears, picking up tone, and body language.

10. James Madison (1809-1817)

Madison had strong moral authority and is well-regarded by historians. "What can you take from the story of President Madison and apply to today's world to make you a leader? First, always believe in yourself and never doubt your abilities. Each day when President Madison went to the Constitutional Convention meetings, he stood up and rallied for a democratic government with the election of congressmen directly by the people.

Secondly, stay true to yourself and stand by your convictions. President Madison stayed true to his belief in freedom for America. And, despite opposition to the war, he stood his ground. He said, "If we lose, we lose independence." People will perceive you as a leader if you stick to your beliefs and do not go back and forth on your ideals. Even those who do not agree with you will respect you for your steadfast loyalty and convictions. Lastly, know when to stay and know when to run. Even the best leaders must give up the fight at some point for the sake of their people. Think carefully about your decisions and of the consequences down the road. Is the fight worth it?" (22, *Photo from White House Web Site*)

"An executive coach who attended a dinner that had as its speaker, Bill Clinton, noticed seven leadership techniques he used to connect with his audience. (*Library of Congress Photo 23*)
Know your stuff. Clinton backed up with stats and specifics. People connect with leaders who are well-informed.
Talk to individuals. Clinton avoids coming off like the smartest guy in the room. It feels like he is just talking to you.
Be Optimistic. Clinton evokes a can-do spirit of optimism. Fact-based optimism connects with people.
Boil It Down. When leaders can boil down their themes to memorable takeaways, they connect with people.
Make It Personal. making it personal connects with people.
Tell Stories. Clinton is a master storyteller and included at least one compelling story in every answer.

Treat People with Respect. People notice when leaders treat the least powerful people with profound respect." (24)

Thomas found another article on presidential leadership published in American Government. "According to the article, some common leadership qualities that a good President may have would be a strong vision for the country's future, an ability to put their own times in the perspective of history, effective communication skills, the courage to make unpopular decisions, crisis management skills, character and integrity, wise appointments, and ability to work with Congress." (25)

Democrats want a president who will cut a deal. Republicans by prefer a president who stands on principle, even if it means things do not get done. Most said an ideal president would have a background in business. Service in the military was a clear asset among Republicans where Democratic views were more mixed.

Thomas found another article on presidential leadership published in American Government. "According to the article, some common leadership qualities that a good President may have would be a strong vision for the country's future, an ability to put their own times in the perspective of history, effective communication skills, the courage to make unpopular decisions, crisis management skills, character and integrity, wise appointments, and ability to work with Congress." (26)

CHAPTER 21

President's Resume

After reading all the articles on presidential rankings and leadership, Jim asked Thomas what he thought would be the qualifications for a great President. "There is a lot of information to compile and analyze Jim. "Perhaps the best way to find out is to write a job description. Jim gave Thomas a puzzling look. "I know what you are thinking Jim. How do we write one? With all the information we gathered, we had a good start! "

Before writing a job, description or resume for the ideal presidential candidate, however, we should understand what a president can and cannot do. "A president can make treaties with the approval of the Senate, veto and sign bills, represent our nation in talks with foreign countries, enforce the laws that Congress passes, act as Commander-in-chief during a war, call out troops to protect our nation against an attack, make suggestions about things that should be new laws, lead his political party, entertain foreign guests, recognize foreign countries, and grant pardons.

On the other side of the spectrum Jim, a president cannot make laws, declare war, decide how the federal money will be spent, interpret laws, and choose Cabinet members or Supreme Court Justices without Senate approval." (1)

"Furthermore Jim, the President has many responsibilities and powers vesting in him or her according to that which is listed on the web site of the White House. Let me read it to you."

"The President is both the head of state and head of government of the United States of America, and Commander-in-Chief of the armed forces.

Under Article II of the Constitution, the President is responsible for the execution and enforcement of the laws created by Congress. Fifteen executive departments — each led by an appointed member of the President's Cabinet — carry out the day-to-day administration of the federal government. They are joined in this by other executive agencies such as the CIA and Environmental Protection Agency, the heads of which are not part of the Cabinet, but who are under the full authority of the President. The President also appoints the heads of more than fifty independent federal commissions, such as the Federal Reserve Board or the Securities and Exchange Commission, as well as federal judges, ambassadors, and other federal offices. The Executive Office of the President (EOP) consists of the immediate staff to the President, along with entities such as the Office of Management and Budget and the Office of the United States Trade Representative.

The President has the power either to sign legislation into law or to veto bills enacted by Congress, although Congress may override a veto with a two-thirds vote of both houses. With these powers come several responsibilities, among them a constitutional requirement to "from time to time give to the Congress Information of the State of the Union and recommend to their Consideration such Measures as he shall judge necessary and expedient." Although the President may fulfill this requirement in any way he or she chooses, Presidents have traditionally given a State of the Union address to a joint session of Congress each January (except in inaugural years) outlining their agenda for the coming year.

The power of the Executive Branch is vested in the President of the United States, who also acts as head of state and Commander-in-Chief of the armed forces. The President is responsible for implementing and enforcing the laws written by Congress and, to that end, appoints the heads of the federal agencies, including the Cabinet. The Vice President is also part of the Executive Branch, ready to assume the Presidency should the need arise.

The Cabinet and independent federal agencies are responsible for the day-to-day enforcement and administration of federal laws. These departments and agencies have missions and responsibilities as widely divergent as those of the Department of Defense and the Environmental Protection Agency, the Social Security Administration and the Securities and Exchange Commission. Including members of the armed forces, the Executive Branch employs more than four million Americans.

The Constitution lists only three qualifications for the Presidency — the President must be at least 35 years of age, be a natural born citizen, and must have lived in the United States for at least 14 years. And though millions of Americans vote in a presidential election every four years, the President is not, in fact, directly elected by the people. Instead, on the first Tuesday after the first Monday in November of every fourth year, the people elect the members of the Electoral College. Apportioned by population to the fifty states — one for each member of their congressional delegation (with the District of Columbia receiving 3 votes) — these Electors then cast the votes for President. There are currently 538 electors in the Electoral College.

Until the 22nd Amendment to the Constitution, ratified in 1951, a President could serve an unlimited number of terms. Franklin Delano Roosevelt was elected President four times, serving from 1932 until his death in 1945; he is the only President ever to have served more than two terms." (2)

"When researching the qualities of past presidents Jim, I also came across an article in Executive Network written by Dominic Fitch titled "The personality traits of a true leader, what to learn from great US Presidents. (3) In the article, Fitch defines the abilities and qualifications that a great president should possess." Thomas continues reading to Jim what his research revealed.

"An array of good qualifications, an impressive CV, and a long political career are excellent qualities, but these aspects alone are not quite enough. The following are some of the personality traits that are commonly associated with prominent Presidents.

CHARISMA A charismatic figure can have a massively positive impact on their team members and followers. Having a personality and attitude that is charming, likeable, and inspiring can win over even the toughest of critics. Example is John Kennedy

ASSERTIVENESS is an indicator of presidential success. On average, US presidents are more assertive than 80% of the American population. Among the most resolute and influential Presidents were Jackson, Wilson, and the two Roosevelts.

COMMITMENT AND RESILENCE Navigating your team through stormy periods often require to keeping yourself and your staff focused and positive such as Franklin Roosevelt

HANDLE STRESS AND CONTROL IMPULSES, the ability to keep their composure and deal with stress. Daily tense situations are the White House's daily agenda, and it takes an individual that can maintain a cool head - to respond to challenges.

OPENESS: Openness is strongly connected to conscientiousness and extroversion to general intelligence and brilliance. This trait is also tied to a willingness to question traditions and pioneer change, putting moral authority as a priority." (3)

"Based upon what a president can and cannot do as well as the characteristics used to rank the top fourteen presidents, we should be voting for a candidate that best embodies good leadership qualities Jim. Problems usually ensue when a presidential candidate is a career politician, especially when they cannot relate to the plight of the people.

Honesty, Integrity, and honor are three characteristics at the top of the job description list, and you cannot have one without the other two. Most historians will agree that these traits are what made Abraham Lincoln and George Washington great and respected leaders. Having trust in a president keeps their constituents focused on the vision set by the president. Franklin D. Roosevelt said "confidence thrives on honesty, on honor, on the sacredness of obligations, on faithful protection, and on unselfish performance. "(4) Without a president being trustworthy or honest, an image of chaos and doubt will envelop him or her."

"*Military expertise*: In these troubled times, it would be prudent for our candidate to have served in the military or at least once held a civilian position in the Department of Defense. Most if not all presidents have had to deal with a conflict that requires their deploying our military. Making a wrong decision could lead to a nuclear confrontation. Washington and Eisenhower understood how to direct and use the military when a crisis arose."

"*Business expertise*: As the livelihood of the American people is dependent upon a healthy economy, our candidate should have a strong background in the business sector. One of the top concerns of Americans today is the economy."

"Selecting the right cabinet and administrators is also necessary Jim. A president must have a good judge of character for selecting knowledgeable cabinet members with a proven track record in their assigned cabinet position as well as staff. Dwight Eisenhower once said that what made him a great general was the quality of people that he chose to serve under him. It is also of prime importance that our candidate can encourage and accept differences in pinion and healthy debate."

"*Administrative Skills*: The president must be able to have the skills to manage and evaluate the performance of their staff and cabinet. They need to be good followers to be good leaders.

"*Team builder and player:* When it comes to being a leader, no one is an island. The president needs to form the right team when a crisis arises, putting the team before themselves when and if necessary. For a team to accomplish its purpose, the president must make them feel fulfilled. When we talk about a team, we must also include coalitions of countries and leaders.

"*Empathy*: A leader cannot press upon their people to succeed without giving them the proper tools to do so. The result will be to push their people away rather than towards their goals."

"*Of solid character and common sense*: The virtues, principles, and character makeup of a presidential candidate will ultimately influence their behavior. Having insight and being able to quickly analyze events during a crisis are everything. A president needs to have both courage and a sense of decency. "

"*Being of sound mind* capable of making sound decisions: A president must have sound mental capacities, being able to comprehend what is before them while at the same time, having the memory and sharpness to recall what went before. Without this, it leaves our country vulnerable to attack and leaves us at a disadvantage when dealing with adversaries.

"*Being a motivator and not an instigator*: No one likes a bully or an agitator Jim. My father continually reminded me of how to gain cooperation by saying to me "You can gain much more with sugar than with vinegar."

"*A vision and a keen sense of direction*: A presidential candidate needs to clearly put forth their vision to the people for them to follow. They also need to have a good grasp of history, so they do not lead our country into the failures of the past." "The candidate must have a good sense of how to avoid confrontations and differences with other countries. They need to learn from successes and mistakes, discern right from wrong, and avoid what may become a catastrophic event."

"*Foreign relations:* The ideal candidate should be highly versed in foreign affairs and have a good grasp of international diplomacy. They should understand how to avoid conflict and what it takes to build solid relationships and coalitions with other countries. They must display a stature of confidence and forthrightness if they are to command the respect of other world leaders. They should keep their word and be compromising rather than threatening when dealing with others. They must possess excellent negotiating skills and make changes where necessary. A bonus would be when a president has a keen sense of discerning when other leaders are sincere and truthful or not."

"*Empowering people and states*: A president needs to adhere to the basic management principle of delegating the authority to his or her people to accomplish their assignments. When doing so, they must realize that they retain the responsibility to see that the work gets done. Harry Truman said it best when he had the slogan on his desk that "the buck stops here."

"*A presidential candidate must be a good communicator as well as a good listener:* A great president must clearly communicate and have the ability and willingness to also listen to make the right decisions. He or she needs to be willing to keep the American people current on all issues. They must be open to weighing both sides of an issue and options without making hasty decisions."

"Pro-active instead of reactive: Too many of our presidents were more reactive rather than pro-active when it came to resolving a crisis. The best way to avoid catastrophic events is to first identify what may befall a nation and have an operations plan in place. The military is incredibly good at doing this by having operation plans (OPPLANS) in place for what they may perceive to be a pitfall further down the road. They also need to exercise and change them.

"Having the courage and foresight to make unpopular decisions. On the spot decisions may have to be made because timing is of the essence and the circumstances may warrant it."

"Ability and willingness to delegate. According to John C. Maxwell, renowned author on Leadership, "If you want to do a few trivial things right, do them yourself. If you want to do great things and make a significant impact, learn to delegate." A great leader needs to delegate tasks so they can focus on others.

"Humility and being humble in a president are necessary, Jim. A president will gain more from their staff and the people by suppressing their own ego. By admitting they do not know all the answers, a president will gain more knowledge and solutions to problems from their staff and cabinet. The ideal presidential candidate needs to share credit and accept blame."

"I realize what we just covered on what leadership qualities the American people should be looking for in a candidate when going to the polls Jim but when voting for a president, we should not just be concentrating only on their campaign promises and resume, we should vote on who they will be selecting as their team, especially cabinet members, and their vice president. It is also important that their spouse supports and shares their values.

"When doing so, however, I cannot stress enough that their anointed vice president must wear the same cloak. The stark reality is that the vice president is only one heartbeat away from becoming president. Realizing this revelation, the voters must look at the prospective team members of a presidential candidate and how they conduct themselves when seeking the highest office in the land. The demeanor of a prospective candidate and who they surround themselves with will reflect on how they will conduct themselves if elected as our next president. Perhaps a quote from President Eisenhower once said about leadership says it best: "You have got to have something in which to believe. You must have leaders, organization, friendships, and contacts that help you to believe that, and help you to put out your best."

"We need to get away from contentious debates that are beginning to mimic a talent show Jim. Presidential candidates should be elected on their qualifications not their popularity." Too many times in the past, the American people have been short changed when it comes to the appointment of qualified staff and cabinet members of a president. It is becoming prevalent for an appointment to a cabinet post or key agency is payback in return for financial or campaign support."

"Another area we must look at is how the size of the Federal government has grown over the years and where there is waste in government. When president Washington took office, he selected highly qualified people to serve in only four key cabinet posts. This number has significantly multiplied with many unneeded staff and agencies. There is also a duplication of cabinet departments that could be eliminated such as Commerce and Education. Most states have similar cabinet departments that mirror the Federal side. These departments may have been created to centralize control at the Federal level. By doing so, they infringe on states' rights and force inappropriate and ineffective decisions at the local and state levels. The states have a better grasp on local needs where the Federal bureaucracy is too distant to apply what works and does not work."

"The Government Accountability Office (GAO) releases an annual report on government duplication, fragmentation, and overlap. Since 2011 GAO has highlighted 440 different actions that Congress, and the president could take to reduce this wasteful spending" The wasteful spending of the federal government is compounded by the dramatic rise in the debt ceiling. Without our having a say, our government proposes to obligate each of us to repay $93,000 of the proposed debt ceiling of $32.4 trillion." (5) "To avoid burdening our children with insurmountable debt Jim, Americans should demand that elected officials eliminate wasteful spending and elect those who prioritize debt reduction. Reducing the national debt should be Included in every presidential debate.

"I found an interesting article on "how other countries reduced debt and deficits." "Overall, a rough guideline that emerges is that deficit reduction efforts should primarily be focused on spending reduction, with 60 percent or more of a plan's savings coming from spending cuts and 40 percent or less from revenue increases. The types of spending cuts and tax reforms also matter. Reductions in social spending, as opposed to public investment, tend to produce more lasting fiscal improvements.

Other factors important for success include the public's perception that the government will fulfill its commitments, and that the adjustment will be gradual, not with large structural policy changes. Research further supports the idea that fiscal consolidations based on spending cuts have had fewer negative effects on GDP than tax increases. Fiscal adjustments based on tax increases reduced investment and business confidence." (6)

"Let us now look at what the people want in their next president Jim. When both parties search for what they perceive to be their ideal candidate, they should listen to what the people want. A University of Suffolk poll published by USA Today provides insight into what the voters want in their next president. "The director of the Suffolk Political Research Center said the job posting for a president could go something like this: "Wanted – a governor with business experience and willing to compromise to get things done. Military experience is a bonus."

The poll revealed that "Younger voters were more likely to prefer younger presidents. Most voters volunteered that gender does not matter. Younger voters were the least tethered to a party.

CHAPTER 22

Party Platforms

Looking at Jim, Thomas wanted to look at an overview of the Republican and Democrat platforms. "Many Americans do not even know the finite difference between ideologies Jim. They should understand the difference when they go to the polls."

The Republican Party traces its roots to the 1850s. During the 20th and 21st centuries the party came to be associated with laissez-faire capitalism, low taxes, and conservative social policies. The party acquired the acronym GOP, widely understood as "Grand Old Party. The party's official logo, the elephant, is derived from a cartoon by Thomas Nast from the 1870s. (1). Republican Party won its first national victory under Lincoln." (2)

As for the Democrat party, many contend that it has gotten away from its original roots. "Historically it has been the party of labor, minorities, and progressive reformers. The party adopted its present name during the presidency of Andrew Jackson. The origins of the Democratic donkey can be traced to the 1828 presidential campaign of Andrew Jackson. During that race, opponents of Jackson called him a jackass." (3) The modern Democratic Party generally supports a strong federal government with powers to regulate business.

"A Pew Research Center analysis finds that, on average, Democrats and Republicans are farther apart ideologically today than at any time in the past 50 years. There are now only about two dozen moderate Democrats and Republicans left on Capitol Hill, versus more than 160 in 1971-72.

- Both parties have moved further away from the ideological center. Democrats on average have become more liberal, while Republicans have become more conservative.

- The geographic and demographic makeup of both congressional parties has changed. Nearly half of House Republicans now come from Southern states, while nearly half of House Democrats are Black, Hispanic or Asian/Pacific." (4)

REPUBLICAN PARTY PLATFORM (4)

Rebuilding the Economy and Creating Jobs, wherever tax rates penalize thrift or discourage investment and wherever current provisions of the code are disincentives for economic growth, they must be changed. Curb corporate welfare.

Our Tax Principles, wherever current provisions of the code are disincentives for economic growth, must be changed.

A Competitive America, we look to broaden our trade agreements with countries which share our values and commitment to fairness, along with transparency.

Freeing Financial Markets, The Republican vision for American banking calls for establishing transparent, efficient markets where consumers can obtain loans at reasonable rates.

Responsible Homeownership and Rental Opportunities, our goal is to advance responsible homeownership while guarding against the abuses that led to the housing collapse.

The Federal Reserve, The Federal Reserve's monetary policy should be transparent through an annual audit of the Federal Reserve, so it remains insulated from political pressures and its decisions are based on sound economic principles.

Fair and Simple Taxes for Growth, getting our tax system right will be the most crucial factor in driving the entire economy back to prosperity. The current tax code is rightly the object of both anger and mockery. Its length is exceeded by its complexity.

A Winning Trade Policy, we envision a worldwide multilateral agreement among nations committed to the principles of open markets in which free trade will truly be fair trade for all.

America on the Move, we will remove legal roadblocks to public-private partnership agreements that can save the taxpayers' money and bring outside investment to meet a community's needs.

Building the Future: Technology, we envision government as a partner with individuals and industries in technology areas so that every American can participate in the global economy.

Building the Future: Electric Grid, we support expedited processes and the expansion of the grid so that consumers and businesses have access to affordable/ reliable electricity.

Start-up Century: Small Business and Entrepreneurship, we recommend the enactment of a commission to secure the integrity of our currency.

Workplace Freedom for a 21st Century Workforce, it impels us to challenge labor laws that limit workers' freedom and lock them into the workplace rules of their ancestors. Minimum wage is an issue that should be handled at the state and local level.

A Federal Workforce Serving the People, we urge Congress to bring federal compensation in line with standards of American employees. Union representatives in the federal workforce should not be paid to conduct union business on the public's time.

Reducing the Federal Debt, A strong economy is one key to debt reduction, but spending restraint must be vigorously pursued.

We the People, we reaffirm the Constitution's fundamental principles: limited government, separation of powers, individual liberty, and the rule of law. We denounce bigotry, racism, anti-Semitism, ethnic prejudice, and religious intolerance.

The Judiciary, Foreign laws and precedents should not be used to interpret our Constitution or laws, nor should foreign sources of law be used in state courts' adjudication of criminal or civil matters. We therefore oppose the adoption of treaties that would weaken or encroach upon American sovereignty.

Administrative Law, we call on Congress to begin reclaiming its constitutional powers from the bureaucratic state by requiring that new federal regulations be approved by Congress. We affirm that courts should interpret laws as written by Congress rather than allowing executive agencies to rewrite them.

Defending Marriage Against an Activist Judiciary, Traditional marriage, and family, based on marriage between one man and one woman, is the foundation for a free society and has for millennia been entrusted with rearing children and instilling cultural values.

The First Amendment: We pledge to defend the religious beliefs and rights of conscience of all Americans and to safeguard religious institutions against government control. We support the right of the people to conduct their businesses in accordance with their religious beliefs and condemn public officials who proposed boycotts against businesses that support traditional marriage.

The First Amendment: Constitutionally Protected Speech, we agree with Thomas Jefferson that "To compel a man to furnish contributions of money for the propagation of opinions is sinful."

The Second Amendment: We uphold the right of individuals to keep and bear arms, a natural inalienable right that predates the Constitution and is secured by the Second Amendment.

The Fourth Amendment: Liberty and Privacy, Americans overseas should enjoy the same rights as Americans residing in the United States, whose private financial information is not subject to disclosure to the government except as to interest earned.

The Fifth Amendment: Protecting Human Life, we oppose the use of public funds to perform or promote abortion or to fund organizations. We are proud to be the party that protects human life.

The Fifth Amendment: Intellectual Property Rights, we call on Congress and state legislatures to enact reforms to protect law-abiding citizens against abusive asset forfeiture tactics.

The Fifth Amendment: Protecting Private Property, private property may not be "taken for public use without just compensation." We call for strong action by Congress to enforce intellectual property laws against all infringers,

The Ninth Amendment: this provision codifies the principle that our national government derives its power from the governed and that all powers not delegated to the government are retained by the people. We call upon legislators to give full force it.

The Tenth Amendment: Federalism as the Foundation of Personal Liberty, every violation of state sovereignty by federal officials is not merely a transgression of one unit of government against another; it is an assault on the liberties of Americans.

Honest Elections and the Electoral College, we oppose the National Popular Vote Interstate Compact and any other scheme to abolish or distort the procedures of the Electoral College.

Honest Elections and the Right to Vote, we pledge to protect the voting rights of every citizen, as well as their rights of conscience when they are harassed or denied a job because of their contributions to a candidate or a cause. We support state efforts to ensure ballot access to all legitimate voters.

Abundant Harvests, we must also ensure that domestic policies do not compromise our global competitiveness through overregulation and undue interference. We believe in promoting active, sustainable management of our forests.

A New Era in Energy, we support the development of all forms of energy that are marketable in a free economy without subsidies. We support the enactment of policies to increase domestic energy production, including production on public lands.

Environmental Progress, we firmly believe environmental problems are best solved by giving incentives for human ingenuity and the development of new technologies, not through top-down, command-and-control regulations that stifle economic growth.

Making Government Work for the People, we pledge to make government work for the people, rather than the other way around.

Balancing the Budget. Republican budgets will prioritize thrift over extravagance and put taxpayers first.

Preserving Medicare and Medicaid, we intend to save Medicare by modernizing it, empowering its participants, and putting it on a secure financial footing. We will preserve Medicaid.

Saving Social Security, Saving Social Security is our moral obligation to those who trusted in the government's word.

Protecting Internet Freedom, we will consistently support internet policies that allow people and private enterprises to thrive, so that the internet does not become the vehicle for a dramatic expansion of government power.

Immigration and the Rule of Law, because "sanctuary cities" violate federal law and endanger their own citizens, they should not be eligible for federal funding.

Reforming the Treaty System, we intend to restore the treaty system specified by the Constitution: The president negotiates agreements, with ratification requiring two-thirds of the senate.

Internal Revenue Service, we support making the federal tax code so simple and easy to understand that the IRS becomes obsolete and can be abolished.

Audit the Pentagon, we urge Congress to demand the same accountability from the Pentagon and Department of Defense.

Improving the Federal Workforce, we call for renewed efforts to reduce government responsibilities, and we urge particular attention to the bloated public relations budgets.

Advancing Term Limits, our national platform has repeatedly endorsed term limits for Members of Congress.

Regulation: The Quiet Tyranny, we will revisit existing laws that delegate too much authority to regulatory agencies and review all current regulations for possible reform or repeal.

Crony Capitalism and Corporate Welfare: We applaud the Republican Members of Congress who have taken the lead in fighting crony capitalism and urge others to rally to their cause.

Honoring Our Relationship with American Indians, we support efforts to ensure equitable participation in federal programs by American Indians, including Alaska Natives and Native Hawaiians, and to preserve their culture and languages.

Americans in the Territories, we call for the appointment of a commonwealth and territories advisory committee consisting of representatives from all five U.S. territories.

The Territory of Puerto Rico, we support the federally sponsored political status referendum authorized and funded by an Act of Congress in 2014 to ascertain the aspirations of Puerto Rico.

Preserving the District of Columbia, Statehood for the District can be advanced only by a constitutional amendment.

American Values, the question is whether we are going to reinvigorate the private sector institutions under citizen control or allow their continued erosion by the forces of centralized social planning. The Republican Party stands with the people.

Marriage, Family, and Society, we urge marriage penalties to be removed from the tax code and public assistance programs.

A Culture of Hope, we urge greater state and local responsibility for, and control over, public assistance programs.

Education: A Chance for Every Child, Maintaining American preeminence requires a world-class system of education in which all students can reach their potential.

Academic Excellence for All, we strongly encourage instruction in American history and civics by using the original documents of our founding fathers.

Choice in Education, we support the English First approach and oppose divisive programs that limit students' ability to advance in American society.

Title IX, we emphatically support the original meaning of Title IX that affirmed "no person in the United States shall, on the basis of sex, be excluded from participation in, be denied the benefits of, or be subjected to discrimination under any education program or activity receiving Federal financial assistance."

Improving Higher Education, we call on state officials to preserve our public colleges, universities, and trade schools as places of learning and the exchange of ideas.

College Costs, accreditation should be decoupled from federal financing, and states should be empowered to allow an array of accrediting and credentialing bodies to operate.

Restoring Patient Control and Preserving Quality in Healthcare, we will make homecare a priority in public policy and will implement programs to protect against elder abuse.

Protecting Individual Conscience in Healthcare, we call for a permanent ban on federal funding and subsidies for abortion and healthcare plans that include abortion coverage.

Better Care and Lower Costs: Tort Reform, we support state and federal legislation to cap non-economic damages in medical malpractice lawsuits.

Putting Patients First: We urge Congress to reform the FDA and pass legislation to give all Americans with terminal illnesses the right to try investigational medicines not yet FDA approved.

Advancing Research, we support cutting federal and state funding for entities that endanger women's health by performing abortions in a manner inconsistent with federal or state law.

Advancing Americans, we oppose the non-consensual withholding of care or treatment from people with disabilities, including newborns, the elderly, and infirm, just as we oppose euthanasia and assisted suicide.

Ensuring Safe Neighborhoods: we applaud the networking sites that bar sex offenders from participation. We urge prosecution of child pornography, which is linked to human trafficking.

Combatting Drug Abuse, we look for an expeditious agreement between the House and Senate on the Comprehensive Addiction and Recovery Act, which addresses the opioid epidemic.

A Dangerous World, Concomitantly, we honor, support, and thank all law enforcement, first responders, and emergency personnel for their service.

Confronting the Dangers, to keep our people safe, we must secure our borders, enforce our immigration laws, and properly screen refugees and other immigrants entering from any country.

Supporting Our Troops: We owe it to the American people and to those who fight our wars that we remain the strongest military on earth and be prepared to defeat any adversary under any circumstances on any battlefield. We must ensure that the nation keeps its commitments to those who enlisted.

Honoring and Supporting Our Veterans: America has a sacred trust with our veterans, and we are committed to ensuring them and their families' care and dignity.

Citizen Soldiers: we recommend a permanent line item for National Guard affairs, one that is not eliminated by the President and reinstated by Congress.

America: The Indispensable Nation, we affirm our party's tradition of world leadership established by President Eisenhower and followed by every Republican president since.

Challenges of a Changing Middle East, it is the responsibility of our government to advance policies that reflect Americans' desire for a relationship between America and Israel.

U.S. Leadership in the Asian Pacific, A Republican president will work with all regional leaders to restore mutual trust while insisting upon progress against corruption and the narcotic trade.

Renewing the European Alliance, we urge greater attention in U.S. diplomacy, trade, and strategic planning, to the nations of Eurasia, formerly parts of the Soviet Empire.

Family of the Americas, we express our solidarity with all the peoples of the Western Hemisphere

Africa: we stand in solidarity with those African countries now under assault by the forces of radical Islam.

Sovereign American Leadership our continued participation in the United Nations should be contingent upon the enactment of long-overdue changes in the way that institution functions.

Defending International Religious Freedom, a Republican administration will quickly designate the systematic killing of religious and ethnic minorities a genocide and will work with the leaders of other nations to condemn and combat genocide.

America's Generosity: we pledge to encourage more involvement by the most effective aid organizations and trusting developing peoples to build their futures through their own values.

Advancing Human Rights, America's continuing participation in the international campaign against human trafficking merits our support.

Liberty to Captives: Combatting Human Trafficking, we call for greater scrutiny of overseas labor contractors to prevent abuses against temporary foreign workers brought to the United States.

Cybersecurity in an Insecure World. We will explore the possibility of a free market for Cyber-Insurance and make clear that users have a self- defense right to deal with hackers as they see fit.

Protection Against an Electromagnetic Pulse, protect the national grid and encourage states to take the initiative to protect their own grids expeditiously.

Confronting Internet Tyranny, A Republican administration will champion an open and free internet based on principles of free expression and universal values.

After analyzing the Republican platform, Thomas downloaded a copy of the **Democratic platform** that was adopted at the last presidential convention.

DEMOCRAT PARTY PLATFORM (5)

The first declaration stated: Protecting Americans and recovering from Covid-19. Democrats will save lives by using every available tool to beat back this pandemic, and lead a global effort to prevent, detect, and respond to future pandemic threats.

Democrats believe the federal government should pick up 100 percent of the tab for COBRA insurance. We will re-open the Affordable Care Act marketplaces and aggressively enforce non-discrimination protections in the Americans with Disabilities Act and other civil rights laws. We will impose rigorous oversight on big corporations seeking financial assistance.

Building a stronger and fairer economy Democrats commit to forging a new social and economic contract with the people—a contract that invests in the people and promotes shared prosperity, not one that benefits only big corporations and the wealthiest few.

Protecting Workers and Families and Creating Millions of Jobs Across America. Democrats believe that it is a moral and an economic imperative that we support working families by rebuilding the American middle class for the 21st century.

Raising Wages and Promoting Workers' Rights Democrats will fight to raise wages for working people and improve job quality and security, including raising federal minimum wage. Democrats will recognize unions with majority sign-up and protect all private-sector workers' right to strike.

We will increase funding to the Equal Employment Opportunity Commission and increase its authority to initiate directed investigations into civil rights violations, violations of the rights of people with disabilities, and violations against LGBTQ+ people, especially transgender women of color. Federal contractors should be required to develop plans to recruit and promote people of color, women, LGBTQ+ people with disabilities, and veterans.

Enacting Robust Work-Family Policies, Democrats will implement paid sick days and a high-quality, comprehensive, and inclusive paid family and medical leave and make major investments in quality, affordable childcare.

Investing in the Engines of Job Creation, we will invest in resilient, sustainable, and inclusive infrastructure and launch a clean energy revolution and will repair, modernize, and expand our highways, roads, bridges, and airports, including by installing 500,000 public charging stations for electric vehicles. We will invest in high-speed rail and modernize our public schools.

Putting Homeownership in Reach and Guaranteeing Safe Housing, we support eliminating the racial wealth gap in America. Democrats will greatly expand the number of affordable, accessible housing. Democrats are committed to ending homelessness in America and provide Section 8 housing support for every eligible family and will keep landlords from discriminating against voucher recipients. We will act to end homelessness among veterans and will enact strong protections for lesbian, gay, bisexual, transgender, and queer youth, especially Black, Latino, and Native American LGBTQ+ youth.

Leveling the economic playing field Democrats believe The U.S. economy is rigged against the American people. Democrats will take decisive action to level the playing field for people of color, working families, women, small business owners, and others.

Reforming the Tax Code to Benefit Working Families, Democrats will reform the tax code to be more progressive and equitable. Democrats will reform the tax code to be more progressive and equitable and reduce barriers for working families to benefit from tax breaks.

Ending Poverty, Democrats remain committed to ending poverty Protecting Consumer Rights and Privacy, Democrats will support efforts to eliminate the use of forced arbitration clauses in employment and service contracts.

Guaranteeing a Secure and Dignified Retirement Democrats will reject every effort to cut, privatize, or weaken Social Security, including attempts to raise the retirement age,

Achieving universal, affordable, and quality health care Democrats will keep up the fight until all Americans can access secure, affordable, high-quality health insurance.

Securing Universal Health Care Democrats believe we need to protect, strengthen, and build upon our bedrock health care programs and will empower the states to use Affordable Care Act.

Bringing Down Drug Prices and Taking on the Pharmaceutical Industry Democrats will take aggressive action to ensure that Americans do not pay more for prescription drugs than people in other advanced economies.

Reducing Health Care Costs and Improving Health Care Quality We will make it easier for working families to afford high-quality insurance in the Affordable Care Act marketplaces and support policies that increase medical and dental therapists.

Expanding Access to Mental Health and Substance Use Treatment Democrats will aggressively enforce the federal mental health and substance use disorder parity law and ensure that health insurers cover mental health and substance use treatment.

Expanding Long-Term Care Services and Supports, Democrats will work to eliminate waiting lists for home and community-based care.

Eliminate Racial, Gender, and Geographic Health Inequities, we will expand access to health by extending Affordable Care Act coverage to Dreamers and remain committed to end the HIV/AIDS epidemic, which affects communities of color and the LGBTQ+.

Protecting Native American Health, we will make mandatory and work toward full funding for the Indian Health Service.

Securing Reproductive Health, Rights, and Justice, we believe every woman should be able to access high-quality reproductive health care services, including safe and legal abortion. We recognize that quality, affordable health care; medically accurate, LGBTQ+ inclusive, age-appropriate sex education.

Protecting and Promoting Maternal Health, we will expand postpartum Medicaid coverage to a full year after giving birth.

Protecting LGBTQ+ Health, we will take action to guarantee that LGBTQ+ people have full access to needed health care and require that federal health plans provide coverage for gender confirmation surgery, and hormone therapy. "Gender affirming surgery is the surgical procedure(s) by which a transgender or non-binary person's physical appearance and functional abilities are changed to align with the gender they know themselves to be."

Strengthening and Supporting the Health Care Workforce, we will invest in community health worker care-forces around the nation and increase opportunities for community health workers.

Investing in Health Science and Research Democrats also support increasing funding for research into health disparities by race, ethnicity, gender, gender identity, sexual orientation, age, geographic area, and socioeconomic status.

Protecting Communities and Reforming criminal justice system Democrats believe we need to overhaul the criminal justice system from top to bottom. Police brutality is a stain on the soul of our nation. Democrats believe we must prevent law enforcement from becoming entangled in lives of Americans.

Healing the Soul of America, Protecting Americans' Civil Rights, Democrats are committed to ending discrimination based on race, ethnicity, national origin, religion, language, gender, age, sexual orientation, gender identity, or disability status.

Achieving Racial Justice and Equity, Democrats will ensure federal data collection and analysis is adequately funded and designed to allow for disaggregation by race and ethnicity.

Protecting Women's Rights, Democrats will fight to guarantee equal rights for women and believe they should have access to quality reproductive health care, including abortion.

Protecting LGBTQ+ Rights, we will fight to enact the Equality Act and outlaw discrimination against LGBTQ+ people.

Protecting Disability Rights, Democrats will fully enforce the Americans with Disabilities Act.

Honoring Indigenous Tribal Nations, Democrats recognize and support the sovereignty of Tribal Nations

Ending Violence Against Women we are committed to ending sexual assault, domestic abuse, and other violence against women.

Ending the Epidemic of Gun Violence Democrats will enact universal background checks, end online sales of guns and ammunition, and close loopholes to buy and possess firearms,

Supporting Faith and Service We condemn the campaign to demonize and dehumanize the Muslim faith community.

Supporting Press Freedom Democrats are concerned about the corporate consolidation in the media industry. We support public funding for the National Endowment for the Arts

Combating the Climate Crisis, we can and must build a thriving, equitable, and globally competitive clean energy economy that puts workers and communities first and leaves no one behind.

Restoring our Democracy, We stand united against the Republican campaign to disenfranchise voters through onerous voter ID laws, unconstitutional and excessive purges of the voter rolls, and closures of polling places in low-income neighborhoods, on college campuses, and in communities of color.

Reforming the Broken Campaign Finance System Democrats will work with Congress on legislation to strengthen the public funding system for all federal candidates and crack down on foreign nationals who try to influence elections.

Building an Effective, Transparent Federal Government Democrats will establish a commission on federal ethics to aggressively enforce and strengthen federal ethics laws.

Making Washington, D.C. the 51st State Democrats unequivocally support statehood for Washington, D.C.

Guaranteeing Self-Determination for Puerto Rico Democrats will help restructure and provide relief from Puerto Rico's remaining debt burden.

Supporting the U.S. Territories, we believe the territories should be treated equally with respect to important federal programs.

Strengthening the U.S. Postal Service Democrats are wholly committed to supporting a public USPS.

Creating a 21st Century immigration system Democrats support policies and programs to make it easier for qualified immigrants and their families to become full and equal citizens, including increasing funding for culturally appropriate immigrant inclusion and citizenship, legal support, and adult education.

Providing world class education, Democrats believe that all children across the United States should have access to high-quality early childhood education programs. Democrats will ban for-profit private charter businesses from receiving federal funding and make public universities tuition-free for students whose families earn less than $125,000.

Renewing American Leadership Democrats will ensure that the reinvention of American leadership abroad prioritizes and accelerates our renewal at home.

Revitalizing American Diplomacy Democrats will revitalize American diplomacy to ensure that the United States remains the world's pivotal power and a force for peace and prosperity.

Rebuilding America's Tool of First Resort Democrats believe that diplomacy should be our tool of first resort.

Reinventing Alliances Democrats will repair and reinvent our alliances to advance mutual priorities and deal with new challenges.

International Institutions Democrats believe that American security and prosperity are enhanced when the United States leads in shaping rules, forging agreements, and steering institutions.

Foreign Assistance and Development Democrats will devote the resources and implement the reforms necessary to further multiply the impact of foreign assistance.

Transforming Our Armed Forces for the 21st century Democrats believe our military is—and must be—the most effective fighting force in the world.

Ending Forever Wars Democrats know it is time to bring nearly two decades of unceasing conflict to an end.

Securing our Competitive Edge Democrats believe the military should be the best-trained, best-equipped, and most effective fighting force in the world. Ending the forever wars

Keeping Faith with Our Veterans and Military Families We will protect and enhance opportunities for anyone who can meet the standards to serve in combat roles and its veterans deserve the world's best health care.

Civil-Military Relations Democrats believe that healthy civil-military relations are essential to our democracy and to the strength and effectiveness of our military.

Climate Change Democrats will immediately rejoin the Paris Climate Agreement and commit the U.S, to do its fair share.

Technology Democrats believe that American diplomatic leadership is critical to maximizing the benefits of technological innovation while minimizing its risks and dislocations.

Nonproliferation Democrats believe the U.S. has a moral responsibility and national security imperative to prevent and eliminate the spread of nuclear, chemical, and biological weapons.

Terrorism So long as violent extremists continue to plot attacks on our homeland and our interests, Democrats will maintain a vigilant focus on counterterrorism.

Democracy and Human Rights Democrats will make gender equality a key foreign policy priority and work to achieve gender parity across our national security team and will protect sexual and reproductive health and rights, including access to reproductive care and abortion services. We will restore the

United States' position of leadership on LGBTQ+ issues and we will amplify the voices of LGBTQ+ persons around the world.

Advancing American Interests- Global Economy and Trade. Democrats will fight for every American job and will make sure American workers have a fair shot in the global economy.

Africa Democrats will revitalize our partnerships across Africa to unleash enormous potential for growth and innovation and address together challenges and stresses across the continent.

Americas Democrats will reaffirm the importance of North America to U.S. global economic competitiveness, and we will work with our regional and international partners to address the root causes of migration.

Asia-Pacific as a Pacific power, the United States should work closely with its allies and partners to advance our shared prosperity, security, and values—and shape the unfolding Pacific.

Europe Democrats will reinvigorate the transatlantic partnership to repair the damage of the Trump era and preempt the risks of broader structural divergence between the U.S. and Europe.

Middle East Democrats believe it is past time, however, to rebalance our tools, engagement, and relationships in the Middle East away from military intervention—leading with diplomacy to lay the groundwork for a more peaceful, stable, and free region.

CHAPTER 23

First Presidential Debate

Both Thomas and Kennedy, having a resounding standing in the polls of 18% and confirmed by the commission they were eligible for the debates, they started preparing for the first one.

All four candidates sent representatives to discuss the format of the debates. After much discussion, all four agreed on two debates even though Thomas and Kennedy thought the electorate deserved more.

After looking at some of the strategies of Trump and Biden now and in the past, Thomas decided to focus his attention on what is of major concern to the American people. He found an article in "The Hill" that noted numerous issues that will define the 2024 election. "Preserving Social Security and Medicare. The issue of education, including targeting educational curriculum and parents' rights to decisions made by schools. Even in key races this year, Democrats are seeking to put the issue of abortion front and center once again. The candidate's stance on foreign policy will weigh in especially with two overseas wars in progress. Immigration and the border may feature prominently." (1)

The hour of the Debate had arrived. The moderators introduced Biden, Trump, Kennedy, and Thomas. Biden was situated at the far-left podium, next came Thomas, then Kennedy, and to the far right was Trump. As Biden's political philosophy was far left and Trump was far right, their far left and right locations seemed appropriate. The moderators went over the rules for the debate.

First question went to Biden. "Democrats across the country are distancing themselves from the White House, and polls indicate widespread frustration with your handling of immigration and the border, creating a liability for your re-election. (4)

Do you feel you have taken the necessary steps to stop illegal immigration, and do you support the Border Wall?

Biden's answer: "On my first day in office, I sent Congress a comprehensive piece of legislation that would completely overhaul what has been a broken immigration system for a long time: cracking down on illegal immigration; strengthening legal immigration; and protecting Dreamers, those with temporary protected status, and farmworkers." (5) "My administration moved forward with the border wall as required by Congress, even though I consider it ineffective." (4)

The moderators then turned to Trump for his response to the border crossings by illegal immigrants. "My administration was finalizing a plan to end the rampant abuse of our asylum system — it is abused — to halt the dangerous influx, and to establish control over America's sovereign borders. Under this plan, the illegal aliens will no longer get a free pass into our country by lodging meritless claims in seeking asylum. Instead, migrants seeking asylum will have to present themselves lawfully at a port of entry. We will hold them — for a long time, if necessary. The only long-term solution to the crisis is for Congress to overcome open borders obstruction. And we will end catch-and-release. We are not releasing any longer." (6)

It was now Thomas's turn. Looking at Trump and Biden, Thomas and said that "According to both your plans Mr. Presidents, they were never fully implemented or failed."

"Let me read you a news article from CNN about your handling the border crossing President Biden, a news media that has strongly supported you in the past but now report your reluctance to act on protecting our borders. "The Department of Homeland Security put together a plan months ago to deal with thousands of migrants arriving at the border. But the plan is dead for now, officials tell CNN, in part after the White House grew hesitant over the complicated planning."

"It has been an endless cycle since President Biden took office, according to administration officials and sources close to the White House. Agency officials dream up a plan but then struggle to get White House approval."

"Interior assistance and community support is something the White House is only serious about discussing when encounter rates rise," was told to CNN. (8)

Not letting up on Biden, Thomas reads another article. "Let me read you another article by Associated Press confirming your failed policies, President Biden."

"New York Mayor Eric Adams went to Mexico this week to implore would-be migrants not to come. He has accused the Biden administration of not providing enough money or resources for the city to process migrants, "The president and the White House have failed New York City on this issue." (9)

Thomas points at President Trump stating, "you never completed the wall Mr. Trump, and you said you were going to get Mexico to pay for it. To quote your words according to an article in Business Insider and said on stage, you said," "I will build a great wall, and I will make Mexico pay for that wall," "Mark my words." "The article further reads Mr. Trump that you were quoted as saying," "Trump recently told a rally that the wall is "almost complete" — while your campaign website says 216 miles have been completed. Mexico border is almost 2,000 miles long. " (10)

The moderator reminded Thomas that the question was what you would do to protect our borders. Without hesitation, Thomas gave his answer. "First, I would make certain that immigrants follow the basic laws of immigration which come under Homeland Security (DHS). Secondly, we need to involve the Mexican and central American governments in stemming the flow of immigrants. We must apply more pressures on the Mexican government to crack down on the cartels that are exploiting illegal immigrants and to stop the southern border flow. If Mexico cannot do it alone, we need to offer Mexico the support of our drug intervention teams. Thirdly, we need to make it a team approach to curbing the flow of illegal aliens. Besides homeland security, we need to include other federal agencies, state, and local authorities. Central American countries need to be members of the team. If these other countries do not step up, we need to terminate their foreign aid. The United States needs to craft a border security plan that are agreed upon and enforced by all. Fifty-five percent of illegal immigrants come from Mexico, which has no border patrol."

"When the federal government neglects to control the border, the resulting illegal immigration imposes an "unfunded mandate" on the states. The states must spend money on a problem created by the federal government without receiving federal reimbursement. The United States needs to remove the incentives that entice immigrants to enter illegally. This would include suspending their claim of political asylum." (11)

"The Texas Army National Guard is composed of approximately 19,000 soldiers, and the Arizona National Guard has 5,000. Instead of serving their two-week training period, the states need to structure it so they can perform their annual training guarding our borders, all at no additional costs to the states."

Thomas points to a web site on his computer. "I would also like to site an article that appeared on the web site of the Heritage Foundation quite some time ago titled "15 Steps to Better Border Security: Reducing America's Southern Exposure, the Heritage Foundation. The author, Jena Baker McNeill, is a homeland security policy analyst. She suggests some of what I just proposed." "Stepping up the Border Enforcement Security Taskforce (BEST). BEST is a program that couples U.S. federal, state, and local law enforcement with Mexican law enforcement to share information and collaborate on matters such as border crime. Security and Prosperity Partnership (SPP). Created in 2005, the SPP works as a forum to increase security between the U.S., Canada, and Mexico. In some areas, erecting fences is the best way to tackle the illegal-entry problem. But the cost makes it important to use fencing only in areas with a low "melting point." (12) Melting point is the time it takes for an individual to cross the border and "melt" into a landscape unnoticed. Another suggestion is using SBI net (Secure Border Initiative), which deploys a combination of both infrastructure and technology, such as cameras, radars, sensors, and towers, along 387 miles of border, the goal of creating a "virtual fence" to detect people as they attempt to cross the border illegally. SBI instituted a program to identify illegal aliens in prisons so they could be deported instead of being released in the U.S.

"Another suggestion is the Immigration and Nationality Act (INA), which allows DHS to enter assistance compacts with state and local governments. The best way would be to encourage states to organize State Defense Forces (SDFs), volunteer organizations dedicated to assisting the federal government in a number of activities, including border control." (13)

Lastly it was Kennedy's turn. Looking over at Thomas, Kennedy said "Ditto." "I agree with most of what Mr. Jefferson just said and I would like to add something." "What I'm going to do as president, I'm going to secure the border," he said in remarks, just after a showing of "Midnight at the Border," a documentary on Kennedy Jr.'s visit to the Arizona-California border with Mexico. "And I am going to make an easier, faster, simplified path to citizenship for people who are here illegally.

"On immigration, Kennedy echoed many conservatives' perspectives on what is seen as a "border crisis," in which "ruthless criminal cartels" have made drugs and human smuggling what he says is a multibillion-dollar business, according to his website. He blames fellow Democrats and his opponent, Biden, and current border enforcement rules for escalating the situation. He said that appointing "more efficient" asylum judges are needed to resolve cases at the border "on the day that immigrants show up." (14)

The next question to answer was given to Trump. **"What do you propose to bolster the economy?"**

Trump begins his speech by expressively waving his hands. "Let us look at some of the facts. Less than two years ago when I was in office, gas, gasoline, that thing called gasoline, now nobody wants to even talk about it, was $1.87 cents a gallon. And now it is five, six, seven, and even in some places, eight and $9 a gallon. Only going to get worse. We gave you the largest tax cuts and regulation cuts in American history, even larger than the Reagan tax cuts that once held the record by a lot. The radical Democrats intend to impose the largest tax hike in American history. And they are working feverishly to pile on more regulations at levels never seen before." (15)

"My plan will embrace the truth that people flourish under a minimum government burden, and it will tap into the incredible unrealized potential of our workers. If we lower our taxes, remove destructive regulations, unleash the vast treasure of American energy, and negotiate trade deals that put America First, then there is no limit to the number of jobs and prosperity we can unleash. America will become the world's great magnet for innovation and job creation." (16)

The moderator then turned to Biden for his answer. The Democrat and self-professed "most pro-union president" often say the economy should be built "from the middle out and the bottom up," rather than the trickle-down economic theory, and powered by union jobs. "I meant what I said when I said I am going to be the most pro-union president in American history. And I make no apologies for it. One of the reasons I ran for President was to rebuild the backbone — the backbone of this country, the middle class; to grow the economy from the middle out and the bottom up, not from the top down. I signed the Bipartisan Infrastructure Law, making the case that to have the strongest economy in the world, we must have the best infrastructure. It is Bidenomics." (18)

It was now Kennedy's turn. "Primary platform" on the economy would be cutting military spending and reinvesting that money into domestic spending and development. "Again, what we were told was a peace dividend after the collapse of the Soviet Union. ... We were going to cut our military budget from about $600 billion a year to $200 billion a year. You know, I can see a lot of problems with those issues, which I think are obvious to anybody. And it is a real departure from American free market capitalism. I would like to try to give this system a chance to work. Thirty-five percent of Americans ... are not making enough money to pay for basic human needs and that means those Americans are sitting on the precipice of a cliff, that they're inches away from, or on top of, becoming homeless." (20)

The moderators turn to Thomas. "I agree with what Mr. Kennedy with exceptions. Let us first discuss President Biden's Bidenomics and President Trump's future economic plans."

Under President Bidens plan "Pay increases did not keep up with inflation for much of the pandemic, leaving low- and middle-income households struggling to keep up. But inflation-adjusted disposable income – a broader category that includes Social Security, investments, and other income – is now running ahead of its pre-crisis level." (21) The most salient feature of Bidenomics consists of the cross agency, whole of government seduction of youths and the able-bodied adult population into reliance on big government programs like loan relief, free childcare, housing interventions at taxpayer expense, and much more. Bidenomics entrenches government control, comes with strings attached." (22)

As for President Trump's effect on the economy, I would like to point to articles about his economic plans, focusing on his trade policies. " His protectionist trade policies have hurt American businesses, workers and farmers, with no benefits to show, even by the president's own favorite measures. Recent deficit data unabashedly reject President Trump's approach to trade." (23)

Thomas bases his way of growing the economy on what he researched. He reads an article from Investopedia that he very much supports. "There is no singular answer to what makes an economy strong. Several factors working together contribute to strong economies. In the United States, economic growth often is driven by consumer spending and business investment. Other factors help promote consumer and business spending and prosperity. Having more cash means companies have the resources to procure capital, improve technology, grow, and expand. All these actions increase productivity, which grows the economy." (25)

The next question goes to you President Trump. **How will you curb inflation?**

"Under the Trump administration, we had the greatest economy in the history of the world with no inflation. No inflation. Biden created the worst inflation in 47 years. We are at 9.1%, but the actual number is much, much higher than that. And it is going higher and higher all the time. It is costing families nearly $6,000 a year, bigger than any tax increase. We created seven million new jobs with the lowest unemployment rates for American, and we had the best rates ever. We had the lowest rates, unemployment for Americans, for African Americans, for Hispanic Americans, and for Asian Americans; We were beating China so badly. We had a record 164 million people working, far more than we have today. We achieved the largest poverty reduction in 50 years. We lifted seven million people off food stamps, and we lifted ten million people off welfare. Under Biden, there are still 4 million people who have not returned to the labor force. Real wages are collapsing." (26)

As the moderators turned towards Biden, it was now his turn to step up to the plate on curbing inflation. "According to an article in PBS, the president has blamed inflation on issues such as supply chains and Russia's 2022 invasion of Ukraine, while Republican lawmakers say the run-up in prices was triggered by the $1.9 trillion in coronavirus relief that Democrat Biden signed into law in 2021. Inflation remains a sore point for Biden's approval ratings ahead of next year's election."

Shuffling his papers, President Biden begins his response on inflation. "We know that prices are still too high for too many things, that times are still too tough for too many families, Biden said. "But we've made progress." Our economy is stronger and better than any industrial nation in the world right now. But we have more work to do, we have a plan that is turning things around. The Inflation Reduction Act is a part of that plan." (28)

Thomas uses his laptop on the podium to look up the Inflation Reduction Act. The name of the plan is misleading and the question to President Biden pertains more so to the inflation of prices? "The Inflation Reduction Act directs new federal spending toward reducing carbon emissions, lowering healthcare costs, funding the Internal Revenue, and improving taxpayer compliance." (29)

President Biden continues his plan to bring costs down by referring to his Build Back Better Plan. "The significance of the plan is to bring down costs and strengthen the middle class (30)

Thomas again goes to his laptop for an explanation of Biden's "Build back better plan." "The plan called for $100 billion in funding for American energy infrastructure, aiming to transition the country to 100% carbon-free electricity production by 2035. It intended to support the construction of transmission lines." (31)

Next to provide his input on inflation was Kennedy. "Kennedy believes that associating the dollar and U.S. debt obligations with hard assets could rejuvenate the dollar's strength and help curb inflation. In an ironic twist, Bitcoin might be the very tool we use to rescue the U.S. dollar, he emphasized in his recognition of the cryptocurrency's potential. "Every individual should have complete control over their wallet. We are committed to ensuring Americans can operate Bitcoin nodes within their residences." (32)

Thomas knew he was next. To start, Thomas read a Washington Post and Forbes articles, "Trump vows massive new tariffs if elected, risking global economic war." Trump has taken to describing as the creation of a "ring around the U.S. economy," could represent a massive escalation of global economic chaos, surpassing the international trade discord that marked much of his first administration. (33) "Research finding companies found that U.S. economy paid a heavy price for the Trump administration's protectionist trade policies." (34)

His next goal was to show the fallacies in President Bidens plan to combat inflation. "Before the crisis in Ukraine, the Administration dismissed inflation as "transitory. When it became obvious higher prices were here to stay, the Biden Administration attempted to shift blame onto everyone but themselves. The Administration also falsely claimed that inflation is part of a global trend – which has been debunked by the San Francisco Federal Reserve Bank." (35)

Thomas then reads an article that appeared in the Washington Examiner in March of this year. "The cost of food at home increased 10.2% this past year, electricity increased 13.3%, shelter (rent) increased 8.1%, and transportation services increased 14.6%. These are all items that are critical to working Americans and drive a significant portion of their household budgets. Car payments, too, are becoming more unaffordable." (36)

Thomas did not leave Kennedy's comments on inflation from his critique. "As for Mr. Kennedy's comments on controlling inflation, I agree with him that every individual should have complete control over their wallet, but I do not necessarily believe that Bitcoin is a solution to controlling inflation. Referring to an article that appeared on Nasdaq.com, Thomas notes that "Bitcoin has potential as an inflation hedge due to its fixed supply and decentralized nature. However, the inherent volatility, regulatory uncertainties, and relatively short historical record compared to traditional hedges add a level of risk. (37) Thomas looks over at Kennedy, "How can using Bitcoin lower inflation if a huge number of Americans have little or no understanding of it?"

The moderators noted that the next question came from the audience. Two-thirds of Americans view the affordability of health care as an excessively big problem for the country today.

What are your plans to make the cost of health care more affordable? President Biden, your turn first.

"We have continued to build on the success of the Affordable Care Act by investing in improvements to the health care system. We continue to see that these investments are paying off through record-breaking enrollment overall and a notable increase in Hispanic/Latino enrollment." The Administration invested $98.9 million in Navigator grant funding for the 2023 Open Enrollment Period to help reduce health disparities." (39)

Kennedy chimed in before the moderators turned to him. "In contrast to a Medicare for all system favored by many Democratic politicians, Kennedy has stated that his "highest ambition would be to have a single-payer program ... where people who want to have private programs can go ahead and do that but to have a single program that is available to everybody. He also opposes the prospect of nationalizing the pharmaceutical industry." (40)

The moderators next turned to President Trump. "My plan expands affordable insurance options, reduces the cost of prescription drugs, will end surprise medical billing, increases fairness through price transparency, streamlines bureaucracy, accelerates innovation, strongly protects Medicare, and protects patients with preexisting conditions. By contrast, the Democrat Party is pushing a socialist nightmare. Their plans will ration care, deny choice, putting Americans on waitlists, driving the best doctors out of medicine, and delaying lifesaving cures." (41)

When it was Thomas's turn, he noted that "millions are being pushed off the Medicaid rolls, undoing the biggest health care coverage expansion since Obamacare. Nearly four million Americans have been cut from Medicaid in the last three months, most of whom lost their insurance over paperwork issues. The number is projected to balloon to 15 million by this time next year, according to official estimates, though some now fear the final toll will be even bigger. The impact is likely to reverse meaningful progress on health coverage and poverty that the White House once trumpeted as a direct benefit of its policies. In Arkansas, more than 300,000 have lost coverage — including more than 108,000 children. "(42)

Looking at President Trump, Thomas states. "During his 2016 campaign, President Donald Trump repeatedly said he was for "insurance for everybody" and promised to "take care of everybody" and to lower costs. Almost four years later, the Trump administration's record falls far short of these promises: The number of uninsured Americans has swelled, his administration has chipped away at the consumer protections guaranteed by the Affordable Care Act (ACA)." (43)

Changing his stance from Trump to Kennedy, Thomas offers some insight on a single payer health system. "Whenever Americans lapse into their periodic "conversations" on health reform, a single-payer health system is proposed by some as the panacea and condemned by others as "socialized medicine. In single-payer health systems, the entire population shares one health insurance carrier, usually the central or provincial government. Single-payer health systems typically are just social insurance grafted onto pluralistic delivery systems." (44) Single-payer health insurance would also lead to rationing and long waiting times for medical services and costs have escalated so far beyond estimates that additional financial support is required. "(45)

Thomas then offers what he feels are solutions to providing affordable health care in America. "The primary reason that the US needs health care reform is that we pay more for health care than any other country in the world; yet our health outcomes are below that of other western nations. A Price Waterhouse Coopers study reported that our complex, fragmented health care delivery system wastes $210 billion per year on unnecessary billing and administrative costs. We need to change our focus from disease management to prevention and health promotion. To change our focus to prevention we need more primary care physicians, family physicians, and general internists. Eliminate unnecessary tests and procedures. Much of the excessive treatment and unnecessary testing occurs at the end of life. We must encourage all citizens to have living wills to avoid unwanted procedures at the end of life. Our government must control the prices of prescription drugs as is done in nearly every other nation. Drug companies can charge whatever they wish in the US. Citizens of other nations pay 20% to 40% less for prescription drugs compared with what Americans pay. We must ensure that all physicians have cost-effective practice patterns that avoid unnecessary tests and better control the cost of prescribed drugs." (46)

The moderators move on to the question of providing military and relief aid to Ukraine. **How much lethal aid should the United States provide to Ukraine?**

The moderators directed President Biden to be the first to answer. Looking at his notes, President Biden began his answer. "The United States will continue our work, together with partners all around the world, to support Ukraine's ability to defend itself against Russia's aggression, to uphold the foundational principles of the UN Charter, and to help the Ukrainian people build the secure, prosperous, and independent future they deserve. Our commitment to Ukraine's independence is unwavering and enduring." (47)

Trump interrupts with his rebut. "I want everybody to stop dying. They are dying. Russians and Ukrainians. I want them to stop dying. (48) "I referenced reports that have indicated that U.S. stockpiles of missiles and ammunition have become depleted as the country continues providing weapons to Ukraine. "The Democrats are sending another $40 billion to Ukraine, yet America's parents are struggling to even feed their children." (49)

Kennedy interrupts Trump with his opinion concerning Ukraine. "The United States' role in the Russia-Ukraine war is "terrible for the Ukrainian people." "We have neglected many, many opportunities to settle this war peacefully," Kennedy said, "I think the way that we have conducted the war is bad ... is terrible for the Ukrainian people." We were told this was a humanitarian exercise. ... But when President Biden was asked why we are over there, he said for regime change of President Vladimir Putin. Kennedy referenced comments from Defense Secretary Austin among the U.S.'s goals in aiding Ukraine is to "see Russia weakened. That is the opposite of a humanitarian mission." (50)

Thomas intently listened to Trump's and Kennedy's comments continually nodding his head in agreement. He decided to chime in. "I agree with all what President Trump and Mr. Kennedy just said. As to President Biden, I only partially agree. I would like to read an OPED letter that I sent to new media across the entire country."

"The recent speech by Russia's President Vladimir Putin referencing new nuclear threats is best rebuked by comments from a former leader of the Soviet Union, Mikhail Gorbachev in 2017. "Politicians and military leaders sound increasingly belligerent and defense doctrines more dangerous. ... It all looks as if the world is preparing for war." Mr. Gorbachev also said, "While state budgets are struggling to fund people's essential social needs, military spending is growing. Money is easily found for sophisticated weapons whose destructive power is comparable to that of weapons of mass destruction.

Nine countries possess more than 15,000 nuclear weapons and the U.S. and Russia possess approximately 93 percent which could be quickly launched. Each is far more powerful than the bomb dropped on Japan, which killed approximately 140,000 innocent people. Our country alone has spent more than $20 billion per year on nuclear weapons. If only 1 percent of the nuclear arsenals were launched, over twenty-one million people would perish as well as the environment of any survivors."

Thomas reminisced about his service during 9-11. "As one who served at the highest level of the military at the Pentagon during 9/11, I know all too well what the result can be if world leaders continue to rattle their sabers. Such irresponsible rhetoric could at least lead to "boots on the ground." We need to ask ourselves if we are prepared to put our loved ones in those boots and to continue this frivolous spending on weapons of mass destruction, ignoring so many other pressing needs of our people. "A quote by former President Harry Truman could best sum up what the result could be if we continue down this path of nuclear proliferation and the unnecessary build-up of the world's military — "If we do not abolish war on this earth, then surely one day, war will abolish us from the earth."

Thomas kept his rebuttal going by reading an excerpt published by Europa. "To support Ukraine itself, since the start of the war, the EU and our Member States have made available over $91 billion* in financial, military, humanitarian, and refugee assistance, with this increasing regularly." (51) "With this in mind, I would ask President Biden if he ever asked and received a detailed accounting of the money the American people have invested in Ukraine. The question I also have is referencing the President of Ukraine always referring to what may or may not be on the negotiation table. For all the money we and other nations have invested, the President needs to insist that we have our people sitting at that table. Another question our President needs to pondered is do the people of Crimea want to stay with Ukraine? "Over ninety five percent of the Crimea people voted to secede from Ukraine." (52)

Another point that comes to mind is that many Americans are right when saying that the President, being the commander in chief of the military, should have served in the military. Let me read another OPED letter that I wrote about President Biden approving the use of cluster bombs in Ukraine.

What next Mr. President, nuclear weapons?

"As one who served at the Pentagon, I am shocked that the President agreed to supply Ukraine with cluster bombs after he had our UN Ambassador publicly condemn them. Especially as many UN nations have banned such weaponry. Cluster bombs can saturate an area the size of several football fields with its Shrapnel hitting nearby innocent people. They pose an ongoing threat after being dropped by leaving unexploded remnants that become landmines, fatal to innocent people for years to come. What next will President Biden approve, nuclear weapons?"

"The thought that Russia would move onto other NATO countries like Poland without resistance from other countries is a fallacy. If that would happen, Russia knows that the United States and other NATO allies would have to defend according to the North Atlantic Treaty!" To quote directly from the Treaty. "We reaffirm our iron-clad commitment to always defend each other and every inch of Allied territory. We will continue to ensure our collective defense from all threats, no matter where they stem from." (53)

I would like to also read you another OPED I wrote about the war against the Hamas.

A scalpel is better than a sledgehammer.

"In response to unprovoked attacks on its people, the Israelis are justified to go after those responsible. Terrorist like Hamas must be brought to justice and irradicated from the face of the earth. When doing so, however, the Israelis must be careful to not wreak havoc on or displace innocent families. Reportedly, the Israeli airstrikes have killed over 2,300 people, wounded over 9,000, and displaced one million people. With 169,000 active soldiers and the call up of 360,000 reservists, the Israelis can readily destroy Hamas by using precision ground warfare instead of widespread air attacks that also kills the innocent. If not, countries of the world will construe the Israeli tactics as one of revenge rather than an intent to invoke justice. Killing and displacement of innocent civilians will only portray the Israelis in the same light as the terrorists and continue to fester the hate that now exists between Israel and its neighbors."

Following the analogy by Thomas, the moderators moved onto the last question. The U.S. national debt passed $33 trillion in September 2023. Tax cuts, stimulus programs, and increased government spending on defense can cause the national debt to rise sharply. Looking at the debt-to-gross-national-product (GDP) ratio of a country shows whether the nation can pay back its debt. In January 2023, the U.S. hit its debt limit; in June 2023, the debt ceiling was suspended in a legislative compromise to avoid default. **How will the four of you reduce the national debt?** President Trump. You are first.

"I would borrow, knowing that if the economy crashed, you could make a deal," Trump told CNBC. Trump later clarified that comment to say he would offer to buy the bonds back at a discount from investors in hopes of refinancing them at lower rates. If trouble arose, he added, he could get investors to accept reduced payments for their Treasury holdings." (54)

"I say to the Republicans out there — congressmen, senators — if they don't give you massive cuts, you're going to have to do a default," said Trump. "And I do not believe they are going to do a default because I think the Democrats will absolutely cave, will absolutely cave because you do not want to have that happen. But it is better than what we are doing right now because we're spending money like drunken sailors." (55)

Referring to what he said when president. "I am renegotiating all our deals, the big trade deals that we are doing so badly on. With China, $505 billion this year in trade. New deals would spur economic growth and allow the U.S. to pay off its trillions of dollars in debt." (56)

"As president, Donald Trump would sell off $16 trillion worth of U.S. government assets to fulfill his pledge to eliminate the national debt in eight years, senior adviser with the campaign Barry Bennett said. "The United States government owns more real estate than anybody else, more land than anybody else, more energy than anybody else," Bennett told Chris Jansing Sunday on MSNBC. "We can get rid of government buildings we're not using; we can extract the energy from government lands, we can do all kinds of things to extract value from the assets we hold." (57)

The moderators then turned to Biden for his answer. "Today, my administration announced that this year the deficit fell by $1.4 trillion — the largest one-year drop in American history — $1.4 trillion decline in the deficit. On my watch, things have been different. The deficit has come down both years that I have been in the office. And I just signed legislation that is going to reduce it even more in the decades to come. "I might note parenthetically: In my first two years, I reduced the debt by $1.7 trillion." (58)

Now it was Kennedy's turn. "Well, number one, we must unravel the warfare business, the warfare machine that is bankrupting our country that and, you know, Paul Kennedy was the Yale historian that, has done this history of the decline of empires. Every empire in the last five hundred years, its debt now is overextending its military abroad. We have spent eight trillion dollars on wars over the past 20 years since 2002 that have gotten us nothing that have made it less safe to be an American." (59)

The moderators called on Thomas for his answer. Thomas referred to his research. "The primary reason for the deficit falling by $1.7 trillion under Biden was that the deficit had skyrocketed to a record high of about $3.1 trillion in fiscal 2020 during the early stage of the pandemic under then-President Donald Trump. The increase happened largely because of temporary, bipartisan pandemic spending. After much of the temporary spending expired on schedule, the deficit plummeted to about $1.4 trillion in fiscal 2022 under Biden."

"We've described Biden's previous deficit boasts as misleading or missing key context. But he went further in his Wednesday speech in Las Vegas on lowering prescription drug costs, delivering a version of the story that is just not true. *E*xperts say the deficit fell in 2021 and 2022 primarily because of expiring pandemic spending, not Biden's own policies, which had the net effect of worsening the deficit." (60)

"One of President Donald Trump's lesser known but profoundly damaging legacies will be the explosive rise in the national debt that occurred on his watch. The financial burden that he is inflicted on our government will wreak havoc for decades, saddling our kids and grandkids with debt. The national debt has risen by almost $7.8 trillion during Trump's time in office. That's nearly twice as much as what Americans owe on student loans, car loans, credit cards and every other type of debt other than mortgages, combined, according to data from the Federal Reserve Bank of New York. It amounts to about $23,500 in new federal debt for every person in the country. The growth in the annual deficit under Trump ranks as the third-biggest increase, relative to the size of the economy, of any U.S. presidential administration, according to a calculation by the Urban-Brookings Tax Policy Center." (61)

Having the last answer to the last question of the night, Thomas took a deep breath. He then closed his laptop and began to speak. "First, let us look at the fact that no elected official or presidential candidate has the courage to tackle such a hot potato or even discuss it at great length and why is that? It is because some of them created the problem in the first place. That is why many of their constituents do not even know what makes up the national debt."

The national debt ($34.06 Trillion) is the total amount of outstanding borrowing by the U.S. Federal Government accumulated over the nation's history. It is the amount. money the federal government has borrowed to cover the outstanding balance of expenses incurred over time.

"The federal government needs to borrow money to pay its bills when its ongoing spending activities and investments cannot be funded by federal revenues alone. The national debt is composed of distinct types of debt, including non-marketable or marketable securities (i.e., Treasury Bonds) and whether it is debt held by the public or debt held by the government itself (known as intragovernmental). The U.S. has carried debt since its inception. Debts incurred during the American Revolutionary War amounted to $75 million, primarily borrowed from domestic investors and the French Government for war materials." (62)

"As of January 2023, the five countries owning the most US debt are Japan ($1.1 trillion), China ($859 billion), the United Kingdom ($668 billion), Belgium ($331 billion), and Luxembourg ($318 billion)." (63)

Petr G Peterson Foundation identifies One of three recommendations outlined by the Nasdaq (64) may be logical and most palatable, growing our way out of national debt. If this is implemented, however, our government will have to make significant cuts in and control expenditures while the growth catches up to monetary surpluses. I think the third, "default on the national debt," one is out of the question. By defaulting on national debt, our country and its borrowing power will lose credibility and create economic instability. Such an initiative could create recessions, unemployment, and social unrest.

1. Economically growing your way out of national debt plays a pivotal role in diminishing a nation's debt by generating heightened tax revenues that can be used for debt reduction.

2. By devaluing the nation's currency through inflation, the government can effectively repay a fixed amount of debt. This approach was employed by the United States post-World War II.

Another ploy used by the United States to pay down debt was implemented in 1795. In 1795, the United States was finally able to settle its debts with the French Government with the help of an American banker who privately assumed French debts at a higher interest rate. He then resold the debt at a profit on U.S. markets. The United States no longer owed money to foreign governments, although it continued to owe money to private investors." (65)

"The selling off some government assets has also been proposed, particularly by you President Trump." According to a story reported by NBC News back in 2016, one of your senior advisers with your campaign said that you would sell off $16 trillion worth of U.S. government assets to fulfill his pledge to eliminate the national debt in eight years. Andrew Jackson did this during his Presidency." (66) "I would advocate this if it were vacant buildings and not treasures such as national park land."

Looking into the cameras, Thomas closes with "whoever becomes president is going to have to make difficult decisions which may be unfavorable to their constituents. I did not create it but I at least have the courage to discuss it. For the sake of those who come after us, we need to demand that the president and congress reduces the National Debt. If not, our country could be forced into financial default."

Immediately following the debate, the polls revealed that a large percentage of Americans agreed with Thomas and Kennedy. After a lengthy debate and perusing excerpts from many news articles, Thomas began to realize that much of their political philosophies closely matched one another. Both are moderates.

Thomas walked across the stage to greet Kennedy. Kennedy spoke first. "I was about to go over to greet you, Thomas. It is surprising how much we agree on." "Likewise, Bobby. The way it now stands, it will be extremely difficult for either of us running as independents to capture the White House." "The United States has a history of rejecting independent candidates. In fact, the last president to win without a party's backing was George Washington, and he did it before there were political parties. The last third-party candidate to make it to the White House was Abraham Lincoln with the newly formed Republican Party. A third-party candidate to pull more than single digits of popular vote was Ross Perot," (67)

Looking at Thomas with his hand on his chin, Bobby nodded his head in agreement, giving Thomas the opportunity to put forth the suggestion that they meet. "Are you open for a meeting to discuss how we may collaborate Bobby?" Once again, Bobby nodded his head in agreement. "Then let's plan to meet before we return to the campaign trail. I will call you in a couple days."

CHAPTER 24

Assassination Attempt

Not long after the first debate, the Republican party held their convention in Milwaukee. There was no surprise that Trump was unopposed for the party's nomination. The mystery that was unraveled was the selection of Ohio Senator, JD Vance.

Vance has undergone a dramatic — and, in the eyes of his critics, highly dubious — political transformation: from blue-collar bard and self-described "Never Trump" conservative to hard-edged MAGA loyalist and dogged defender of the former president. Vance says he's had a genuine change of heart about Trump; his critics say he's cynically molded himself to the times. In the Senate, Vance has cultivated a dual identity as key Trump ally and leader of the GOP's populist-national wing. His name when he was born was James Donald Bowman. Vance wrote in the introduction to *Hillbilly Elegy,* his bestselling 2016 memoir about his life growing up in a working-class family in post-industrial Ohio. In November 2022, he was elected to the United States Senate from Ohio with the help of over $10 million in donations from Thiel. It was his first public office. (1)

Vance describes himself as "pro-life," but during his 2022 Senate campaign said he would like the issue to be left to the states. Vance is one of the leading congressional Republican voices against U.S. aid to Ukraine. While running for the Senate in 2022, Vance said on the campaign trail that he thought the 2020 election was "stolen from Trump." And earlier this year, Vance told ABC News he still questions the results of the 2020 election. Vance has taken a hard line on immigration; he has often decried a "crisis" at the southern border and called for funding and constructing a border wall. Like Trump, Vance wants to "drain the swamp". In a 2021 podcast, Vance advised Trump to, "fire every single mid-level bureaucrat, every civil servant in the administrative state, replace them with our people," and then potentially defy the Supreme Court if the president was sued." (2)

Following the Republican convention, "A growing number of Democratic lawmakers have begun to call for President Biden to withdraw from the race in the wake of his debate performance last month. On Capitol Hill, they have been weighing arguments about whether Mr. Biden should be the party's nominee. So far, 31 House Democrats and four Senate Democrats have directly called on the president to exit the race. (3)

Still, many congressional Democrats have publicly expressed support for Mr. Biden since the debate. Some lawmakers have called for the party to unequivocally back the president, including prominent members of the powerful Congressional Black Caucus. The president sent a letter to Democrats in Congress saying he is "firmly committed" to staying in the race and making clear that "I wouldn't be running again if I did not absolutely believe I was the best person to beat Donald Trump in 2024." (4)

Early next morning, Martin and Thomas meet for a strategy meeting. Martin is the first to comment on the possibility of Biden dropping out of the race. "Bidens pulling out of the race changes the person Thomas, but it does not change the progressive, socialistic, and liberal platform of the Democratic party. We need to closely monitor how the Republican party responds to whoever may fill the void if Biden drops out."

"Republicans need to prepare for the very real possibility that Joe Biden is forced out of the 2024 race. What does that mean? It means that it's time the GOP stopped obsessing about Joe Biden's age and focus on his disastrous policies instead. Biden's policies have hurt average Americans; under this president, the country has become poorer and less safe, while children have lost ground academically. He has richly earned the lowest approval ratings since Jimmy Carter. How does that constitute a successful presidency? Gearing up for next year's elections, Republicans should call out Biden's inability to secure our borders, and his party's complicity. They must focus on his mulish war on our oil industry, the explosion in the federal deficit and out-of-control spending, his administration's damaging allegiance to teachers' unions, the corruption that has rippled through our law enforcement agencies and the perversion of our justice system. Democrats have done an excellent job of portraying Republicans as "MAGA extremists"; the tables can and should be turned. The GOP should attack Democrats as the extremists they are extremists on abortion, bail reform, immigration and climate change. Ignatius applauds Biden for having "in a polarized nation governed from the center out." "How can he make that case for this most divisive and extreme of all presidents? Republicans must expose the damage done by these policies and remind voters that Democrats across the land have been in lockstep with Biden, endorsing his failed approaches." As Vice President Harris has not spoken out against his policies, she shares his failures and approaches.

"Abortion is not the only issue on which Democrats are guided to extreme positions by the progressive left. Bail reform and misguided "social justice" initiatives have led to unprecedented thievery and lawlessness in cities like San Francisco and New York. Biden has also led his party down a green path of no return, upending our auto industry and threatening to ban gas stoves, incandescent light bulbs, workable dishwashers and ceiling fans.

Inflation has not disappeared. In fact, thanks in part to Biden's extreme climate agenda, backed by most Democrats, and to his antagonism toward Mohammed bin Salman, the de facto ruler of Saudi Arabia, oil and gasoline prices are up 35 percent since early June while gasoline prices have climbed 18 percent.

Astonishingly, even as oil prices soar, Biden has doubled down on efforts to restrict U.S. future production by canceling important leases in Alaska and ramping up fees on oil producers.

The GOP should clobber Democrats in 2024. They will run on the White House's embrace of far-left programs that have left voters worse off. Biden has pushed these progressive initiatives, but he is not solely to blame, his fellow Democrats are responsible, too." (3)

Martin continues his hypothesis, as to what candidates may replace if Biden drops out of the race. "The most likely replacement would be Vice President Kamala Harris, who was dismissed by Washington Post columnist David Ignatius as a poor candidate." (3) "She evidently said when she was a prosecutor that 18-24 years olds are stupid." "In the video clip, Harris says: "What else do we know about this population, 18 through 24? They are stupid. That is why we put them in dormitories. And they have a resident assistant. They make bad decisions." (5)

Martin and Thomas were suddenly interrupted when the news is reporting an assassination attempt on Trump. "The FBI said Friday that Donald Trump was hit by a bullet, or a fragment from one, fired by the would-be assassin. "What struck former President Trump in the ear was a bullet, whether whole or fragmented into smaller pieces," the bureau said in a statement.

The department's confirmation Friday that the former president was struck in the ear by a bullet marks its latest attempt to quell a political uproar. The new statement is the most direct yet from federal law enforcement about Trump's injury, though it changes little in practical terms." (6)

CHAPTER 25

Biden Abdicates

Approximately seven days following the assassination attempt, the news media reports another shocking story. "Despite Biden's insistence that he was not dropping out of the race, Martin and Thomas stood looking at one another in shock when it was announced Sunday that he was withdrawing from it. "Just two days after announcing he was prepared to return to the campaign trail, President Joe Biden announced Sunday that he is dropping out of the race, taking members of his staff by surprise. Furthermore, he endorsed Kamala Harris as his replacement. With his electoral delegates and endorsement of Harris, it is a lock that Harris will become the Democratic candidate for President. The question bodes is who she will pick as her running mate. "Two frontrunners have emerged in the race to be presumptive Democratic presidential nominee Kamala Harris's second in command: Pennsylvania Gov. Josh Shapiro and Arizona Sen. Mark Kelly." (1)

"Kelly, along with Pennsylvania Gov. Josh Shapiro, are Hill Democrats' two top picks to join Harris on the ticket, according to interviews with 30 Democratic lawmakers and senior aides. They both have won multiple elections in swing states, and lawmakers believe they have the most to offer in helping the party beat Donald Trump. Still, while there's a sense that Shapiro would bring executive experience to the ticket that Harris lacks, others — including in Harris' own orbit — think Kelly would be critical to addressing Harris' weakness on immigration." (2) Other dark horses are Governors Tim Walz of Minnesota and Andy Beshear of Kentucky.

Biden's decision to withdraw from the reelection campaign came in the wake of repeated White House statements, and declarations from Biden himself, that he would remain in the race and was confident that he could defeat former President Donald Trump's reelection bid. Yet those assurances did little to decrease the public pressure from an increasing number of his fellow Democrats for Biden to move aside in favor of a stronger candidate. Not only did the list of Democratic congressional members echoing the call for Biden to withdraw grow to at least 40, staunch Biden supporters like Sen. Joe Manchin, I-W.Va., upped their public calls for the 81-year-old president to end his presidential campaign." (3)

After getting over the shock of the announcement, Martin and Thomas refocused on the tasks at hand. Although the first debate covered numerous key issues, Martin noted that it did not include others that would be of prime importance to voters. "Should another debate occur, we need to review those key issues. Even though Biden has dropped out, his legacy remains and must be adopted by whoever becomes the anointed nominee."

Martin ticks off Harris's negative stances on major issues. A week after announcing her run for president, Kamala Harris has yet to tell voters how she will address the key issues facing the nation.

"The vice president's platform will be in the same vein as that of President Joe Biden, whom she has supported for the past four years. The electorate should assume without a doubt that the debate answers given by Biden is the same as the answers that would be given by Harris. In essence just interchange the two in the recent debate.

Harris is expected to put her own stamp and style on matters ranging from abortion to the economy to immigration. Also, she'll have to walk a fine line of taking credit for the administration's accomplishments while not being jointly blamed by voters for its shortcomings.

"In the leadup to her 2020 presidential run, Harris tried to build a coalition of more moderate liberals and progressives — in particular, she attempted to build left-wing bona fides by supporting the two legislative building blocks of a progressive agenda, the Green New Deal and Medicare for All (though her M4A plan differed from other progressives'). But progressives nevertheless latched onto the "Kamala is a cop" rhetoric in an attempt to leverage the perception on the left that Harris' pro-law enforcement background made her unfit to be the Democratic nominee — and thus should be discredited as an opportunistic progressive." (4)

Before returning to the business at hand, Thomas insisted that for the sake of the country, it was imperative for him to send a letter to the editor denouncing the nomination of Kamala Harris.

"The plethora of leading democrats who support Kamala Harris as their presidential candidate is a travesty and disservice to the American people. Her record of chaos among her staff, failure when it comes to protecting our borders, lack of military prowess, questionable decision making, and giddy demeanor speaks volumes about her incompetence. How could she dawn the mantle of the presidency when her performance as vice president is lack luster and she may go down in history as one of the worst vice presidents of the millennium. According to a survey of scholars by a highly respected newspaper, Harris was rated in the bottom half of vice presidents. Out of an average of 538 polls, she has a disapproval rating of 50.4%. Once again, party politics prevails over that which is best for our precious country!"

Word finally came in that Kamala Harris chose Governor Tim Walz of Minnesota as her running mate. "As governor of Minnesota, he has enacted policies to secure abortion protections, provide free meals for schoolchildren, allow recreational marijuana and set renewable energy goals. The newly announced running mate to Vice President Kamala Harris, has worked with his state's Democratic-controlled Legislature to enact an ambitious agenda of liberal policies: free college tuition for low-income students, free meals for schoolchildren, legal recreational marijuana, and protections for transgender people. Mr. Walz signed a bill last year that guaranteed Minnesotans a "fundamental right to make autonomous decisions" about reproductive health care on issues such as abortion, contraception and fertility treatments. Another bill he signed legally shields patients, and their medical providers, if they receive an abortion in Minnesota after traveling from a state where abortion is banned. Mr. Walz supports a path to citizenship for undocumented immigrants." (5) "As Minnesota's governor, he signed bills that provided health insurance coverage regardless of immigration status and made undocumented immigrants eligible for state driver's licenses. He also signed a bill that allowed the state's nearly 81,000 undocumented immigrants to receive free tuition at a state university. As governor, he signed a bill that enshrined the right to abortion into the state's statutes. Known as a champion of progressivism, his selection was celebrated by top progressives, including Sen. Bernie Sanders of Vermont and Rep. Alexandria Ocasio-Cortez of New York." (6)

CHAPTER 26

Campaign Promises

Thomas thought it made more sense to compare the campaign platforms of President Trump and Vice President Harris. He found several articles.

President Trump's political philosophies and promises.

According to an article that Thomas found on NBC news (1), Former president Trump proposed numerous initiatives.

"Former President Donald Trump is firing a fusillade of policy proposals into the GOP presidential primary, including to toughen penalties for teens who break the law. Order the direct election of school principals. Build ten new cities on federal land — and tent cities for the homeless.

But the main purpose, some close advisers to Trump say, is to offer primary voters a forward-looking vision that emphasizes what he plans to do — a notable shift from his 2020 campaign, which centered on "promises made, promises kept," and a response to conservatives who worry he's too focused on the past. Dubbed "Agenda47," Trump's developing platform mixes new, recast, and recycled planks — some of which simply did not get much attention in the last election — to give his campaign a fresher look. Trump has struggled to generate the kind of attention he received during his past campaigns, even as most polls show him to be the GOP's presidential front-runner.

Trump has called for overhauling federal standards for disciplining minors, punishing doctors who provide gender-affirming care and barring any federal agency from promoting "the concept of sex and gender transition at any age" or using "misinformation" and "disinformation" when describing domestic speech.

Much of Trump's appeal has always been how he sells his ideas. Trump did not just talk about immigration, he created a "build the wall" brand. Rather than get into the weeds of how he wanted to reform the government, Trump pledged to "drain the swamp." And much of his success with this forward-looking agenda may, again, be whether he is able to make his ideas marketable.

Terry Sullivan, who was Sen. Marco Rubio's 2016 presidential campaign manager, said more so than the policy rollout, he sees the biggest difference between Trump's current campaign and his prior efforts is an increased emphasis on holding smaller events and doing more traditional politicking in early states." (1)

Thomas then found a BBC article on Trump's promises as to whether he delivered them. (2)

Promise to cut taxes: Trump promised to lower the corporate tax rate and bring in huge tax cuts for working Americans. *(Delivered on his promise)*

Promise on Paris Climate Deal: As a candidate, Mr. Trump derided climate change as a hoax concocted by China, and the regulations of Paris as stifling to American growth.

Delivered on Promise:

Promise to Replace the Judiciary: "I am looking for judges and have actually picked 20 of them. They'll respect the Second Amendment and what it stands for and what it represents."

Delivered on Promise:

Promise to repeal and replace Obamacare: One of Mr. Trump's trademark rally pledges was to repeal and replace Obamacare. Republicans have not been able to pass or repeal.

Promise to build a border wall paid for by Mexico: His vow to build a wall along the US-Mexican border was one of the most controversial of Mr. Trump's campaign promises. Mr. Trump also insisted that Mexico would pay for it. *Not delivered on Promise.*

Promise to bomb IS: During a speech in Iowa in November 2015, Mr. Trump warned that he would, using an expletive, bomb the so-called Islamic State group into obliteration. *Delivered on Promise:* Dropped the biggest non-nuclear bomb in Afghanistan.

Promise to move Israeli Embassy: Mr. Trump pledged during his campaign to move the embassy from Tel Aviv to Jerusalem, a divided city which both Israelis and Palestinians claim. *Delivered on Promise:*

Promise on Military Spending: "I'm going to build a military that's going to be much stronger than it is right now. It is going to be so strong; nobody is going to mess with us," *Delivered on Promise.*

Promise to cut regulations: Just a month before his election win in November 2016, Mr. Trump said he could cut as many as 70% of US federal regulations if elected. *Delivered on Promise:* The president has slashed through regulations.

Promise to bring troops home: Mr. Trump has long called for the US to leave the Middle East. *Partially delivered on Promise:* Approximately five hundred, remain.

Promise on Trade Deals: Mr. Trump called NAFTA "a disaster" and warned that the TPP "is going to be worse, so we will stop it". He also pledged to correct the trade deficit with China. *Partially delivered on Promise:* Transpacific Partnership (TPP).

Promise on Muslims ban: Mr. Trump initially promised to ban all Muslims entering the US. *Partially Delivered on Promise:*

Promise on Cuba: Mr. Trump said in September 2016 that he would reverse the deal President Barack Obama had struck to reopen diplomatic relations and improve trade. *Partially delivered on Promise:* **R**eimposed some trade and travel restrictions.

Promise on China: Mr. Trump repeatedly pledged to label Beijing a "currency manipulator" on his first day in office. *Partially delivered on Promise:*

Promise on National Debt: Donald Trump told the Washington Post in 2016, and promised to clear the country's then-$19tn national debt "over a period of eight years". *Promise not delivered:* Increased the national debt ceiling in 2017.

Political philosophies and promises of Vice President Harris

"In policy proposals, speeches and rallies, she has voiced support for continuing many of President Joe Biden's measures, such as providing tax credits to middle-class and lower-income families, lowering drug costs and eliminating so-called junk fees. Vice President Harris describes her vision as "an opportunity economy" that focuses on strengthening the middle class and punishes bad actors who try to unfairly raise costs.

Generally, her agenda contains an amped-up series of progressive proposals, though her campaign has confirmed that she's moved away from several of her more notable left-leaning stances from her 2020 presidential run, such as her interest in a single-payer health insurance system and a ban on fracking.

Harris is also expected to put her own stamp and style on matters ranging from abortion to the economy to immigration, as she aims to walk a fine line of taking credit for the administration's accomplishments while not being jointly blamed by voters for its shortcomings.

"On the Economy, "her proposals include Tax breaks for homebuilders with the goal of building 3 million new housing units in four years.

A ban on price gouging in the food sector, singling out meat prices in particular. Work with states to ban the use of medical debt in credit scores. She announced a goal to build 3 million new housing units in four years, proposing $40 billion in tax incentives for home builders to accomplish it. Harris also said she'd ask Congress to pass legislation giving buyers up to $25,000 toward a down payment on their first home.

When it comes to taxes, she is proposing that lower-income adults who do not have children see an expansion of their earned income-tax credit (more on her proposals for those who do have children below). She also vows to protect consumers by pushing a federal ban on corporate price gouging in the grocery and food industries.

She is now pitching an economic agenda focused on using government money and regulations to address higher costs, though most of her plans would require congressional approval. The measures would also prove pricey, and the Harris campaign has not provided many details about the proposals and how she would pay for them. (3)

Work with states to ban the use of medical debt in credit scores! In other campaign speeches, Harris has said she would:
- Ban hidden bank fees
- Hike the minimum wage
- Ban taxes on tips for service and hospitality workers
- Support affordable childcare and paid family leave.

So far, there have been few details on: The overall costs of these new measures and Who would qualify for the various incentives.

The Harris campaign said she would propose hiking the corporate tax rate to 28% up from 21%, a move that would generate billions in revenue to pay for programs. The Harris campaign told Politico that she would not raise taxes on people making less than $400,000 per year.

After the Supreme Court struck down *Roe v. Wade* in 2022, Harris became the administration's leading voice on restoring protections for abortion rights. She has urged Congress to pass legislation to codify *Roe* protections and said she would sign it into law.

Harris has said she backs comprehensive immigration reform with "an earned pathway to citizenship" but she has not spelled out the details. She has backed Biden administration efforts to negotiate lower prescription drug prices for seniors on Medicare. She has said she would address gun violence by urging Congress to pass universal background checks, red flag laws and an assault weapons ban." (4)

According to an article that appeared in the Hill, "If Americans think Joe Biden's economy's bad, then just wait 'til they get Kamala Harris's economy. Over the last four years, Biden's excessive spending has helped stoke the inflation inferno that has consumed average Americans' paychecks. But as big as

Biden has spent, Harris wants to spend even bigger. Not simply dependent on the extreme left, as Biden has been, Harris is one of them and brings their spending priorities with her.

No wonder Americans are dissatisfied with the Biden-Harris economy: They're worse off than they were four years ago. And no wonder they link Biden-Harris to inflation: This administration helped provoke it, and it's continued without interruption throughout its tenure. Congressional Budget Office data show the Biden-Harris appending explosion. Spending soared with COVID, but under Biden-Harris, it essentially stayed at crisis-response levels. During fiscal 2021 through 2024, CBO projects this administration will spend $5.9 trillion over pre-pandemic 2019 levels and run deficits of $7.7 trillion. In 2022, inflation climbed even higher, hitting 9.1 percent in June; by December it was still at 6.5 percent. Throughout 2023, inflation never dropped below 3 percent — not doing so until July 2024, when it hit 2.9 percent. Even this remains well above the Fed's 2 percent target level — and has for 41 consecutive months.

Yet Harris has even bigger spending aspirations than Biden." (5)

CHAPTER 27

The Silent Majority

The former acquaintance of Thomas, Matt, has been intently following Thomas's campaign. After reading his last OPED letter and others, Matt decided to meet up with Thomas at his next campaign rally he was holding in West Virginia. Long before meeting Thomas, Matt was promoting the idea of forming a coalition of majority voters who stood helplessly by while their fate was decided by extreme minority factions throughout the United States. Matt confronted Thomas right after the rally was over. "Hopefully you remember me Thomas" After attempting to recall their meeting, Thomas quickly spoke up. "Yes, Matt, you are the guy I stood in the road handing out Trump and Toomey signs. It's great to see you again." Matt took a firm grasp of Thomas's hand and asked him to join him over dinner.

Sitting in a restaurant in Charleston West Virginia, Matt began the conversation. "Since we last met, I have been thinking of our conversation about ways to organize those voters who consider themselves the independents, the silent majority. Your campaign is a great way to jump start it Thomas and I would like to become part of it."

"The silent majority is the largest part of a country's population that consists of people who are not actively involved in politics and do not express their political opinions publicly." (1) "The term was popularized by U.S. President Richard Nixon in a televised address on November 3, 1969, in which he said, "And so tonight—to you, the great silent majority of my fellow Americans—I ask for your support." In this usage it referred to those Americans who did not join in the large demonstrations against the Vietnam War at the time, who did not join in the counterculture, and who did not participate in public discourse. Nixon, along with many others, saw this group of Middle Americans as being overshadowed in the media by the more vocal minority. " (2) Looking at Thomas, Matt says that the same is happening today.

"In the landscape of American politics, a pronounced and potentially transformative shift is taking place-the rise of the independent voter. Traditionally, our political arena has been dominated by the two-party system, with Democrats and Republicans each outnumbering Independents. However, recent years have witnessed a surge in the number of individuals choosing to declare their independence from party affiliations.

The independent voter, once a silent minority, is rapidly becoming the silent majority. According to various studies, the percentage of registered voters identifying as independents has been steadily increasing and is now at 49% — equaling the combined affiliations of Republicans and Democrats. In 2004, the three affiliations were equal, so the shift is significant. This shift is not confined to a specific demographic but spans across age groups, ethnicities, and socioeconomic backgrounds. What was once considered an almost irrelevant category has evolved into a potentially formidable force." (3)

"Thomas, I see a need for the silent majority to have a public platform to voice their opinions on political elections, issues, and governmental initiatives that will impact their daily lives. One only must frequent coffee shops, public forums, school board meetings, local governmental hearings to sense the frustrating mood across America of the "Silent Majority". They have little to no voice because they are not organized like smaller special interest groups.

"As you know", "An interest group is usually a formally organized association that seeks to influence public policy. Interest group is, any association of individuals or organizations, usually formally organized, that, on the basis of one or more shared concerns, attempts to influence public policy in its favor. All interest groups share a desire to affect government policy to benefit themselves or their causes. Their goal could be a policy that exclusively benefits group members or one segment of society or a policy that advances a broader public purpose." (4)

"Thomas, I further contend that many political candidates of special interest and extremist groups are being elected to local and national offices because their campaigns are being fully funded and they themselves receive the necessary resources to focus on winning those offices. In sharp contrast, candidates having moderate philosophies must raise campaign monies and provide income to support themselves and their families. Moderates are shying away from seeking public office because of hard fought campaigns, low pay, and the relentless demands of the office if elected. This political trend is why America is being overtaken by smaller extremist groups that are not representative of the philosophies and beliefs of the silent majority."

"Far-left extremism in the United States centers around the notion of correcting an injustice but is otherwise broad in its ideological catchment. In the 20th century, U.S. left-wing extremism was synonymous with either communism or causes such as environmentalism. In the 1960s and '70s, the Weather Underground declared war against the U.S. government and carried out a campaign of political violence. According to the FBI, far-left extremism in the United States was most active during the period between the 1960s and 1980s. Special-interest extremism emerged on the far-left in the 1990s, resulting in the promulgation of groups such as the Animal Liberation Front (ALF) and Earth Liberation Front (ELF). The FBI estimated that between 1996 and 2002, these two groups were responsible for 600 criminal acts in the United States that caused more than $42 million in damages." (5)

"One such extremist group is rightly named the Progressive Left." The Progressive left may not be categorized as being a far-left extremists' group, but they do profess socialist ideology. "Reflecting their name, Progressive Lefts have very liberal views across a range of issues – including the size and scope of government, foreign policy, immigration and race. A sizable majority (79%) describe their views as liberal, including

42% who say their views are *very liberal*. Two-thirds of Progressive Left (68%) are White, non-Hispanic, by far the largest share among Democratic-aligned groups. Progressive Left are the second youngest typology group – 71% are ages 18 to 49. Progressive Left are also highly educated, with about half (48%) holding at least a four-year college degree, making it one of the two most highly educated groups overall.

Progressive Left are more liberal than the three other Democratic-oriented groups on many issues. For example, while majorities in all four of these groups favor a bigger government providing more services, Progressive Left are most likely to express this view. When asked a follow-up question about how much bigger the government should be, 63% of Progressive Left say government services should "greatly expand" from current levels.

Their liberal outlook is not limited to issues related to the size and scope of government. Their views on race and racial equality also distinguish them from other typology groups: Sizable majorities say White people benefit from societal advantages that Black people do not have and that most U.S. institutions need to be completely rebuilt to ensure equal rights for all Americans regardless of race or ethnicity.

Progressive Left broadly supports substantial hikes in tax rates for large corporations and high-income households. They are the only typology group in which a majority express positive views of political leaders who describe themselves as democratic socialists. And Progressive Left are more likely than any other group to say there are countries that are better than the U.S.

Although they are one of the smallest political typology groups, Progressive Left are the most politically engaged group in the Democratic coalition. No other group turned out to vote at a higher rate in the 2020 general election, and those who did unanimously voted for Biden. They donated money to campaigns in 2020 at a higher rate than any other Democratic group." (6)

"In Pennsylvania, several far-left candidates emerged as victors in balloting among Democrats. These are not garden-variety liberals. They are self-proclaimed socialists who ran on platforms harshly critical of their merely liberal Democrat opponents." (7) One candidate who recently won the third most powerful office in Pennsylvania ran on the premise that she was not a socialist. To the contrary, she told the former councilman that she was a socialist when standing in his street as his state legislator.

"Another state legislator was a card-carrying member of the radical Democratic Socialists of America, whose activities include Marxist reading sessions, wound up taking two-thirds of the vote in her race against incumbent Democratic state Rep." (7) She later went on to win a congressional seat.

On the other side of the spectrum are the right-wing extremists. "In January 2022, the ADL Center on Extremism identified more than 100 right-wing extremists running for elected office nationwide, and warned that these candidates had the potential to shift what is considered "normal" or "acceptable" in political and social discourse.

The right-wing extremist candidates who won their 2022 primaries subscribe to or espouse a range of extremist and fringe ideologies, including support for QAnon; ties to anti-government extremists like the militia movement and the Constitutional Sheriffs and Peace Officers Association; white supremacy; and antisemitism. Other candidates have sought to undermine the United States electoral system by propagating election conspiracies and participating in the January 6 Capitol attack." (8)

Not soon after President Biden announced that he was no longer a presidential candidate, numerous names, besides vice president Kamala Harris came up as replacement candidates. One such name was Senator Joe Manchin of West Virginia. What caught my interest and respect Thomas was his saying that "I am a candidate for basically speaking to the middle of this country."

Sen. Joe Manchin, the longtime West Virginia Democrat who recently became an independent, told "CBS Mornings" on Monday that he won't be running for president. "I am not going to be a candidate for president, "I am a candidate for basically speaking to the middle of this country." (9)

What also caught my attention was that like me, Senator Manchin changed his party registration to independent for the same reasons as me. "Charleston, WV – Today, U.S. Senator Joe Manchin (I-WV) released the following statement after he registered as an independent at the West Virginia State Capitol.

From my first day in public service in 1982, I have always focused on doing what's best for my state and my country, without regard to party or politics. Throughout my days in elected office, I have always been proud of my commitment to common sense, bipartisanship and my desire to bring people together. It's who I am. It's who I will always be. I have never seen America through a partisan lens." (10)

"When I was first eligible to register as a voter Thomas, I chose to be an independent. I later changed my party affiliation so that I could run against an incumbent in a democratic district. I was a long-time Democrat and a long-time Republican. Like Senator Manchin, I became so disenchanted with both parties that I changed my party affiliation to Independent.

What I am saying Thomas is that the extreme left, and extreme right are eroding the very values our country was founded upon. Hopefully, your and Bobby Kennedy's candidacy will get America back on track of moderate philosophy and where the silent majority will have a voice and save our country from going down a path of chaos and polarization.

Listening intently to what Matt had to say, Thomas replied. "I agree with everything you have said and believe my political philosophy parallels yours and Senator Manchin's. I have also been following RFK Jr's race closely and feel many of his beliefs are the same as mine. I have already approached him about meeting to see if we can collaborate in some way. Perhaps the three of us can meet to see how we can best get our message across to the electorate and the Silent Majority! Give me a few days to see if I can arrange a meeting between the three of us."

CHAPTER 28

Unorthodox Partners

Thomas was woken early in the morning by Martin. Martin was raving about what he was hearing on the news channels and morning newspapers. "If you add your and Kennedy's poll numbers, you both are within striking distance Thomas!" Thomas quickly sat up on his bed slightly confused. "What do you mean we are in striking distance Martin!? Martin thrust a newspaper in the lap of Thomas and turned on the morning news show. "With Biden exiting the race and replaced by Harris, the polls show that you and Kennedy combined are within ten points of Trump and Harris!" Thomas jumps up from the bed excited!

Prior to his meeting the next day with Kennedy, Thomas conferred with his team on some scenarios he may pose to Kennedy. At first, his committee was not on board about joining up with Kennedy. To convince them, Thomas called in Matt to give his team the reasoning why a collaboration with Kennedy would be better than going it alone.

In the meantime, Martin started mapping out a follow-up campaign for Thomas. He pointed out a Gallup Poll last month that he had already knew and that was a record 49% of Americans see themselves as politically independent, which was the same amount as the two major parties put together. "In essence Thomas, you need to attract a good percentage of those independent voters and cut into the bases of the Democratic and Republican voters. The best path we can take now to overcome the shortage of campaign money is for you to stomp across the country to solidify our grass roots campaign and garner as much free press as we can by pumping out news releases and your OPED letters. We also need to get into the talk show circuit and nurture campaign committees across the country. One other key point is that you need to make certain that your campaign stops include every 2nd and 3rd class cities in rural America and especially the swing states. Hitting the staunch democrat populations will only eat up valuable campaign time."

Having his marching orders in hand, Thomas invites Matt to board his campaign bus to join him in the meeting with Kennedy before going on the road again.

Upon his arrival at the hotel, Thomas and Matt were cleared through the front desk and Kennedy's security. Looking back on the tragic shooting of Kennedy's father in a hotel, Kennedy's campaign staff protected him. They did not know what to expect and did not know what exactly to say. Meeting with an opposing candidate was very awkward for Thomas, especially one that was once a member of a party that Thomas considered his opposition. He had formulated in his mind many questions and what he wanted to propose.

Finally reaching the door of Kennedy's hotel room, Thomas and Matt again had to clear through Kennedy's secret service. Before entering, Thomas took a deep breath and tugged on his suit coat to tidy his appearance. Upon entering, however, he found Kennedy in casual dress by himself. Kennedy reached out his hand and began to speak. "Sorry about all the security Thomas but the secret service does not want what happened to my uncle and father befall me." "No problem Mr. Kennedy. I understand." "We can dispense with the formalities Thomas. My family and friends call me Bobby. Who is your friend?" "This is Matt. He is going to work on my campaign."

The three men sat at the table and began having their lunch. Kennedy started the conversation about the assassination attempt on Trump. He was relieved that he was finally granted secret service protection. "Up until then, he was not granted Secret Service protection. Finally secret service showed up on my doorstep. President Biden has directed the Secret Service to protect me following Saturday's attempted assassination of Donald Trump.

The RFK Jr. campaign was requesting Secret Service protection long before the attempt on former President Donald Trump's life. The Kennedy family is painfully aware of how quickly life can be taken by a single attacker — both RFK Jr.'s father, Robert F. Kennedy, and his uncle, John F. Kennedy, were assassinated in the 1960s." (1)

Matt spoke up about protection by the Secret Service. "Twice I was able to get extremely close to two presidents without being challenged. The first was when I was the youngest Program Controller for ABC World News. The first was when a President was speaking at a hotel in New York. I was not yet issued my press pass with photo. The ABC crew said all I had to do was draw one of the generic yellow Press passes that were kept in a cardboard box in the assignment room. I went up to the perimeter of the security and flashed the pass and the police officer never checked it closely. I got close enough to the President and his wife that I could have touched his arm. There was an old-style Lincoln Continental convertible nearby with a secret service sitting in a modified rear seat that was facing backward, looking away from me and the President. He had a fully automatic weapon between his legs. If a shooter shot, the position of the secret service agent gave him no opportunity to stop a shooter in time."

"The second time I got close to a President was when President Bush was campaigning in the North Hills of Pittsburgh. The local Republican party asked me to attend. I showed up dressed in a suit and walked around the inside of the small hall without challenging me. The normal protocol is for everyone to be cleared from the hall and then reenter through metal detectors. I was never asked to leave. After Bush completed his presentation, I stood shoulder to shoulder next to him which allowed me to ask him a few questions while he signed some autographs. Two young men, asking for a photograph, stood one each side of Bush with their arms around his shoulders. None of us were challenged by the Secret Service.

Matt went on about the Secret Service protecting Presidential candidates. "I once watched a documentary where some of the Secret Service that guarded your uncle said, "it is extremely difficult to totally protect anyone." Bobby listened intently with his hand on his chin, followed by all three men standing in silence contemplating what Matt had said.

The three then snapped back to the conversation at hand. Thomas thought the time was right for him to start the conversation about a collaboration between him and Kennedy. "I am certain that you have seen the polls where combined, we both have come within striking distance of Trump and Harris. "I have Thomas, very exciting. The two of us have even done better than Ross Perot did when he ran as an independent. The question now is how we make up the gap. I for one do not want to simply get within striking distance. I want to win!" "Likewise, Bobby. To return our country to it being what American once stood for, it is imperative for one of us to win." "One of us Thomas? I am surprised to hear you say that either one of us would be better in the white house than President Trump or Vice President Harris." "I guess I would have to say that is exactly what I mean Bobby! Even though our politics differ somewhat, we both have the common hope that our country does not go down a road where we have an America divided. I believe that most Americans think like us. Together with them, we make up the silent majority. As far as America is concerned, however, the tail is wagging the dog. A minority of extreme right and left groups are guiding us towards chaos and decaying the values and constitution our country was founded upon.

Matt picks up the conversation where Thomas left off. "I want to stress that you do not necessarily have to win to make a huge difference in the election of future presidents. What you are attempting to do can set the stage for an independent to win in a future presidential campaign if not now. You will also set the stage, a roadmap, for any independent that will seek a major elected office."

"As far as extremism influencing our everyday lives, the extreme left is pushing us towards a progressive socialistic philosophy and the extreme right rejects mainstream conservatism while amplifying "digital hate cultures"—i.e. online content that intentionally promotes hate speech and prejudiced narratives." (2) These philosophies could divide our people into factions." Thomas chimes in. "I believe that either one of us are a far better alternative than Trump or Harris. I suggest we form a pact where one of us can win.

"Luckily there are moderates in Congress." "The Moderate Democrats PAC was formed in 2007 to help support moderate Senate candidates. They believe in using common sense and practical solutions to move the country forward." (3)

Pondering what Thomas just said, Kennedy leans back on his chair and philosophies on which presidential candidate he would support if he discontinued his campaign. "You know Thomas and Matt; I would rather see Trump win if we did not. Although Trump and I differ on some issues, we share a lot of the same beliefs. "Kennedy cited free speech, the war in Ukraine and "a war on our children. These are the principal causes that persuaded me to leave the Democratic Party and run as an independent." (4) "I may even endorse Trump if I discontinue my race for the Presidency!"

Thomas simply replied. "With all the adversities facing President Trump, I thought it best for the good of the country if he would have stepped aside for a more moderate candidate that has a better chance of winning. The problem is that his loyal followers get him through the primary election and those of us who are moderates must agonize through a nail-biting campaign with a possible loss in the general election. The Republican party should have nominated one of their other less controversial and moderate candidates. This is precisely why I am running for the presidency."

"Well then Thomas, how can one of us win?" "The most effective way is to not campaign as individuals but as a team Bobby. We need to formulate a campaign that has a common theme." "What would we call our campaign Thomas?" Getting up from the table, Thomas paces back and forth. People have forgotten how special America is compared to other countries. We need to pick a theme that people can rally around, something like *Save our Country*."

"I like the campaign theme you have come up with and your analogies Thomas. I agree that we can become far more effective by combining our teams. Thomas gathers his thoughts. "I think I have a suggestion, Bobby. Let's start by splitting up the swing states and particularly hold news conferences at the burial place or libraries of former presidents." When visiting each place, we will extol upon the good attributes of each president. We will end our campaign at your uncle's library. Hopefully, we will gain the support of those voters who share our values."

Looking at Thomas, Kennedy agrees and produces another revelation. "I have another idea, Thomas. If one of us receive more electoral votes than the other two, that person will push to install the other as their Vice President. Thomas looks at Kennedy with a weird grin. "Agreed Bobby. Hopefully, we can trust one another to follow through. Kennedy reaches out his hand. "You have my word, Thomas. Matt is our witness, and we will announce it to the media."

Thomas came up with where and how to launch their campaign of *Save our Country*. "Let's announce our campaign in Washington DC in front of the Lincoln Memorial with the backdrop of your uncle's flame flickering from Arlington Cemetery. Let's do it at dusk when the memorial is most inspiring, with its lights shining down on it and on the pool of reflections. We can quote Abraham Lincoln, and we can receive much more news coverage in Washington."

Matt thought it appropriate to tell a story when he roomed with some young FBI agents in New York City. "By the way, Bobby and Thomas, I have a remarkable story about the Lincoln Memorial. When I lived in New York working for ABC World News, I roomed with some young FBI agents. When they first entered the FBI, a bunch of them were sent to Washington for training. Before returning to New York, they went out to celebrate the night before their departure.

"As several of them never visited the Lincoln memorial, they  decided to go in the early morning hours. *(Photo 9)* There was a dozen or more and all of them always weapons concealed on their person. While standing at the foot of Lincoln's statue, a limousine accompanied by two SUV's drove up below the steps. A man came out of the limo surrounded by bodyguards. When the man ascended the stairs and stood at the foot of the monument in reverence, they realized that it was President Nixon with a dozen or more secret service. My friends who were reading the quotes to the side of the monument, turned to look at Nixon while he stood at the foot of the statue. After President Nixon stood in solitude for a brief time, he felt compelled to walk over to explain his presence. "Good evening gentlemen, I often come here late at night when I cannot sleep." He then left with his entourage. Ironically, his secret service did not check out my friends who were also packing concealed weapons. At the time this all happened, the Watergate investigations were ongoing. It was no wonder that he could not sleep."

Thomas chimes in. "I recall a published news story where Nixon visited the Lincoln Memorial late at night. "It was one of the unlikeliest spectacles in Washington history: the President decided to make a spontaneous visit to share what he considered the most beautiful spot in Washington — the Lincoln Memorial by night." (5-6)

It was mid-summer when the two men met up in Washington the night before their news conference. Their campaign teams sent out an advance team to stage the area. The next evening sprouted a warm summer nights breeze with dusk just over the horizon when the two men arrived. To their surprise, there was a large entourage of News media and a couple thousand on lookers. As their people finished setting up, hundreds more gathered. Many were drawn to the mystic of a member of the Kennedy family in their midst.

The time had arrived for their announcement. It was a clear summer night with the moon now shining over Arlington, the pool of reflections, and the flame hovering over JFK's grave. Several other memorials were off to both sides of the Lincoln memorial, including several war memorials. The moon silhouetted the outline of both men. As a courtesy, Thomas allowed Kennedy to start the news conference. Cameras started flashing as soon as Bobby Kennedy walked to the podium with his uncle and father's grave in the background and with the grave's flame flickering in the distance.

Kennedy started his speech. "You see here before you two men that may have some political differences but have a common goal and that is to *SAVE OUR COUNTRY*. Save America from extremists and those that want to indoctrinate our people with political philosophies that can eventually tear our country apart. There are extreme factions that have taken over the two major parties dramatically changing them, straying far from the very fiber of our Constitution and major political parties. They have strayed from putting America first. It is our hope that we can return America back to the principles it was founded upon. We can no longer stand by while Americans are led down a path of biasness and hatred. Today we are announcing a campaign with the slogan *Save our Country,* and we invite the American people to join our crusade." Kennedy motions for Thomas to the podium.

"First, I would like to thank Bobby Kennedy for sharing our vision to preserve the values that America was founded upon. Our campaign is not one of personality or personal political philosophy. It is one of a valiant mission to save the values that our forefathers and veterans gave their life to preserve. With America so close to being divided since the civil war, Abraham Lincoln (Pointing to Lincoln's stature) would be disheartened to see our country is again on the brink of division. If we continue down this path, we could tear our country apart and leave us very vulnerable to those that want to destroy us. It is our intention to bring America back to the middle. We have allowed our freedom of speech to be suppressed far too long and it is time to not only end both discrimination and reverse discrimination."

All the people present gave a resounding applause to Thomas and Kenndy's speech and reached out to shake their hands. Their security looked on with great concern as the people descended on the two candidates. Most everyone in attendance signed up as a volunteer. The news media also surrounded them for more comments and went off to write their stories.

Before Kennedy and Thomas boarded their buses to campaign across America, they visited the gravesite of JFK and his brother's nearby grave. Bobby had visited it many times before, but each time brought back hurtful and joyful memories. *(Photo 10)*

After paying homage to JFK, the two men walked over to the grave of Bobby's father. It bore a simple white cross with a tip of Robert E. Lee's mansion at a distance. Looking over at Bobby, Thomas spotted a tear in the corner of his eye. Thomas comforted Bobby by patting his shoulder.

Looking at Thomas, Bobby repeated a great quote of his fathers.' *Only those who dare to fail greatly can ever achieve greatly. Few will have the greatness to bend history itself, but each of us can work to change a small portion of events.* Turning to Thomas, Bobby stressed that his father's words fit what the two of them wish to accomplish. We have no choice but to succeed Thomas." Staring into the eyes of Kennedy, Thomas emphatically nodded his head in agreement.

The two then went over to President Taft's grave, the only president to serve on the Supreme Court after his term as president. Looking at Thomas, Kennedy told him about a famous quote by Taft which was symbolic of his being both a president and a supreme court justice. *"Presidents come and go, but the Supreme Court goes on forever."*

Before leaving Washington, Bobby and Thomas also stopped by the tomb of Woodrow Wilson which was in the National Shrine. The bishop long ago asked for him to be buried there hoping to make the National Cathedral the American version of Westminster Abbey. Woodrow Wilson created the League of Nations after World War I (1914–18). He presided over ratification of the Nineteenth Amendment, giving women the right to vote, and laws that prohibited child labor. (Britannica) He is quoted as saying about World War 1 *This is a war to end all wars."* (7) Thomas exclaimed "I wonder what he would have said if he were alive today." Both candidates gave one another a hardy handshake and drove through Washington in separate directions.

CHAPTER 29

Trump and Harris Debate

President Trump and Vice President Harris debated in Philadelphia. Although Thomas and Kennedy were eligible and invited to debate, they declined because they felt it better to concentrate their energy on campaigning. The two vice presidential candidates also agreed to a debate. Thomas felt that regardless of the outcome of the debate, the candidates have a record of where they stand on the key issues important to the people.

Following the Trump/Harris debate, Thomas found an excellent comparison published by PBS-WHYY. "This year's presidential race is a genuine contest of ideas between Vice President Kamala Harris and former President Donald Trump — with clear differences on taxes, abortion, immigration, global alliances, climate change and democracy itself. The two candidates have spelled out their ideas in speeches, advertisements and other venues. Many of their proposals lack specifics, making it difficult to judge exactly how they would translate their intentions into law or pay for them. While the candidates agree on not taxing workers' tips, the outcome in November could drastically change the tax code, America's support for Ukraine, abortion access and the commitments made to limit the damage caused by climate change.

Harris wants middle class tax cuts, tax hikes on the wealthy and corporations, a restoration of abortion rights and a government that aggressively addresses climate change, among other stances.

Trump wants to accomplish much of what he couldn't do during a term that was sidetracked by the global pandemic. The Republican wants the extension and expansion of his 2017 tax cuts, a massive increase in tariffs, more support for fossil fuels and a greater concentration of government power in the White House.

How each candidate stands on the top ten issues:

ABORTION

Harris: The vice president has called on Congress to pass legislation guaranteeing in federal law abortion access, a right that stood for nearly 50 years before being overturned by the Supreme Court. Like Biden, Harris has criticized bans on abortion in Republican-controlled states and promised as president to block any potential nationwide ban should one clear a future GOP-run Congress. Harris was the Democrats' most visible champion of abortion rights even while Biden was still in the race. She has promoted the administration's efforts short of federal law — including steps to protect women who travel to access the procedure and limit how law enforcement collects medical records.

Trump: The former president often brags about appointing the Supreme Court justices who overturned Roe v. Wade. After dodging questions about when in pregnancy he believes the procedure should be restricted, Trump announced last spring that decisions on access and cutoffs should be left to the states. He has said he would not sign a national abortion ban into law if one landed on his desk and recently said he would not try to block access to abortion medication. He told Time magazine that it should also be left up to states to determine whether to prosecute women for abortions or to monitor their pregnancies. He has also said that, if he wins, he wants to make IVF treatment free for women.

CLIMATE/ENERGY

Harris: As a senator from California, the vice president was an early sponsor of the Green New Deal, a sweeping series of proposals meant to swiftly move the U.S. to fully green energy that is championed by the Democratic Party's most progressive wing. Harris also said during her short-lived 2020 presidential campaign that she opposed offshore drilling for oil and hydraulic fracturing. But during her three and a half years as vice president, Harris has adopted more moderate positions, focusing instead on implementing the climate provisions of the Biden administration's Inflation Reduction Act. That provided nearly $375 billion for things like financial incentives for electric cars and clean energy projects. The Biden administration has also enlisted more than 20,000 young people in a national "Climate Corps," a Peace Corps-like program to promote conservation through tasks such as weatherizing homes and repairing wetlands. Despite that, it's unlikely that the U.S. will be on track to meet Biden's goal of cutting greenhouse gas emissions in half by 2030 — a benchmark that Harris hasn't talked about in the early part of her own White House bid.

Trump: His mantra for one of his top policy priorities: "DRILL, BABY, DRILL." Trump, who in the past cast climate change as a "hoax" and harbors a particular disdain for wind power, says it's his goal for the U.S. to have the cheapest energy and electricity in the world and has claimed he can cut prices in half within a year of his potential return to office. He'd increase oil drilling on public lands, offer tax breaks to oil, gas and coal producers, speed the approval of natural gas pipelines, open dozens of new power plants, including nuclear facilities, and roll back the Biden administration's aggressive efforts to get people to switch to electric cars, which he argues have a place but shouldn't be forced on consumers. He has also pledged to re-exit the Paris Climate Accords, end wind subsidies and eliminate regulations imposed and proposed by the Biden administration targeting energy-inefficient kinds of lightbulbs, stoves, dishwashers and shower heads.

DEMOCRACY/RULE OF LAW

Harris: Like Biden, Harris has decried Trump as a threat to the nation's democracy. But, in attacking her opponent, the vice president has leaned more heavily into her personal background as a prosecutor and contrasted that with Trump being found guilty of 34 felony counts in a New York hush money case and in being found liable for fraudulent business practices and sexual abuse in civil court. The vice president has also talked less frequently than Biden did about Trump's denial that he lost the 2020 presidential election and his spurring on the Jan. 6, 2021, assault on the Capitol. When she's interrupted during rallies with supporters' "Lock him up!" chants directed at Trump, Harris responds that the courts can "handle that" and that "our job is to beat him in November."

Trump: After refusing to accept his loss to Biden in 2020, Trump hasn't committed to accepting the results this time around. He's repeatedly promised to pardon the Jan. 6 defendants jailed for assaulting police officers and other crimes during the attack on the Capitol, and recently threatened to jail lawyers, election officials, donors and others "involved in unscrupulous behavior" surrounding November's vote, again stoking unfounded fears. He vows to overhaul the Justice Department and FBI "from the ground up," aggrieved by the criminal charges the department has brought against him. He also promises to deploy the National Guard to cities such as Chicago that are struggling with violent crime and in response to protests and has also vowed to appoint a special prosecutor to go after Biden.

FEDERAL GOVERNMENT

Harris: Like Biden, Harris has campaigned hard against "Project 2025," a plan authored by leading conservatives to move as swiftly as possible to dramatically remake the federal government and push it to the right if Trump wins back the White House. She is also part of an administration that is already taking steps to make it harder for any mass firings of civil servants to occur. In April, the Office of Personnel Management issued a new rule that would ban federal workers from being reclassified as political appointees or other at-will employees, thus making them easier to dismiss. That was in response to Schedule F, a 2020 executive order from Trump that reclassified tens of thousands of federal workers to make firing them easier.

Trump: The former president has sought to distance himself from "Project 2025," despite his close ties to many of its key architects. He has nonetheless vowed his own overhaul of the federal bureaucracy, which he has long blamed for blocking his first term agenda, saying: "I will totally obliterate the deep state." The former president plans to reissue the Schedule F order stripping civil service protections. He says he'd then move to fire "rogue bureaucrats," including those who" weaponized our justice system," and the "warmongers and America-Last globalists in the Deep State, the Pentagon, the State Department, and the national security industrial complex." Trump has also pledged to terminate the Education Department and wants to curtail the independence of regulatory agencies like the Federal Communications Commission. As part of his effort to cut government waste and red tape, he has also pledged to eliminate at least 10 federal regulations for every new one imposed.

IMMIGRATION

Harris: Attempting to defuse a GOP line of political attack, the vice president has talked up her experience as California attorney general, saying she walked drug smuggler tunnels and successfully prosecuted gangs that moved narcotics and people across the border. Early in his term, Biden made Harris his administration's point person on the root causes of migration. Trump and top Republicans now blame Harris for a situation at the U.S.-Mexico border that they say is out of control due to policies that were too lenient. Harris has countered that Trump worsened the situation by killing a bipartisan Senate compromise that would have included tougher asylum standards and hiring more border agents, immigration judges and asylum officers. She said she would bring back that bill and sign that law, saying that Trump "talks the talk, but doesn't walk the walk" on immigration. The vice president has endorsed comprehensive immigration reform, seeking pathways to citizenship for immigrants in the U.S. without legal status, with a faster track for young immigrants living in the country illegally who arrived as children.

Trump: The former president promises to mount the largest domestic deportation in U.S. history — an operation that could involve detention camps and the National Guard. He'd bring back policies he put in place during his first term, like the Remain in Mexico program and Title 42, which placed curbs on migrants on public health grounds. And he'd revive and expand the travel ban that originally targeted citizens from seven Muslim-majority countries. After the Oct. 7 Hamas attack on Israel, he pledged new "ideological screening" for immigrants to bar "dangerous lunatics, haters, bigots, and maniacs." He'd also try to deport people who are in the U.S. legally but harbor "jihadist sympathies." He'd seek to end birthright citizenship for people born in the U.S. whose parents are both in the country illegally.

ISRAEL/GAZA

Harris: Harris says Israel has a right to defend itself, and she's repeatedly decried Hamas as a terrorist organization. But the vice president might also have helped defuse some backlash from progressives by being more vocal about the need to better protect civilians during fighting in Gaza. More than 40,900 Palestinians have been killed in the Israel-Hamas war in Gaza, according to the Health Ministry in the Hamas-ruled territory. The ministry does not distinguish between civilians and militants in its count but says that women and children make up just over half of the dead. Israel says it has killed more than 17,000 militants in the war. Like Biden, Harris supports a proposed hostage for extended cease-fire deal that aims to bring all remaining hostages and Israeli dead home. Biden and Harris say the deal could lead to a permanent end to the war and they have endorsed a two-state solution, which would have Israel existing alongside an independent Palestinian state.

Trump: The former president has expressed support for Israel's efforts to "destroy" Hamas, but he's also been critical of some of Israel's tactics. He says the country must finish the job quickly and get back to peace. He has called for more aggressive responses to pro-Palestinian protests at college campuses and applauded police efforts to clear encampments. Trump also proposes to revoke the student visas of those who espouse antisemitic or anti-American views and deport those who support Hamas.

LGBTQ+ issues

Harris: During her rallies, Harris accuses Trump and his party of seeking to roll back a long list of freedoms including the ability "to love who you love openly and with pride." She leads audiences in chants of "We're not going back." While her campaign has yet to produce specifics on its plans, she's been part of a Biden administration that regularly denounces discrimination and attacks against the LGBTQ+ community. Early in Biden's term, his administration reversed an executive order from Trump that had largely banned transgender people from military service, and his Education Department issued a rule that says Title IX, the 1972 law that was passed to protect women's rights, also bars discrimination based on sexual orientation or gender identity. That rule was silent on the issue of transgender athletes.

Trump: The former president has pledged to keep transgender women out of women's sports and says he will ask Congress to pass a bill establishing that "only two genders," as determined at birth, are recognized by the United States. He promises to "defeat the toxic poison of gender ideology." As part of his crackdown on gender-affirming care, he would declare that any health care provider that participates in the "chemical or physical mutilation of minor youth" no longer meets federal health and safety standards and bar them from receiving federal money. He'd take similarly punitive steps in schools against any teacher or school official who "suggests to a child that they could be trapped in the wrong body." Trump would support a national prohibition of hormonal or surgical intervention for transgender minors and bar transgender people from military service.

NATO/UKRAINE

Harris: The vice president has yet to specify how her positions on Russia's war with Ukraine might differ from Biden's, other than to praise the president's efforts to rebuild alliances unraveled by Trump, particularly NATO, a critical bulwark against Russian aggression. The Biden administration has pledged unceasing support for Ukraine against Russia's invasion. The government has sent tens of billions of dollars in military and other aid to Ukraine, including a tranche of aid that totaled $61 billion in weapons, ammunition and other assistance that is expected to last through the end of this year. The administration has maintained that continuing U.S. assistance is critical because Russian leader Vladimir Putin will not stop at invading Ukraine. Harris has said previously that it would be foolish to risk global alliances the U.S. has established and decried Putin's "brutality."

Trump: The former president has repeatedly taken issue with U.S. aid to Ukraine and says he will continue to "fundamentally reevaluate" the mission and purpose of the NATO alliance if he returns to office. He has claimed, without explanation, that he will be able to end the war before his inauguration by bringing both sides to the negotiating table. (His approach seems to hinge on Ukraine giving up at least some of its Russian-occupied territory in exchange for a cease-fire.) On NATO, he has assailed member nations for years for failing to hit agreed-upon military spending targets. Trump drew alarms this year when he said that, as president, he had warned leaders that he would not only refuse to defend nations that don't hit those targets, but "would encourage" Russia "to do whatever the hell they want" to countries that are "delinquent."

TARIFFS/TRADE

Harris: The Biden-Harris administration has sought to boost trade with allies in Europe, Asia and North America, while using tariffs and other tools to go after rivals such as China. The Democratic administration kept Trump's tariffs on China in place, while adding a ban on exporting advanced computer chips to that country and providing incentives to boost U.S. industries. In May, the Biden-Harris administration specifically targeted China with increased tariffs on electric vehicles and steel and aluminum, among other products.

Trump: The former president wants a dramatic expansion of tariffs on nearly all imported foreign goods, saying that "we're going to have 10% to 20% tariffs on foreign countries that have been ripping us off for years." He's suggested tariffs as high as 100% on Chinese goods. He treats these taxes as a way to fund other tax cuts, lower the deficit and possibly fund childcare — though the tariffs could raise prices for consumers without generating the revenues Trump promises. He would also urge Congress to pass legislation giving the president authority to impose a reciprocal tariff on any country that imposes one on the U.S. Much of his trade agenda has focused on China. Trump has proposed phasing out Chinese imports of essential goods including electronics, steel and pharmaceuticals and wants to ban Chinese companies from owning U.S. infrastructure in sectors such as energy, technology and farmland.

TAXES

Harris: With much of the 2017 tax overhaul expiring at end of next year, Harris is pledging tax cuts for more than 100 million working- and middle-class households. In addition to preserving some of the expiring cuts, she wants to make permanent a tax credit of as much as $3,600 per child and offer a special $6,000 tax credit for new parents. Harris says her administration would expand tax credits for first-time homebuyers and push to build 3 million new housing units in four years, while wiping out taxes on tips and endorsing tax breaks for entrepreneurs. Like Biden, she wants to raise the corporate tax rate to 28% and the corporate minimum tax to 21%. The current corporate rate is 21% and the corporate minimum, raised under the Inflation Reduction Act, is at 15% for companies making more than $1 billion a year. But Harris would not increase the capital gains tax as much as Biden had proposed on investors with more than $1 million in income.

Trump: The former president has promised to extend and even expand all the 2017 tax cuts that he signed into law, while also paying down the debt. He has proposed cutting the overall corporate tax rate to 15% from 21% — but only for companies that make their products in the U.S. He would repeal any tax increases signed into law by Biden. He also aims to gut some of the tax breaks that Biden put into law to encourage the development of renewable energy and EVs. Trump has proposed eliminating taxes on tips received by workers — a policy embraced by Harris, who would also raise the minimum wage for tipped workers — as well as eliminating taxes on Social Security benefits. He also wants to lower the cost of housing by opening up federal land to development. Outside analyses suggest that Trump's ideas would do much more to increase budget deficits than what Harris would do, without delivering the growth needed to minimize any additional debt.

After reading the article, Thomas decided to write another OPED letter: "Hopefully, the American people will look beyond the two hours debate we just witnessed. Presidential candidates should stand the same test as any job applicant. In particular, the candidate should have a proven and lengthy record of successes. We have a clear vision of President Trumps track record. As to Vice President Harris, she cannot simply dismiss herself from what transpired while serving alongside President Biden. Make no mistake that the two are glued at the hip. With America in two wars, our borders more porous than ever, possibility of a recession, and families struggling with inflation; the American people need to do due diligence when selecting our next President. They need to set aside personalities and seriously look at track records and what candidates have to offer. They should answer Ronald Reagan's question when he ran for President, "Are you better off today than you were four years ago."

While writing it Thomas kept thinking that either he or RFK would make a better President than either Trump or Harris.

CHAPTER 30

On The Road Again

A day after returning to the campaign news of Thomas's and Kennedy's announcement to collaborate went ballistic. It was aired and published in every newspaper, on every television-radio station including the major networks. Talk show hosts were clamoring for them to call in for an interview. Thomas's and Kennedy's staff were overloaded with fielding requests from the news media. Contributions to their fund-raisers swelled every day, mostly from small grass-roots contributors. Kennedy and Thomas's press agents scheduled interviews with the news media and talk show hosts as they crisscrossed America. They received far more free coverage than Biden and Trump combined.

Meantime, Trump, and Harris were stunned that Thomas and Kennedy were fast becoming a phenomenon among the news media. In sharp contrast, the two of them were not the talk of the country and received little coverage. Their campaign managers started to closely track Thomas and Kennedy.

As Thomas rode to his first stop, the news was still abuzz about the illegal immigrants infiltrating our borders and straining the resources of border towns. Thomas thought an OPED letter would be appropriate to help stem the tide of illegal immigrants. He sent out his OPED letter across the country: OPED Letter on *Unarmed Invasion at our borders.*

"In times of crisis, four presidents ordered the closure of our borders. The 9-11 terrorists entered our country illegally by using forged passports. One can only wonder how many terrorists, criminals, or people infected with contagious diseases could be embedded among the illegal immigrants. Resources of our border towns have been taxed beyond catastrophic proportions. Article

1of the constitution guarantees the states the sovereign power to repel an invasion and defend against imminent danger. The illegal immigrants might be likened to "unarmed invaders." With millions of apprehended illegals, the president should exemplify his predecessors and empower border states with the authority and resources to defend themselves."

His letter was printed across the United States, especially in the Border states. Letters agreeing to his OPED letter started to roll into his campaign headquarters. Before making any stops, Kennedy and Thomas sent out press releases announcing each stop. An overwhelming gathering of news media and well-wishers greeted them at each stop and hundreds more were signing on as volunteers.

Thomas's first stop on the campaign trail was the memorial library of William McKinley in Niles Ohio. McKinley was one of the few presidents that was assassinated. His most memorable quote was *War should never be entered upon until every agency of peace has failed."* (1) McKinley's quote resonated with Thomas. He noted that it is the leaders who start wars, not the people and wars never start with peace, they only end with it after their countries are devastated and their people suffer needless casualties.

First stop on Kennedy's list was in Lancaster to visit the grave of President Buchanan. "He was an advocate for states' rights and minimized the role of the federal government preceding the Civil War. Historians and scholars rank Buchanan as among the worst presidents. He remains the only President to be elected from Pennsylvania and to remain a lifelong bachelor." (2) His quote was *Honest conviction is my courage; the Constitution is my guide.* Kennedy stressed that many elected officials placate special interest groups instead of adhering to the constitution.

Kennedy then went onto Virginia where his first stop was at George Washington's Mt. Vernon. A famous quote of his was *"Still I hope I shall always possess firmness and virtue enough to maintain (what I consider the most enviable of all titles) the character of an honest man."* The main topic of Kennedy's speech was about how many elected officials have lost their way, violated their oath of office, and unlike Washington, have not been up front and honest with their constituents.

Before going onto Montpellier, the home of the 4th president, James Madison, Kennedy campaigned in the city of Richmond.

He visited the resting places of James Monroe, the fifth president of the United States and the tenth president, John Tyler. They are enshrined in Hollywood cemetery overlooking the James River. The principal feature of James Monroe's tomb is an architecturally unusual cast iron cage known by many as the birdcage (Photo 11). Napoleon offered a surprised Monroe and Livingston the entire territory of Louisiana for $15 million. The Louisiana Purchase encompassed 530,000,000 acres of territory in North America" (4) and was one of the smartest real estate deals ever made. Kennedy reflected particularly on one of his most famous quotes, *"Knowledge will forever govern ignorance, and a people who mean to be their own governors, must arm themselves with the power knowledge gives."* He stressed that many of us are one issue voters and need to educate ourselves on the broad issues confronting us. We need to not allow one issue to cloud that which is best for our country.

Dubbed "His Accidency" by his detractors, John Tyler became the tenth President of the United States when President William Henry Harrison died in April 1841. Tyler died a member of the Confederate House of Representatives." (5) One of his most famous quote was *"I can never consent to being dictated to," highlights his strong belief in the importance of individual liberty and independence.* As the 10th President of the United States, Tyler firmly rejected the notion of being controlled or dictated by others. Kennedy stressed that the presidency should never become a pulpit for a dictator and the president should answer to the people, not the other way around.

Due to Richmond's role as capital of the South, the cemetery contains the burials of many officials of the confederacy and is considered the unofficial National Confederate Cemetery." (3)

The trip to Montpellier took Kennedy through small towns where people greeted him with excitement that a Kennedy was in their town. Upon arriving at James Madison's Montpellier, Kennedy drew a large crowd of admirers where he held a news conference in front of the mansion. One of Madison's famous quotes was *"The accumulation of all powers, legislative, executive, and judiciary, in the same hands, whether of one, a few, or many, and whether hereditary, self-appointed, or elective, may justly be pronounced the very definition of tyranny."* Kennedy again used Madison's quote to stress that he and Thomas believe that any candidate for the presidency should never perceive that the presidency grants to him or her dictatorial powers.

While Kennedy campaigned in the South, Thomas went on to campaign in Cleveland, visiting inner city neighborhoods and attending media and talk show interviews. The final resting place of the 20th president of the United States, Garfield, is in Cleveland. Garfield's Presidency was impactful but cut short when he was assassinated. One of his famous quotes was *"The truth will set you free, but first it will make you miserable.* Thomas recoined Garfield's quote by saying that "the truth may make you miserable at first, but a president must be prepared to accept whatever misery that may befall him or her so that truth and honesty will prevail over the misery in the long run. Not following this simple rule will only lead to a lasting misery that will imprison what virtues and integrity you may possess."

There were three more presidential memorials in the state of Ohio that Thomas chose to visit. Because they were in rural areas, it gave Thomas the chance to firm up more rural votes.

Rutherford B. Hayes presidential library and museum is in Spiegel Grove Ohio. "President and Mrs. Hayes are buried within the grounds of Spiegel Grove. A granite tombstone, made from granite quarried from the Hayes homestead in Vermont, marks their burial site. Their son, a Medal of Honor recipient, is buried next to his parents. Hayes most famous quote was Wars will remain while human nature remains. I believe in my soul in cooperation, in arbitration; but the soldier's occupation we cannot say is gone until human nature is gone." (6) Addressing a crowd that gathered at Haye's tomb, Thomas expounds on Hay's quote. Looking back at history, those leaders who sought war harbored ambitions and ego that clouded their sense of righteousness. Going back to the beginning of time, these ambitious leaders-built armies at the expense of the needs of their people. Not only did their people experience the ravage of war but leaders like Napoleon, Hitler, Hussein, and Gaddafi paid the ultimate price by being forced from power and the loss of their lives. Sooner or later, all tyrannical leaders pay the ultimate price.

After visiting with and supplying some local independent committee people with signs, Thomas continued his journey through rural Ohio to North Bend Ohio, the final resting place of William Henry Harrison. "Harrison died one month after taking office and is known as the president with the longest inauguration speech, and the shortest term. (7) His quote: *There is nothing more corrupting, nothing more destructive of the noblest and finest feelings of our nature, than the exercise of unlimited power.* Talking to the audience and news people, Thomas emphatically states *that a people's love for their leader can turn quickly into disdain if that leader does not relinquish some of his power to his people. A good example would be the abdication and execution of the last czar of Russia when he refused to give more power to his parliament.*

Thomas resumed his campaign trip through rural Ohio, greeting people in small towns and cities on his way to Marion Ohio where Warren Harding and his wife are buried. "Harding's campaign promised a return to "normalcy," rejecting the activism of Theodore Roosevelt and the idealism of Woodrow Wilson." (8) His most famous quote was his plea for normalcy, "*America's present need is not heroics but healing; not nostrums but normalcy; not revolution but restoration...not surgery but serenity.*" While there, Thomas guest appeared on two talk shows. He noted that when Warren Harding became president, our country had gone through some horrific war years and our people yearned for peace and tranquilly. No nation can bear extended times of turmoil and ravage, including America.

After greeting some residents in the town of Marion, Thomas suggested to his team that they campaign in Illinois, starting with Chicago. Because Illinois has not voted Republican at the presidential level since 1988 when George H. W. Bush won the state, they did not want to spend a lot of time. They headed to Lincoln's tomb because they wanted to liken the ideals of Thomas to the ideals closely held by Abraham Lincoln.

Kennedy worked his way through the southern states, starting with Kentucky visiting the memorial of Zachory Taylor. Because of Taylor's obscurity, he did not arouse the interest of the media. Taylor's most famous quote was *I have always done my duty. I am ready to die. My only regret is for the friends I leave behind me. Never judge a stranger by his clothes."*

When meeting with the news media, Thomas compared one of Taylor's attributes to himself and Kennedy and that is they favored a strong and sound banking system and thought that Andrew Jackson had foolishly destroyed the Second Bank of the United States. Jackson's use of party politics to award patronage seemed dishonest and corrupt to Taylor." (9)

When Thomas arrived for a second visit at Lincoln's Tomb *(Photo 12)*, they were pleasantly surprised to see that all their hard work was not in vain. Lincoln's Tomb in Oakridge Cemetery is the second most visited cemetery after Arlington Cemetery. Besides throngs of news media, there were thousands of towns people that showed up. So that everyone could see him, Thomas climbed atop his bus with a microphone in hand. "Lincoln gave his life to save the union. He refused to let it split apart. Like Lincoln, Bobby Kennedy and I want to save our country that is being torn apart by progressive extremists and right-wing radicals. We invite all to join us in saving America and preserving the constitution. Thomas then quoted a passage from the New Testament paraphrased by Lincoln. "a house divided against itself cannot stand."

While Thomas was working across the Midwest, Bobby Kennedy was continuing his trek through the South. He spent days in the Carolinas before moving over to Tennessee. His first stop was Nashville, the burial place of the seventh president, Andrew Jackson. "Jackson laid the framework for democracy, paid off the national debt, gained new lands for America, strengthened relationships with foreign nations globally and issued a new currency." (10) Kennedy emphasized that like Andrew Jackson, he and Kennedy will place a priority on paying down the debt."

After crisscrossing the Carolinas, Kennedy canvassed the rural areas before heading to Atlanta and the museum of President Carter. Working his way thru the rural areas of Georgia, Kennedy is well received. Having a Kennedy amongst them drew out many people. "The Carter's property features a pond Jimmy helped dig and a magnolia tree transplanted from a sprout from a tree that Andrew Jackson planted on the lawn of the White House nearly two hundred years ago." (11)

Kennedy asks his driver to pull up alongside the road facing the house. Disembarking, he thought he could see someone peering through the front windows of his bus. One of Carter's secret service people comes out to greet Kennedy. With the bus painted with Kennedy all over it, the secret service lady felt comfortable that it was Kennedy and confirmed that it was Jimmy Carter peering through the window. Knowing that Jimmy Carter served in the Navy, Kennedy slowly raises his hand in a salute to him. He could faintly see Jimmy saluting back from the window. Kennedy motions his driver to move on to Florida.

Kennedy stressed that Carter exemplified the humanitarian aspects of a president and that every candidate that seeks the presidency should bear the same trait.

On the other side of the country, Thomas, and his entourage stomps through Missouri and head for President Truman's library and museum in Independence Missouri. "One of his quotes we can all learn from is "Three things can ruin a man: power, money and women, I never wanted power, I never had any money, and the only woman in my life is up at the house right now." (12)

Looking at Jim, Thomas exclaims. "You know Jim, Harry Truman said what many of us have been saying all along. "Today discrimination applies to all no matter of color or ethnicity. Is reverse discrimination not rampant today? Yet no one is talking about it or standing up for those that are being victims of reverse discrimination." Jim shakes his head in agreement.

Kennedy swings down through Florida starting in Jacksonville and working his way through rural areas towards Orlando. As Kennedy once made a four-minute televised speech in Spanish, Kennedy was welcomed with arms open by the large Hispanic population in Florida. While campaigning in Tallahassee, he encountered Governor Ron DiSantis at a labor meeting. Kennedy told him that both he and Thomas held him in high regard and wished he would have stayed in the race.

The next states Kennedy visited were Louisiana and Alabama. Alabama housed the William J. Clinton presidential library and museum. After canvassing the state, Kennedy stopped by the library out of curiosity to compare it to his uncle's library. To his surprise, President Clinton happened to be on site. They sat talking about Kennedy and Thomas's campaign. What Kennedy and Thomas liked most about Clinton was like themselves, he was a moderate. He never expressed extreme right or left tendencies. They wished one another goodbye, and Kennedy moved onto the next states. He finally reached Texas, the home of the Lyndon Baines Johnson Presidential Library.

"Texas is a huge state with the most border exposed to illegal immigrants. The Texas border makes up about half of the U.S. – Mexico border, stretching 1,254 miles from the Gulf of México to El Paso. Four Mexican states share borders with the state of Texas." (13) Texas is America's most-populous Republican state with Republicans controlling every statewide office. Kennedy crisscrossed the state and ended up in Austin, the home of the LBJ's Presidential Library. It was difficult for Bobby to visit LBJ's library because President Johnson and Robert F. Kennedy Sr. fought over the course of nine years was for the soul of the

Democratic Party. Two of President Johnson's most famous quotes are *"Yesterday is not ours to recover, but tomorrow is ours to win or lose"* and *"Being president is like being a jackass in a hailstorm. There is nothing to do but to stand there and take it."* (14) With a quote like this, Bobby did not know where to even start his speech. He therefore improvised the best he could. A question did come from one of the news people about the contentious interaction between his father and LBJ. That's when he used LBJ's saying to respond. "I think LBS's quote says it all about is pertinent to how I feel about their relationship. "Anyone that dawns the mantle of the presidency needs to put past adversities behind them to accomplish greater things tomorrow. Thomas and I are not running to stroke our egos, we are running to save our country from its people being polarized by right and left extremists.

Bobby Kennedy took a few hours to tour the library before leaving to canvass other parts of Texas and to reach the George H.W. Bush presidential library and Museum in College Station. "The Bushes are buried at college station, but their library is not scheduled to open until June of 2024. President Bush was the first sitting vice president to ascend to the presidency since 1837 and was on the second American president to serve a full term without party control in both chambers of Congress." (15) A famous quote by George Bush was *"I have spoken of a thousand points of light, of all the community organizations that are spread like stars throughout the Nation, doing good. We will work hand in hand, encouraging, sometimes leading, sometimes being led, rewarding."* Kennedy stressed to the audience and news media that a great president recognized that he or she cannot do it alone and must draw upon the expertise of others. They must have the keen insight to recognize and draw upon the expertise and talents of others to accomplish tasks that are put before them. In essence, they must know when to follow as well as when to lead.

Before leaving Texas, Kennedy visited the George W. Bush presidential library in Dallas Texas, the son of the 41st president of the United States. The Native Texas park is a 15-acre urban park on the grounds of the George W. Bush Presidential Center.

The park, featuring a one-mile network of trails, reflects the President and Mrs. Bush's longstanding commitment to environmental conservation and restoration. He was the president that guided us through the 9/11 terrorist attacks on New York and the Pentagon. Two of his quotes were *"Leadership to me means duty, honor, country. It means character, and it means listening from time to time." "We will not waver, we will not tire, we will not falter, and we will not fail."* (16) Kennedy told the people that gathered to hear him that a good leader must be a good listener. "A great leader needs to listen to the advice of others before acting. He does not know if Trump and Harris are good listeners, but he has no doubt that both he and Thomas are."

As Bobby Kennedy started to work his way up through Oklahoma, New Mexico, and Midwest states; Thomas started his trek through Kansas and Colorado. Kansas is gaining in unaffiliated registered voters while the two major political parties are losing.

Of prime importance was for him to reach the Dwight D. Eisenhower presidential library and Museum in Abilene. With Thomas serving at the Pentagon and Eisenhower's military record, Thomas felt he could draw a large entourage of News media and curious onlookers. As was custom, Thomas's people distributed news releases announcing his visit. The response was outstanding, thousands of people showed up along with News people across the state. He also received invitations to appear on three of the top talk shows in the state.

Bringing to the Presidency his prestige as commanding general of the victorious forces in Europe during World War II, Dwight D. "Eisenhower obtained a truce in Korea and worked incessantly during his two terms to ease the tensions of the Cold War. He pursued the moderate policies of "Modern Republicanism," pointing out as he left office, "America is today the strongest, most influential, and most productive nation in the world." Two of his famous quotes were, "*I hate war as only a soldier who has lived it can, only as one who has seen its brutality, its futility, its stupidity.*" "*I have said time and again there is no place on this earth to which I would not travel, there is no chore I* would not undertake if I had any faintest hope that, by so doing, I would promote the general cause of world peace." (17)

Addressing the huge crowd that had gathered to hear him speak, Thomas said "As one who served during the Iraqi Freedom War and Noble Eagle homeland defense, I can relate to what Eisenhower is telling us. A great president must discern between wars that are waged in protection of our homeland and those wars that we need to avoid because they serve no purpose or not in our realm of responsibility. Two that immediately come to mind are Vietnam and Afghanistan."

After scouring most of the western states, Thomas's bus went from the northern to the southern tips as well as the east and west borders of California on a whistle stop tour. He realized that it would be a foregone conclusion that the democratic candidate would win the electoral votes of California. Thus, it would be a waste of time to spend too much time in California. The main reason he came to California was to gain press coverage when visiting the Nixon and Regan presidential libraries.

The distance between the two was only sixty-three miles so he could hold both new conferences in the morning or afternoon. "During the 1970s President Nixon appointed more women to high-level positions in the Executive Branch than all his predecessors, fought against the discrimination of women, and ultimately advanced their condition in American Society." (18) One of his quotes exemplifies his commitment to advancing the cause of women. *In this era of great challenges and potentials, the nation—in the private sector as well as in government at all levels—needs the capabilities and brainpower of every single American. The full and equal participation of women is crucial to the strength of our country.* Engraved on his tombstone is a quote "The greatest honor history can bestow is title of peace maker." (19)

Thomas had an outstanding turnout. for his news conference where like Nixon, he pledged to advance the cause of women in government and business. He also said that he and Kennedy wanted their administration to be known as peace makers instead of war hawks.

Right after finishing his news conference, news came across that Iran backed militants suspected of attacks on U.S. Troops. After reviewing the White House's response that it intended to deliver an attack on Iran, Thomas decided to write an OPED piece on it and read it at the news conference.

"First the White House allowed an unidentified balloon to drift across our country before shooting it down. Now it violated the basic principle of surprise when delivering a blow to the enemy. By the white house broadcasting its intent to attack Iran backed militants gave the enemy ample time to relocate leadership and targets of interest. As one who served at the Pentagon during 9-11, we never gave the enemy advanced warning of when, where, or how we would attack. By doing so, we knew it would also place our pilots at risk and prompt the enemy to strike again. Most important, our leadership in Washington must answer the question as to why these militants were allowed to imbed themselves in Iraq, a country that we supposedly liberated? Eradicating them was long overdue. If our leadership does not become more proactive instead of reactive, terrorists will have the freedom to continue their deadly assaults on us and other countries of the free world!"

Thomas's team sent the OPED piece across the country before he went on to the Ronald Reagan Library. The *Reagan Library* is one of California's most beautiful and unique destinations. Ronald "Reagan signed a sweeping immigration reform bill into law. It was sold as a crackdown: There would be tighter security at the Mexican border, and employers would face strict penalties for hiring undocumented workers." (20) It was the perfect place for Thomas to reaffirm his commitment to stop the flow of illegal immigrants. One way might be to issue VISAs to those who pass a stringent background check and where prospective employers are willing to employ ten or more and assume responsibility for them. Those that cannot pass the background checks will be immediately returned to their respective countries of origin.

He suggested another way to stem the flow of illegal immigrants was to have reserve units take turns guarding the borders by performing their two-week annual duty at the borders. With Texas having 290 reserve units, the units can provide ample coverage and save Texas considerable money.

Thomas started to work his way back East, canvassing the northern states while Kenndy started north with his goal to reach a huge labor convention in Michigan. With Kennedy's stance being strong pro-union, Thomas thought it would be far more productive for Kennedy to speak at the labor conference.

Thomas was well received in Utah, Nevada, Oregon, and Washington. "For the first time ever, nonaffiliated voters in Oregon outnumber Democrats, having long ago outdistanced Republicans." (21) "In Nevada, nonpartisan voters are officially the largest group of registered voters in the state, according to July voter registration data released earlier this month." (22) With the number of registered independent voters, Thomas believed that he and Kennedy could win three of the four states.

Thomas continued his journey by canvassing the states that bordered the Canadian border and those neighboring states like Iowa and Nebraska. Iowa housed the Herbert Hoover Presidential Library and Museum. "The permanent galleries tell the story of Hoover's fifty years of public service and the large temporary gallery features changing exhibits. The whirlwind successes of Hoover's first months in office did not last. A stock market crash in October 1929 signaled the beginning of the relentless economic collapse that became known as the Great Depression." His 1928 U.S. presidential campaign slogan of Herbert Hoover was rather condescending when the people were during a depression. "*A chicken in every pot and a car in every garage*" One of his famous quotes was "*Freedom is the open window through which pours the sunlight of the human spirit and human dignity.*" (23)

Standing before on-lookers, Thomas echoed his concerns that no presidential candidate is putting forth a plan to get the debt and inflation under control.

The campaign called for Thomas and Kennedy to rejoin one another on the boarder of New York to complete their blitz of the United States. Realizing that due to the staunch democratic registrations in major cities, New York would not be one in their column of winners. On the other hand, former presidents were enshrined throughout New York that could be used as a drawing card from which to garner national news coverage.

The first one they visited upon meeting up was the burial place of Martin Van Buren, the eighth president of the United States. "Van Buren devoted himself to maintaining the solvency of the national Government. He opposed not only the creation of a new Bank of the United States but also the placing of Government funds in state banks. He fought for the establishment of an independent treasury system to manage Government transactions. As for Federal aid to internal improvements, he cut off expenditures so completely that the Government even sold the tools it had used on public works. (24) His famous quote was "*As to the presidency, the two happiest days of my life were those of my entrance upon the office and my surrender of it.*" "*The people under our system, like the king in a monarchy, never dies.*" "*It is easier to do a job right than to explain why you didn't.*"

Using Van Buren's quote, Thomas and Kennedy profess their commitment to not linger in any elected office, including the Presidency. They further commit to enacting term limits for elected officials. "In fact, according to the last five national polls on this issue, 82 percent of Americans want term limits. That includes support from 89 percent of Republicans, 76 percent of Democrats and 83 percent of independents. This is not a left or right issue; this is an American issue." (25)

Next, they moved onto the burial place of Chester A. Arthur, the 21st president of the United States. He signed the Pendleton Civil Service Act. "The Pendleton Act provided that federal government jobs be awarded based on merit and that government employees be selected through competitive exams. The act also made it unlawful to fire or demote for political reasons employees who were covered by the law." (26) One of his most interesting quotes was *I may be president of the United States, but my private life is nobody's damned business*. Thomas used Arthur's example of the civil service act to promise that they would make certain that reverse discrimination would not be tolerated and no longer would any American be discriminated against due to race, ethnicity, or affirmative action policies. "Government Jobs, especially presidential appointments, will be solely based on merit and qualifications."

They stopped at Millard Fillmore's burial place because one of his quotes was apropos to the main theme of their campaign. Addressing a gathering of well-wishers, Thomas and Kennedy emphasized some famous quotes of Fillmore which said, " *An honorable defeat is better than a dishonorable victory. May God save the country, for it is evident that the people will not.?* (27) "The sayings emphasized the focus of our campaign, "Wake up America-the people need to join us to *SAVE OUR COUNTRY*." "Also, we will win only with honor and valor."

Next was the commander of the armies during the civil war and 18th president of the United States, Ulysses S. Grant. *One of his most famous quotes was I have never advocated war except as a means of peace. On the facade of the Tomb is the epitaph*, "LET US HAVE PEACE," a quote taken from Grant's letter accepting the Republican nomination for president that would characterize the ultimate aims of his public career. (28) Standing at the entrance to the Tomb before a throng of reporters, Kennedy and Thomas assert "We will never commit the United States to a war that is not directly related to the defense of the United States or shed the blood of our youth and waste tax dollars on senseless wars that have no end state." "The U.S. needs to make critical and time-sensitive decisions regarding the future of its wars in Afghanistan, Iraq, Syria, and Yemen – as well as in its broader struggle with terrorism and extremism, and its dealings with Iran. The U.S. is now trapped in four "failed state" wars where there are no clear prospects for lasting "victory" unless the current threats can be defeated at the military level and the host country can both develop forms of politics and governance that can create an enduring peace and make enough progress in recovery and development to sustain peaceful stability." (29)

Their next stop was the final resting place of Teddy Roosevelt. His tomb stone had no quotes or the fact that he was the 26th president of the United States. It only bore a seal. "With

Save Our Country

the assassination of President McKinley, "Theodore Roosevelt, not quite forty-three, became the youngest President in the Nation's history. He brought new excitement and power to the Presidency, as he vigorously led Congress and the American public toward progressive reforms and a strong foreign policy. He won the Nobel Peace Prize for mediating the Russo-Japanese War."

Some of Theodore Roosevelt's most effective achievements were in conservation. enormously to the national forests in the West, reserved lands for public use, and fostered: great irrigation projects. "Some of his quotes were *"Speak softly and carry a big stick; you will go far" Life is a great adventure…accept it in such a spirit. I recognize the right and duty of this generation to develop and use the natural resources of our land; but I do not recognize the right to waste them, or to rob, by wasteful use, the generations that come after us.*" (31) Standing to the side of Teddy Roosevelt's headstone, Thomas, and Kennedy pledge to protect our environment, especially our National Parks. "Like Teddy Roosevelt, we will peacefully negotiate but if the results do not benefit the American people, we are capable of having the strength to do whatever necessary to bring about a fair and just resolution." Simultaneously threatening with the "big stick", or the military, ties in heavily with the idea of Realpolitik, which implies a pursuit of political power that resembles Machiavellian They also noted that a great president listens to his advisors and the needs of his people, weighing all options before acting. Being boisterous and brash is not what they perceive will bring about good results.

Arriving next at the Hyde Park home of Franklin Delano Roosevelt, Thomas and Kennedy Walk the grounds and through Roosevelt's beloved rose garden before giving their news conference. "Franklin Delano Roosevelt, also referred to as FDR, was the only president elected to the office four times, serving from 1933 until his death in 1945. Roosevelt led the United States through two of the greatest crises of the 20th century: the Great Depression and World War II. "(32) The most famous quotes of Franklin D. Roosevelt were *"The only thing we have to fear is fear itself." "I have seen war. I have seen war on land and sea. I have* seen blood running from the wounded...I have seen the dead in the mud. I have seen cities destroyed...I have seen children starving. I have seen the agony of mothers and wives. I hate war." "Among American citizens, there should be no forgotten men and no forgotten races." (33) Standing over the grave of Franklin and Eleanor Roosevelt, Kennedy and Thomas said that like Roosevelt, one of their primary goals was to keep America working and out of wars. "It is time that we place the well-being of our people over the ravages that war brings. "Never again will we allow the blood of our youth be needless wasted in baseless wars that are not directly in defense of our country or those of our allies."

As time was fleeting, they needed to move on to their next stop, New Jersey. They traversed the state north to its south and east to west, and to the grave site of President Grover Cleveland. "Cleveland was the first Democrat elected after the Civil War in 1885, our 22nd and 24th President Grover Cleveland was the only President to leave the White House and return for a second term. He was the only President married in the White House. Cleveland was also known for honesty, self-reliance, integrity." (34)

Standing over the grave surrounded by news media, Thomas and Kennedy said, "If President Cleveland can win with support from people of all parties, so can we!" Like Cleveland, they also subscribe to limited government, economic and political freedom.

They moved on to campaign in Vermont and New Hampshire. Vermont was the burial place of Calvin Coolidge. When they arrived at his burial site, they were amused to find that like many presidents of long ago, the headstone of Calvin Coolidge was remarkably simple and did not indicate his being a former president of the United States. President Calvin Coolidge signs into law the Immigration Act of 1924, the most stringent U.S. immigration policy up to that time in the nation's history. The quota provided immigration visas to two percent of the total number of people of each nationality in the United States as of the 1890 national census. (35) Some of his quotes included: *I have noticed that nothing I never said ever did me any harm. Nothing in this world can take the place of persistence. Talent will not; nothing is more common than unsuccessful men with talent.*

Genius will not; unrewarded genius is almost a proverb. His campaign slogan was "*Keep Cool and Keep Coolidge*" Thomas emphatically stated that they want to follow the lead of Coolidge when it comes to reducing the debt and restricting illegal immigration.

Thomas and Kennedy noted that it is surprising that illegal immigrants are not made to adhere to U.S. Immigration Laws. As published on the White House web site, "In order to be eligible, noncitizens must – as of June 17, 2024 – have resided in the United States for 10 or more years and be legally married to a U.S. citizen, while satisfying all applicable legal requirements. On average, those who are eligible for this process have resided in the U.S. for 23 years." (36)

Thomas further points out that according to the Pew Research Center, "The unauthorized immigrant population in the United States grew to 11.0 million in 2022." (37) Kennedy and Thomas noted that this recent increase occurred during the current administration. Under their administration, they pledge that this trend will stop!"

Moving onto New Hampshire, New Hampshire is noted for its moderate politics and its status as a prominent swing state.

New Hampshire houses the grave of Franklin Pierce, the fourteenth president of the United States. In his Inaugural he proclaimed an era of peace and prosperity at home, and vigor in relations with other nations. (37) One of his famous quotes was *If your past is limited, your future is boundless*, meaning if you are not bound by your past, you are free to create any future you want. Thomas and Kennedy proclaimed that they will not isolate the United States from other nations, and it is imperative that we build solid and friendly relationships with other nations." (38)

The last state on their whirlwind tour of America was Massachusetts, which housed the grave sites of John Adams and John Quincy Adams.

John Adams and his son John Quincy Adams, along with their wives, are entombed beneath the United First Parish Church (also called the church of the presidents) at Quincy Massachusetts.

"His contemporaries would describe John Adams as honest, straightforward, and plainspoken. His greatest contribution came in the form of his ability to rally Americans around the cause of independence. His contemporaries would describe him as honest, straightforward and plainspoken. As a delegate, diplomat, politician, husband, father and friend, he was known to share his opinions with anyone and everyone, especially if he disagreed with their point of view—he was ever certain that his opinion was always correct." (39) Some of his quotes are *How strangely will the Tools of a Tyrant pervert the plain Meaning of Words! Mankind is governed more by their feelings than by reason. May none but honest and wise Men ever rule under this roof.*

Thomas and Bobby promised that, like John Adams rallied Americans around the cause of independence, "we will restore unity in America. "Like John Adams, a great president always seeks out other people's views when making major decisions even if he or she disagrees with them. We will do the same."

"John Quincy Adams, son of John and Abigail Adams, served as the sixth President of the United States from 1825 to 1829 and was a member of multiple political parties over the years. John Quincy Adams played a leading part in the U.S. acquisition of Florida and establishing the northern boundary of the United States. Formulating, among other things, what came to be called the Monroe Doctrine." (40) Some of his quotes include, *Courage and perseverance have a magical talisman, before which difficulties disappear, and obstacles vanish into air.* "*If your actions inspire others to dream more, learn more, do more and become more, you are a leader.*

One of the news people broke into their speech, asking for an impromptu statement. Thomas and Bobby, "You're not going to condemn people for exercising their right to free speech and presenting their opinions?' Thomas responded. "I for one am not supportive of the progressive socialist's suppression of people speaking their mind. "The First Amendment of the constitution provides that Congress makes no law respecting an establishment of religion or prohibiting its free exercise. It protects freedom of speech, the press, assembly, and the right to petition the Government for a redress of grievances."

It was only days before the general election and the polls now showed Kennedy and Thomas in a dead heat with the other two major party candidates.

CHAPTER 31

The Votes Are Counted

Kennedy and Thomas retreated to their combined headquarters and got on the phones to major donors and leaders that influenced large blocks of voters. They needed to obtain more donations to reinforce their messages through targeted ads. They worked feverishly alongside volunteers and campaign staffers working the phones for donations and votes while their campaign managers identified which states they needed to target with television ads. On the other side of the spectrum, they were being bombarded with negative campaign ads trying to confuse the voters. The headquarters were abuzz with more volunteers coming in every day. Their State and local headquarters were lit up with enthusiasm after they saw the polls reporting a dead heat.

The day before the general election has now arrived. Thomas and Kennedy met up at the JFK library Columbia Point in Boston Massachusetts. With polls showing the two of them within striking distance, multitudes of news media showed up to listen to their last news conference. Although some of the Kennedy clan initially did not agree with some of Bobby's stances, a good many of them showed up to lend their support. "Robert's presidential aspirations have roiled the Kennedy family. Ahead of his brother's announcement in April, Chris said in an interview with POLITICO there was "robust intra-family dialogue" about Robert running. "All of us shared with him our candid thoughts. It's what a big Irish Catholic family will do." (1)

Kennedy started the News conference. He talked about how he and Thomas joined up with one another because they shared the same ideals and hope for restoring America to what our forefathers envisioned. He also reiterated his reason for leaving

Save Our Country

the democratic party to run as an independent for president. Kennedy said there is corruption "in the leadership of both political parties" and said he wants to "rewrite the assumptions and change the habits of American politics." Allies of both major parties have questioned whether Kennedy would be a spoiler against their candidate. "The truth is, they're both right," Kennedy said onstage Monday to roaring applause. "My intention is to spoil it for both of them." (2)

Next it was Thomas's turn to address the news media. "Standing here at the JFK library humbles me. As a child, I watched him being nominated by a party that was once a party Once known as the party of the "common man," the early Democratic Party stood for individual rights and state sovereignty." (3) I watched every news story that came out on him while running for the presidency and during his presidency. I agree with JFK's beloved first lady when she was the first to refer to the John F. Kennedy administration as Camelot. *"There will be great presidents again ... but there will never be another Camelot again- Jacqueline Kennedy"* (4)

Thomas discusses their travels across America. "As we traveled the country, the news media reported our stances on issues and our vision for America. Thus, there is no need to reiterate them. Our campaign theme, "Wake up America-save our country," says it all. As to which of us may be elected president matters not? What matters most is that together we can preserve the freedoms, values, and ideals that our great country was found upon. We need to protect the constitution handed down by our forefathers and reject socialistic ideas and especially progressive socialism. Such philosophies have proven to be the downfall of great nations." "Economist Milton Friedman argued that socialism, by which he meant state ownership over the means of production, impedes technological progress due to competition being stifled. He noted that "we need only look to the United States to see where socialism fails" by observing that the "most technologically backward areas are those where government owns the means of production". (5)

"Some have said that a third party or independent candidate cannot win the presidency. As Robert Kennedy and I stand here before you, we echo the words of John Fitzgerald Kennedy, "If not us, who? If not now, when?"

'I would like to read some of my OPED letters. Some of you may have published them. The first letter is titled *"The American people are once again faced with choosing the lesser of two evils as their President, only this time it is far worse than ever before."*

"Many Americans like me sit helplessly by while minority factions in the two major parties thrust upon us two candidates that are unfit to occupy the White House. Vice President Harris failure to follow to protect our borders when assigned the responsibilities and Trump's legal entanglements should readily disqualify both from dawning the mantel of the presidency. Especially as one is passively docile, and the other is aggressively dictatorial. Lest I remind the American people that our president has his trigger finger on a nuclear and military arsenal that could destroy us and other nations by simply giving a series of command codes. In times like this when the world is in chaos, we desperately need leaders that can make sound and rational decisions. One misguided order or wrongful threat to an adversary could cause a domino effect of catastrophic proportions. From what we have witnessed thus far from the two leading presidential candidates, neither of the two should be reelected to the highest office in the land."

"How about the insurmountable debt being created by our elected leaders. When Americans says they are debt free, they are sadly mistaken. Without our having a say, our government proposes to obligate each of us to repay $93,000 of the proposed debt ceiling of $32.4 trillion. The national debt has now reached 128% of our economic output and after the United States, the next three largest economies in the world combined is a third less than our outstanding debt. To avoid burdening our children with insurmountable debt, Americans need to demand the elimination of wasteful spending and elect those that prioritize debt reduction."

"I would also like to also comment about a former speech by Russia's president Vladimir Putin threatening nuclear attacks, which was rebuked by the last leader of the Soviet Union. Nine countries possess more than 15,000 nuclear weapons and the U.S. and Russia possess approximately 93 percent which could be quickly launched. Each is far more powerful than the bomb dropped on Japan, which killed approximately 140,000 innocent people. Our country alone has spent more than $20 billion per year on nuclear weapons. If only one percent of the nuclear arsenals were launched, over twenty-one million would perish as well as the environment of any survivors. As one who served at the Pentagon during 9-11, I know all too well what the result will be if world leaders continue to rattle their sabers. Such irresponsible rhetoric could at least lead to boots on the ground. We need to ask ourselves if we are prepared to put our loved ones in those boots and to continue this frivolous spending on weapons of mass destruction while ignoring other pressing needs of our people."

"Besides major issues like the invasion of our borders by illegal immigrants, I would like everyone to think back and envision Media images of the past where thugs and unruly mobs broke into shop windows and descended upon communities where law abiding people had to defend themselves while liberals including the current Vice President publicly called to defund the police. "CNN —Vice President Kamala Harris voiced support for "defund the police" in a radio interview in June 2020 amidst nationwide protests for police reform, just months before denouncing the movement after she had joined the Biden presidential campaign." (6)

"Lastly, let me reflect on a presidential candidate's stance where a presidential candidate made about evaluating the mental acuity of elder statesmen a key part of their opening campaign pitch. I concur with older voters being irked by such a stance. Some of our greatest leaders were over the age of seventy. I think, however, that the American people should demand that anyone running for a higher office should provide proof of their passing an acuity test, regardless of their age."

The news media scrambled to reach out to their News Bureaus to report what was said by Kennedy and Thomas's OPED Letters. Their report was broadcasted across the television networks and in newspapers throughout the country and well received by the American people. It was too late to take another poll. The people were ready to go to their respective voting places. Thomas was preparing to return home when Kennedy invited him to count the returns at his family's compound in Hyannis Port. At first, Thomas thanked him but felt compelled to join his supporters in his hometown. Kennedy suggested that he could use his campaign aircraft to spend the day in Pennsylvania and fly to his family's compound at Hyannis Port when the voting polls close.

Thomas insisted that he did not want to impose on Kennedy's family. "You will not be imposing Thomas. We will use my grandmother's house which is not occupied now. You can bring whoever you can get on your bus. Thomas accepted his offer thinking that it would show more resolve for them to be seen together in the afternoon rather than at night, especially as more voters turned out in the evening. Thomas boarded Kennedy's airplane for the flight back home to greet and thank his volunteers.

The next day, the east coast voting polls opened before those in the Midwest and West. Mail-in votes were already in hand or on their way to be counted, depending on the election laws. Whatever the outcome, Thomas and Kennedy agreed not to question or challenge the results. Both Thomas and Kennedy greeted the news media in their respective polling places early in the morning. Their message was to the people was unchanged, "hopefully the American people will wake up and save our country.

After voting first thing, Thomas's campaign manager Martin called him to prepare for a whistle stop tour. Puzzled, Thomas asked him what he meant by a whistle stop tour? Martin gave Thomas his marching orders. "You are boarding an aircraft and doing "touch and goes" in the major swing states throughout the Midwest down through some cities in Texas. I have urged Kennedy's manager to ask him to do the same. They will be covering the swing states in the Northeast and some in the south.

We have sent out press releases to the news media in the cities where you will be visiting highlighting our slogan "Wake up America, save our country. You will then fly to meet Kennedy in Hyannis Port."

The candidates of the two major parties returned to their headquarters after voting and planned not to stay there while the vote was counted.

As soon as Thomas and Kennedy voted, they boarded their planes and started their whirlwind whistle stops. Abbey joined Thomas while Kennedy's lovely wife joined him. The news media ate it up. It was the first-time presidential candidates continued to campaign using a whistle stop tactic. At every stop, throngs of new people met them. They spent no more than a half hour at each stop and never left the airports. Their plane would taxi to a gate and with Abbey and Kennedy's wife by their sides, they gave a rallying speech immediately inside the waiting room of each gate. Exit interviews of voters revealed that their desire to reach out to the people at the last minute reinforced their reason for casting a vote in their favor.

The time had arrived for them to meet up in Hyannis Port. Both of their planes touched at the same time. Meeting up inside the gate, throngs of well-wishers met them. Working the crowds of people and reaching out to shake their hands, both men held up their hands in a clasped show of solidarity before boarding SUVs for the Kennedy compound. They were greeted by security at the entrance to the Kennedy compound. "

The Kennedy Compound *(Photo 13)* became a U.S. National Landmark.

Ethel Kennedy still owns and resides in the home she lived in with her late husband, while the Big House was donated to the Edward M. Kennedy Institute for the United States Senate in 2013. The first, and now largest, of the Kennedy Compound abodes is the aptly named "Big House. With eleven bedrooms, a sauna, a pool, a tennis court, and a basement movie theater, it eventually became known as the Big House. In the '50s, the Kennedys purchased two more properties adjacent to the Big House. Robert and Ethel bought their home in 1955, while John and Jackie acquired what would later be called the "President's House" in 1957. With these new additions, the Kennedy Compound now totaled six acres of waterfront property." (7)

The entourage of the two candidates use the Big House as it was large enough to accommodate them and their family and friends. Thomas and Kennedy along with their ladies and campaign managers sat in the same living room that JFK and Jacqueline once sat in while waiting for election returns. Later, they would join their family and friends in a larger room in another part of the house.

"The living room, to the right from the front door and across the hall from the dining room, was probably the first room that you would have been brought to when visiting the family. Although the clues may be subtle, the room is furnished with signs of Mr. and Mrs. Kennedy's wealth, education, and culture. Mrs. Kennedy was an accomplished musician and her piano sits in the corner. On the walls hung prints of famous works of art that she had seen on her overseas travels and studies in Europe. There are *National Geographic* magazines, books, a newspaper, and a *Literary Digest*, which show that the family valued reading. There are also many family portraits - of Mrs. Kennedy with her children, as well as the Fitzgerald family." (8)

At nine o'clock in the evening, the first large block of returns started coming in and the network news stations started to report. Thomas and Kennedy were tense waiting for the first results. Thirty percent of the votes were reported in the first hour, approximately forty-five million votes. The breakdown had President Trump in the lead with thirteen million votes, Vice President Harris with twelve million, Thomas, and Kennedy evenly split the remaining twenty million votes. Kennedy and Thomas spouted long faces. The three major networks were not ready to declare any states in favor of anyone candidate. Martin chimed in. "Are you kidding me, why are you two looking so down? That is a great showing. The urban areas always come in first and because they are heavily democrat, those votes would favor the democratic candidate."

In the next hour, another twenty million votes were tallied, a little over forty percent of the votes were now counted. Two of the networks called New York's 28 electoral votes in Harris's column and Florida's 30 electoral votes went to Trump. Michigan's 15 electoral votes went to Kennedy. Pennsylvania's 19, Thomas's home state, was called for Thomas. That gave Harris 28 votes, Trump 30, Thomas 19, and Kennedy 15.

As the night wore on, more votes were counted, and select states were declared as won by each candidate. The next vote totals gave Delaware's 3 electoral votes, and DC's 3 to Harris. Missouri's 10, and west Virginia's 4 to Trump. It was a given from the beginning that Kennedy would win Massachusetts's 11 electoral votes. Louisiana's 8 was earmarked for Thomas. That gave Harris 34 votes, Trump 44, Thomas 27, and Kennedy 26.

Within the half hour, another round of votes came in and the networks declared the winners of the reporting states. It was no surprise that Harris was declared the winner of California's 54 electoral votes. Trump won North Carolina's 16 and Kennedy was declared the winner of Washington's 12 electoral votes. Arizona's 11 electoral votes were declared for Thomas. The electoral tally was now 88 electoral votes for Harris, Trump 60, Kennedy with 38, and Thomas had 38.

With the Democrat and Republican having a lead on Thomas and Kennedy, friends and family could see that they were on edge. Abbey and Kennedy's wife went over to console them. Martin was fixated on the computer with the IT guys checking the vote counts of the television networks.

It was approaching midnight, and the networks declared Illinois's 19 electoral votes for Harris. Surprisingly Walz's home state of Minnesota, 10 electoral votes, went to Trump. Colorado's 10, and Indiana's 11 also went to Trump. Thomas won Tennessee's 11 electoral votes, North Dakota's 3, and South Dakota's 3. The networks declared Georgia's 16 electoral votes, and Arkansas's 6 for Kennedy. The totals were now 107 electoral votes for Harris, ninety-one for Trump, fifty-five for Thomas, and 60 for Kennedy.

One of the television anchors said that according to election laws, you need 270 electoral votes to win the presidency.

Martin chimed in. Thats not true. "Normally it does take 270 electoral votes to win but if neither candidate gets a majority of the 538 electoral votes, the election for President is decided in the House of Representatives, with each state delegation having one vote. Most of the states, 26 states, are needed to win. Senators would elect the Vice-President, Each Senator casts a single vote, and the votes of a majority of the whole Senate, 51 or more, are necessary to elect. "This is known as a contingent election. A contingent election is used to elect the president or vice president if no candidate receives a majority of the whole number of Electors appointed. A presidential contingent election is decided by a special vote of the United States House of Representatives, while a vice-presidential contingent election is decided by a vote of the United States Senate. During a contingent election in the House, each state delegation votes in block to choose the president instead of representatives voting individually. Senators, by contrast, cast votes individually for vice president.

The contingent election process is specified in Article Two, Section 1, Clause 3 of the United States Constitution. The procedure was modified by the 12th Amendment in 1804, under which the House chooses one of the three candidates who received the most electoral votes, while the Senate chooses one of the two candidates who received the most electoral votes. The phrase "contingent election" is not in the text of the Constitution but has been used to describe this procedure since at least 1823." (9)

Contingent elections have occurred three times in American history: in 1801, 1825, and 1837. "In 1800, In the election of 1800, the Federalist Incumbent John Adams ran against the rising Republican Thomas Jefferson. The extremely partisan and outright nasty campaign failed to provide a clear winner because of a constitutional quirk. Presidential electors were required to vote for two people for the office of president and vice-president. The individual receiving the highest number of votes would become president. Unfortunately, Jefferson and his vice-presidential running mate Aaron Burr both received the identical number of electoral votes, and the House of Representatives voted to break the tie. When Adam's Federalists attempted to keep Jefferson from the presidency, the stage was set for the first critical constitutional crisis of the new American federal republic." (10)

It was now past midnight, and all were waiting for the reporting of more votes. Suddenly a new count was reported. Connecticut's 7 electoral votes were declared for Harris. Montana's (4) and Idaho's (4) went to Trump. Kennedy was declared the winner of Kansas's 6 electoral votes. Ohio's 17 electoral votes and New Hampshire's 4 went to Thomas. The tally now stood at 114 electoral votes for Harris, 99 for Trump, 66 for Kennedy, and 76 for Thomas.

It was well into the early hours of the morning and still no more counts had been reported. As it now stood, both Harris and Trump were leading in electoral votes. Kennedy and Thomas decided to take a walk outside. Walking along the beach and staring at the stars over the ocean, Thomas started philosophizing about the formation of the Universe and the presence of God in it. Kennedy mentioned that his father once told him that sometimes you must put yourself in the palm of God's hand and accept the outcome. Looking at Bobby, Thomas reminisced about an OPED letter he wrote about our earth in relation to space exploration and how long it may survive.

The letter went something like this Bobby. "The renowned physicist Stephen Hawkins has confirmed what I have been saying to friends, family, and students for years-we must look to the universe for ways to preserve our heritage and the human race. Mr. Hawkins estimates that we have 1,000 years to migrate to another planet in our solar system before the Earth is no longer habitable.

It is sad that since John F. Kennedy, no president or presidential candidate for that matter, has placed a high priority on space exploration. Not once did the debate moderators put forth questions to us about space exploration and specifically whether we had a plan to save our civilization when our Earth spins out of existence.

We are so intent on protecting that which we have built and those who will carry on our heritage, yet we seem to be so very shortsighted by not placing more emphasis on space exploration, the only gateway to the survival of the life as it now exists on Earth. If we continue to ignore the inevitable destruction of the Earth, those whom we love and all that we love and all that we have built will perish, and there will be no trace that we ever existed."

"Your letter is quite thought-provoking Thomas. Hopefully, one of us will become president and can do something to make our space program more robust."

"Thanks Bobby. If only one of us ran as an independent, we may have been in the lead by five electoral votes. Martin emerges from the house. Sensing that they are stressed about the vote count, he steps between the two of them and places his hands on each of their shoulders. "We have not lost yet. Many of the states that need to report are independent in nature. Note this. A recent Gallup polling found that a record 49% of Americans see themselves as politically independent — the same as the two major parties put together. (11) If either one of you win, you are going to face far more adversities as president." Both Thomas and Kennedy nodded their heads in agreement while Martin went back inside to count more returns. (*Library of Congress Photo*)

Looking at Thomas, Bobby told him that his uncle's election was close and not decided until the next day. "The 1960 Presidential race of Kennedy and Nixon was too close to call until the final ballots were tallied. Results were not official until noon the following day." (12) Just then, a shooting star shot overhead. Looking upwards, Thomas exclaimed. "Maybe that's a sign in our favor Bobby!"

Suddenly at that very moment, they heard loud cheers coming from the house. Running back into the house, they both stared in shock at the large monitor set up for the guests. The networks were reporting on the remaining states. All but one state,

New Mexico with five electoral votes, had now reported. New Mexico was having difficulty counting because there was a mechanical problem with their computers which tabulated the votes.

The networks reported that Harris won only three more states, Hawaii's 4 electoral votes, Rhode Island's 4, and Vermont's 3. The total states won for Harris was 8 states and the District of Columbia, giving her a total of 125 electoral votes. Trump added Kentucky's 8 electoral votes, Oklahoma's 7, Wyoming' 3, and Maryland's 10 to his column of wins. Total states won for Trump was thirteen with a total of 127 electoral college votes. Kennedy won New Jersey's 14 electoral votes, Virginia's 13, South Carolina's 9, Alabama's 9, Mississippi's 6, Nebraska's 5, Oregon's 8, and Wisconsin's 10. Kennedy, having won fourteen states gave him a total of 140 electoral votes. Thomas won Maine's 4 electoral votes, Utah's 6, Nevada's 6, Alaska's 3, Texas's 40, and Iowa's 6. The final total for Thomas was 141 electoral votes and the Total states he won was the same as those won by Kennedy.

The result was that Thomas and Kennedy each won more states and electoral votes than Harris and Trump. Even if the major party candidates won the yet to be reported 5 electoral votes of New Mexico, the tally showed that they could not surpass the number of electoral votes won by either Thomas or Bobby.

As for Kennedy and Thomas, the one last state not yet reporting would decide which of the two could be the next president of the United States. Of course, this was predicated upon each state of the Congressional causes casting their one vote according to the will of their constituents, which should be either Thomas or Kennedy. Once the president is voted upon, the selection of the vice president would then be in the hands of the United States Senate. Out of respect for the wishes of their constituents, they should select either Thomas or Kennedy as president and the other one as vice president, depending on which one wins New Mexico.

Looking at one another, Thomas and Kennedy showed great concern that the Congress and Senate would vote the will of the electorate. Just then, Matt and Martin came into the room and spoke to them both. "You two are losing site of the big picture. Regardless of how the Senate and Congress vote, you two have done much more than winning the most electoral votes. You have set the stage for independent third-party candidates to win major offices for years to come. Besides giving a road map to independents where they can win political campaigns, you have given a voice to the silent majority. You have given the people what they want and that is a third and independent party!" "Sixty-three percent of U.S. adults currently agree with the statement that the Republican and Democratic parties do "such a poor job" of representing the American people that "a third major party is needed." This is the highest increase since Gallup first asked the question in 2003." (13)

Looking at Matt and Martin and everyone that surrounded them, Thomas and Kennedy high fived one another. Their wives came over and gave them a big hug and kiss. Family members and friends surrounded Bobby and Thomas as soon as the networks declared that they had garnered the most electoral votes. The News Media anxiously waited to interview them, while throngs of people gathered just outside the compound. They received congratulatory phone calls from Trump and Harris. Together, they walked outside the gates to speak to the News Reporters and well-wishers. Immediately, black SUVs loaded with more secret service security showed up to secure the perimeter. For Kennedy and Thomas, it reminded them of those days when Bobby's uncle and father walked among well-wishers despite secret service protection.

Ignoring the concerns of the Secret Service, the two of them  walked among those gathered outside, shaking hands with everyone. Despite Secret service agents immediately surrounding them, they pushed through them to greet well-wishers and the news media. *(Library of Congress photo 14)* The mood and atmosphere were electrifying, reminiscent of the days when John F. Kennedy greeted well-wishers after he was declared the winner of the presidency. They continually clasped one another's hands and raised them in victory. Finally, one of the reporters asked what they wanted to say to the people of America. As the secret service people looked on with great consternation, Thomas and Kennedy climbed on top of one of their campaign buses. First, they thanked the American people and their volunteers for all their show of confidence in them. Looking at one another, they again raised one another's hands and called out to the people, "join our quest to "SAVE OUR COUNTRY!"

REFERENCES

CHAPTER 1, Roots

1. The Jefferson Monticello.org, The life of Sally Hemmings
2. Encyclopedia Virginia, Thomas Jefferson, and his family
3. The Jefferson Monticello. On Slavery FAQs-Property
4. The Jefferson Monticello, Meet people.
5. Britannia, Martha Jefferson, wife of Thomas Jefferson
6. The Jefferson Monticello.org, The life of Sally Hemmings
7. The Jefferson Monticello.org, The life of Sally Hemmings
8. The Jefferson Monticello.org, The life of Sally Hemmings
9. Wikipedia, Jefferson-Hemmings controversy
10. WordPress.org, –Jefferson's grief over his wife's death and his promise to her. Edward Bacon, April 2012
11. George Washington's Mt. Vernon, Life of the Enslaved
12. Wikipedia, "An act to authorize the freeing of slaves".
13. Wikipedia, Thomas Jefferson, and Slavery
14. National Park Service
15. Wikipedia, Jefferson's Blood – The Memoirs of Madison Hemings". Frontline. WGBH-TV
16. Miller Center, Thomas Jefferson, Campaigns/Elections, Peter Onuf

CHAPTER 2, The Encounter

1. Monticello.org and various sources
2. Library of Congress, Jefferson's library Collection
3. The Jefferson Monticello, Jefferson's Libraries
4. The Jefferson Monticello, Jefferson's Libraries
5. Library of Congress, Jefferson's Library Exhibition
6. Library of Congress, Thomas Jefferson Libraries
7. Library of Congress, Thomas Jefferson Libraries
8. The Jefferson Monticello, Jefferson's Libraries
9. Raptis Rare Books
10. Jefferson Monticello, could members of the enslaved community at Monticello read and write?

11. The Jefferson Monticello
12. Encyclopedia.com, Thomas Jefferson's Plan
13. The Jefferson Monticello, Jefferson's Bill for the More General Diffusion of Knowledge
14. Massachusetts Institute of Technology
15. Lemelson MIT, Thomas Jefferson Patent System
16. Thirteen PBS, Slavery and the making of America.
17. Monticello Digital classroom, School house at Tuckahoe
18. History.com, In Early 1800s American Classrooms, Students Governed Themselves
19. Thomas Jefferson autobiography, Monticello
20. NPR, Americas one room schools
21. Family Tree.com, One Room school houses

CHAPTER 3, First love

1. Monticello, Games in the Parlor
2. Monticello, The life of Sally Hemmings
3. Monticello, The life of Sally Hemmings
4. Monticello, Thomas Jefferson and Sally Hemmings, a brief account
5. Encyclopedia Virginia, Notes on the State of Virginia
6. Monticello, Jefferson attitude towards slavery
7. Monticello, Jefferson attitude towards slavery
8. NBC News, Historians uncover slave quarters of Sally Hemings at Monticello, by Michael Cottman, July 2017

CHAPTER 4, Boxing Lessons

1. DBPedia, About bare-knuckle boxing
2. Monticello, The Great Clock
3. Monticello.org, Weather Observations-Thomas Jefferson
4. Monticello, Textile workshop
5. Effective self-defense, Practical ways to defend yourself.
6. Monticello, Jefferson's religious beliefs
7. Colonial Williamsburg.com, Comparing horsepower.
8. Monticello, Thomas Jefferson, and Sally Hemmings
9. New York Times, Interracial intimacies

CHAPTER 5, Discovered

1. Hammond-Howard House Museum, 18th century marriage, by Tara Owns

2. PBS, the real rules of courtship: Dating in the Regency Era
3. FragranceX, Fashion and courtship in the Victorian era
4. Harvard University, how many copies were made of the Declaration of Independence? By Jesse Greenspan, 2013
5. Library of Congress, Declaring Independence, Drafting the Documents Timeline
6. Monticello.org, Jefferson's attitude towards slavery

CHAPTER 6, War of independence

1. University of Illinois Library, American Newspapers
2. USS Constitution Museum, The War, September 5, 1812
3. American Battlefield Trust, War of 1812 Facts, May 2017
4. Brandy Heritage Center, Jefferson during the War of 1812
5. National Guard Bureau, Presidential series, Jefferson
6. American Battlefield Trust, War of 1812 facts
7. National Geographic, Roads, canals, and rails in the 1800s
8. Old Fort Niagara.org, History and collections
9. Andrew Jackson's Heritage, Rounding up Jackson's motley troops.
10. National Archives, War of 1812 Discharge Certificates
11. Andrew Jackson's Hermitage, War of 1812
12. Bill of Rights Institute, Old Hickory: Andrew Jackson and the Battle of New Orleans
13. Trvia-Library.com, U.S. President Andrew Jackson early life and description
14. American Battlefield Trust, Equipment in the war of 1812
15. Joint Base Langley-Eustis, War of 1812-Part of Army's proud history
16. Bill of Rights Institute, Old Hickory: Andres Jackson and the Battle of New Orleans
17. American Battlefield Trust, New Orleans battle facts
18. National Archives, War of 1812 Discharge Certificates
19. National Park Service, Wounded soldier contend with crude treatments.
20. History.com, Francis Scott Key pens "The Star-Spangled Banner"
21. Veteran Soldiers, A brief history of wounded veterans in America, By Sidra Montgomery and Meredith Kleykamp

CHAPTER 7, War hero returns
1. National Park Service, wedged between slavery and freedom: African American equality deferred.
2. World population Review, Slave states
3. Welcome to William and Mary
4. Library of Congress, Runaway fugitive slave ads
5. Wikipedia, History of the University of Virginia
6. College Stats.org, The first 10 U.S. Colleges to go co-ed.
7. University of Virginia, Women at the University of Virginia- Exhibitions
8. Monticello.org, Founding of the University of Virginia
9. University of Virginia, History, Office of the Executive VP and Provost
10. American Battlefield Trust, Slavery in Colonial America
11. US History.org, Slave life and slave codes

CHAPTER 8, True love
1. Monticello, Jefferson's cause of death
2. US Department of Veteran Affairs, Bounty Land Warranted

CHAPTER 9, A sad loss
1. Monticello, Jefferson's last words
2. Washington Post, Visiting Monticello, Jefferson's home.
3. Thomas Jefferson Monticello, Thomas Jefferson Funeral
4. Monticello, Thomas Jefferson, and Sally Hemings
5. American consumer credit counseling, Presidential Debt
6. Monticello, Jefferson's Gravestone

CHAPTER 10, Winds of War
1. National Park Service, Causes-Civil War
2. PBS, Causes of the Civil War
3. History Channel, The Louisiana Purchase was driven by a slave rebellion.
4. Louisiana State Museum, Civil War
5. American Battlefield Trust, 10 facts, what everyone should know about the civil war.
6. United States Senate, Civil war begins.
7. National Park service, Civil War series
8. History.com, Congress passes Civil War Conscription Act
9. American Battlefield Trust, Gettysburg, Adams County

10. Army Heritage Center Foundation, Answering the call, The Personal Civil War Equipment
11. American Battlefield Trust, Civil War Medical Articles
12. American Battlefield Trust, Civil War casualties
13. Essentialcivilwarcurriculum.com, Civil War Pensions, by Kathleen L. Gorman

CHAPTER 11, Time Marches on

1. Virginia museum of History, Robert E. Lee after the war
2. Arlington National Cemetery, Robert E. Lee's plantation
3. National Archives, Emancipation Proclamation
4. Library of Congress, Civil War and Reconstruction
5. Purdue University, Analysis of Kennedy Nixon Debates
6. National Park Service, Camelot, three women who shaped JFK's Legacy
7. National Park Service, Theodore White's interview with Jackie Kennedy
8. United States Mint, Fort Knox Bullion Depository
9. Oregon Live, thirteen ways Secret Service keeps the president safe, by Anna Marum
10. Richard Nixon Library, President Nixon's unplanned visit to the Lincoln Memorial
11. History.com, How Nixon's 1972 visit to China changed the balance of cold war power, by Dave Roos, Feb 2022
12. Wikipedia, Prisoner of Second Avenue

CHAPTER 12, Enter Politics

City of Pittsburgh, The Honorable David L. Lawrence

1. Rand Corporation, understanding how Teachers influence students they do not teach.
2. US News, Vermin Supreme, a Joke Presidential candidate, gets 240 votes, New Hampshire Rachel Dicker
3. Andrew Rafferty. It's official, Trump wins GOP Presidential Nomination. NBC News
4. Forbes, Americans suddenly more conservative than liberal on social issues, by Molly Bohannon, staff reporter, 2023

CHAPTER 13, Nominations

1. History.com. Here's how third-party candidates have changed elections.

Save Our Country

2. The Hill, Third-party presidential candidates who changed American history.
3. Gallup, support for third U.S. Political Party by Jeffrey m. Jones, 2023.
4. History.com. President Nixon calls on the silent majority.
5. Wikipedia, Libertarian Party
6. Gallup, Party Affiliation
7. LSE Blog, What Happened? The 2020 election showed that Libertarians have a long way, by Rob Ledger and Peter Finn
8. Libertarian Party Platform, as adopted by convention, May 2022
9. Abraham Lincoln
10. Ballotpedia, Ballot access for Presidential candidates
11. Wikipedia, the making of the president by Joe McGinnis, Britannica, by Kalisa Hauschen
12. Richard Nixon Presidential Library
13. JFK Museum library, the making of the president by Theodore H. White
14. Britannica, the making of the President, 1968
15. History.com, how Ross Perot brought populism back to Presidential Politics, by Suzanne McGee 2020
16. Politics, Stack exchange.com, How do I hire a campaign manager?
17. The Commission on Presidential Debates, (CPD), an overview
18. AP News, Hamas surprise attack out of Gaza stuns Israel and leaves hundreds of dead in fighting, retaliation, by Josef Federman and Issam Adwan
19. Gallup, Support for Third U.S. Political Party up to 63%
20. AP News, how independents and third-party candidates could threaten Democrats and Republicans in 2024, by Steve Peoples
21. Britannica, United States presidential election of 1992, by Michael Levy
22. World Population Review, Most conservative states, 2024
23. Robert C. Byrd Center

CHAPTER 14, Marching Orders

1. Pew Research Center, what to know about the Iowa Caucuses, by Drew DeSilver, Jan 2020
2. USA.gov, How Presidential primaries and caucuses work
3. Fair Vote, Presidential campaign strategies based on Swing States, by Chris Beaulier, 5/2012
4. Boston Globe, The story behind Mitt Romney's loss in the presidential campaign to President Obama, by Michael Kranish, Dec 2012

CHAPTER 15, Super Tuesday

1. USA Today, when is Super Tuesday? By Sudiksha Kochi
2. Congressional Research Service, Rules-Statutes to safeguarding classified Materials, 2023
3. CNN Poll, Trump narrowly leads Biden in rematch by Jennifer Agiesta and Edward Dovere
4. Associated Press, A year from 2024 election, Biden strategy memo says he'll revive 2020 themes, draw contrast to Trump, by Zeke Miller and Will Weissert, Nov 2023
5. Kennedy 24.com web site
6. 18 USC 3056A: Power, authorities, and duties of United States Secret Service

CHAPTER 16, THE candidates meet

1. CBS News, Georgia 2020 election results, Biden is presumptive winner by LaCrai Mitchell
2. CNN Politics, RFK Jr argues that Biden is more of a threat to democracy than Trump, By Aaron Pellish, CNN, April 2024
3. Wikipedia, Politics of Colorado
4. Wikipedia, 2020 United States presidential election in California

CHAPTER 17, Swing States

1. CBS News, Georgia 2020 election results, Biden is presumptive winner by LaCrai Mitchell
2. Wikipedia, Politics of Colorado
3. Wikipedia, 2020 United States presidential election in California

CHAPTER 18, Border Crisis

1. PBS News Hour, Smugglers are steering migrants into the hot Arizona Desert, posing new Border Patrol challenges, Sept 2023
2. US News, AP, Smugglers are steering migrants into the hot Arizona Desert, posing new Border Patrol challenges, Sept 2023 BY ANITA SNOW
3. Santa Fe New Mexican, New Mexico border city says it is suffering consequences of illegal immigration, by Daniel J. Chacon, Sept 2023
4. Texas Counties Net, Texas Counties: Comparing the 2020 Presidential Election to 2016, by David Carson, Nov 2020
5. The Texas Tribune, Texas Legislature tries again with bills making illegal border crossings a state crime, by Uriel Garcia, Nov 2023
6. The Texas Tribune, San Antonio and other Texas cities confront the spillover from the border migration crisis, by Jay Root, July of 2019
7. Office of Texas Governor, Greg Abbott, Press release, May 2023, Operation Lone Star Surges Border Resources as Title 42 Ends
8. Migration Policy Institute, Shifting Patterns and Policies Reshape Migration to U.S.-Mexico Border in Major Ways in 2023, by Colleen Putzel-Kavanaugh and Ariel G. Ruiz Soto, October 2023
9. Reuters, Immigration issue heats up, by Jarrett Renshaw and Andrea Shalal, Jan 2023
10. AZ Central, Timeline: Donald Trump's five visits to the boarder as president by Alexis Egeland, April 2019
11. PBS News Hour, Biden meets border officials in El Paso on first stop of visit to U.S.-Mexico border, by Colleen Long, Associated Press, Jan 2023
12. The Texas Tribune, Joe Biden tours El Paso for first border visit of his presidency, By Uriel J. Garcia and Sneha Dey, Jan 2023
13. Statista, Countries with the largest immigrant population worldwide in 2020

14. New York Times, what can the U.S. Learn from how other countries handle Immigration? By Quoctrung Bui and Gaitlin Dickerson, Feb 2018
15. Statista, Illegal Immigration in the United States, Statistics & Facts, Published by Veera Korhonen, Dec 2023
16. Pew Research Center, Republicans and Democrats have different top priorities for U.S. immigration policy, by J. Baxter Oliphant and Andy Cerda, Sept
17. Jodey Arrington.house, Arrington Fights to Safeguard States' Rights to Defend Against Border Invasion
18. Whitehouse.gov President Biden's Budget Strengthens Border Security, Enhances Legal Pathways, and Provides Resources to Enforce Our Immigration Laws
19. Congressional Research Service, Can the President Close the Border? Relevant Laws and Considerations, April 2019, Ben Harrington Legislative Attorney, Author
20. CBS News U.S. Mexican Border wall, what it really looks like, by Jessica Learish

CHAPTER 19, Debate Eligible

1. National Park Service, A plot to steal the Remains of Lincoln

CHAPTER 20, Top ten Presidents

1. Sienna College Research Institute, American Presidents: Greatest and Worst
2. C-Span, Presidential Historian Survey 2021
3. Sienna College Research Survey, CBS News, Presidents ranked from Word to Best by Elisha Fieldstadt, Sept 2022,
4. The White House, Franklin Delano Roosevelt
5. Scholar works, Grand Valley State University, Hauenstein Center for Presidential Studies
6. Lincoln Heritage Museum, Lincoln Character qualities
7. Mt. Vernon, 10 Thing you really ought to know about George Washington
8. Washington Papers, George Washington genius in Leadership, by Richard Stazesky
9. Constitution Rights Foundation, what made George Washington a great leader.

10. The White House, Theodore Roosevelt
11. Miller Center, Theodore Roosevelt-Impact and Legacy, By Sidney Milkis
12. The White House, Thomas Jefferson
13. The Jefferson Hour, On Jefferson and Leadership, by Clay S. Jenkinson, August 2018
14. Eisenhower Presidential Library, honesty
15. Addison Leadership Group, 5 Things strong Leaders do, By John Addison
16. American Historama, Harry Truman
17. Harry S. Truman Library and Museum, Decision to drop the Atomic Bomb
18. Wagner College, Lyndon B. Johnson, Wagner Faculty, by Connor Nolan
19. Harvard Business Review, Lessons in Power: Lyndon Johnson Revealed, by Diane Coutu
20. John F. Kennedy presidential library and museum, The Legacy of John F. Kennedy
21. LinkedIn, JFK, and the attributes of Leadership, by Gary Burnison, CEO of Korn Ferry, 2013
22. Tyndall AFB-U.S. Air Forces in Europe and Africa, Leadership Lessons from not so well-known President
23. Gallup News, Biden Ends 2023 with 39% job approval, by Megan Brenan, Dec.2023
24. The White House, James Monroe
25. UVA Miller Center, James Monroe Impact and Legacy, by Daniel Preston, Editor The papers of James Monroe, University of Mary Washington
26. White House web site including photo.
27. Government Executive, seven things' leaders can learn from Bill Clinton about connecting with people, Scott Eblin, Executive Coach
28. American Government, Rating the Presidents

CHAPTER 21, President's Resume
1. Harry S. Truman Presidential library and museum, Keeping the balance, what a president can do and cannot do.

2. The White House, The executive branch
3. Executive Network, The Personality Traits of a True Leader: What to Learn from Great US Presidents, by Dominic Fitch, Feb 2022
4. Brainy Quote, Franklin D. Roosevelt Quotes
5. Government Accountability Office, Duplication and cost savings, U.S. GAO
6. Tax Foundation, how other countries successfully reduced debt and deficits.

HAPTER 22, Party Platforms

1. USA Today, Suffolk University Poll, Dec 2022
2. Britannica, Republican Party, Jan 2024
3. Library of Congress, Constitution and Green parties of the United States
4. The Republican National Committee, The Republican Platform
5. The Democrat National Committee, The Democrat Platform

CHAPTER 23, First Presidential Debate

1. The Hill, seven issues that will define the 2024 election, by Caroline Vakil, Feb 2023
2. Civic Science, Voters prioritize the effectiveness of Congress and Immigration as top 2024 election issues, Oct 2023
3. CNN Politics, GOP presidential candidates prepare for first debate with or without Trump, By Steve Contorno, CNN, Aug 2023
4. AP News, Biden faces more criticism about the US-Mexico border, one of his biggest problems heading into 2024, by Will Weissert and Adreana Gomez Licon, Oct 2023
5. The White House, Jan 2023
6. White House Historical material, Nov 1, 2018
7. Trump's campaign announcement at Key mar a lago
8. CNN Politics, Hail Mary after Hail Mary': Biden administration struggles with border policy, fueling frustration, By Priscilla Alvarez, CNN, Oct 2022

9. AP, Biden is dangling border security money to try to get billions more for Israel and Ukraine, by Colleen Long, Oct 2023
10. Business Insider, A timeline of unfulfilled promises Trump made about his border wall, a cornerstone of his 2016 campaign which has faded from view in 2020, by Mia Jankowicz, Sept 2020
11. Center for Immigration Studies, States Must Pay Health and Education Benefits to Illegal Immigrant families, by Jason Richwine, Jan 2022
12. The Heritage Foundation, report Homeland Security, 15 Steps to Better Border Security: Reducing America's Southern Exposure, Jena Baker McNeill, homeland security analyst.
13. U.S. Citizenship and Immigration Services, Immigration and Nationality Act
14. Los Angeles Daily News, Robert F. Kennedy Jr. pitches tough immigration policies to LA Latinos, By Allyson Vergara, Victoria Ivie, and Ryan Carter
15. Donald Trump speech at Arizona rally, rev.com
16. Time.com, Trumps speech
17. Wikipedia
18. The White House web site, Remarks by President Biden on Bidenomics | Chicago
19. Investopedia, Bidenomics: How Joe Biden's Policies Are Shaping the U.S. Economy, By Nathan Reiff, Nov 2023
20. ABC News, What RFK Jr., now a presidential candidate, has said about Ukraine, vaccines, the economy and more, By Nicholas Kerr, June 2023
21. USA Today, Bidenomics? President tells Americans why his policies are good for their pocketbooks, by Paul Davidson, June 2023
22. Competitive Enterprise Institute, what is wrong with Bidenomics? By Clyde Wayne Crews, Sept 2023
23. The Hill, widening deficit puts Trump's trade fallacies on full display, by Phil Levy Sept 2018
24. Forbes, Trade Wars, Facts, and fallacies, by Steve Hanke, Oct 2019

25. Investopedia, What Are Ways Economic Growth Can Be Achieved? By Greg Depersio, Sept 2023
26. Trump speech, a campaign speech at a rally in South Dakota
27. CNBC, Trump bemoans high interest rates and indicates he might pressure Fed to lower, By Jeff Cox Sept 2023
28. The White House, Remarks by President Biden on the Anniversary of the Inflation Reduction Act.
29. McKinsey and Company, The Inflation Reduction Act, here is what is in it, Oct 2022
30. The White House, Build back better plan.
31. MIT News, Build Back Better, Morgan Bettex, MIT News Office
32. NFT Now, RFK Jr. wants to save the U.S. dollar by using Bitcoin, by Andrew Rossow, July 2023
33. The Washington Post, Trump vows massive new tariffs if elected, risking global economic war, By Jeff Stein, Aug 2023
34. Forbes, Trump's Tariffs were much more damaging than thought, By Stuart Anderson, May 2021
35. Ways and Means House.gov, Fact Check: Nine misleading claims in President Biden's Inflation Denial, May 2022
36. Washington Examiner, The Fallacy of Biden's economic victory lap, By the Washington Examiner, Jerome Powell, Mar 2023
37. Nasdaq, Bitcoin as a Hedge for Inflation-Is it still a good option?
38. Pew Research Center, Majority of Americans are not confident in the safety and reliability of cryptocurrency, by Michelle Faverio and Olivia Sidoti, April 2023
39. U.S. Department of Health and Human Services
40. Jacobin, Populist? RFK Jr does not even support Medicare for all, by Ben Burgis, April 2023
41. National Archives, Remarks by President Trump on the America First Healthcare Plan

42. Politico, Biden's health care wins are being undone — and at the worst possible time, by Adam Cancryn and Megan Messerly, August 2023
43. Center for American Progress, Less Coverage and Higher Costs: The Trump's Administration's Health Care Legacy, By Emily Gee, 2020
44. National Library of Science, why single-payer health systems spark endless debate, By James Madison
45. ATS Journal, Single Payer Health Care, why it is not the best answer, By Michael A. Diamond
46. The American Journal of Medicine, we can reduce health care costs, By James E. Dalen, MD, MPH
47. White House.org
48. CNN Politics, Trump will not commit to backing Ukraine in war with Russia, Jack Forrest, May 2023
49. The Hill, Trump urges pause on Ukraine aid until agencies turn in 'every scrap' of evidence in Biden, by Jared Gans, July 2023
50. The Hill, RFK Kr. Tells US role in war terrible for the Ukrainian people, by Julia Mueller, June 2023
51. Europa, EU assistance to Ukraine, Julia Mueller, June 2023
52. CBS News, Crimeans vote overwhelmingly to secede from Ukraine, join Russia.
53. North Atlantic Treaty Organization-NATO
54. Longview News Journal, Trump proposal for national debt would send rates soaring: Trumps debt proposal for U.S. reckless, By Josh Boak
55. CNBC, Trump urges GOP to let catastrophic debt default happen if Dems do not accept cuts, Mike Calia, May 2023
56. CNN Politics, Trump's debt proposal for U.S. reckless, By Jeremy Diamond, 2016
57. NBC News, Donald Trump's Unusual Plan to Lower the National Debt: Sell Off Government Assets, By Anne L. Thompson and Christina Coleburn
58. PBS News Hour, Biden Lays out 2024 budget priorities.

59. CNBC, Democratic Presidential Candidate Robert F. Kennedy Jr. Speaks with CNBC's Brian Sullivan on "Last Call" Today, Aug 2023
60. CNN Politics,' Biden falsely credits tax that took effect in 2023 for deficit reduction in 2021 and 2022, By Daniel Dale, March 2023
61. ProPublica, Donald Trump Built a National Debt So Big (Even Before the Pandemic) That It will Weigh Down the Economy for Years, By Alan Sloan, Jan 2021
62. Fiscal Data, Treasury.com, Understanding the national debt.
63. USA Facts, Which countries own the most US Debt
64. Peter G. Peterson Foundation, seventy-six options to reduce the federal deficit, Feb 2023
65. Nasdaq, three methods to alleviate National Debt, by Taylor Sohns, MBA, Aug 2023
66. NBC News, Donald Trump's unusual plan to lower the National Debt: Sell off Government Assets, By Anne L. Thompson and Christina Coleburn, April 2016
67. Mt. Vernon, Political Parties, George Washington Mt Vernon

CHAPTER 24, Assassination attempt

1. Politico, 55 things to know about JD Vance, Trumps VP Pick
2. NPR, Where JD Vance stands on key issues, **By Lexis Schapitl, Ben Giles, Destinee Adams**
3. CBS News, here are the democratic law makers calling for Biden to step aside in the 2024 race, by Kaia Hubbard and Melissa Quinn.
4. A growing number of democrats The Hill, Democrats may dump Joe Biden, but they still own his extreme policies, by Liz Peek Opinion Contributor
5. Reuters, Fact check: Kamala Harris quote on young people being "stupid" is missing context.
6. CNN Politics, Trump was struck by bullet in assassination attempt, FBI says, by Evan Perez, Alayna Treene, Hannah Rabinowitz and Holmes Lybrand

CHAPTER 25, Biden Abdicates

1. New York Post, two main front runners emerge for Kamala Harris VP Pick, by Jon Levine
2. Politico, Hill Dems believe this VP contender would help address Harris Giggest Weakness, by Sarah Ferris, Ursula Perano, Adam Cancryn and Anthony Adragna
3. ABC News, what pushed President Biden to withdraw from the reelection race, by Bill Hutchinson, July 22, 2024
4. Politico Nightly, Defining Kamala Harris, by Calder McHugh
5. The New York Times, Where Tim Walz stands on the issues, by Maggie Astor
6. Time, Where Tim Walz stands on the issues, by Nik Popli and Chantelle Lee

CHAPTER 26, Campaign Promises

1. NBC News, Trump blends new policies with old grievances in his 2024 campaign, By Allan Smith and Jonathan Allen, March 2023
2. BBC News, US election 2020: Has Trump delivered on his promises?
3. CNN Politics, Promises Kamal Harris has made so far in her campaign, by Tami Luhby and Way Mullery, CNN
4. NPR Politics, What we know and do not know about the Harris policy agenda.
5. The Hill, Kamal Harris's economy will be even worse than Biden's.

CHAPTER 27, The Silent Majority

1. Merriam Webster Dictionary
2. Nixon's silent majority speech, Address to the nation on the war in Vietnam, Miller Center of Public Affairs
3. Vail daily, Lewis-The new silent majority, by Mark Lewis
4. Britannica, Interest group, by Clive S. Thomas
5. Counter extremism Project, far left extremist groups in the United States
6. Pew Research Center, Progressive Left, very liberal, highly educated and majority White; most say U.S. institutions need to be completely rebuilt because of racial bias.

7. The Hill, who is the farthest left of them all? By Charlie Gerow, Opinion Contributor
8. Anti-Defamation League (ADL), Center on Extremism, Right wing extremism in the 2022 primaries
9. CBS Morning, Senator Joe Manchin says he will not run for president but calls for Democratic mini primary now that Biden's out, by Caroline Linton
10. Joe Manchin, Newsroom-Press releases, Manchin registers as an independent

CHAPTER 28, Unorthodox partners

1. CBS News, Biden orders secret service protection for RFK Jr. following Trump assassination attempt, by Kathryn Watson
2. Counter Extremism Project, far right.
3. Moderate Democratic PAC, About ModSquad
4. NBC Washington, Channel 4, RFK Jr suspends presidential campaign and endorses Trump.
5. Richard Nixon Presidential Library and Museum, Richard Nixon's unplanned visit to the Lincoln Memorial
6. Washingtonian, The Story of the Really Weird Night Richard Nixon Hung out with Hippies at the Lincoln Memorial, Howard Means, May 2016
7. Woodrow Wilson House, The 19th Amendment

CHAPTER 29, Trump and Harris Debate

1. PBS, WHYY, Here's where Kamala Harris and Donald Trump stand on key issues from democracy and immigration to Tariffs and Trade, By Associate Press, Josh Boak, Jill Colvin, Seung Min Kim, Sept 10, 2024

CHAPTER 30 On the road again

1. McKinley presidential library and Museum
2. The White House, President Buchanan
3. Wikipedia, Hollywood Cemetery Richmond, Virginia
4. Office of the Historian, Louisiana Purchase, 1803
5. The White House, President John Tyler
6. Rutherford B. Hayes Library and Museum
7. National Park Service, President Harrison

8. Library of Congress, Warren G. Harding, Republican candidate for President
9. Miller Center, Zachary Taylor: Campaigns and Elections
10. Andrew Jackson Hermitage, Debt.org, Timeline of US Federal Debt since Independence Day
11. People Magazine, All about Jimmy and Rosalynn modest Georgia home
12. Truman Library Institute & White House
13. Texas health and human services, The Texas portion of the U.S. Mexico Border
14. LBJ Presidential Library, The Virginia Pilot, The battle between LBJ & RFK, by Jeff Shesol
15. George Bush Library
16. George W. Bush Library
17. Eisenhower Library
18. Richard Nixon Foundation
19. Nixon Library and Museum
20. NPR, A Reagan, Legacy Amnesty for Illegal Immigrants
21. Willamette Week, Nonaffiliated Oregon voters now outnumbered Democrats and Republicans for the first time
22. Ballotpedia, Partisan affiliation of registered voters
23. Herbert Hoover Presidential Library, the Great Depression
24. The White House, Martin Van Buren, the 8th President of the United States
25. Senate committee on the Judiciary, Opening remarks Tomboulides testimony.
26. National Archives, Pendleton Act of 1883
27. Presidential power.org, Millard Fillmore quotes
28. Grant Monument Association
29. Center for Strategic and International Studies, America's failed state wars in Afghanistan, Iraq, Syria, and Yemen: Still less than half a strategy, by Anthony H. Cordesman
30. The White House, Theodore Roosevelt, the 26th president of the United States
31. National Archives, Theodore Roosevelt

32. Britannica, Franklin D. Roosevelts Achievements
33. National Park Service, Franklin Delano Roosevelt Memorial
34. The White House, Grover Cleveland
35. Office of the Historian, The Immigration act of 1924
36. The White House, Fact Sheet: President Biden Announces new actions to keep families together.
37. Pew Research Center, what we know about unauthorized immigrants living in the U.S. by Jeffrey S. Passel and Jens Manuel Krogstad
38. White House Historical Association, Franklin Pierce
39. Boston Tea Party a Revolutionary experience, John Adams
40. The White House, John Quincy Adams

CHAPTER 31, The Votes are Counted

1. Politico, Kennedy family feud cools as RFK Jr.'s independent run rattles Republicans, By Shia apos, 2023
2. AP News, RFK Jr.'s run for president draws GOP criticism and silence from Democrats.
3. Wikipedia, History of the Democratic Party
4. National Park Service, Commemorating Camelot, three women who shaped JFK's legacy.
5. Wikipedia, on Milton Friedman
6. CNN Politics, Kamala Harris praised defund the police movement in June 2020 radio interview.
7. Women's Wear Daily, Inside the Kennedy Compound, By Hannah Malach, July 2023
8. National Park Service, Kennedy Living room

PHOTOS
Wikimedia Commons, Library of Congress, White House Web Site, Unsplash, and other sites

1. Jeffersons Monticello, in Charlottesville, Va, Wikimedia, https//creative commons.org
2. Field scene around Madge Dale-geograph.org.uk, Wikimedia https//creative commons.org

3. Monticello Study, Library of Congress, 2016853986
4. Thomas Jefferson tomb, Library of Congress
5. Original photographs taken on the battlefields during the Civil War, Wikimedia, Internet Archive book images.
6. Ron DeSantis campaign bus, Gage Skidmore from Surprise, AZ
7. High altitude balloon recovery, Wikimedia, Public domain by Navy sailor or employee https://www.dvidshub.net/image/7620708
8. Mexican Border Wall, Wikimedia, https://creative commons.org
9. Aerial view of Lincoln Memorial, Carol M. Highsmith Archive collection at the Library of Congress
10. RFK gravesite at Arlington National Cemetery, Wikimedia, Public domain, work of U.S. Army soldier or employee
11. James Monroe Tomb, Wikimedia, Public domain, https://en.wikipedia.org/
12. Abraham Lincoln Tomb, Springfield Illinois, Wikimedia, https://en.wikipedia.org
13. Hyannis port MA, Kennedy Compound, Wikimedia Commons, https://en.wikipedia.org
14. Kennedy greeting people, Library of Congress, Hyannis Port Kennedy Compound, Wikimedia, https://en.wikipedia.org/wiki

Stature of Liberty photos by Fabian Fauth and Brandon Mowinkel, Unsplash, and Elcobbola-Wikimedia Commons **Harry Truman** photo from National Archives and Records Administration. Office of Presidential Libraries. Truman Library.

OTHER NOVELS BY MATT DROZD
https://mattdrozdbooks.com

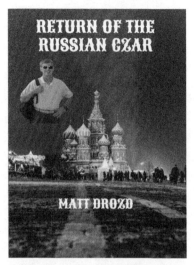

RETURN OF THE RUSSIAN CAZAR A fairy tale like story filled with romance and intrigue. Readers will travel through time starting with Czar Nicholas's 1917 abdication of the Russian throne to the present day of 2023 where Russia's president contrives a sinister plot to deceive the Russian people by thrusting an obscure and unsuspecting descendant of Nicholas's into becoming the Russian Czar. The suspense thickens and twists when it is discovered that the heir to the throne is American born who becomes loved by the Russian people. The author's extensive experience in international and military affairs provides the reader with insight as to what may befall Russia's president if he continues to wage war on Ukraine. He voluntarily deployed into harm's way, to protect our embassies and our troops.

His novels can be purchased on major book websites and outlets. For other information on novels by Matt Drozd, please visit his web site https://mattdrozdbooks.com or YouTube.

Copyright registered @ 2022 by Matt Drozd

COMING SOON

BEHIND THE SCENES OF 911

(Photo provided by Wikimedia Commons)

The Author, Matt Drozd, served at the Pentagon for three Chairman of the Joint Chiefs of Staff, the Secretary of the Air Force, and the Secretary of Defense. While serving at the Pentagon, he also served in the State Department when Colin Powell was Secretary of State. Due to his extensive military and foreign affairs experience, he was referred to be Secretary of the Army. He voluntarily deployed twice into harm's way to protect our troops and embassies. His serving at the highest level of the military and State Department will reveal to the reader what transpired behind the scenes of 9-11. In addition to his military and foreign affairs prowess, the author was the Program Controller for ABC World News. Behind the Scenes is an intriguing look into how our military responded to what became one of the most catastrophic events in our nation's history. Visit **https://mattdrozdbooks.com** to learn when this captivating and exciting book becomes available, and where it, along with other books of the author can be purchased.

Made in the USA
Middletown, DE
10 November 2024